SECOND CHANCES

Thank you, Natalie, for giving me many second chances

(and helping me make this book!)

—Ricky

To Sara, my first, my last and everything in between.

—Max

IMAGE COMICS, INC. • **Robert Kirkman**: Chief Operating Officer • **Erik Larsen**: Chief Financial Officer • **Todd McFarlane**: President • **Marc Silvestri**: Chief Executive Officer • **Jim Valentino**: Vice President • **Eric Stephenson**: Publisher / Chief Creative Officer • **Nicole Lapalme**: Controller • **Leanna Caunter**: Accounting Analyst • **Sue Korpela**: Accounting & HR Manager • **Marla Eizik**: Talent Liaison • **Jeff Boison**: Director of Sales & Publishing Planning • **Lorelei Bunjes**: Director of Digital Services • **Dirk Wood**: Director of International Sales & Licensing • **Alex Cox**: Director of Direct Market Sales • **Chloe Ramos**: Book Market & Library Sales Manager • **Emilio Bautista**: Digital Sales Coordinator • **Jon Schlaffman**: Specialty Sales Coordinator • **Kat Salazar**: Director of PR & Marketing • **Drew Fitzgerald**: Marketing Content Associate • **Heather Doornink**: Production Director • **Drew Gill**: Art Director • **Hilary DiLoreto**: Print Manager • **Tricia Ramos**: Traffic Manager • **Melissa Gifford**: Content Manager • **Erika Schnatz**: Senior Production Artist • **Ryan Brewer**: Production Artist • **Deanna Phelps**: Production Artist • **IMAGECOMICS.COM**

RICKY MAMMONE
writer

MAX BERTOLINI
artist

DC HOPKINS
letters

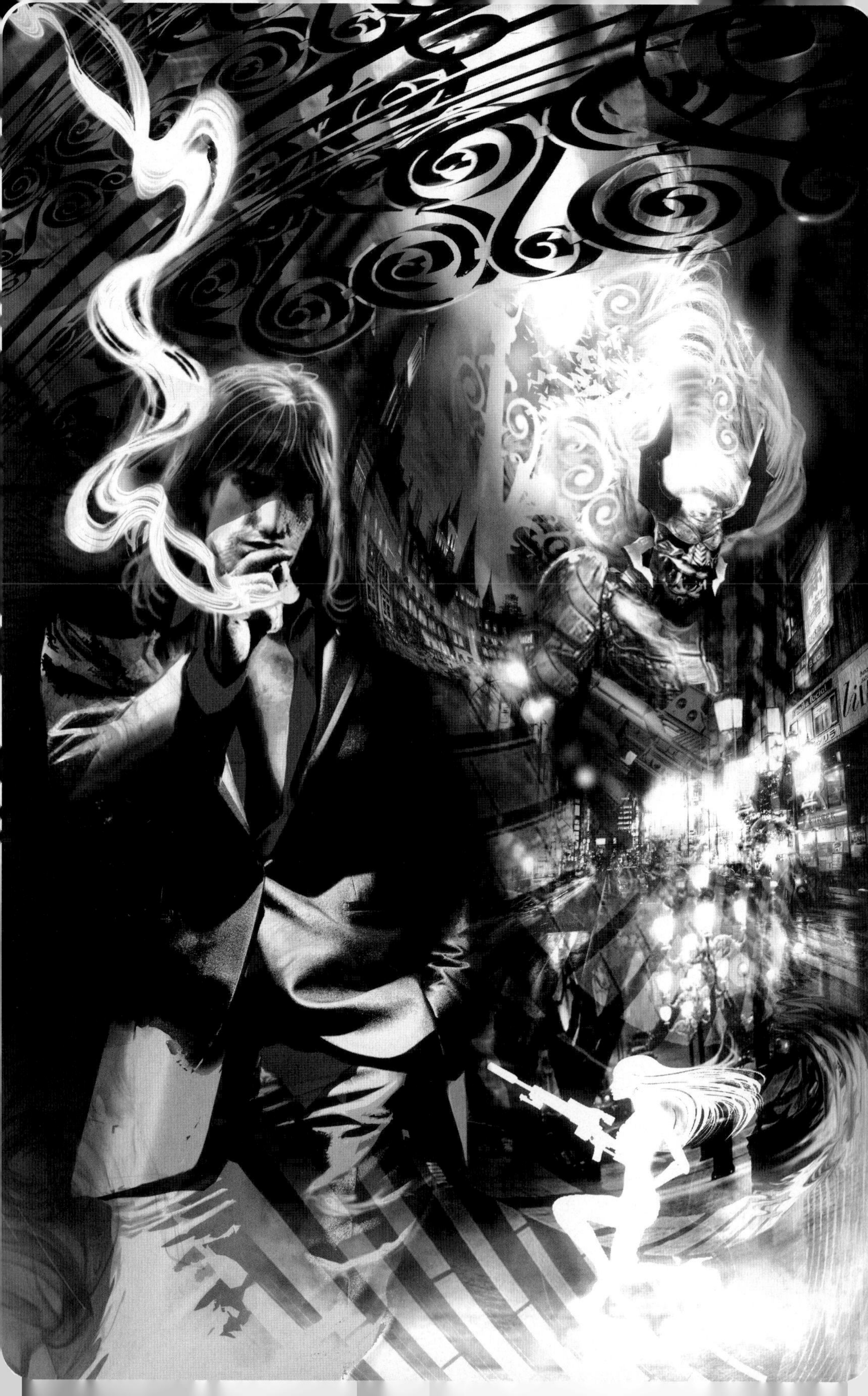

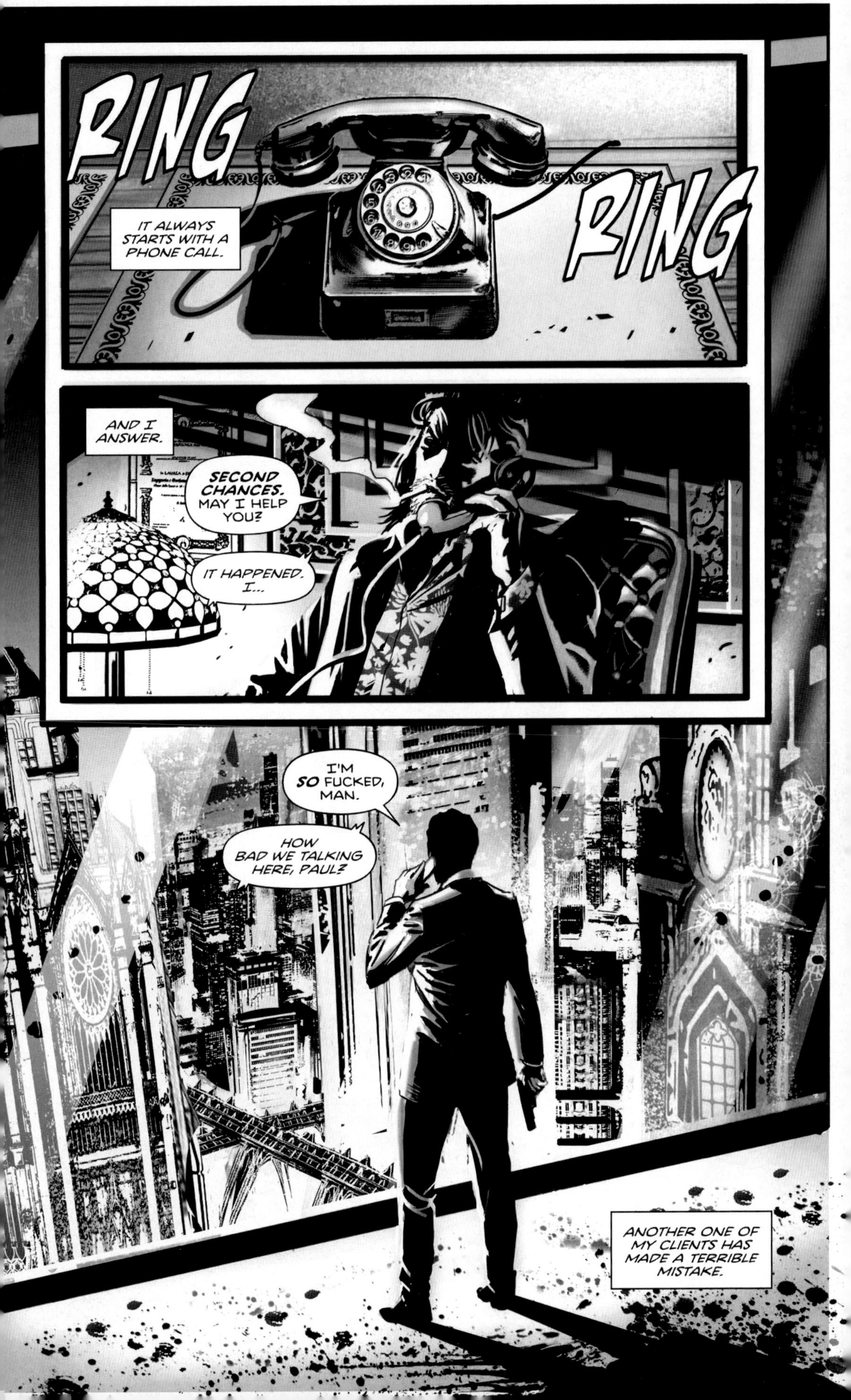
RING
RING
IT ALWAYS STARTS WITH A PHONE CALL.
AND I ANSWER.
SECOND CHANCES. MAY I HELP YOU?
IT HAPPENED. I...
I'M SO FUCKED, MAN.
HOW BAD WE TALKING HERE, PAUL?
ANOTHER ONE OF MY CLIENTS HAS MADE A TERRIBLE MISTAKE.

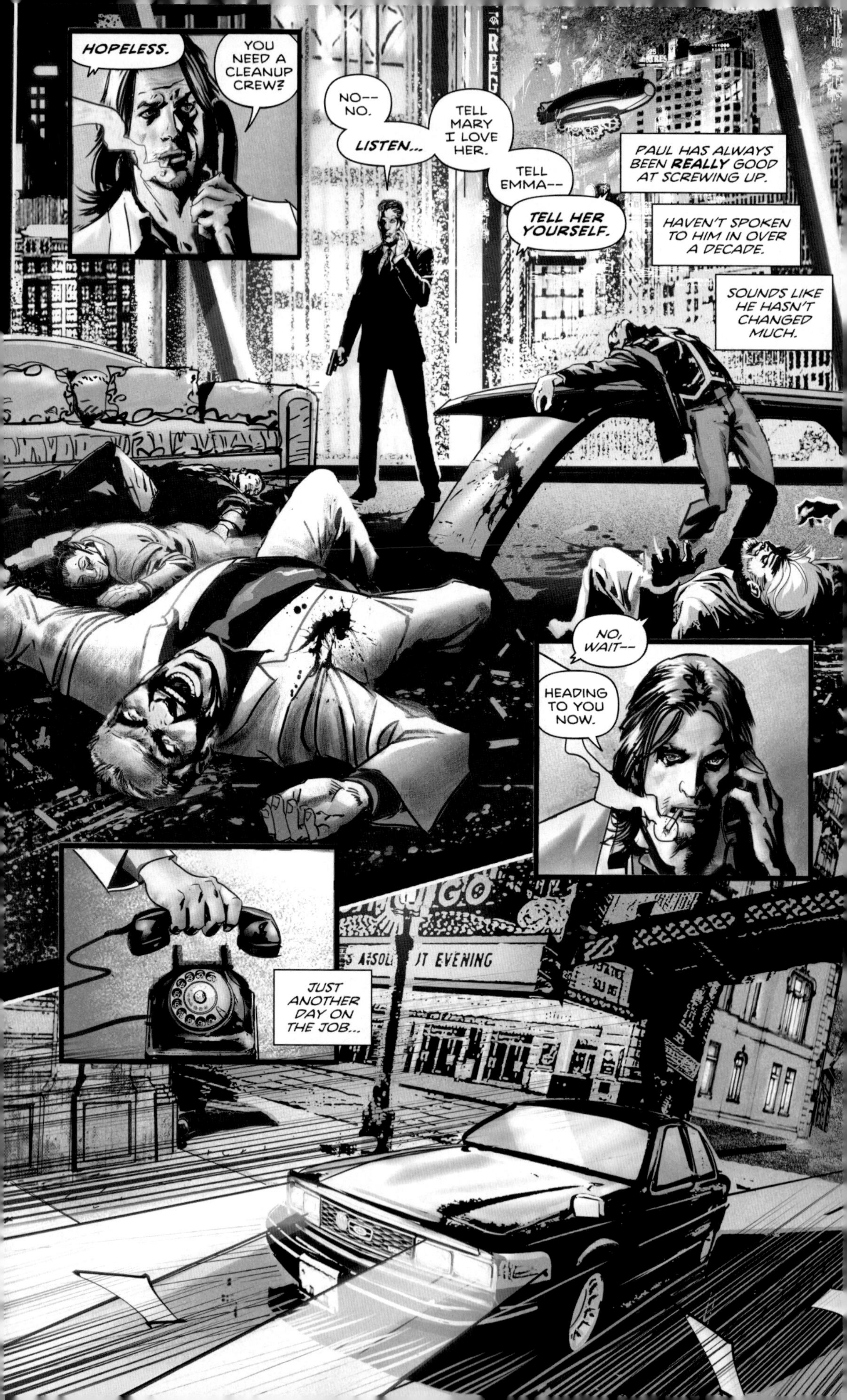
HOPELESS.
YOU NEED A CLEANUP CREW?
NO-- NO.
LISTEN...
TELL MARY I LOVE HER.
TELL EMMA--
TELL HER YOURSELF.
PAUL HAS ALWAYS BEEN **REALLY** GOOD AT SCREWING UP.
HAVEN'T SPOKEN TO HIM IN OVER A DECADE.
SOUNDS LIKE HE HASN'T CHANGED MUCH.
NO, WAIT--
HEADING TO YOU NOW.
JUST ANOTHER DAY ON THE JOB...

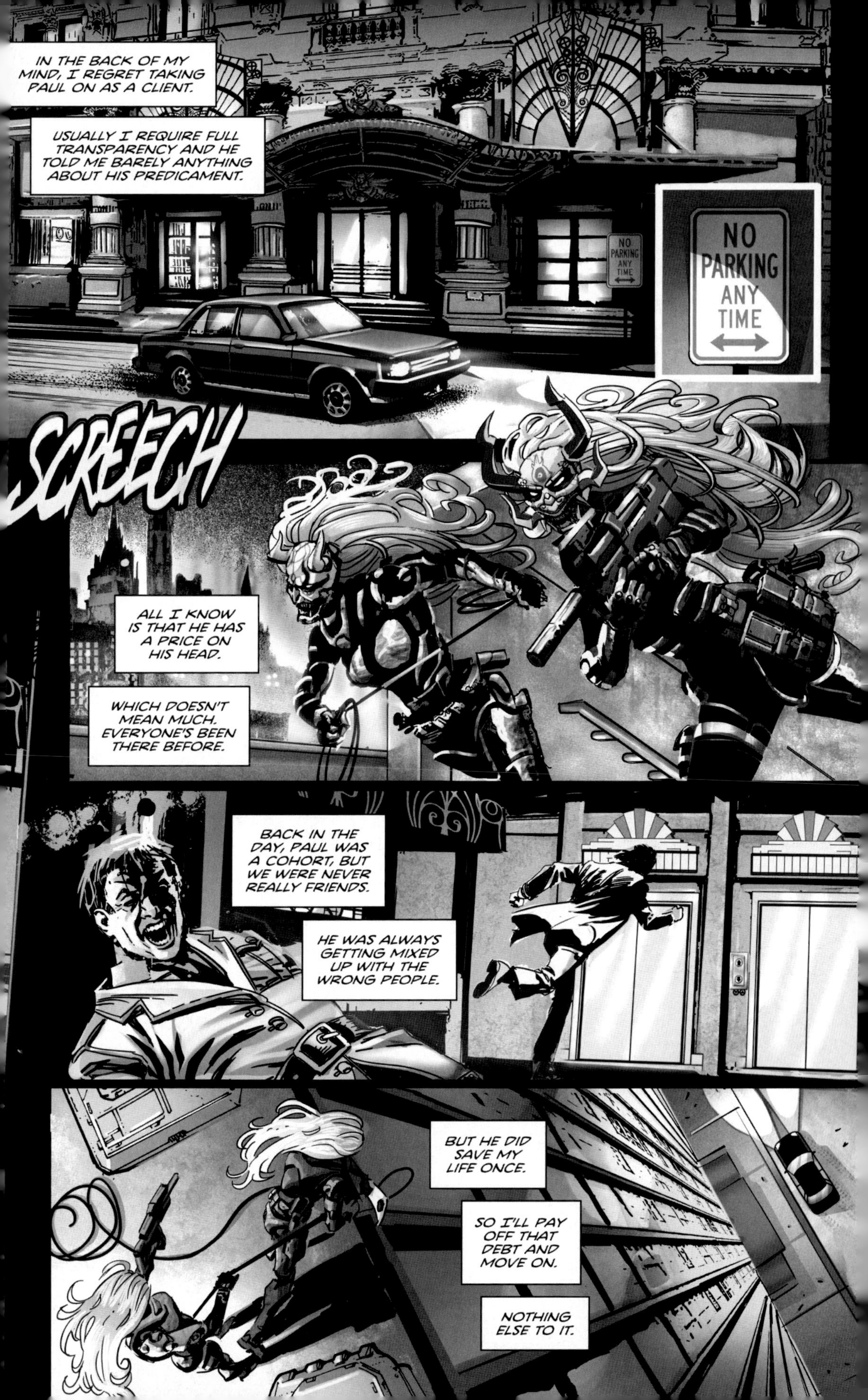
IN THE BACK OF MY MIND, I REGRET TAKING PAUL ON AS A CLIENT.
USUALLY I REQUIRE FULL TRANSPARENCY AND HE TOLD ME BARELY ANYTHING ABOUT HIS PREDICAMENT.
NO PARKING ANY TIME
NO PARKING ANY TIME
SCREECH
ALL I KNOW IS THAT HE HAS A PRICE ON HIS HEAD.
WHICH DOESN'T MEAN MUCH. EVERYONE'S BEEN THERE BEFORE.
BACK IN THE DAY, PAUL WAS A COHORT, BUT WE WERE NEVER REALLY FRIENDS.
HE WAS ALWAYS GETTING MIXED UP WITH THE WRONG PEOPLE.
BUT HE DID SAVE MY LIFE ONCE.
SO I'LL PAY OFF THAT DEBT AND MOVE ON.
NOTHING ELSE TO IT.

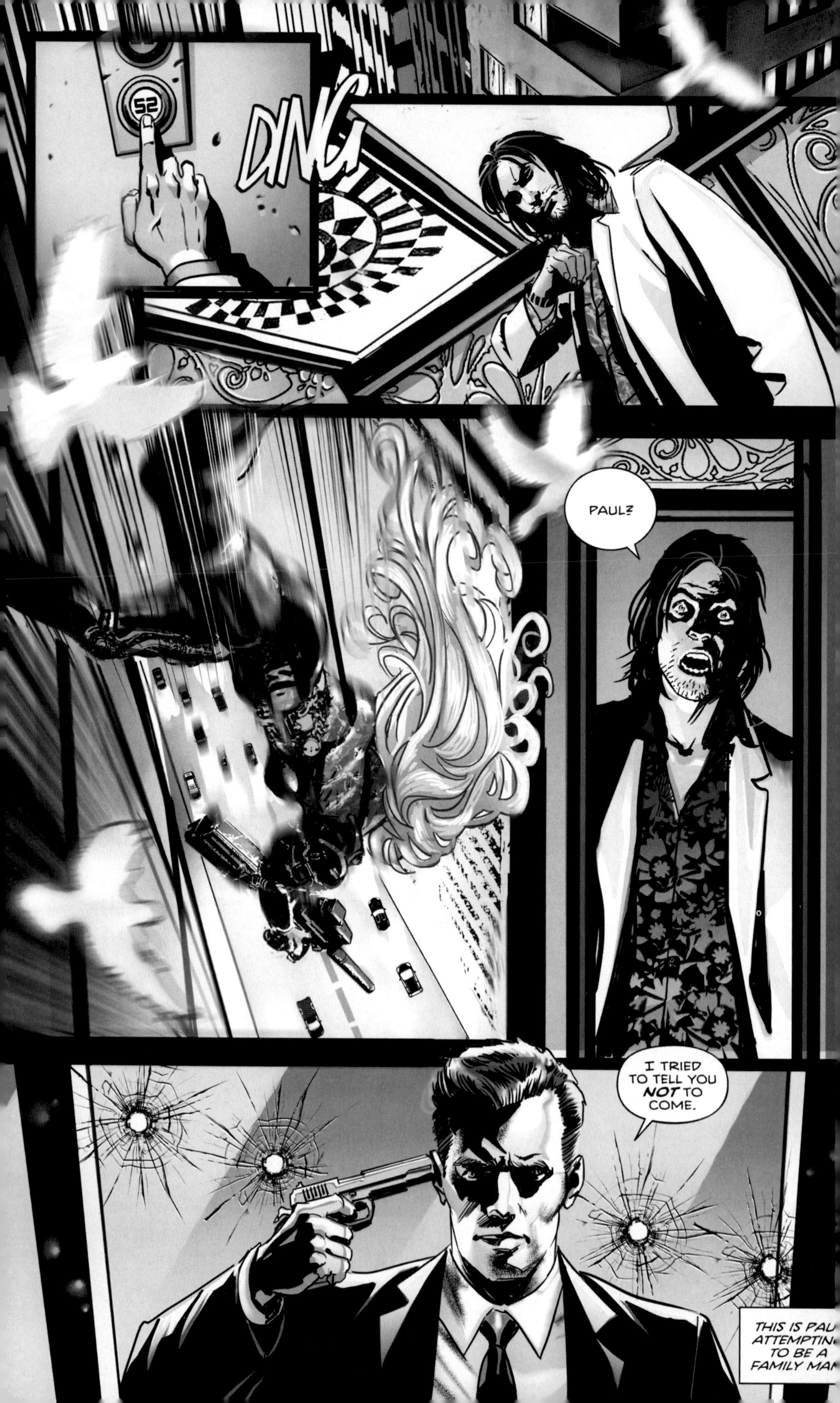
52
DING
PAUL?
I TRIED TO TELL YOU ***NOT*** TO COME.
THIS IS PAU
ATTEMPTIN
TO BE A
FAMILY MA

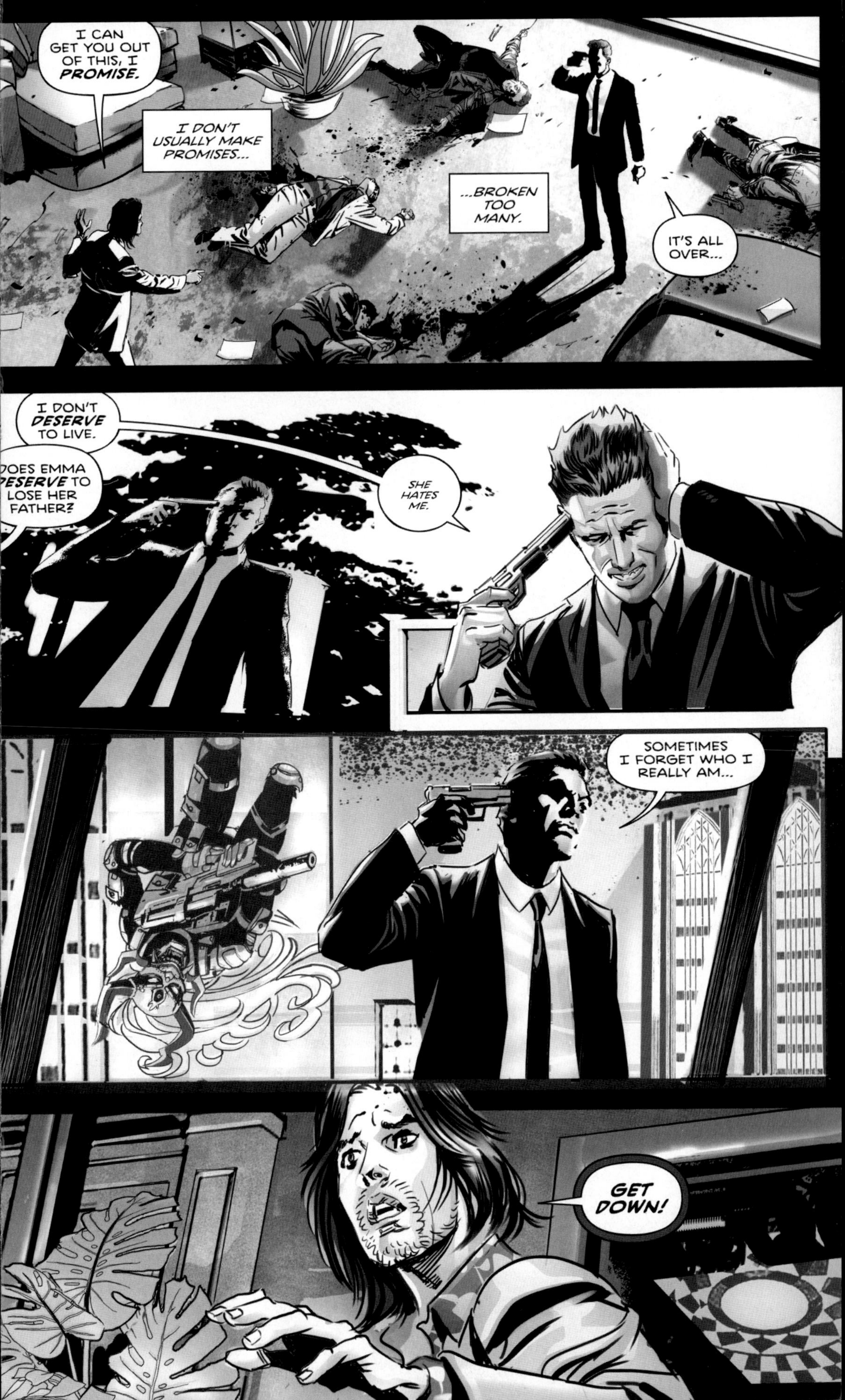

I CAN GET YOU OUT OF THIS, I PROMISE.
I DON'T USUALLY MAKE PROMISES...
...BROKEN TOO MANY.
IT'S ALL OVER...
I DON'T DESERVE TO LIVE.
DOES EMMA DESERVE TO LOSE HER FATHER?
SHE HATES ME.
SOMETIMES I FORGET WHO I REALLY AM...
GET DOWN!

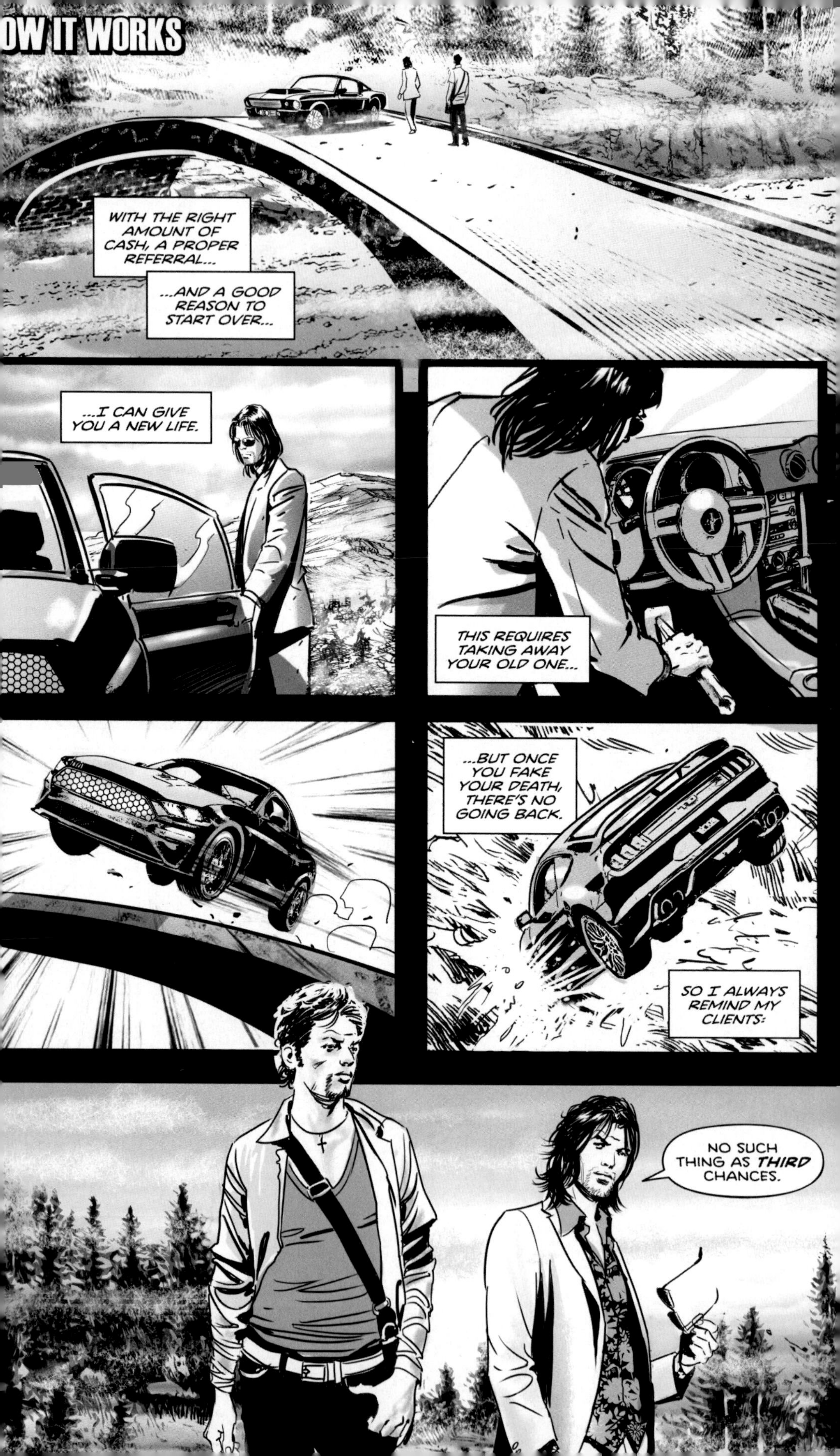
OW IT WORKS
WITH THE RIGHT AMOUNT OF CASH, A PROPER REFERRAL...
...AND A GOOD REASON TO START OVER...
...I CAN GIVE YOU A NEW LIFE.
THIS REQUIRES TAKING AWAY YOUR OLD ONE...
...BUT ONCE YOU FAKE YOUR DEATH, THERE'S NO GOING BACK.
SO I ALWAYS REMIND MY CLIENTS:
NO SUCH THING AS *THIRD* CHANCES.

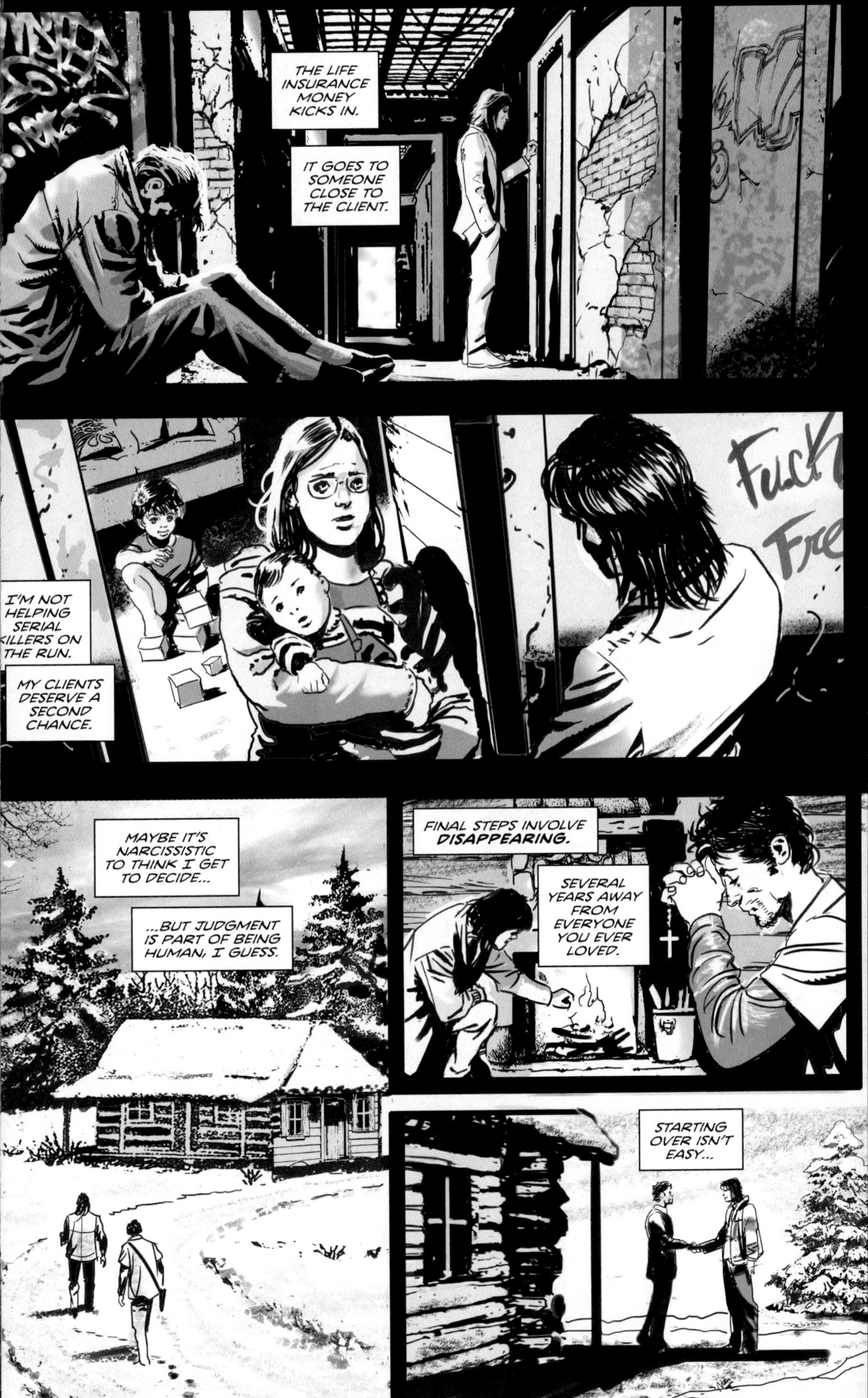
THE LIFE INSURANCE MONEY KICKS IN.
IT GOES TO SOMEONE CLOSE TO THE CLIENT.
I'M NOT HELPING SERIAL KILLERS ON THE RUN.
MY CLIENTS DESERVE A SECOND CHANCE.
MAYBE IT'S NARCISSISTIC TO THINK I GET TO DECIDE...
...BUT JUDGMENT IS PART OF BEING HUMAN, I GUESS.
FINAL STEPS INVOLVE **DISAPPEARING.**
SEVERAL YEARS AWAY FROM EVERYONE YOU EVER LOVED.
STARTING OVER ISN'T EASY...

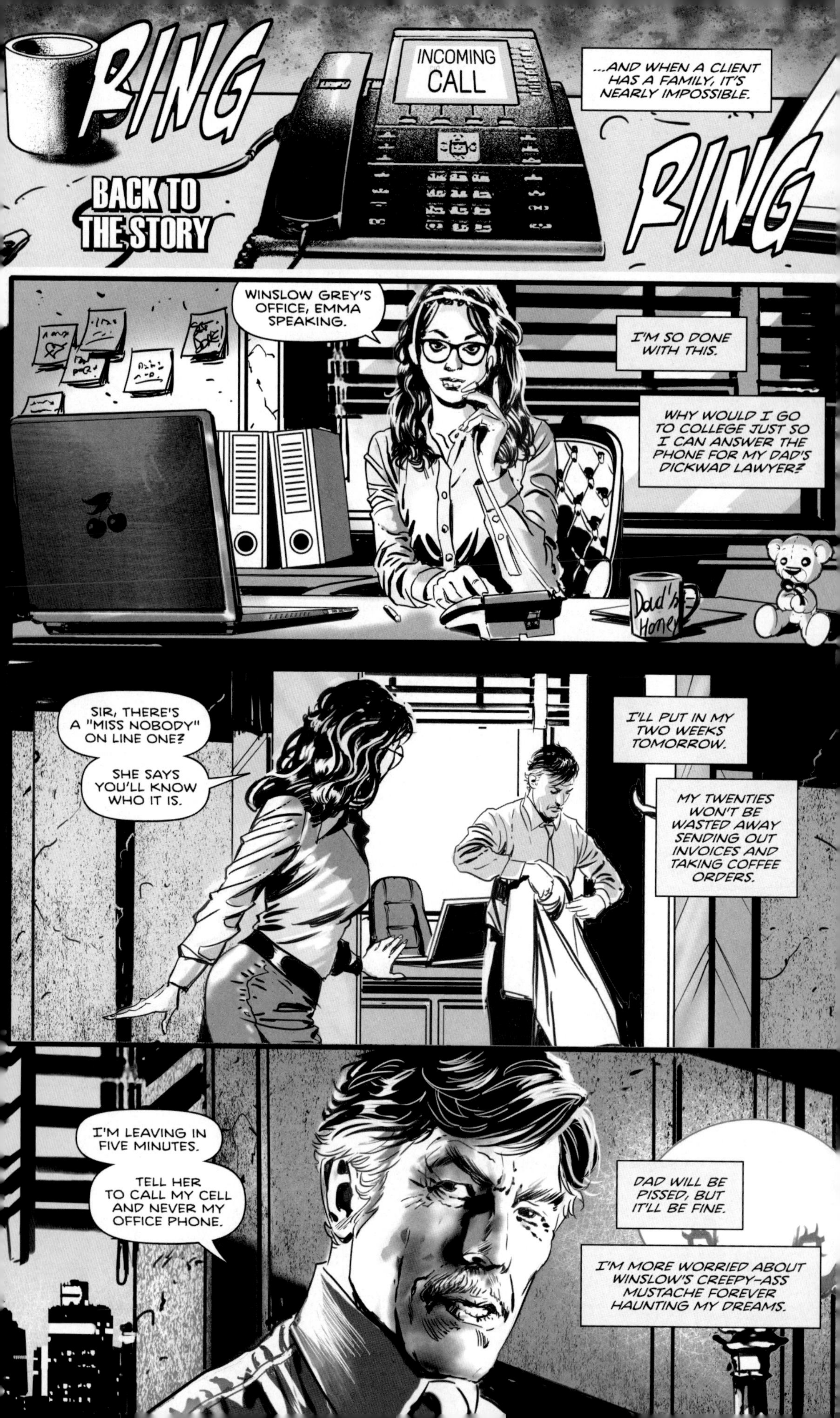
RING
BACK TO THE STORY
INCOMING CALL
...AND WHEN A CLIENT HAS A FAMILY, IT'S NEARLY IMPOSSIBLE.
RING
WINSLOW GREY'S OFFICE, EMMA SPEAKING.
I'M SO DONE WITH THIS.
WHY WOULD I GO TO COLLEGE JUST SO I CAN ANSWER THE PHONE FOR MY DAD'S DICKWAD LAWYER?
Dad's Honey
SIR, THERE'S A "MISS NOBODY" ON LINE ONE?
SHE SAYS YOU'LL KNOW WHO IT IS.
I'LL PUT IN MY TWO WEEKS TOMORROW.
MY TWENTIES WON'T BE WASTED AWAY SENDING OUT INVOICES AND TAKING COFFEE ORDERS.
I'M LEAVING IN FIVE MINUTES.
TELL HER TO CALL MY CELL AND NEVER MY OFFICE PHONE.
DAD WILL BE PISSED, BUT IT'LL BE FINE.
I'M MORE WORRIED ABOUT WINSLOW'S CREEPY-ASS MUSTACHE FOREVER HAUNTING MY DREAMS.

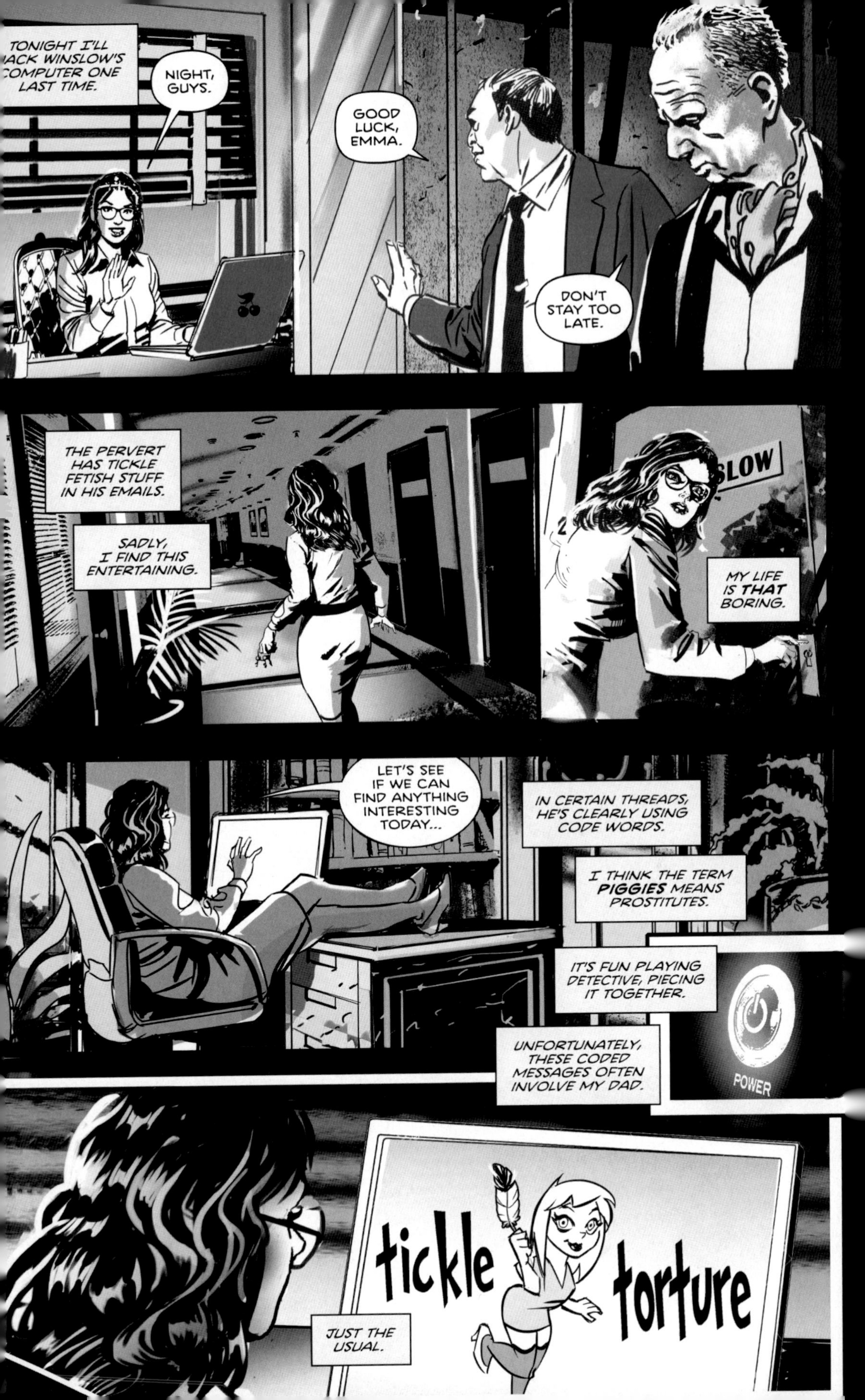
TONIGHT I'LL HACK WINSLOW'S COMPUTER ONE LAST TIME.
NIGHT, GUYS.
GOOD LUCK, EMMA.
DON'T STAY TOO LATE.
THE PERVERT HAS TICKLE FETISH STUFF IN HIS EMAILS.
SADLY, I FIND THIS ENTERTAINING.
SLOW
MY LIFE IS THAT BORING.
LET'S SEE IF WE CAN FIND ANYTHING INTERESTING TODAY...
IN CERTAIN THREADS, HE'S CLEARLY USING CODE WORDS.
I THINK THE TERM PIGGIES MEANS PROSTITUTES.
IT'S FUN PLAYING DETECTIVE, PIECING IT TOGETHER.
UNFORTUNATELY, THESE CODED MESSAGES OFTEN INVOLVE MY DAD.
POWER
tickle torture
JUST THE USUAL.

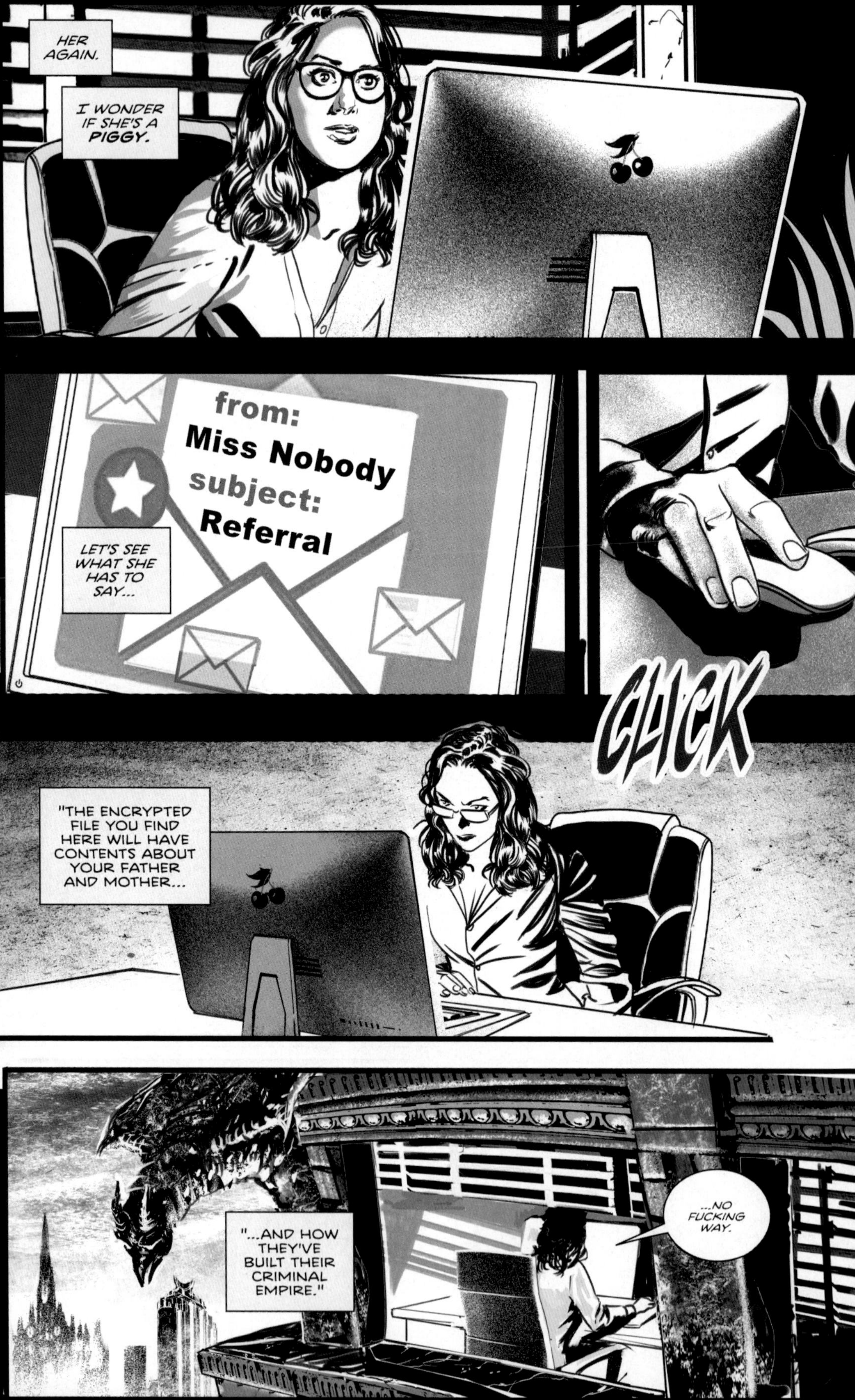
HER AGAIN.
I WONDER IF SHE'S A PIGGY.
from: Miss Nobody subject: Referral
LET'S SEE WHAT SHE HAS TO SAY...
CLICK
"THE ENCRYPTED FILE YOU FIND HERE WILL HAVE CONTENTS ABOUT YOUR FATHER AND MOTHER...
"...AND HOW THEY'VE BUILT THEIR CRIMINAL EMPIRE."
...NO FUCKING WAY.

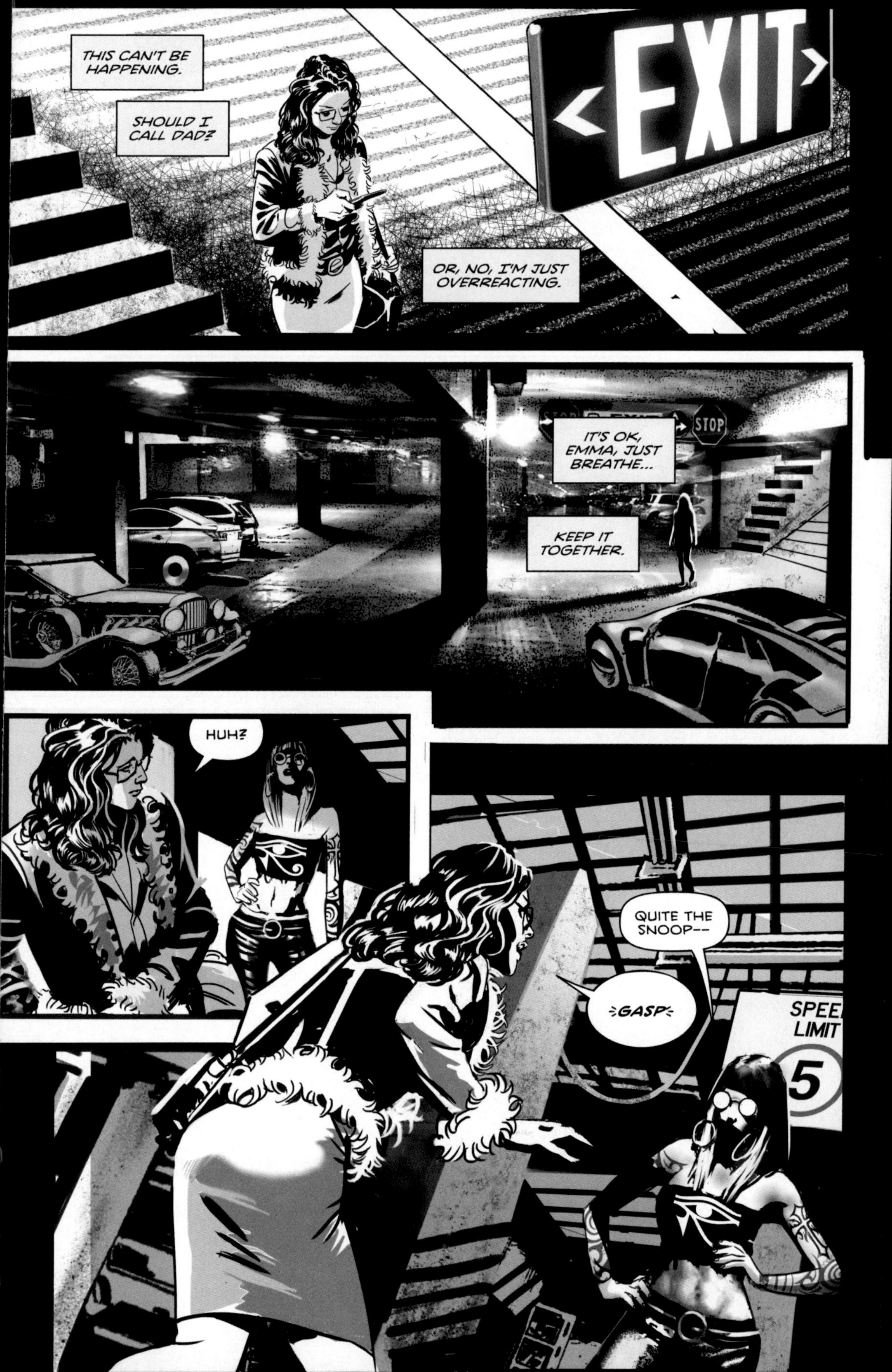
THIS CAN'T BE HAPPENING.
SHOULD I CALL DAD?
EXIT
OR, NO, I'M JUST OVERREACTING.
STOP
IT'S OK, EMMA, JUST BREATHE...
KEEP IT TOGETHER.
HUH?
QUITE THE SNOOP--
GASP
SPEE LIMIT
5

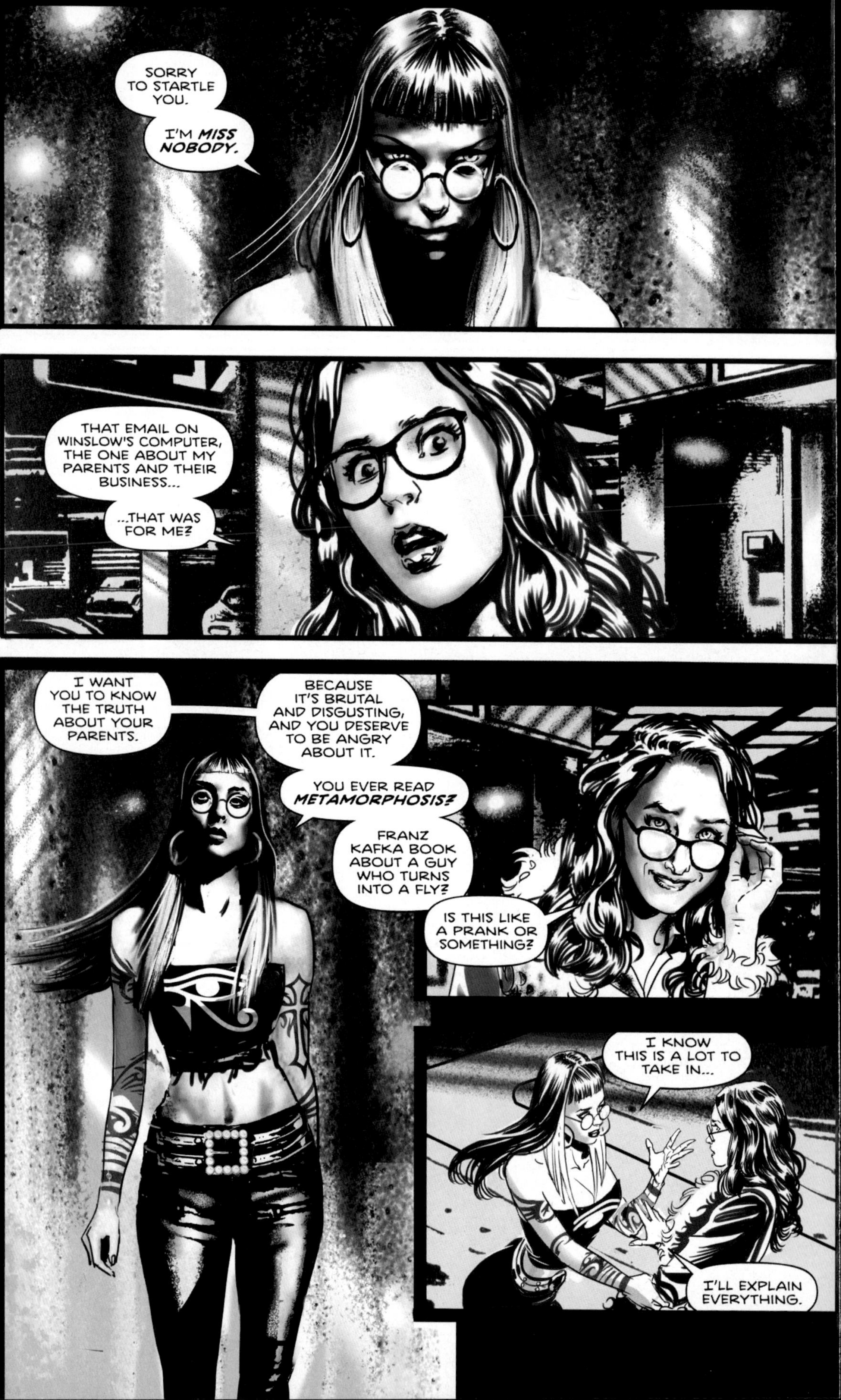
SORRY TO STARTLE YOU.
I'M MISS NOBODY.
THAT EMAIL ON WINSLOW'S COMPUTER, THE ONE ABOUT MY PARENTS AND THEIR BUSINESS...
...THAT WAS FOR ME?
I WANT YOU TO KNOW THE TRUTH ABOUT YOUR PARENTS.
BECAUSE IT'S BRUTAL AND DISGUSTING, AND YOU DESERVE TO BE ANGRY ABOUT IT.
YOU EVER READ METAMORPHOSIS?
FRANZ KAFKA BOOK ABOUT A GUY WHO TURNS INTO A FLY?
IS THIS LIKE A PRANK OR SOMETHING?
I KNOW THIS IS A LOT TO TAKE IN...
I'LL EXPLAIN EVERYTHING.

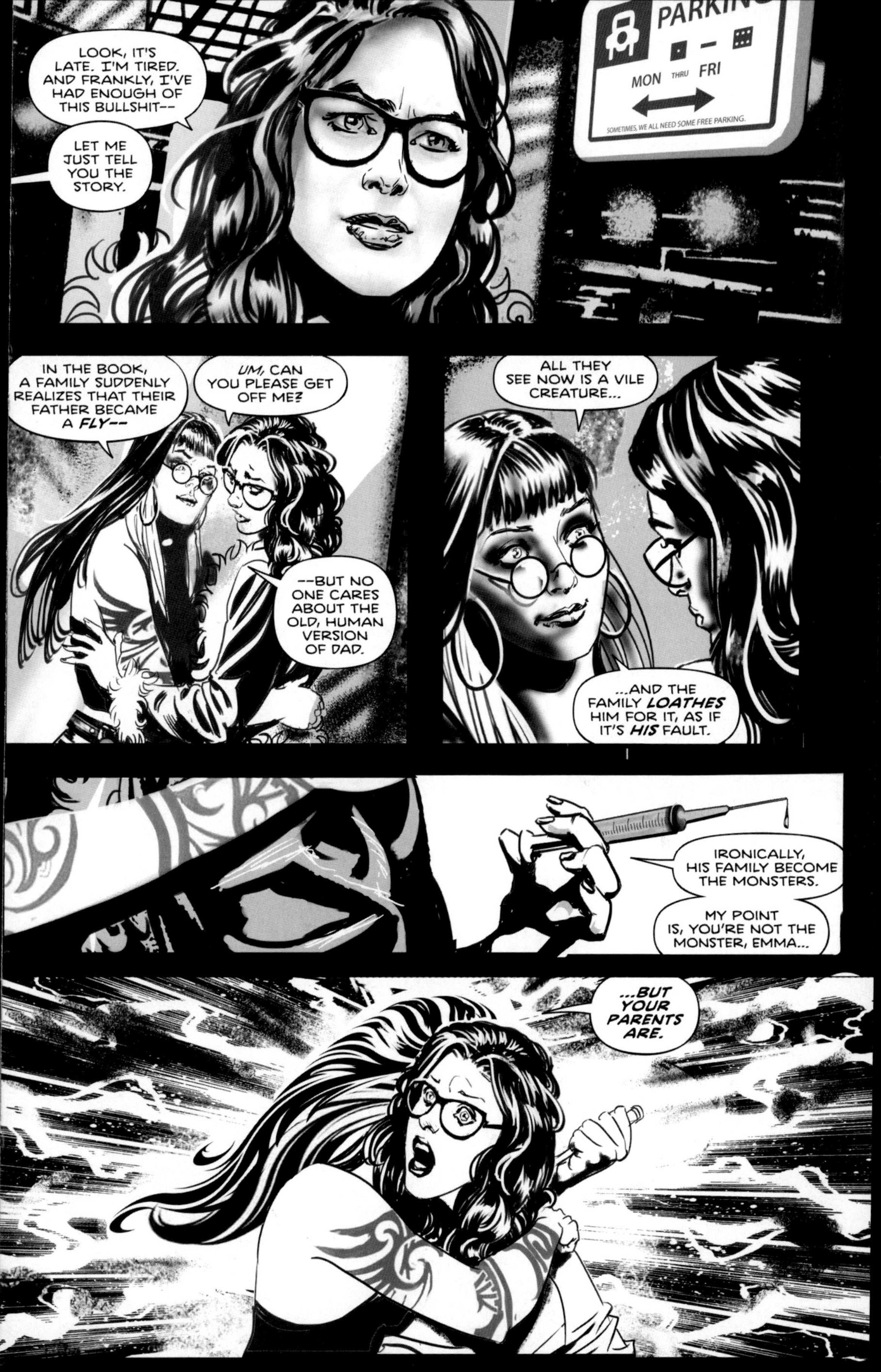

LOOK, IT'S LATE. I'M TIRED. AND FRANKLY, I'VE HAD ENOUGH OF THIS BULLSHIT--
LET ME JUST TELL YOU THE STORY.
PARKING
MON THRU FRI
SOMETIMES, WE ALL NEED SOME FREE PARKING.
IN THE BOOK, A FAMILY SUDDENLY REALIZES THAT THEIR FATHER BECAME A *FLY*--
UM, CAN YOU PLEASE GET OFF ME?
--BUT NO ONE CARES ABOUT THE OLD, HUMAN VERSION OF DAD.
ALL THEY SEE NOW IS A VILE CREATURE...
...AND THE FAMILY *LOATHES* HIM FOR IT, AS IF IT'S *HIS* FAULT.
IRONICALLY, HIS FAMILY BECOME THE MONSTERS.
MY POINT IS, YOU'RE NOT THE MONSTER, EMMA...
...BUT YOUR PARENTS ARE.

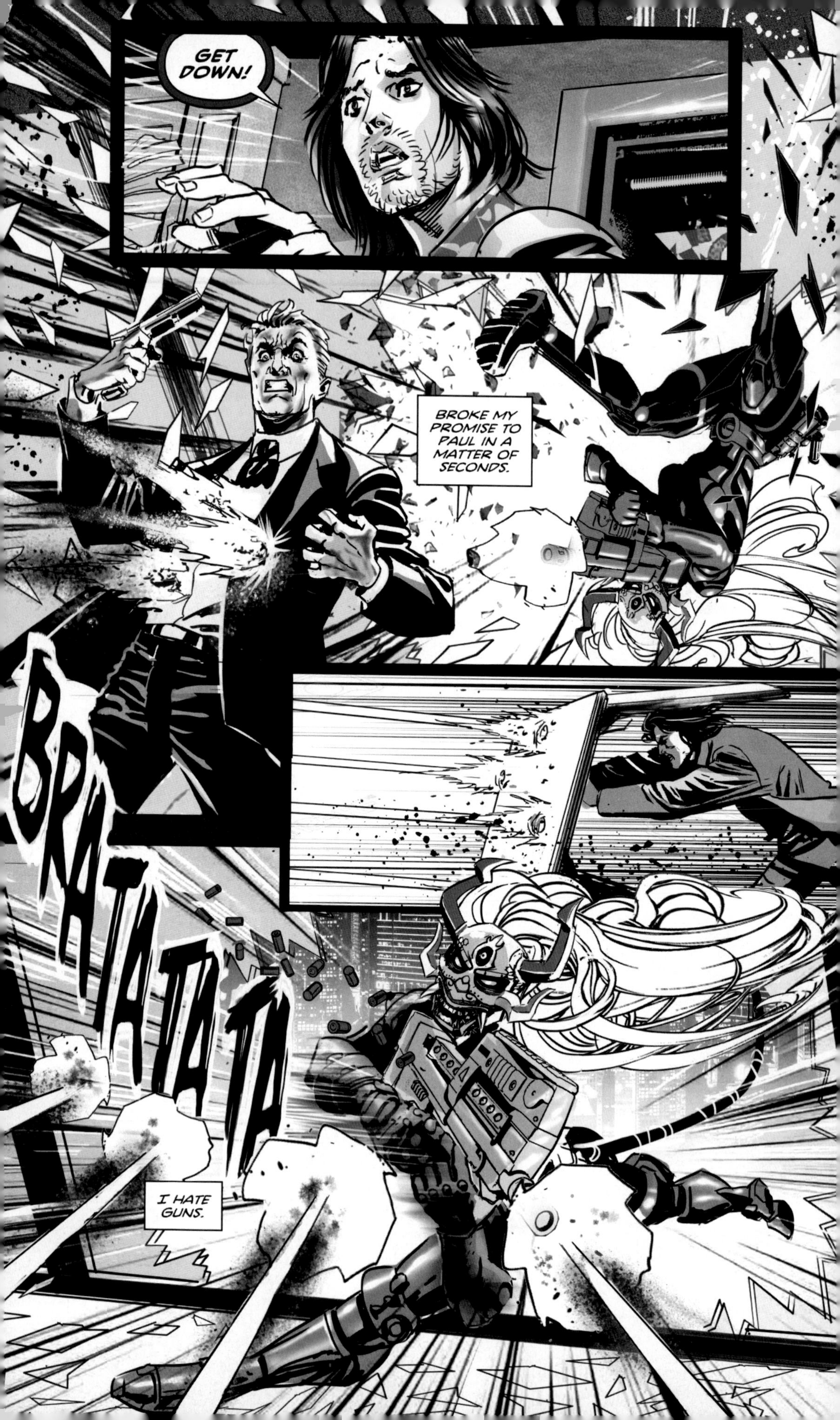
GET DOWN!
BROKE MY PROMISE TO PAUL IN A MATTER OF SECONDS.
BRATATATA
I HATE GUNS.

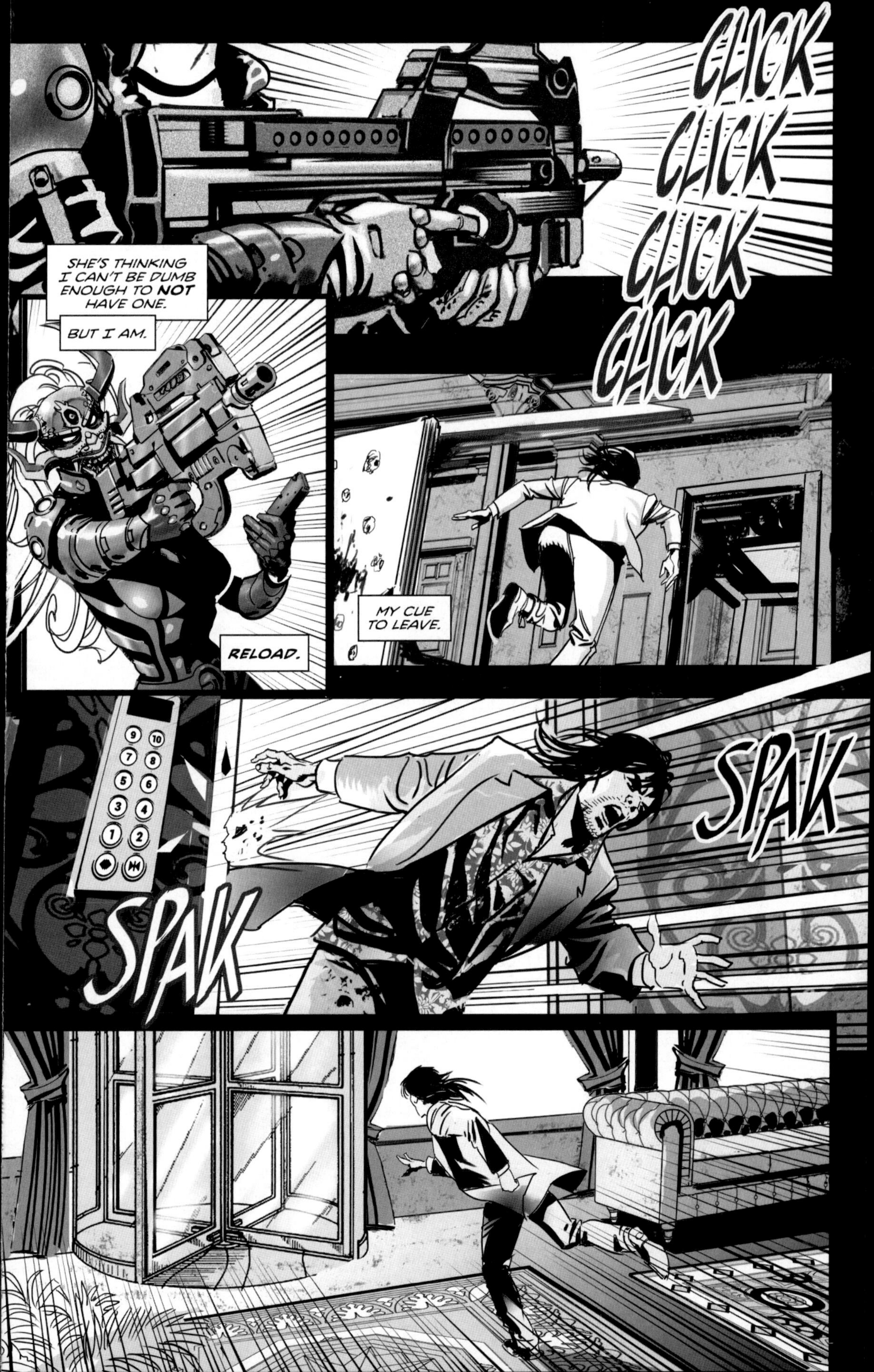
CLICK
CLICK
CLICK
CLICK
SHE'S THINKING I CAN'T BE DUMB ENOUGH TO NOT HAVE ONE.
BUT I AM.
RELOAD.
MY CUE TO LEAVE.
SPAK
SPAK

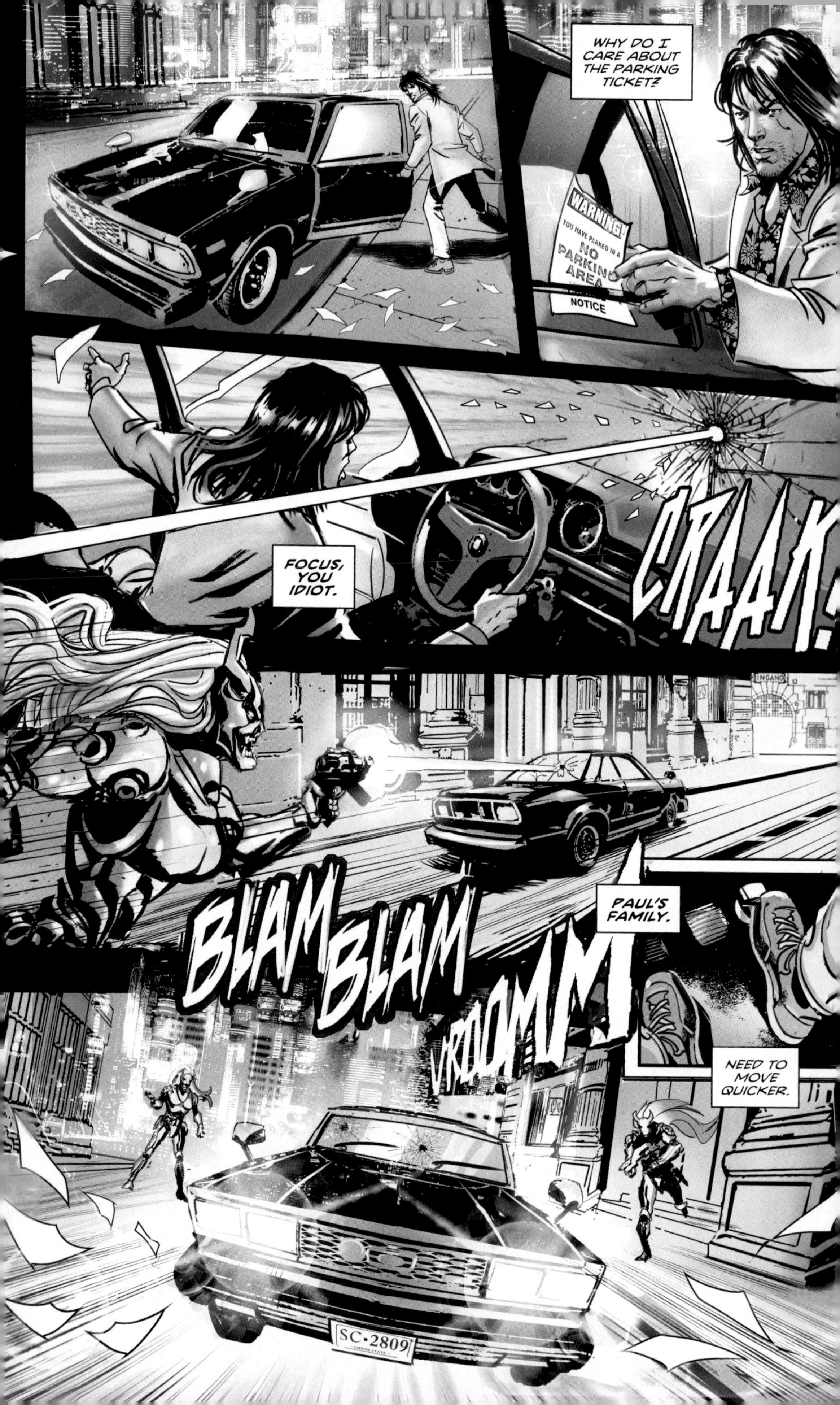

WHY DO I CARE ABOUT THE PARKING TICKET?
WARNING!
YOU HAVE PARKED IN A
NO PARKING AREA
NOTICE
FOCUS, YOU IDIOT.
CRAAAK!
BLAM BLAM
PAUL'S FAMILY.
VROOMM
NEED TO MOVE QUICKER.
SC•2809
EMPIRE STATE

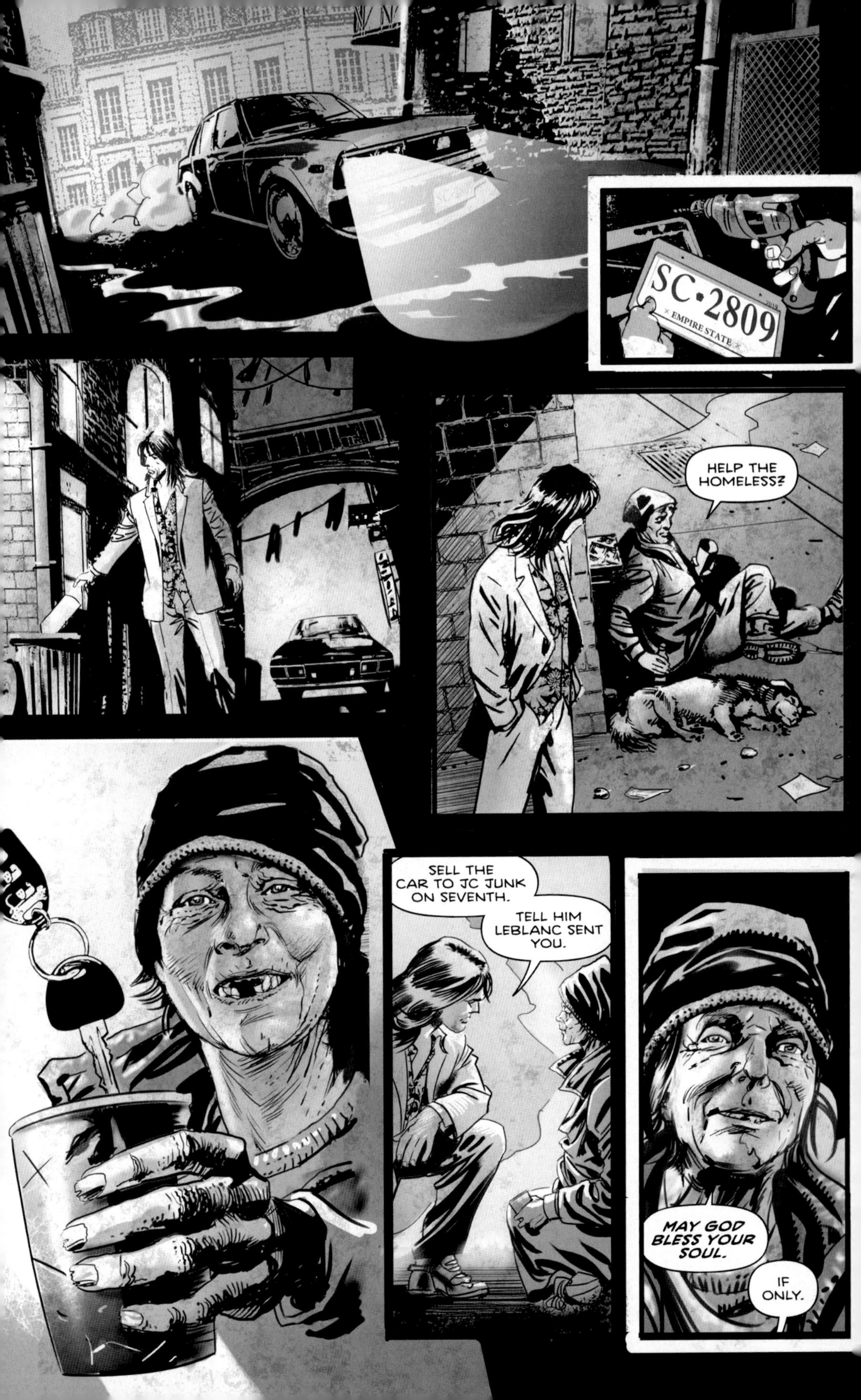
SC•2809
EMPIRE STATE
HELP THE HOMELESS?
SELL THE CAR TO JC JUNK ON SEVENTH.
TELL HIM LEBLANC SENT YOU.
MAY GOD BLESS YOUR SOUL.
IF ONLY.

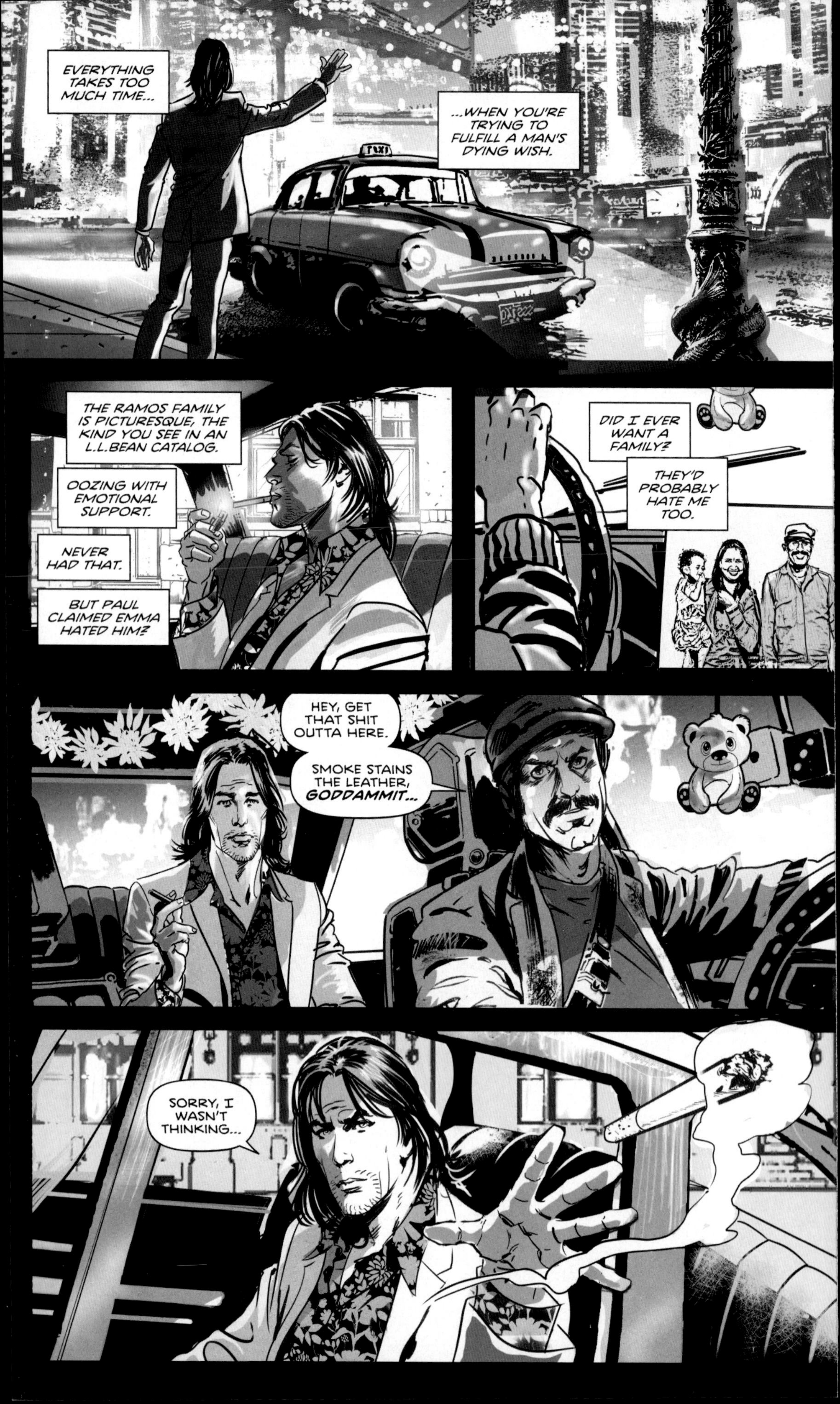

EVERYTHING TAKES TOO MUCH TIME...
...WHEN YOU'RE TRYING TO FULFILL A MAN'S DYING WISH.
THE RAMOS FAMILY IS PICTURESQUE, THE KIND YOU SEE IN AN L.L.BEAN CATALOG.
OOZING WITH EMOTIONAL SUPPORT.
NEVER HAD THAT.
BUT PAUL CLAIMED EMMA HATED HIM?
DID I EVER WANT A FAMILY?
THEY'D PROBABLY HATE ME TOO.
HEY, GET THAT SHIT OUTTA HERE.
SMOKE STAINS THE LEATHER, GODDAMMIT...
SORRY, I WASN'T THINKING...

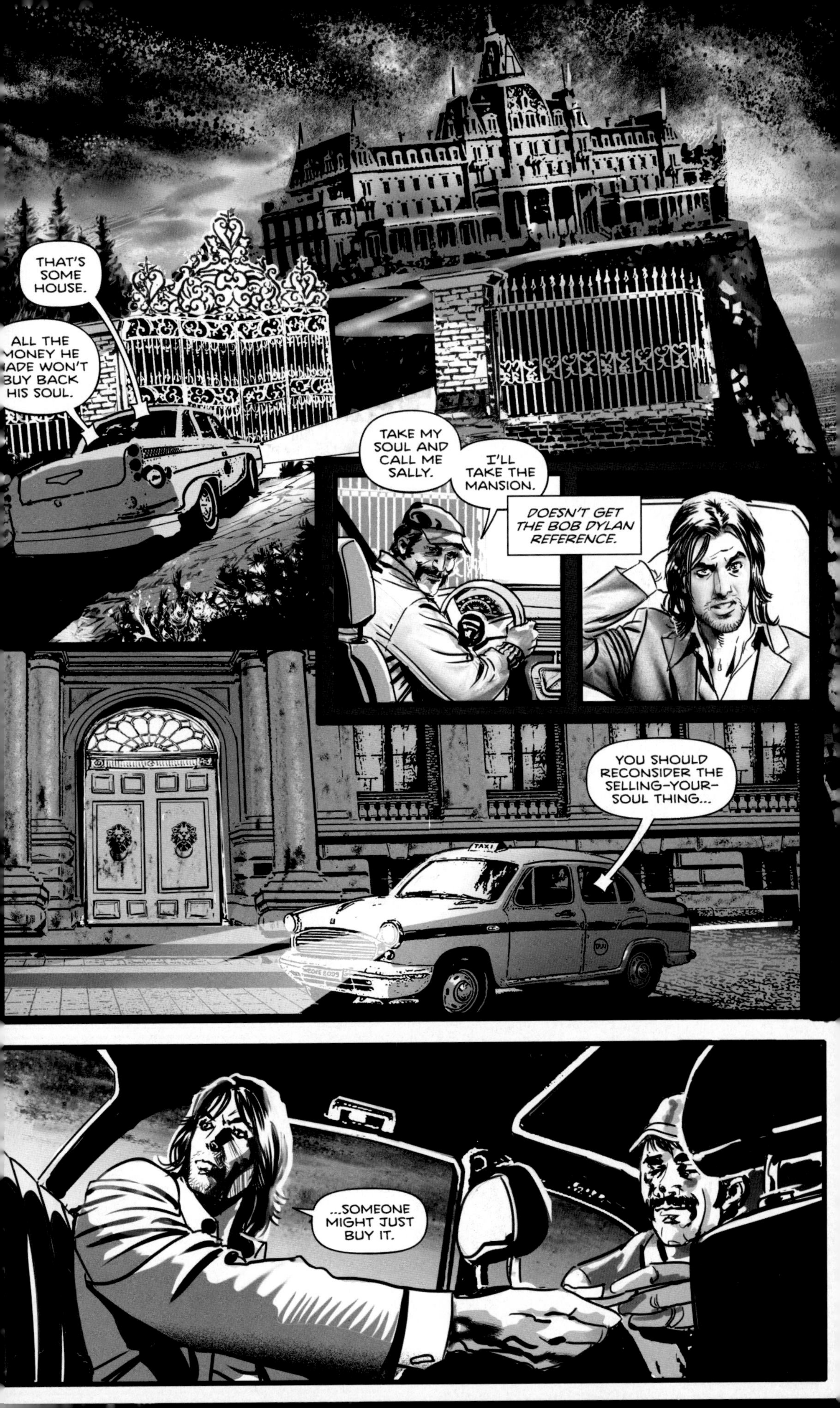
THAT'S SOME HOUSE.
ALL THE MONEY HE MADE WON'T BUY BACK HIS SOUL.
TAKE MY SOUL AND CALL ME SALLY.
I'LL TAKE THE MANSION.
DOESN'T GET THE BOB DYLAN REFERENCE.
YOU SHOULD RECONSIDER THE SELLING-YOUR-SOUL THING...
...SOMEONE MIGHT JUST BUY IT.

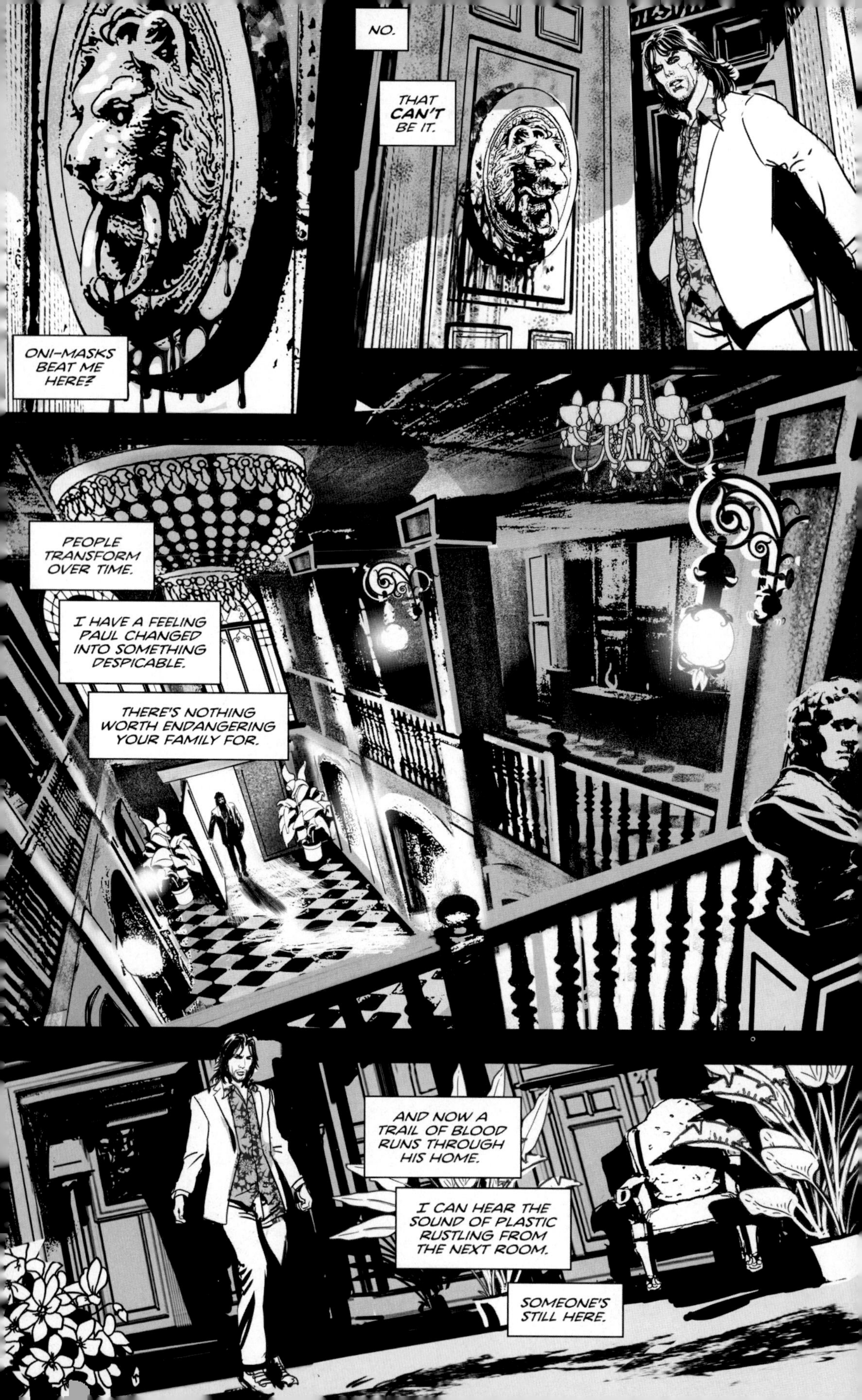
ONI-MASKS BEAT ME HERE?
NO.
THAT CAN'T BE IT.
PEOPLE TRANSFORM OVER TIME.
I HAVE A FEELING PAUL CHANGED INTO SOMETHING DESPICABLE.
THERE'S NOTHING WORTH ENDANGERING YOUR FAMILY FOR.
AND NOW A TRAIL OF BLOOD RUNS THROUGH HIS HOME.
I CAN HEAR THE SOUND OF PLASTIC RUSTLING FROM THE NEXT ROOM.
SOMEONE'S STILL HERE.

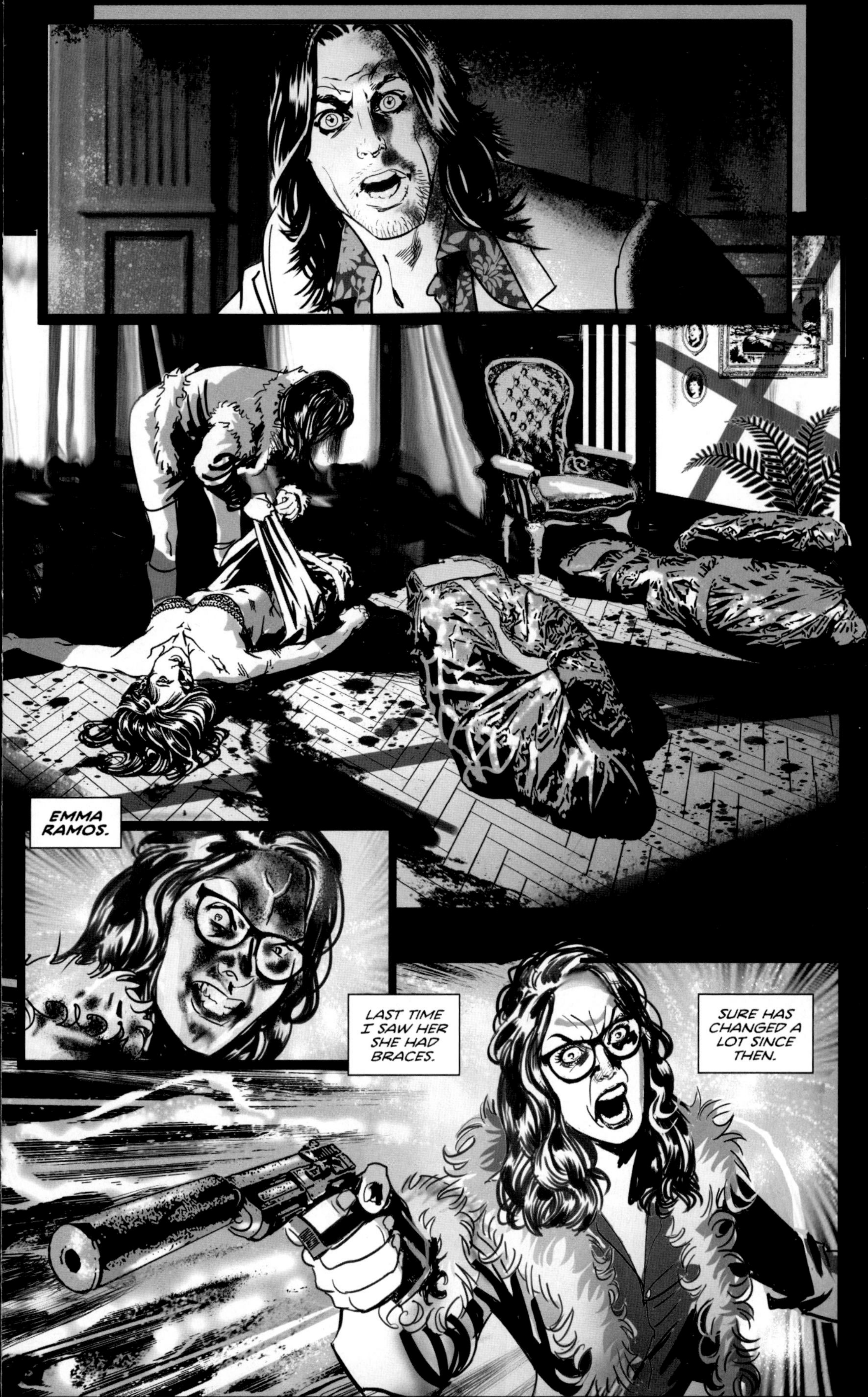
EMMA
RAMOS.
LAST TIME
I SAW HER
SHE HAD
BRACES.
SURE HAS
CHANGED A
LOT SINCE
THEN.

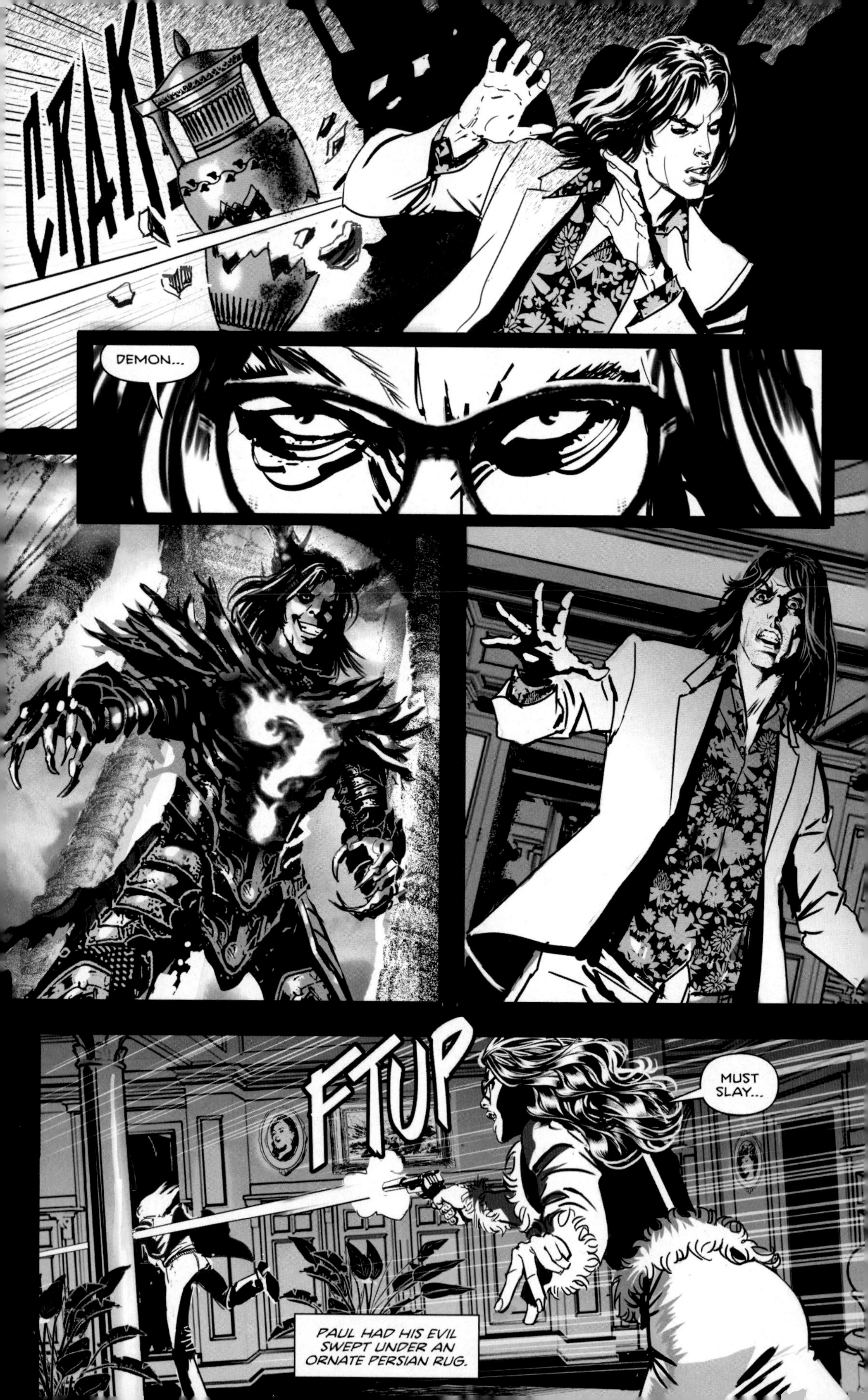
CRAK!
DEMON...
FTUP
MUST SLAY...
PAUL HAD HIS EVIL SWEPT UNDER AN ORNATE PERSIAN RUG.

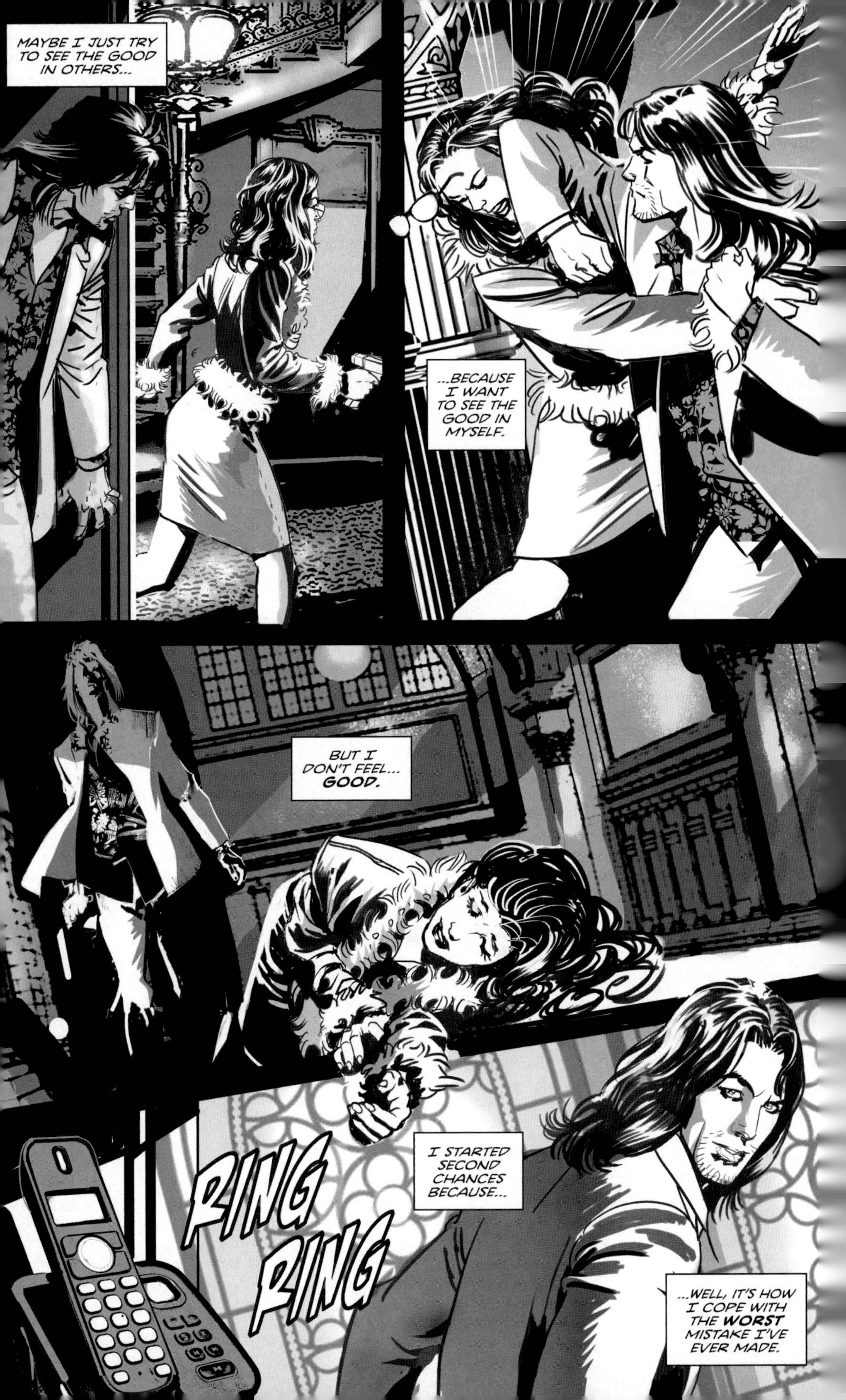
MAYBE I JUST TRY TO SEE THE GOOD IN OTHERS...
...BECAUSE I WANT TO SEE THE GOOD IN MYSELF.
BUT I DON'T FEEL... GOOD.
I STARTED SECOND CHANCES BECAUSE...
RING RING
...WELL, IT'S HOW I COPE WITH THE WORST MISTAKE I'VE EVER MADE.

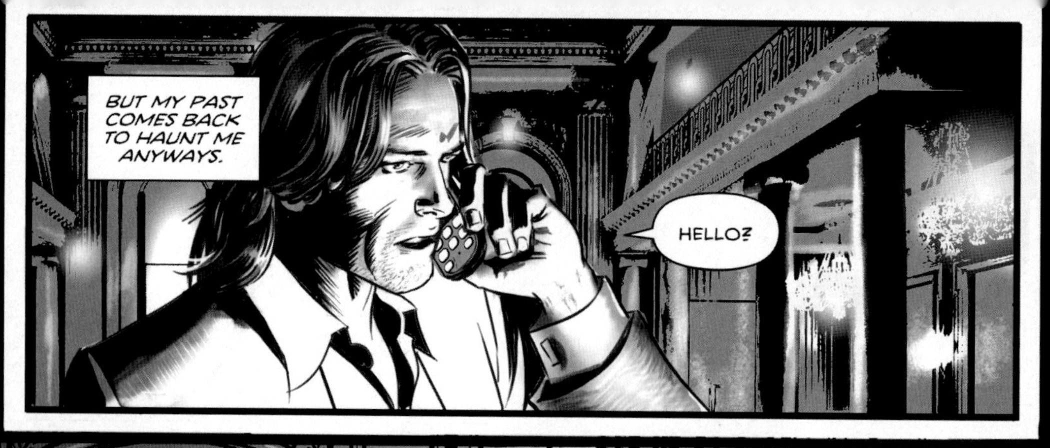
BUT MY PAST COMES BACK TO HAUNT ME ANYWAYS.
HELLO?

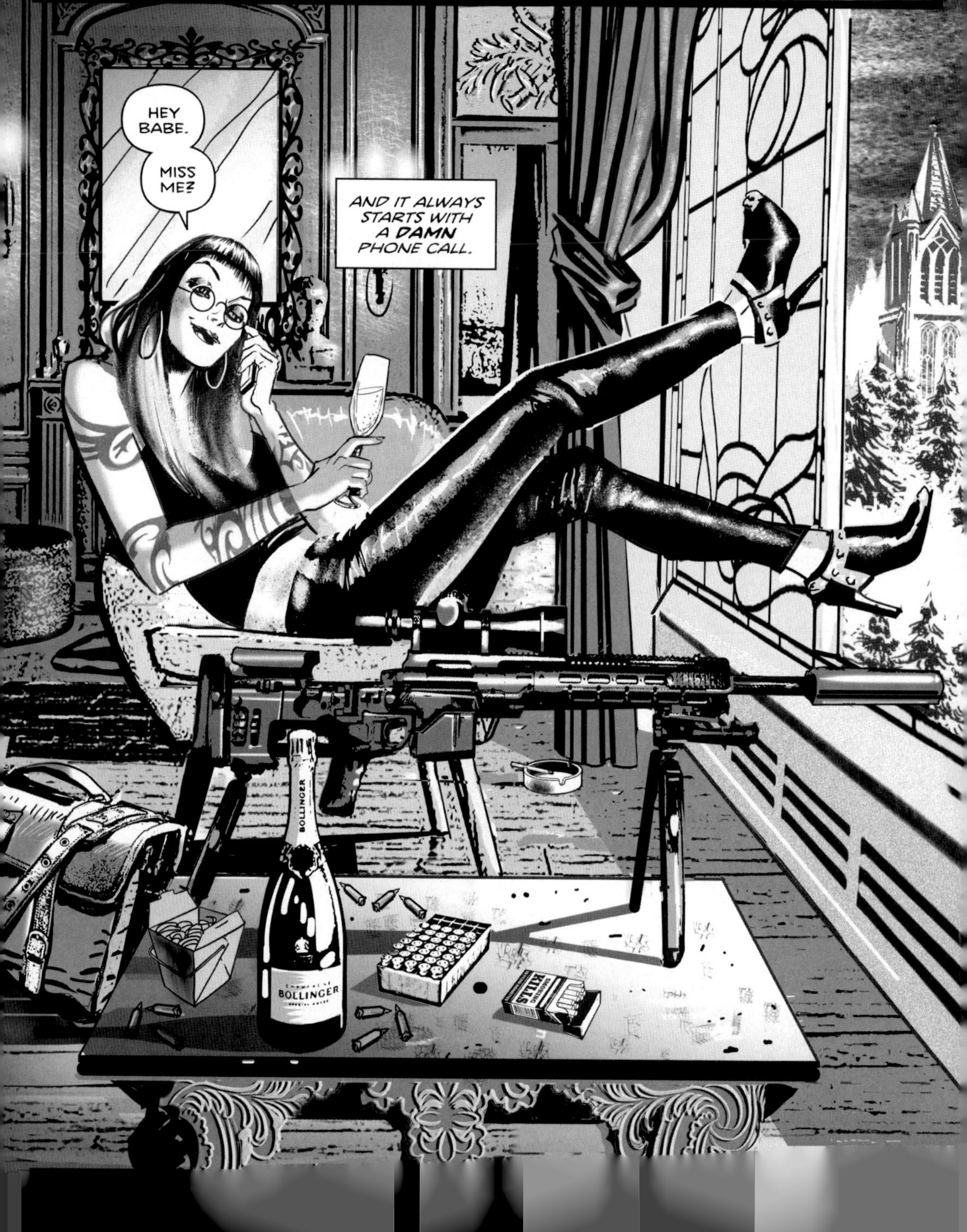
HEY BABE.
MISS ME?
AND IT ALWAYS STARTS WITH A DAMN PHONE CALL.
BOLLINGER

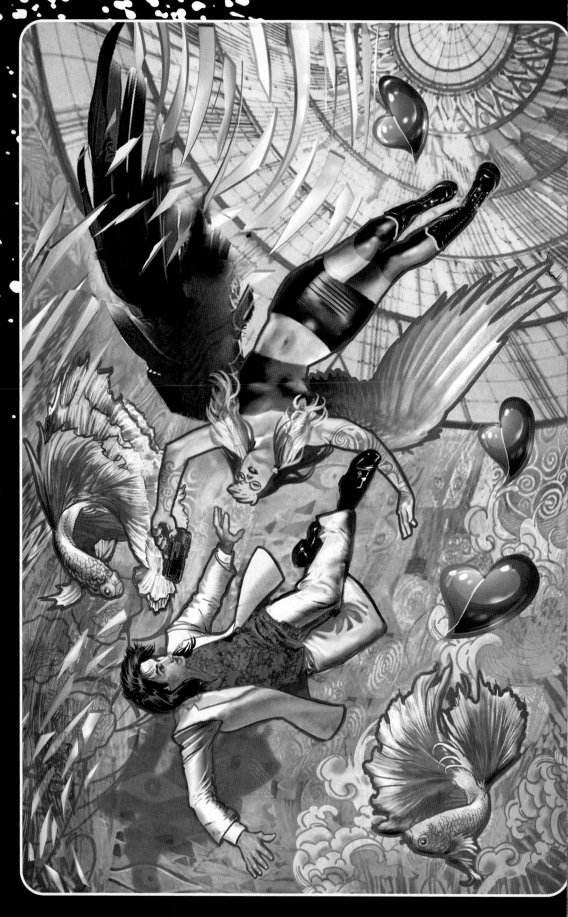

CHAPTER TWO

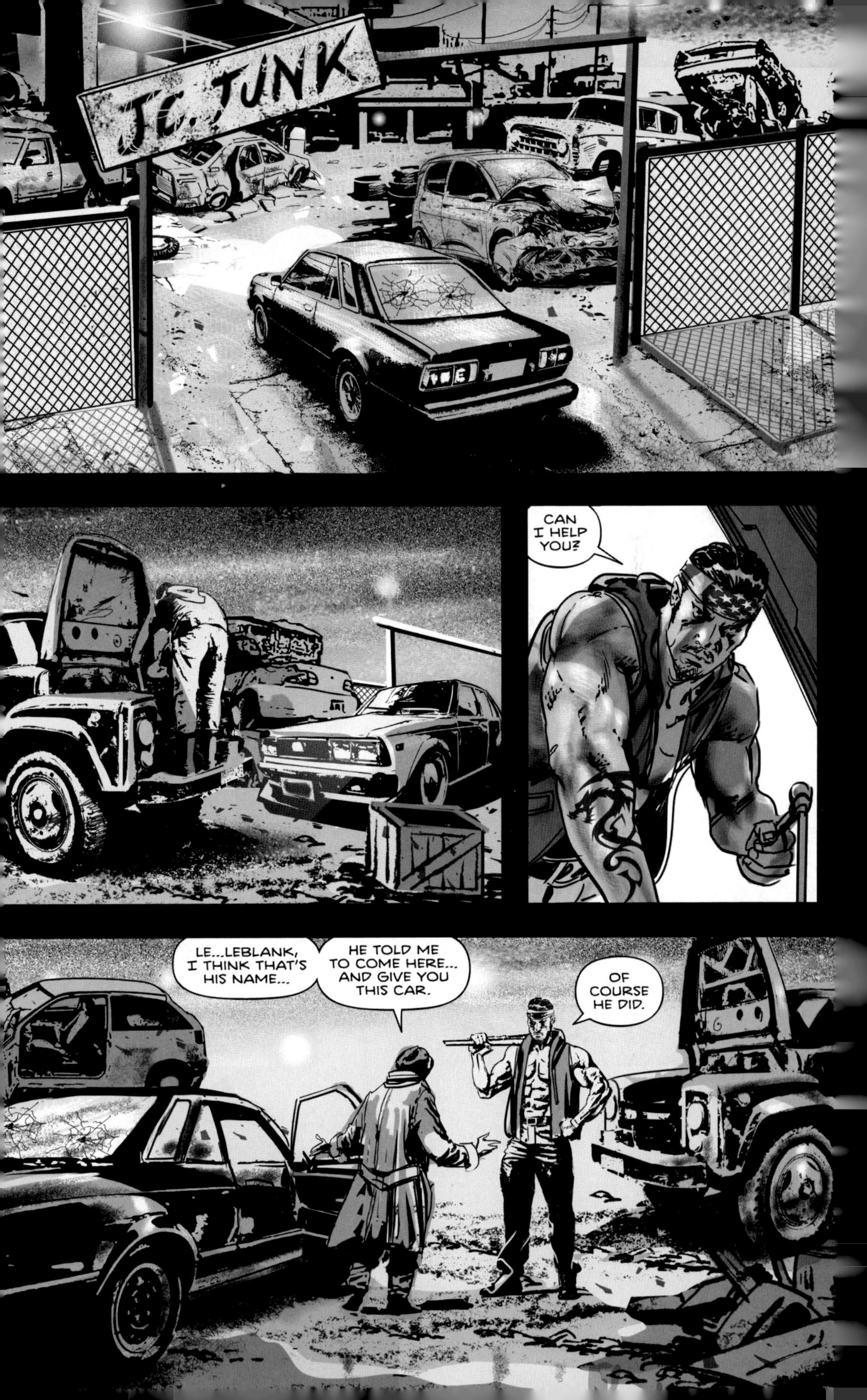

JC. JUNK
CAN I HELP YOU?
LE...LEBLANK, I THINK THAT'S HIS NAME...
HE TOLD ME TO COME HERE... AND GIVE YOU THIS CAR.
OF COURSE HE DID.

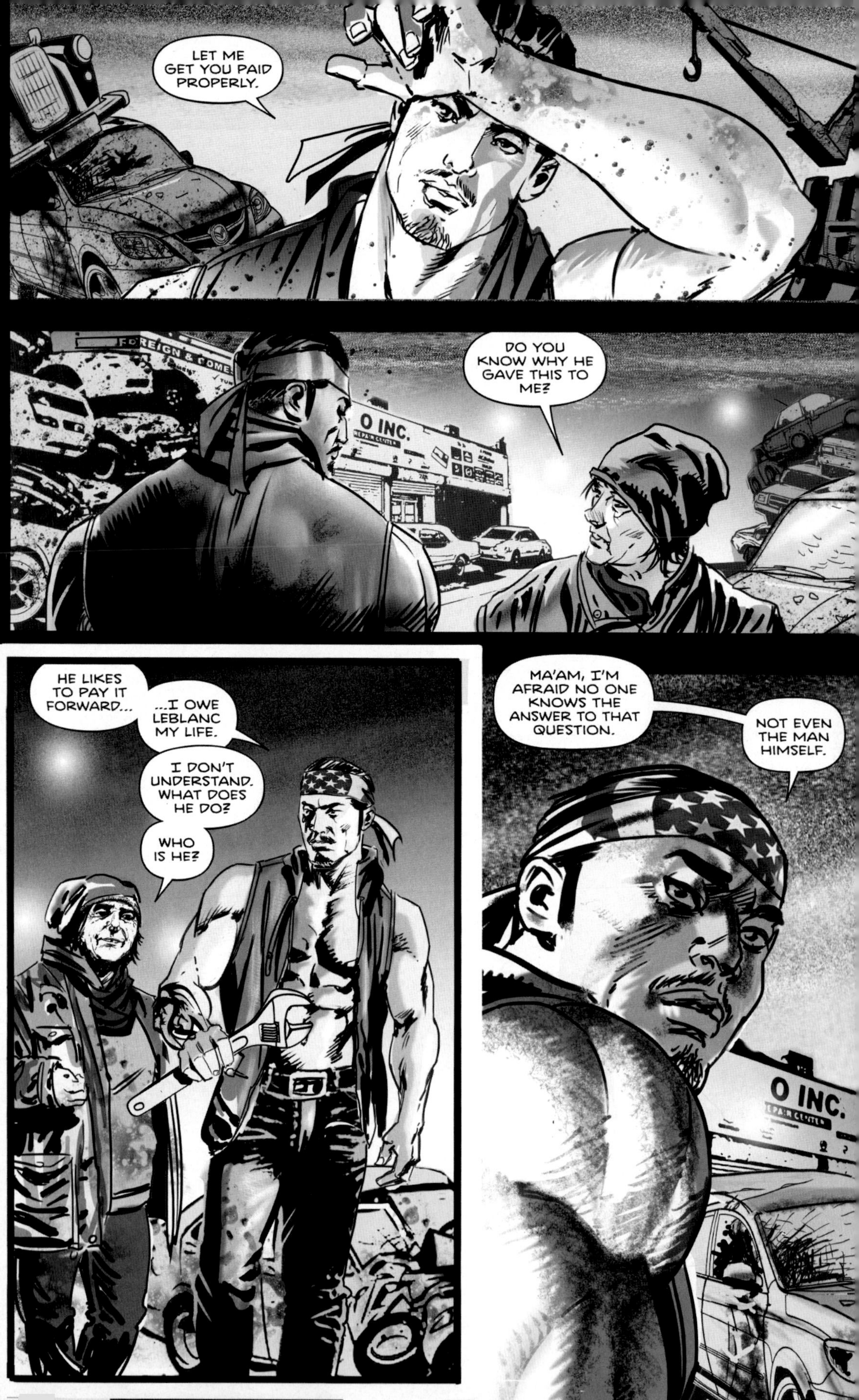
LET ME GET YOU PAID PROPERLY.
FOREIGN & DOME
O INC.
DO YOU KNOW WHY HE GAVE THIS TO ME?
HE LIKES TO PAY IT FORWARD...
...I OWE LEBLANC MY LIFE.
I DON'T UNDERSTAND. WHAT DOES HE DO?
WHO IS HE?
MA'AM, I'M AFRAID NO ONE KNOWS THE ANSWER TO THAT QUESTION.
NOT EVEN THE MAN HIMSELF.
O INC.

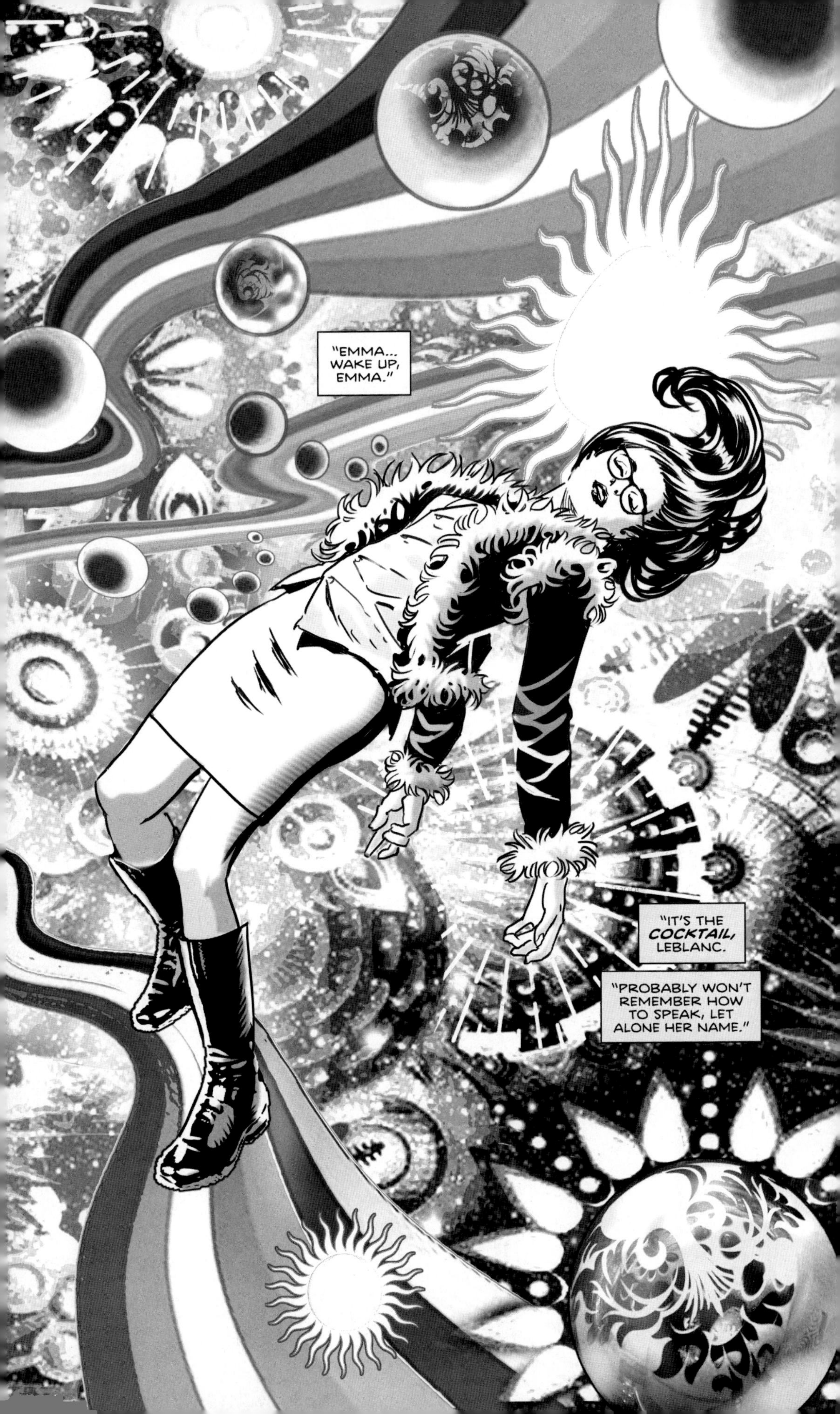
"EMMA... WAKE UP, EMMA."
"IT'S THE COCKTAIL, LEBLANC.
"PROBABLY WON'T REMEMBER HOW TO SPEAK, LET ALONE HER NAME."

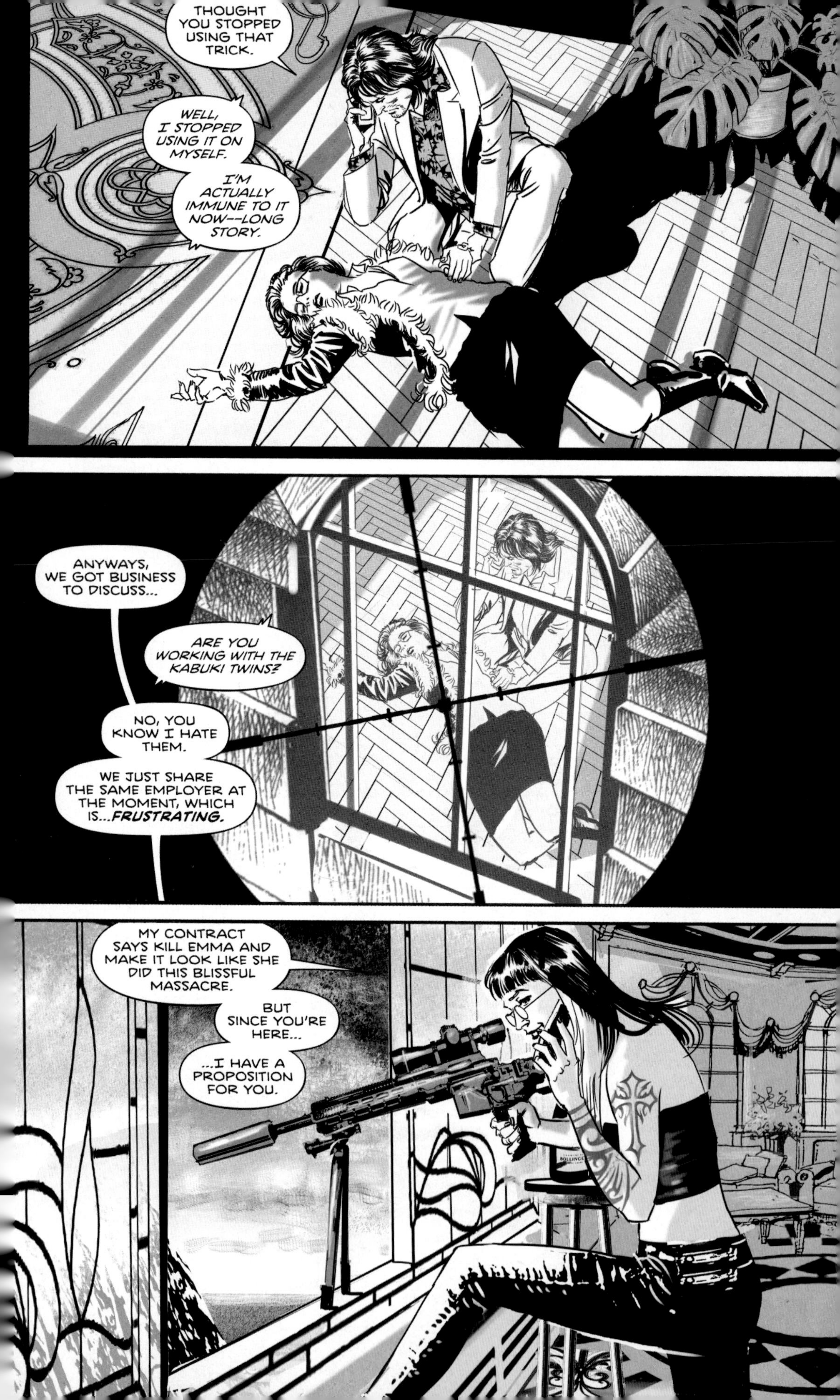
THOUGHT YOU STOPPED USING THAT TRICK.
WELL, I STOPPED USING IT ON MYSELF.
I'M ACTUALLY IMMUNE TO IT NOW--LONG STORY.
ANYWAYS, WE GOT BUSINESS TO DISCUSS...
ARE YOU WORKING WITH THE KABUKI TWINS?
NO, YOU KNOW I HATE THEM.
WE JUST SHARE THE SAME EMPLOYER AT THE MOMENT, WHICH IS...FRUSTRATING.
MY CONTRACT SAYS KILL EMMA AND MAKE IT LOOK LIKE SHE DID THIS BLISSFUL MASSACRE.
BUT SINCE YOU'RE HERE...
...I HAVE A PROPOSITION FOR YOU.

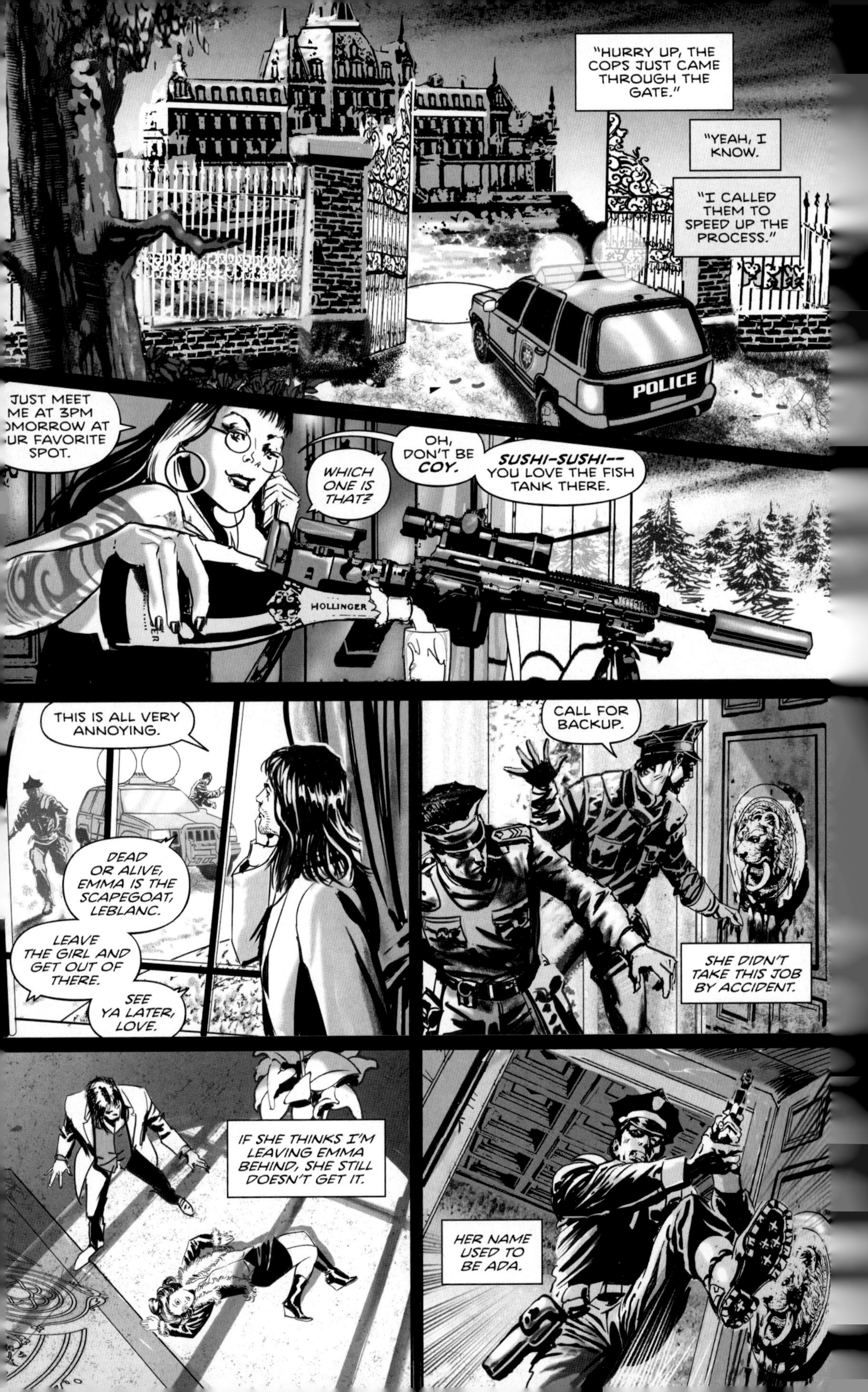
"HURRY UP, THE COPS JUST CAME THROUGH THE GATE."
"YEAH, I KNOW.
"I CALLED THEM TO SPEED UP THE PROCESS."
POLICE
JUST MEET ME AT 3PM TOMORROW AT OUR FAVORITE SPOT.
WHICH ONE IS THAT?
OH, DON'T BE COY.
SUSHI-SUSHI-- YOU LOVE THE FISH TANK THERE.
HOLLINGER
THIS IS ALL VERY ANNOYING.
DEAD OR ALIVE, EMMA IS THE SCAPEGOAT, LEBLANC.
LEAVE THE GIRL AND GET OUT OF THERE.
SEE YA LATER, LOVE.
CALL FOR BACKUP.
SHE DIDN'T TAKE THIS JOB BY ACCIDENT.
IF SHE THINKS I'M LEAVING EMMA BEHIND, SHE STILL DOESN'T GET IT.
HER NAME USED TO BE ADA.

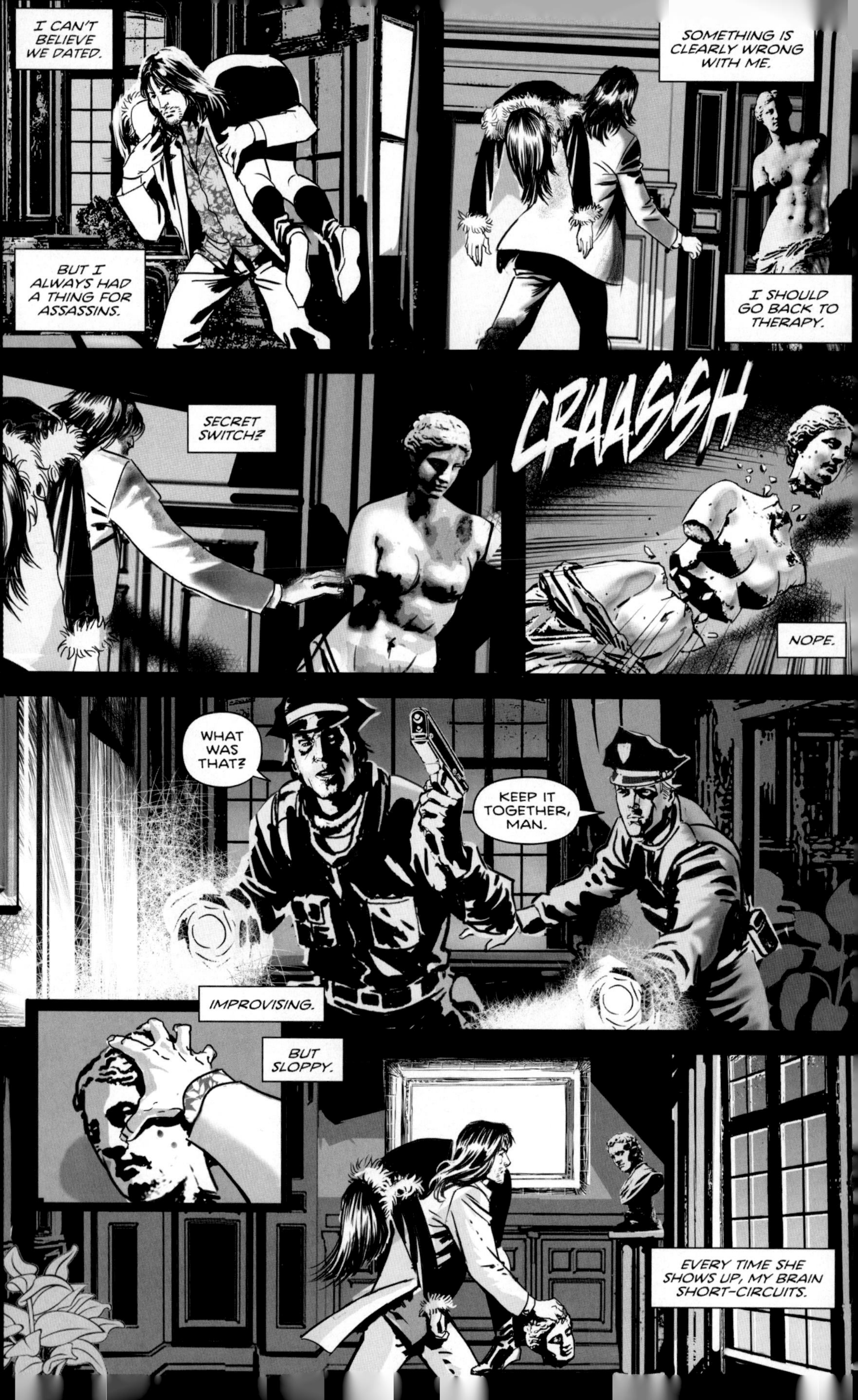
I CAN'T BELIEVE WE DATED.
BUT I ALWAYS HAD A THING FOR ASSASSINS.
SOMETHING IS CLEARLY WRONG WITH ME.
I SHOULD GO BACK TO THERAPY.
SECRET SWITCH?
CRAASSH
NOPE.
WHAT WAS THAT?
KEEP IT TOGETHER, MAN.
IMPROVISING.
BUT SLOPPY.
EVERY TIME SHE SHOWS UP, MY BRAIN SHORT-CIRCUITS.

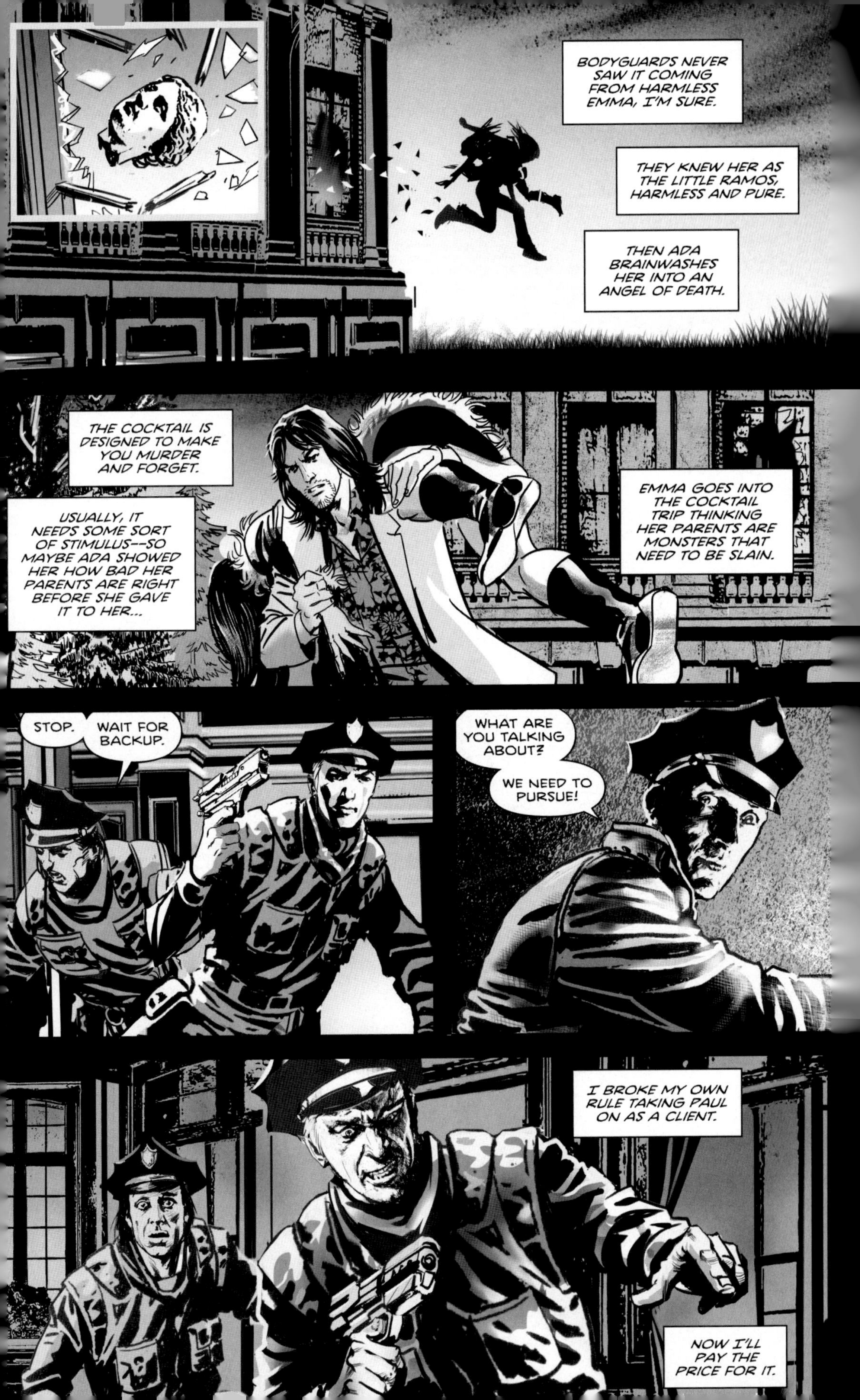
BODYGUARDS NEVER SAW IT COMING FROM HARMLESS EMMA, I'M SURE.
THEY KNEW HER AS THE LITTLE RAMOS, HARMLESS AND PURE.
THEN ADA BRAINWASHES HER INTO AN ANGEL OF DEATH.
THE COCKTAIL IS DESIGNED TO MAKE YOU MURDER AND FORGET.
USUALLY, IT NEEDS SOME SORT OF STIMULUS--SO MAYBE ADA SHOWED HER HOW BAD HER PARENTS ARE RIGHT BEFORE SHE GAVE IT TO HER...
EMMA GOES INTO THE COCKTAIL TRIP THINKING HER PARENTS ARE MONSTERS THAT NEED TO BE SLAIN.
STOP.
WAIT FOR BACKUP.
WHAT ARE YOU TALKING ABOUT?
WE NEED TO PURSUE!
I BROKE MY OWN RULE TAKING PAUL ON AS A CLIENT.
NOW I'LL PAY THE PRICE FOR IT.

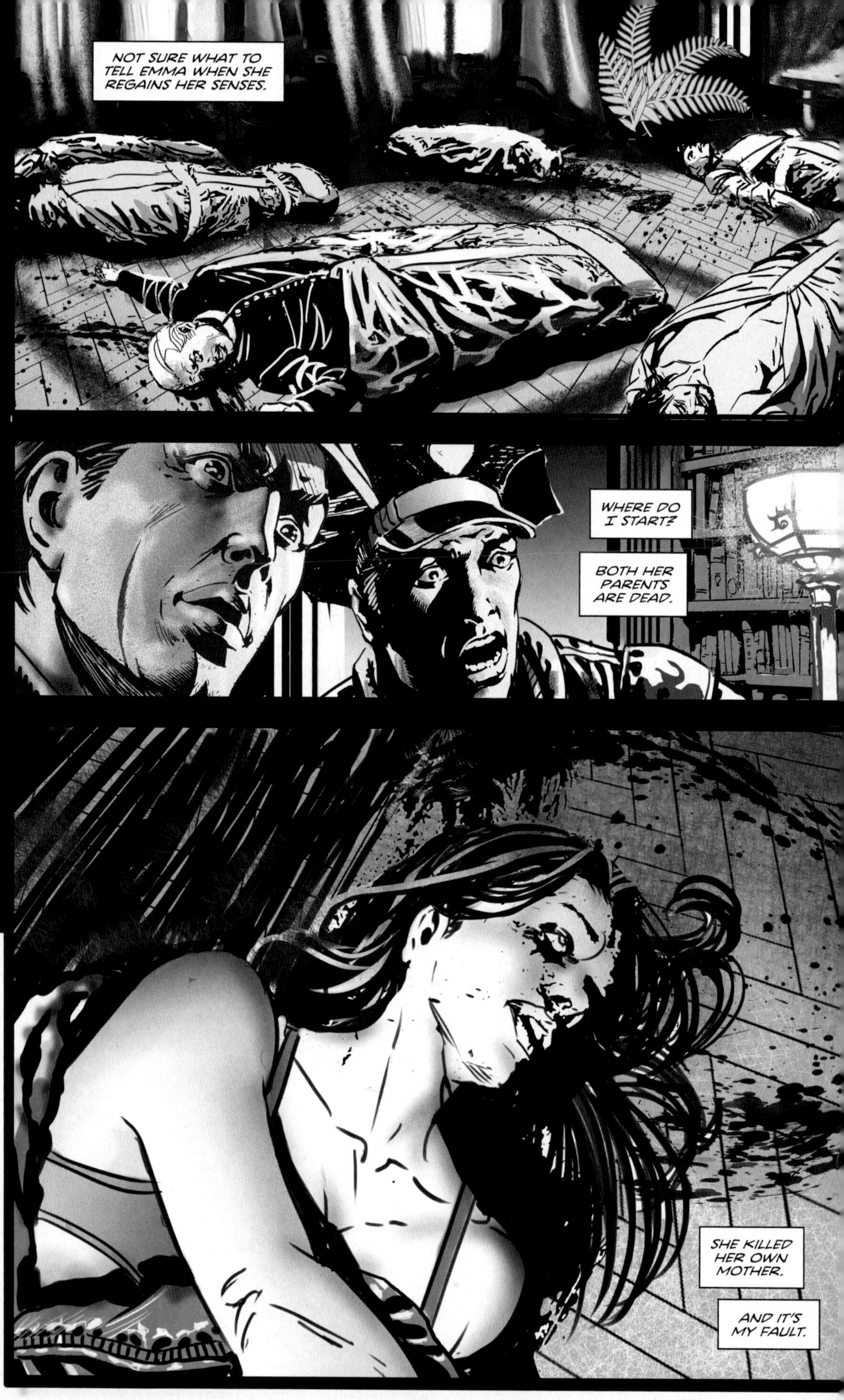
NOT SURE WHAT TO TELL EMMA WHEN SHE REGAINS HER SENSES.
WHERE DO I START?
BOTH HER PARENTS ARE DEAD.
SHE KILLED HER OWN MOTHER.
AND IT'S MY FAULT.

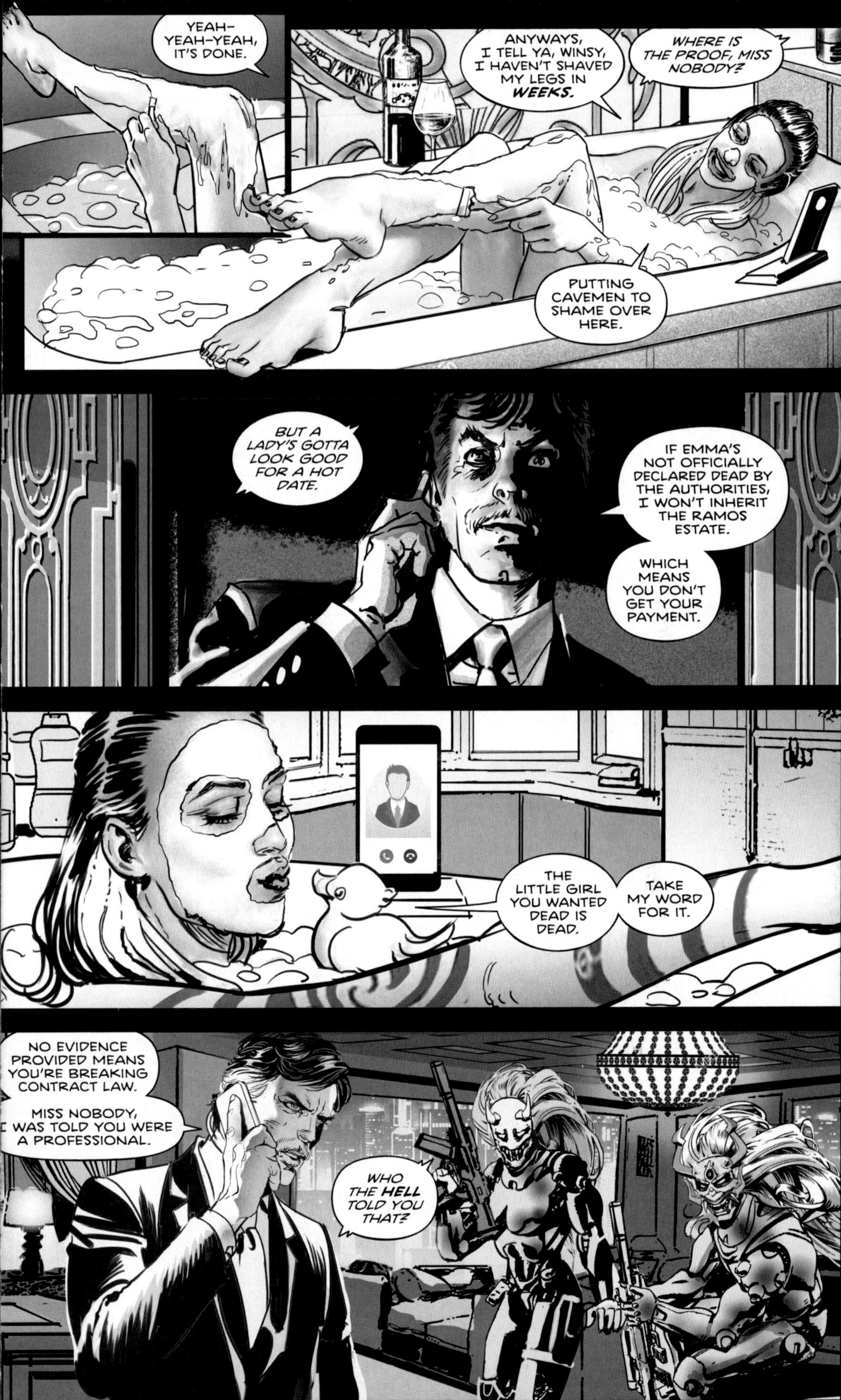

YEAH-YEAH-YEAH, IT'S DONE.
ANYWAYS, I TELL YA, WINSY, I HAVEN'T SHAVED MY LEGS IN WEEKS.
WHERE IS THE PROOF, MISS NOBODY?
PUTTING CAVEMEN TO SHAME OVER HERE.
BUT A LADY'S GOTTA LOOK GOOD FOR A HOT DATE.
IF EMMA'S NOT OFFICIALLY DECLARED DEAD BY THE AUTHORITIES, I WON'T INHERIT THE RAMOS ESTATE.
WHICH MEANS YOU DON'T GET YOUR PAYMENT.
THE LITTLE GIRL YOU WANTED DEAD IS DEAD.
TAKE MY WORD FOR IT.
NO EVIDENCE PROVIDED MEANS YOU'RE BREAKING CONTRACT LAW.
MISS NOBODY, I WAS TOLD YOU WERE A PROFESSIONAL.
WHO THE HELL TOLD YOU THAT?

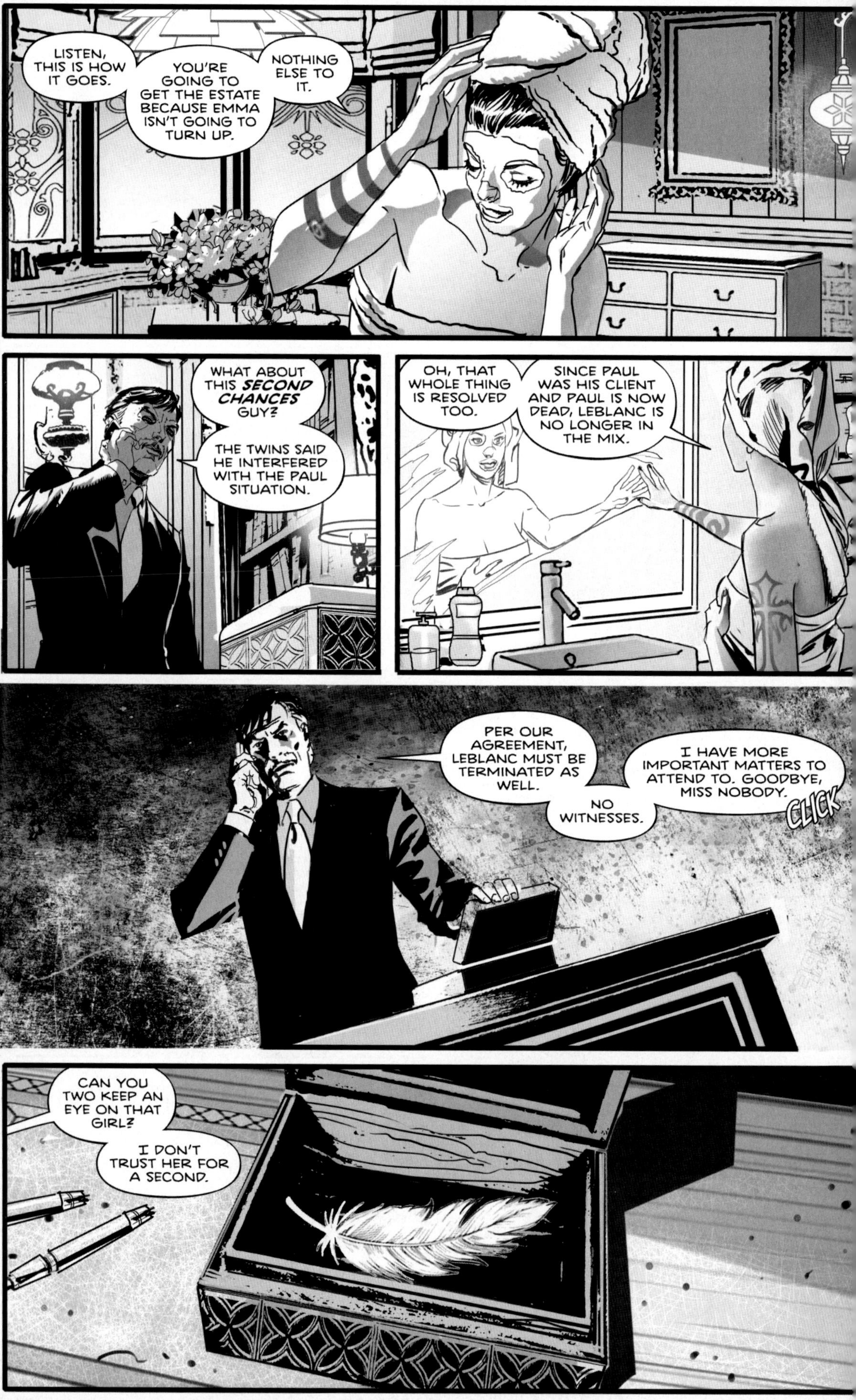

LISTEN, THIS IS HOW IT GOES.
YOU'RE GOING TO GET THE ESTATE BECAUSE EMMA ISN'T GOING TO TURN UP.
NOTHING ELSE TO IT.
WHAT ABOUT THIS *SECOND CHANCES* GUY?
THE TWINS SAID HE INTERFERED WITH THE PAUL SITUATION.
OH, THAT WHOLE THING IS RESOLVED TOO.
SINCE PAUL WAS HIS CLIENT AND PAUL IS NOW DEAD, LEBLANC IS NO LONGER IN THE MIX.
PER OUR AGREEMENT, LEBLANC MUST BE TERMINATED AS WELL.
NO WITNESSES.
I HAVE MORE IMPORTANT MATTERS TO ATTEND TO. GOODBYE, MISS NOBODY.
CLICK
CAN YOU TWO KEEP AN EYE ON THAT GIRL?
I DON'T TRUST HER FOR A SECOND.

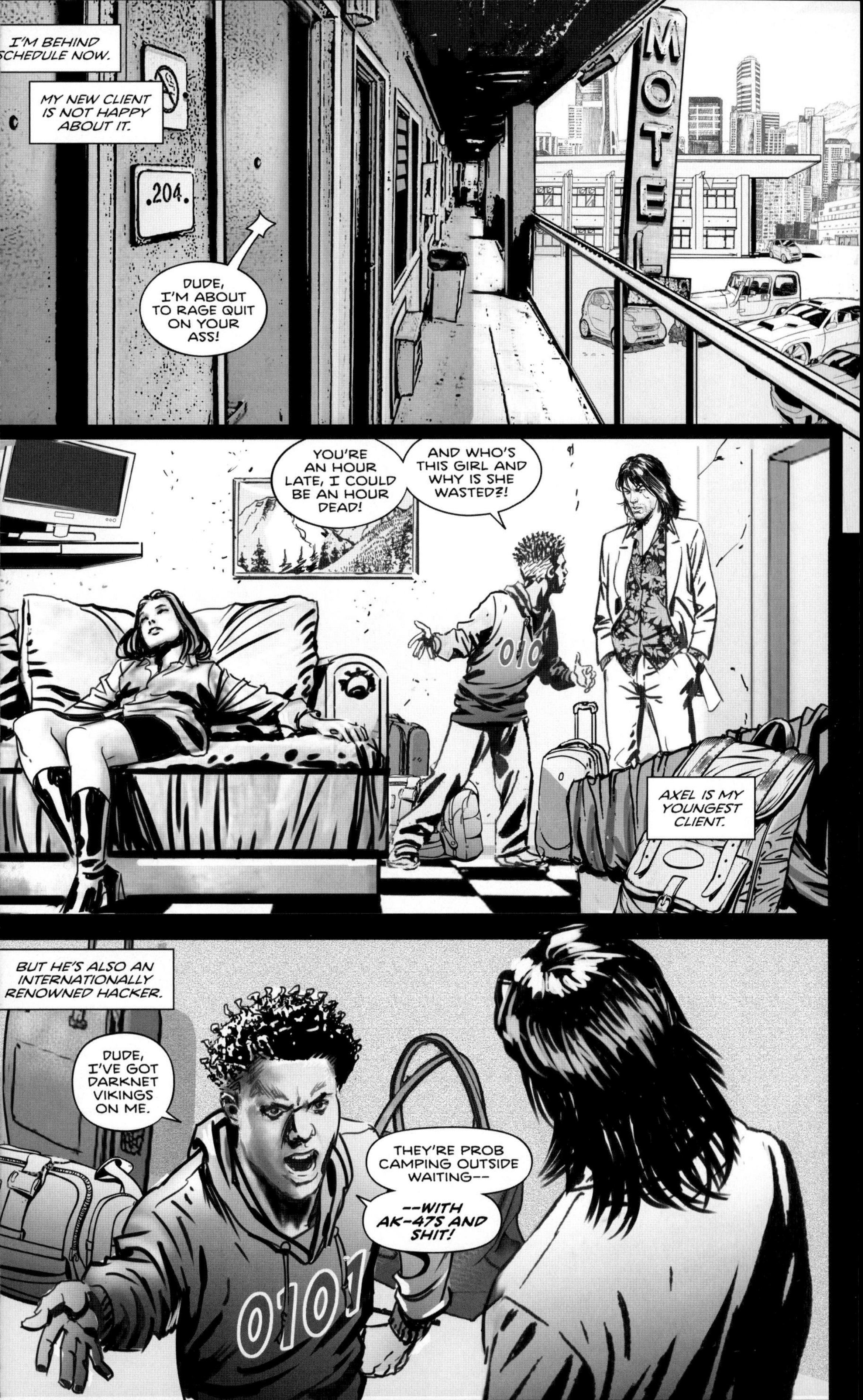
I'M BEHIND SCHEDULE NOW.
MY NEW CLIENT IS NOT HAPPY ABOUT IT.
.204.
DUDE, I'M ABOUT TO RAGE QUIT ON YOUR ASS!
MOTEL
YOU'RE AN HOUR LATE, I COULD BE AN HOUR DEAD!
AND WHO'S THIS GIRL AND WHY IS SHE WASTED?!
0101
AXEL IS MY YOUNGEST CLIENT.
BUT HE'S ALSO AN INTERNATIONALLY RENOWNED HACKER.
DUDE, I'VE GOT DARKNET VIKINGS ON ME.
THEY'RE PROB CAMPING OUTSIDE WAITING--
--WITH AK-47S AND SHIT!
0101

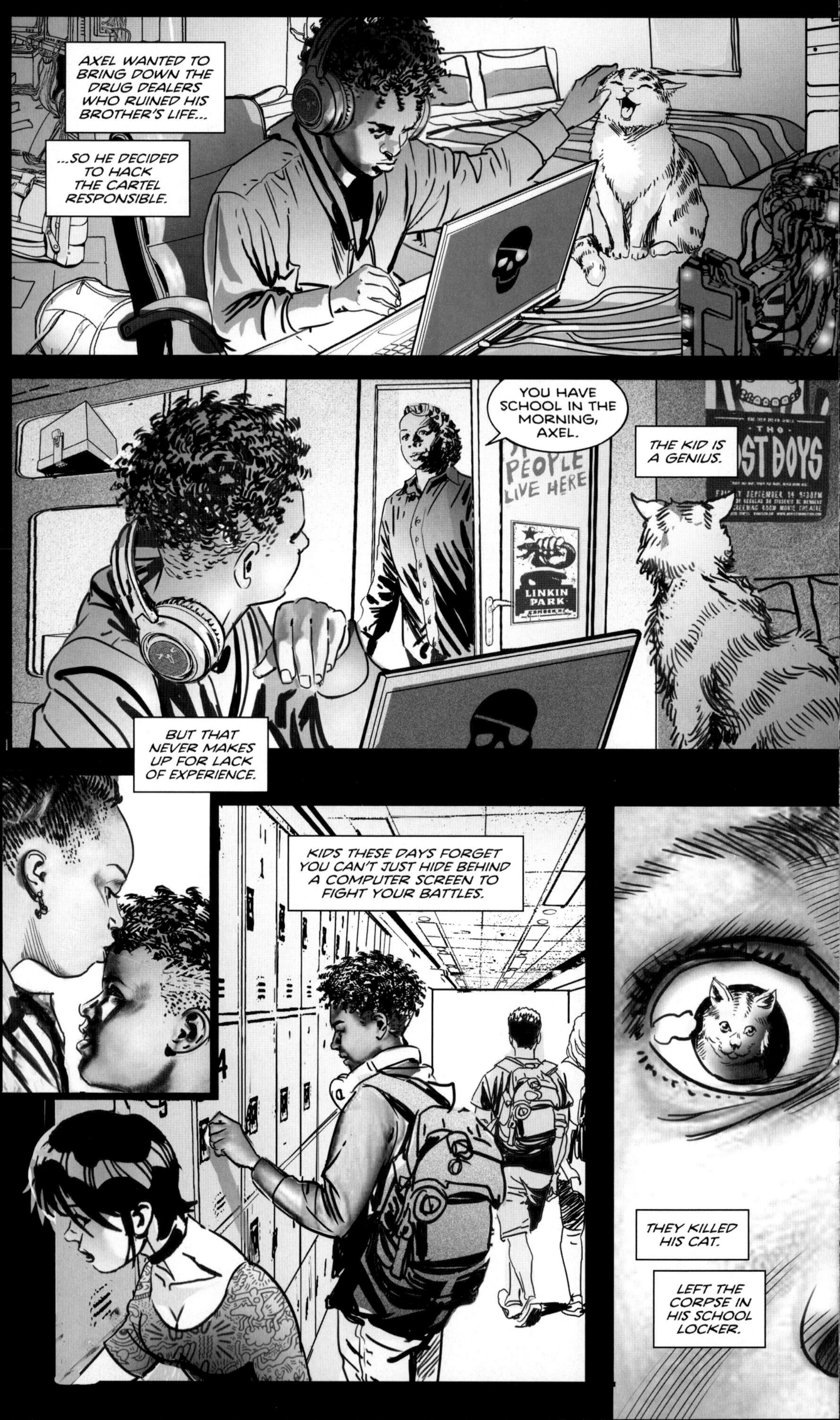
AXEL WANTED TO BRING DOWN THE DRUG DEALERS WHO RUINED HIS BROTHER'S LIFE...
...SO HE DECIDED TO HACK THE CARTEL RESPONSIBLE.
YOU HAVE SCHOOL IN THE MORNING, AXEL.
THE KID IS A GENIUS.
PEOPLE LIVE HERE
LINKIN PARK
BUT THAT NEVER MAKES UP FOR LACK OF EXPERIENCE.
KIDS THESE DAYS FORGET YOU CAN'T JUST HIDE BEHIND A COMPUTER SCREEN TO FIGHT YOUR BATTLES.
THEY KILLED HIS CAT.
LEFT THE CORPSE IN HIS SCHOOL LOCKER.

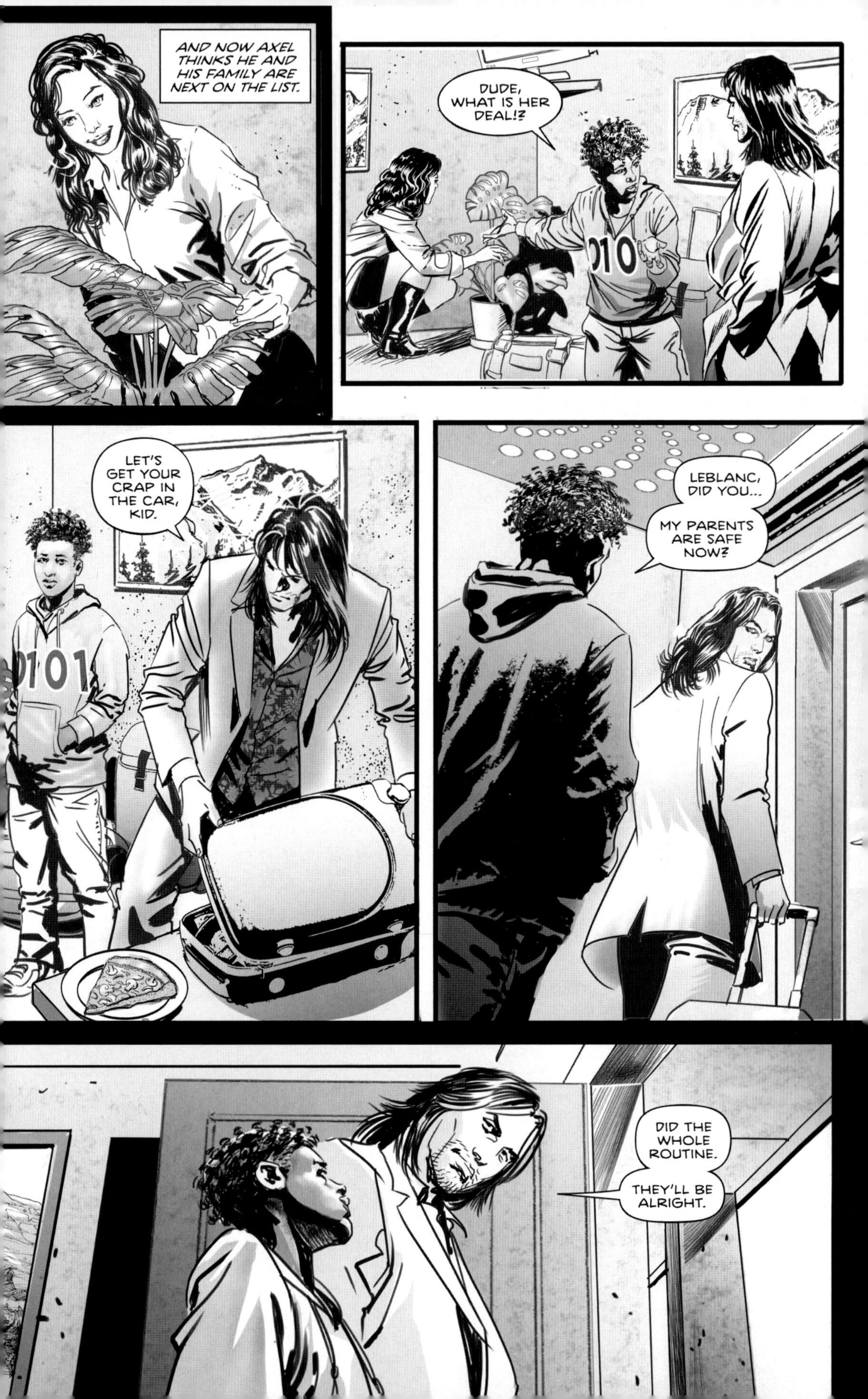
AND NOW AXEL THINKS HE AND HIS FAMILY ARE NEXT ON THE LIST.
DUDE, WHAT IS HER DEAL!?
0101
LET'S GET YOUR CRAP IN THE CAR, KID.
0101
LEBLANC, DID YOU...
MY PARENTS ARE SAFE NOW?
DID THE WHOLE ROUTINE.
THEY'LL BE ALRIGHT.

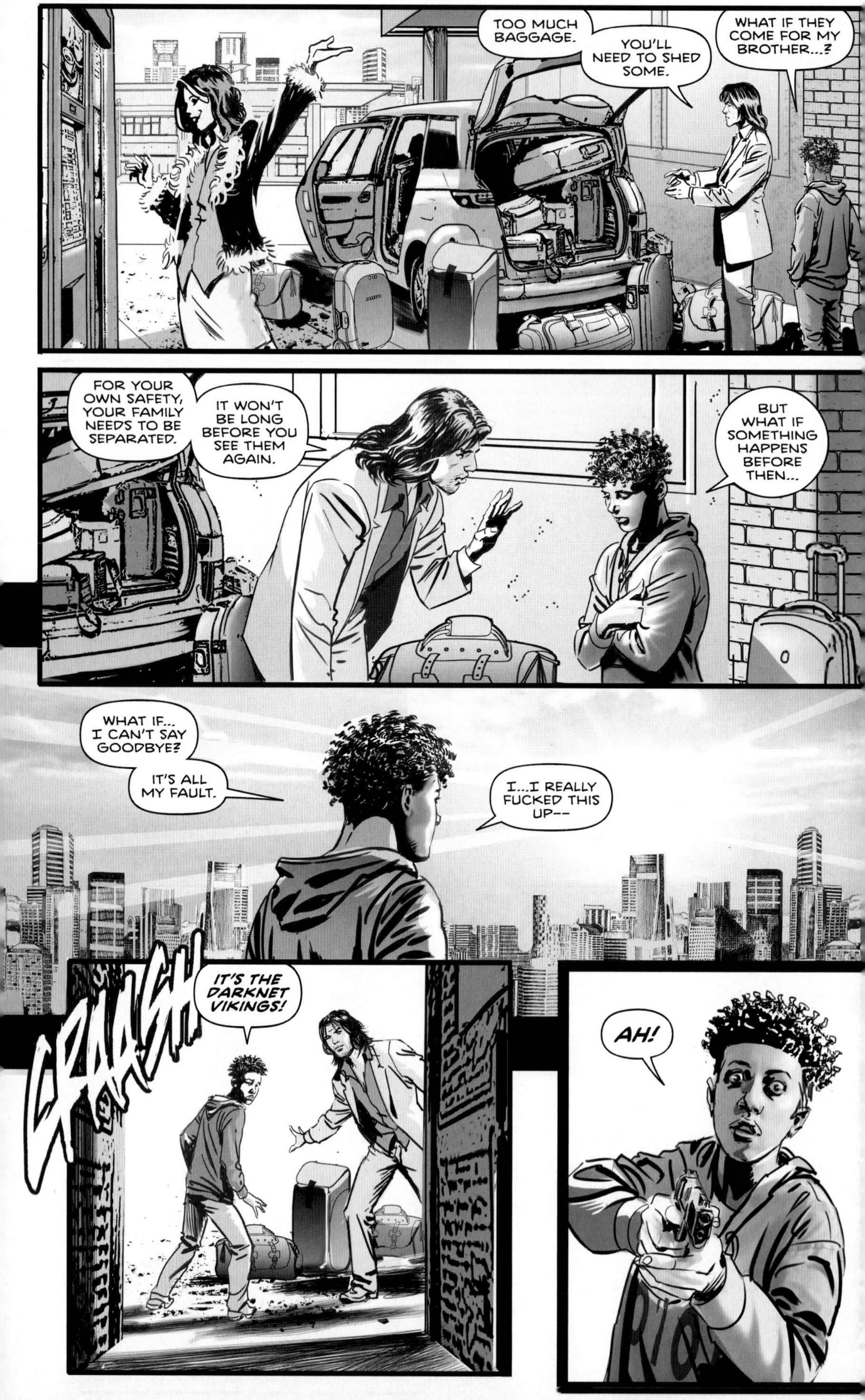
TOO MUCH BAGGAGE.
YOU'LL NEED TO SHED SOME.
WHAT IF THEY COME FOR MY BROTHER...?
FOR YOUR OWN SAFETY, YOUR FAMILY NEEDS TO BE SEPARATED.
IT WON'T BE LONG BEFORE YOU SEE THEM AGAIN.
BUT WHAT IF SOMETHING HAPPENS BEFORE THEN...
WHAT IF... I CAN'T SAY GOODBYE?
IT'S ALL MY FAULT.
I...I REALLY FUCKED THIS UP--
CRASH
IT'S THE DARKNET VIKINGS!
AH!

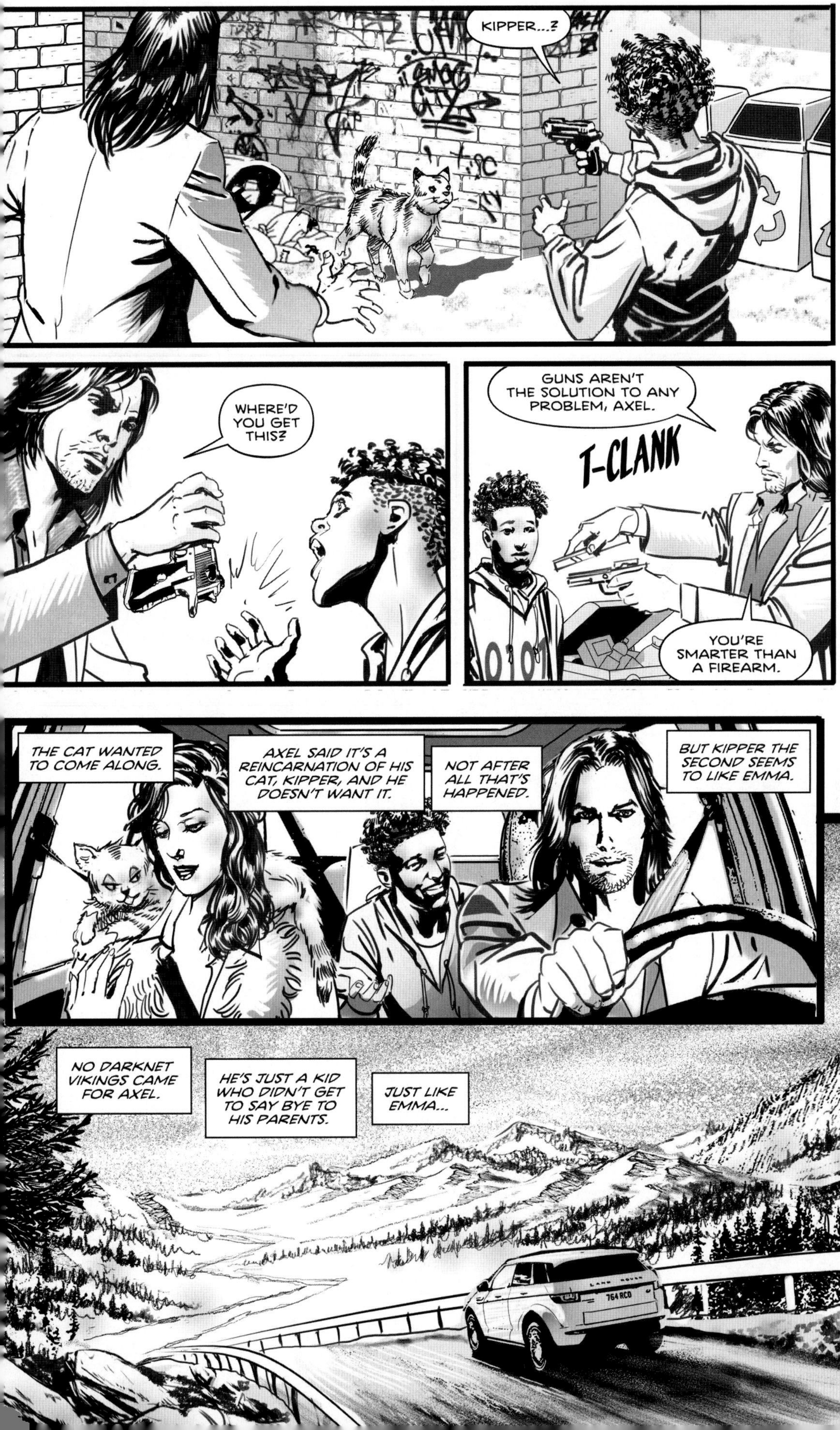

KIPPER...?
WHERE'D YOU GET THIS?
GUNS AREN'T THE SOLUTION TO ANY PROBLEM, AXEL.
T-CLANK
YOU'RE SMARTER THAN A FIREARM.
THE CAT WANTED TO COME ALONG.
AXEL SAID IT'S A REINCARNATION OF HIS CAT, KIPPER, AND HE DOESN'T WANT IT.
NOT AFTER ALL THAT'S HAPPENED.
BUT KIPPER THE SECOND SEEMS TO LIKE EMMA.
NO DARKNET VIKINGS CAME FOR AXEL.
HE'S JUST A KID WHO DIDN'T GET TO SAY BYE TO HIS PARENTS.
JUST LIKE EMMA...

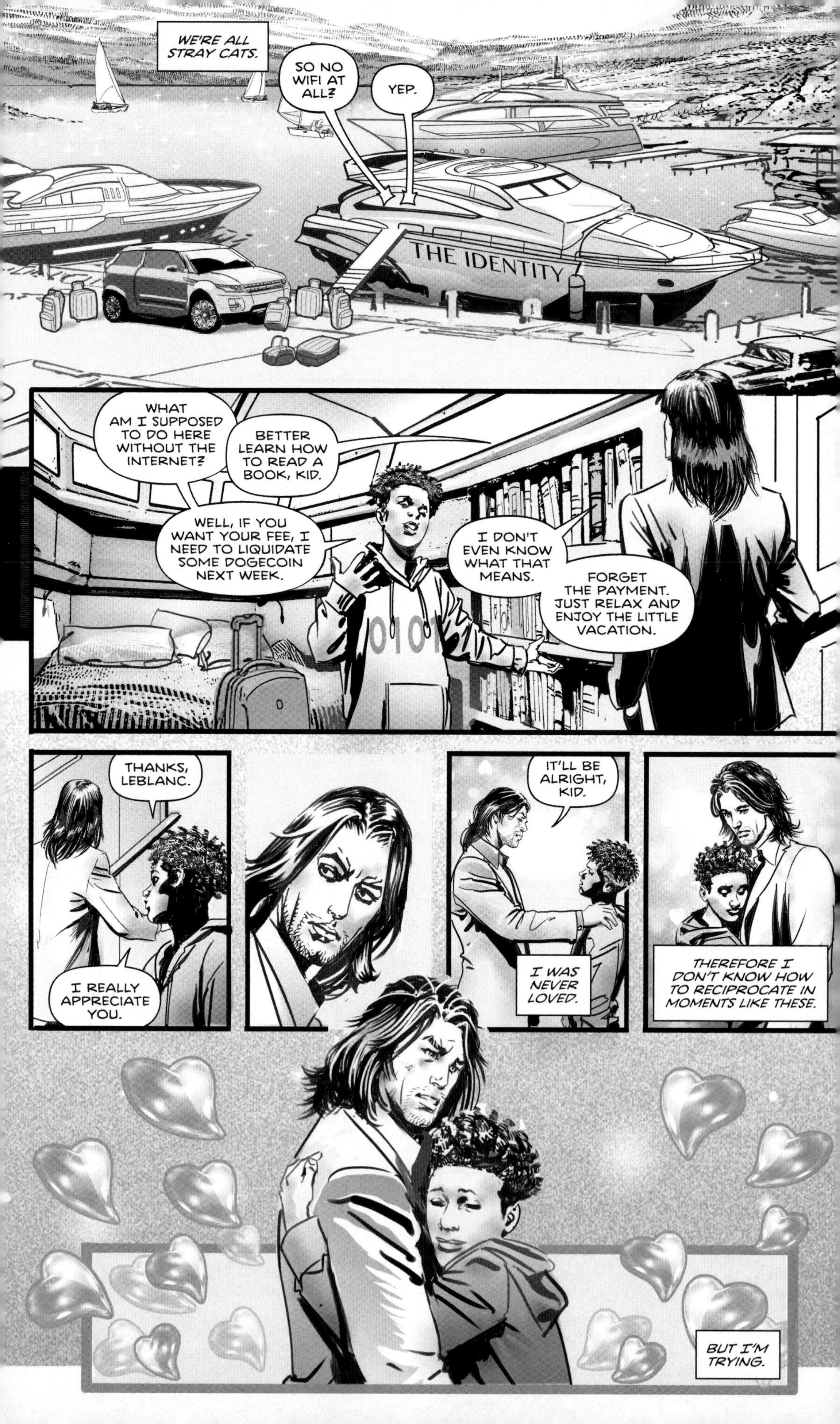
WE'RE ALL STRAY CATS.
SO NO WIFI AT ALL?
YEP.
THE IDENTITY
WHAT AM I SUPPOSED TO DO HERE WITHOUT THE INTERNET?
BETTER LEARN HOW TO READ A BOOK, KID.
WELL, IF YOU WANT YOUR FEE, I NEED TO LIQUIDATE SOME DOGECOIN NEXT WEEK.
I DON'T EVEN KNOW WHAT THAT MEANS.
FORGET THE PAYMENT. JUST RELAX AND ENJOY THE LITTLE VACATION.
THANKS, LEBLANC.
I REALLY APPRECIATE YOU.
IT'LL BE ALRIGHT, KID.
I WAS NEVER LOVED.
THEREFORE I DON'T KNOW HOW TO RECIPROCATE IN MOMENTS LIKE THESE.
BUT I'M TRYING.

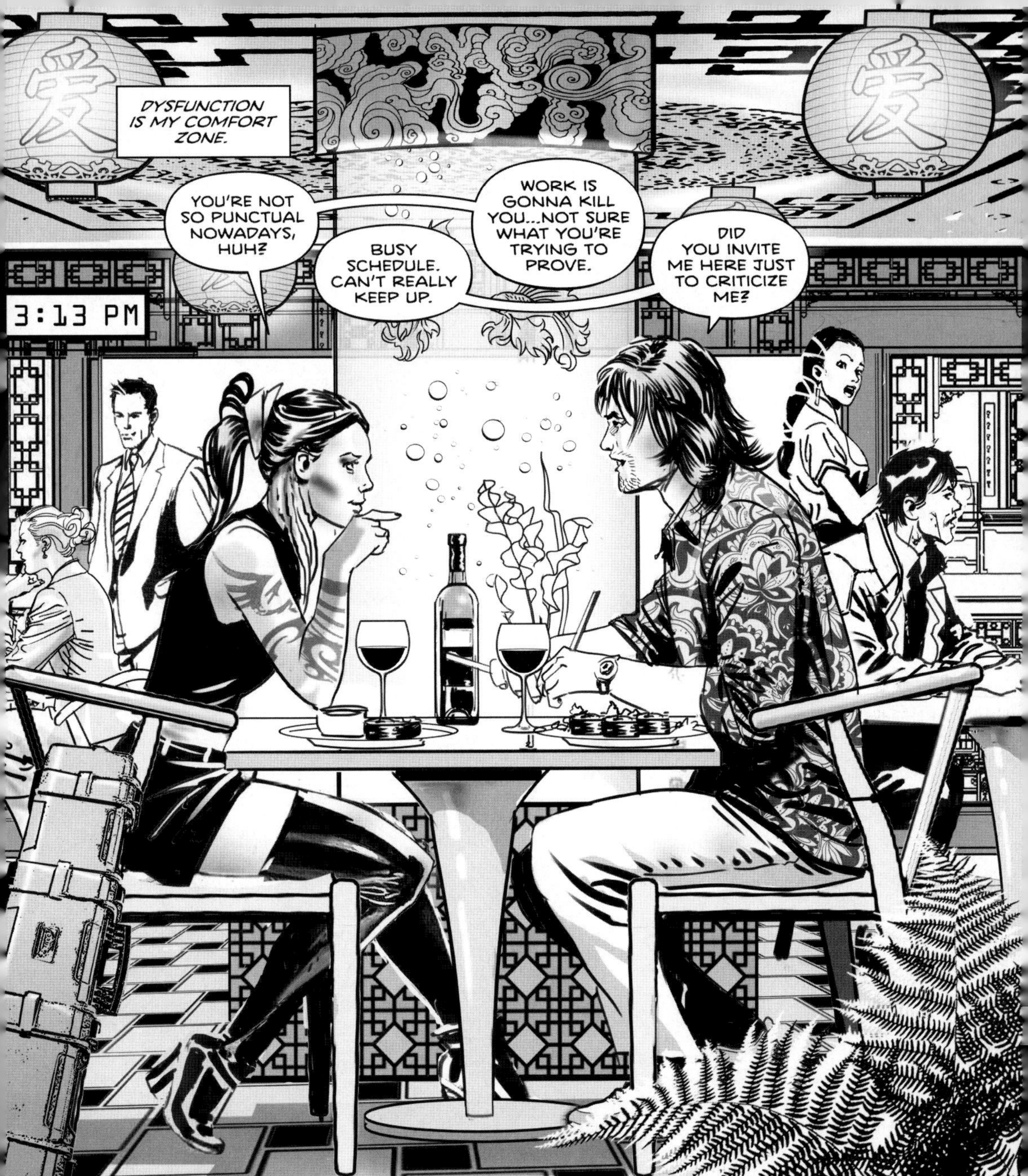
DYSFUNCTION IS MY COMFORT ZONE.
YOU'RE NOT SO PUNCTUAL NOWADAYS, HUH?
BUSY SCHEDULE. CAN'T REALLY KEEP UP.
WORK IS GONNA KILL YOU...NOT SURE WHAT YOU'RE TRYING TO PROVE.
DID YOU INVITE ME HERE JUST TO CRITICIZE ME?
3:13 PM

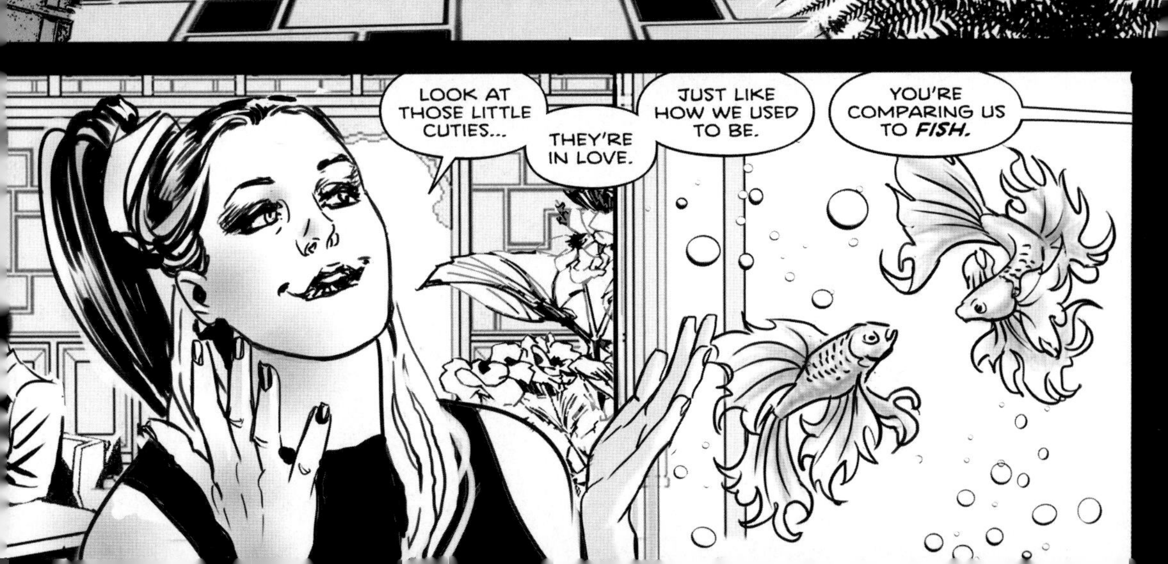
LOOK AT THOSE LITTLE CUTIES...
THEY'RE IN LOVE.
JUST LIKE HOW WE USED TO BE.
YOU'RE COMPARING US TO *FISH.*

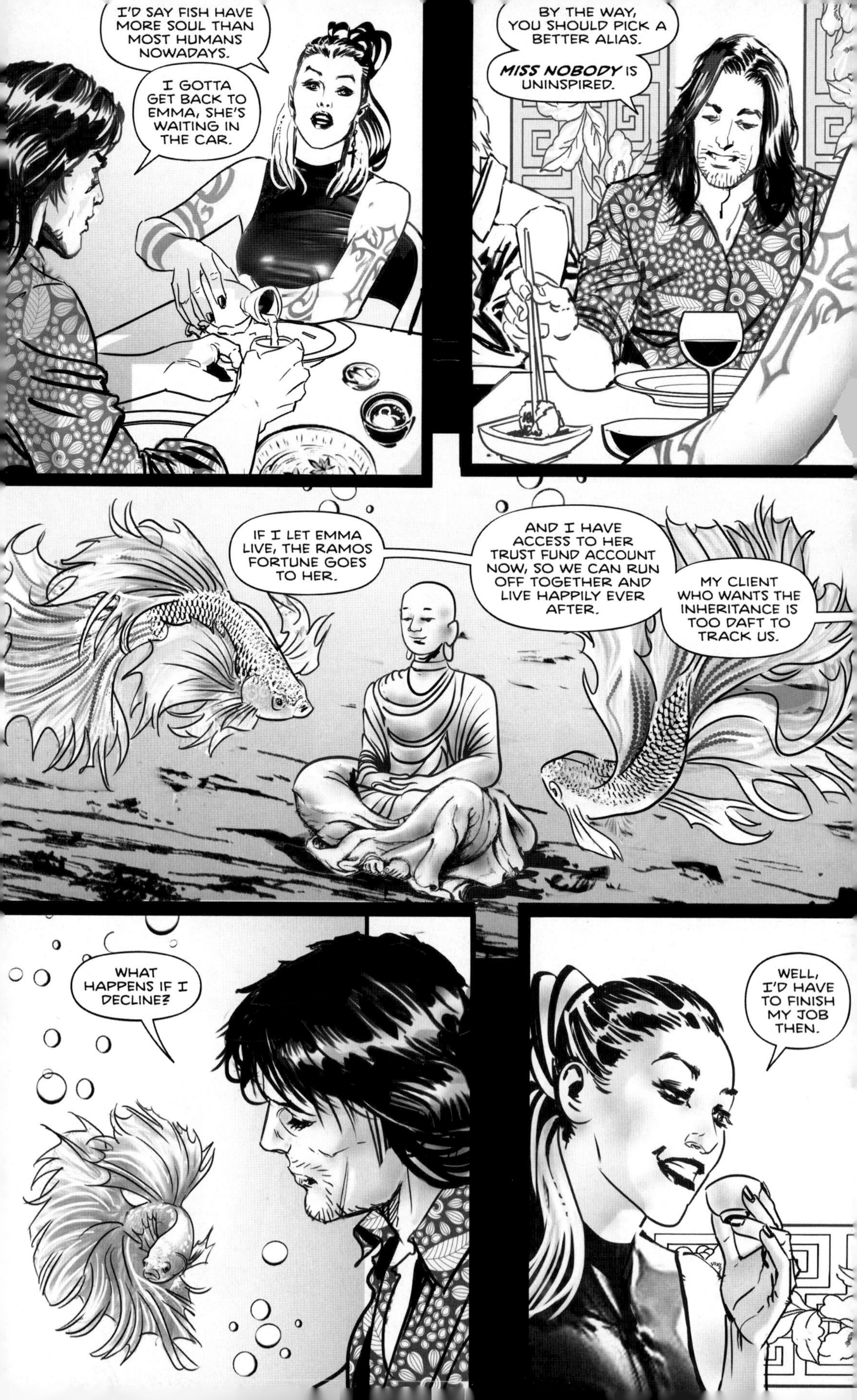

I'D SAY FISH HAVE MORE SOUL THAN MOST HUMANS NOWADAYS.
I GOTTA GET BACK TO EMMA, SHE'S WAITING IN THE CAR.
BY THE WAY, YOU SHOULD PICK A BETTER ALIAS.
MISS NOBODY IS UNINSPIRED.
IF I LET EMMA LIVE, THE RAMOS FORTUNE GOES TO HER.
AND I HAVE ACCESS TO HER TRUST FUND ACCOUNT NOW, SO WE CAN RUN OFF TOGETHER AND LIVE HAPPILY EVER AFTER.
MY CLIENT WHO WANTS THE INHERITANCE IS TOO DAFT TO TRACK US.
WHAT HAPPENS IF I DECLINE?
WELL, I'D HAVE TO FINISH MY JOB THEN.

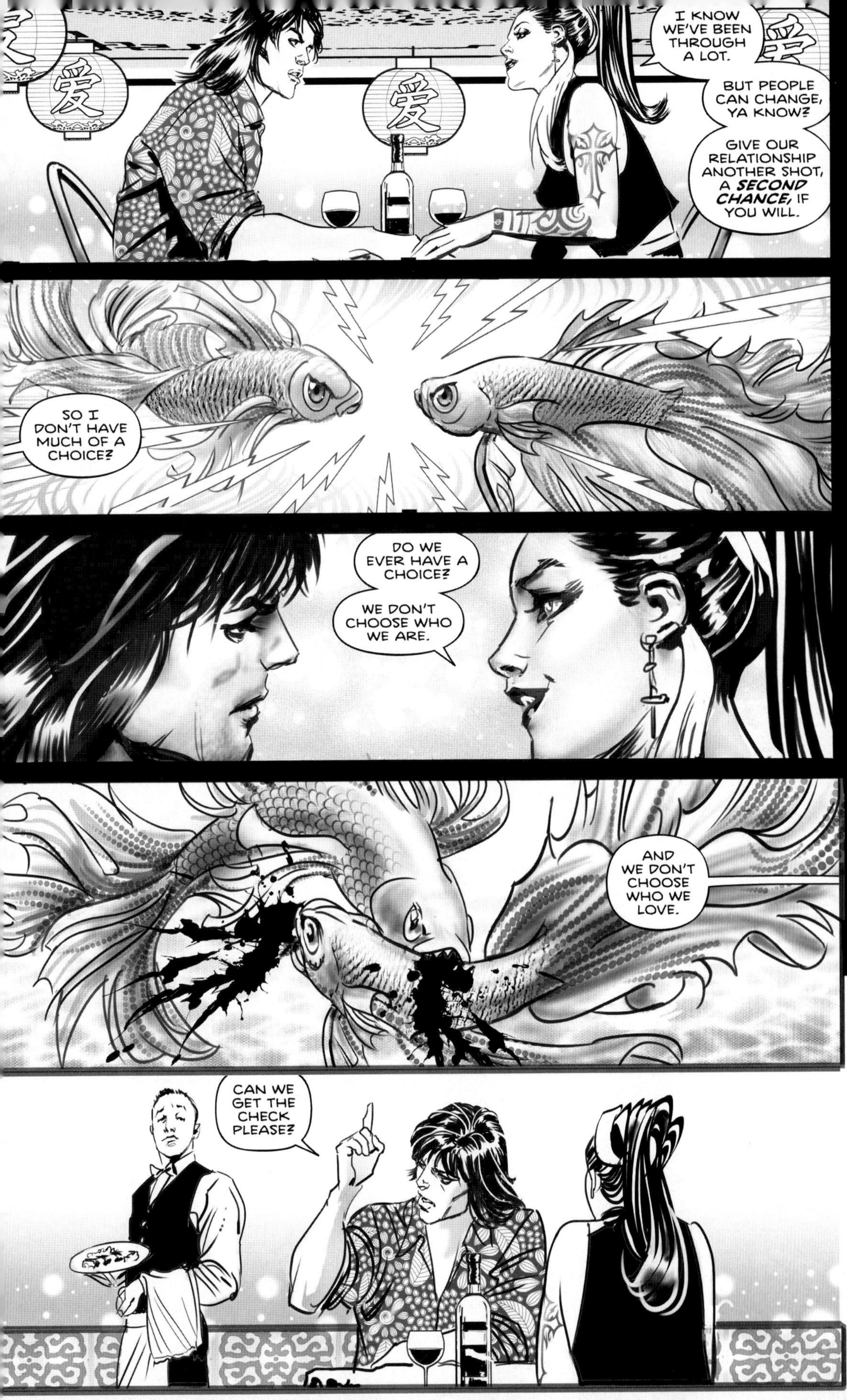

I KNOW WE'VE BEEN THROUGH A LOT.
BUT PEOPLE CAN CHANGE, YA KNOW?
GIVE OUR RELATIONSHIP ANOTHER SHOT, A **SECOND CHANCE,** IF YOU WILL.
SO I DON'T HAVE MUCH OF A CHOICE?
DO WE EVER HAVE A CHOICE?
WE DON'T CHOOSE WHO WE ARE.
AND WE DON'T CHOOSE WHO WE LOVE.
CAN WE GET THE CHECK PLEASE?

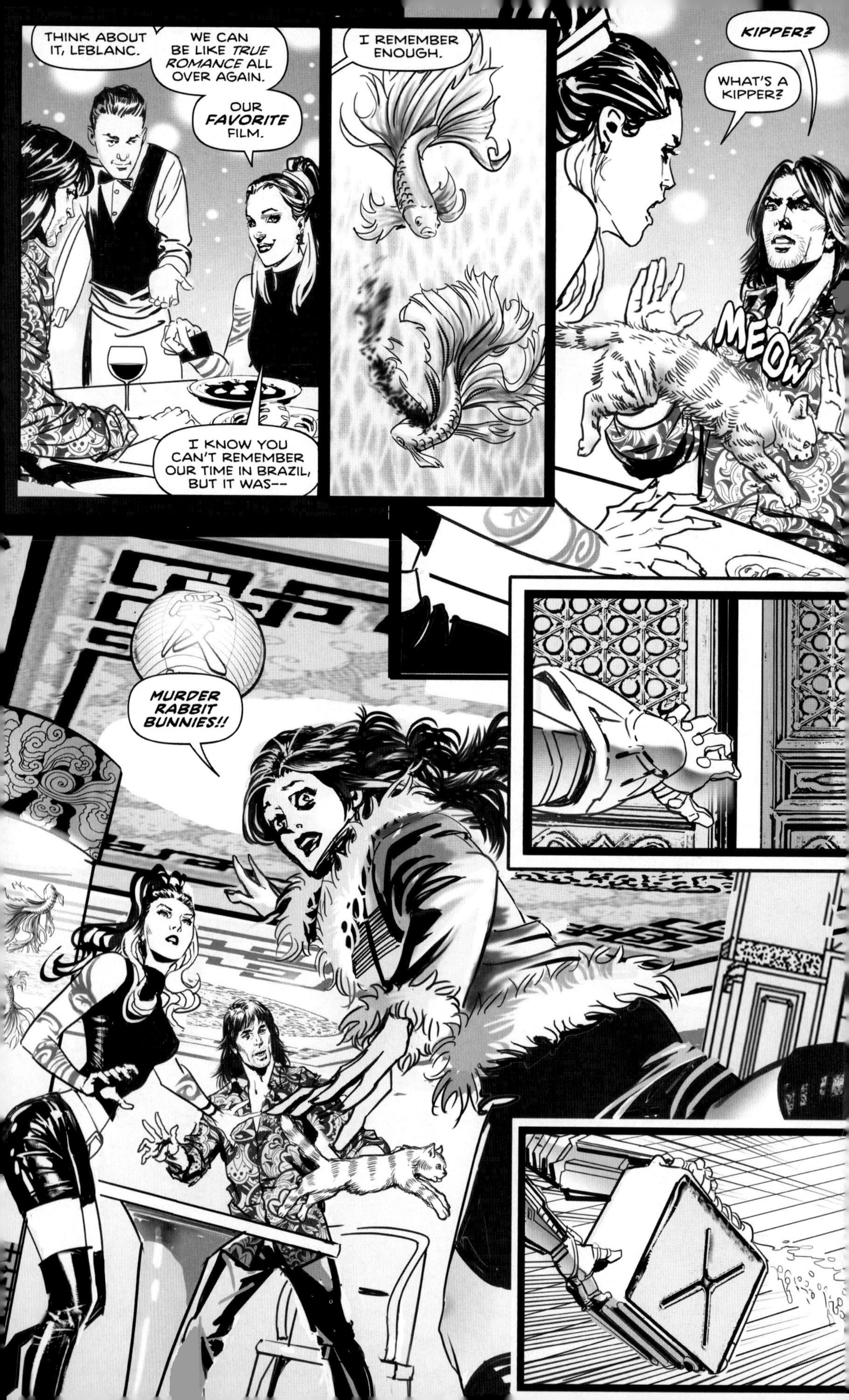

THINK ABOUT IT, LEBLANC.
WE CAN BE LIKE TRUE ROMANCE ALL OVER AGAIN.
OUR FAVORITE FILM.
I KNOW YOU CAN'T REMEMBER OUR TIME IN BRAZIL, BUT IT WAS--
I REMEMBER ENOUGH.
KIPPER?
WHAT'S A KIPPER?
MEOW
MURDER RABBIT BUNNIES!!

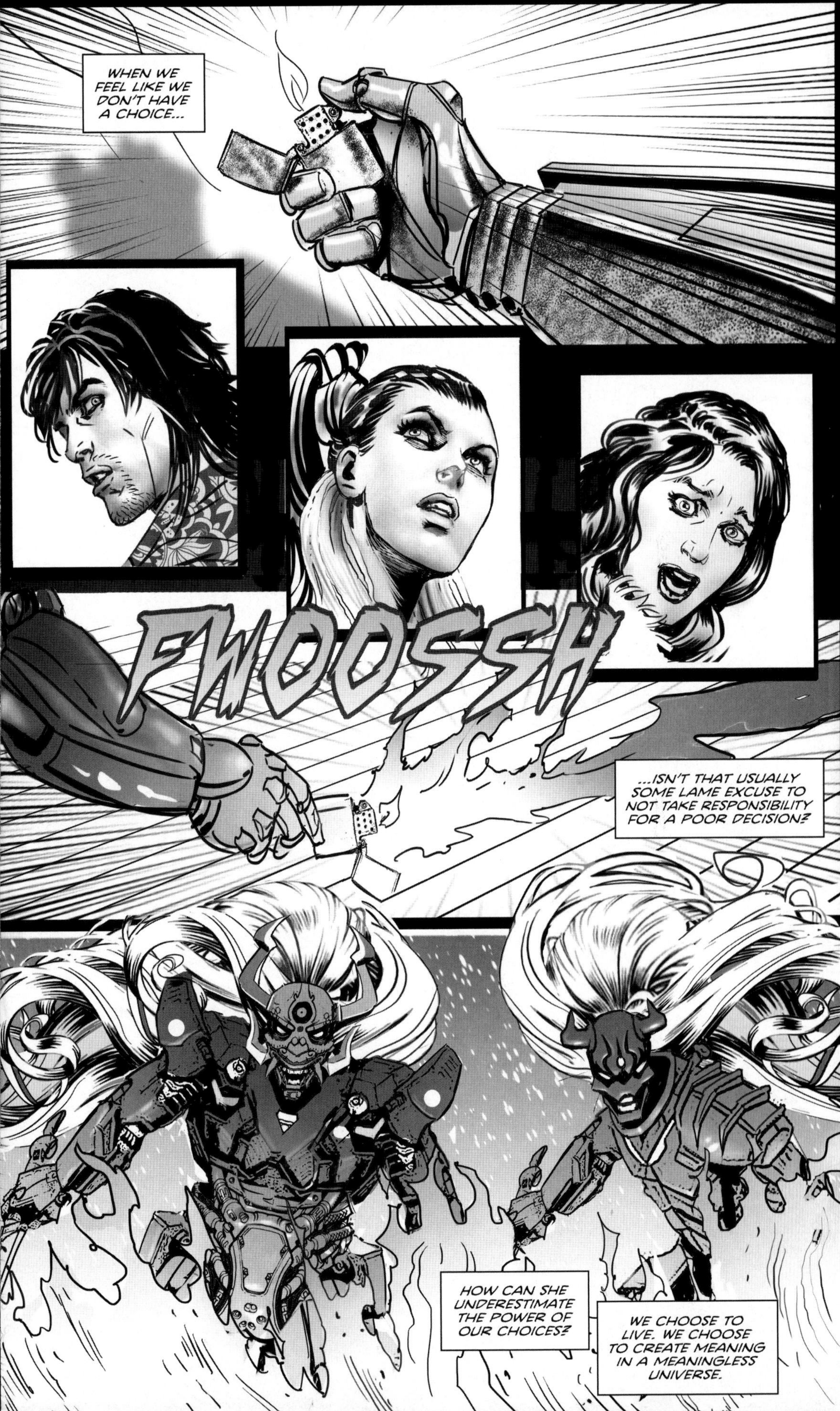

WHEN WE FEEL LIKE WE DON'T HAVE A CHOICE...
FWOOSSH
...ISN'T THAT USUALLY SOME LAME EXCUSE TO NOT TAKE RESPONSIBILITY FOR A POOR DECISION?
HOW CAN SHE UNDERESTIMATE THE POWER OF OUR CHOICES?
WE CHOOSE TO LIVE. WE CHOOSE TO CREATE MEANING IN A MEANINGLESS UNIVERSE.

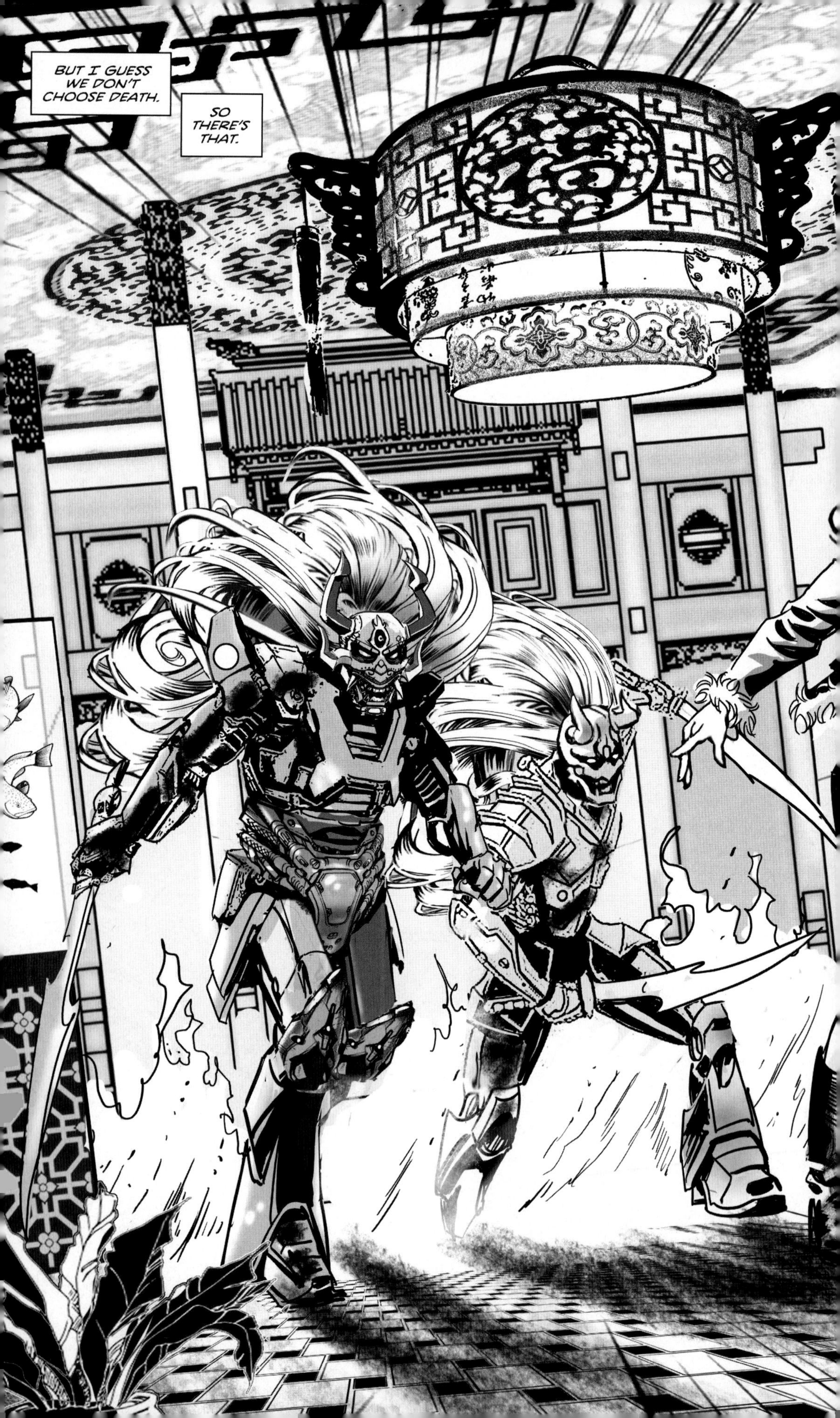
BUT I GUESS WE DON'T CHOOSE DEATH.
SO THERE'S THAT.

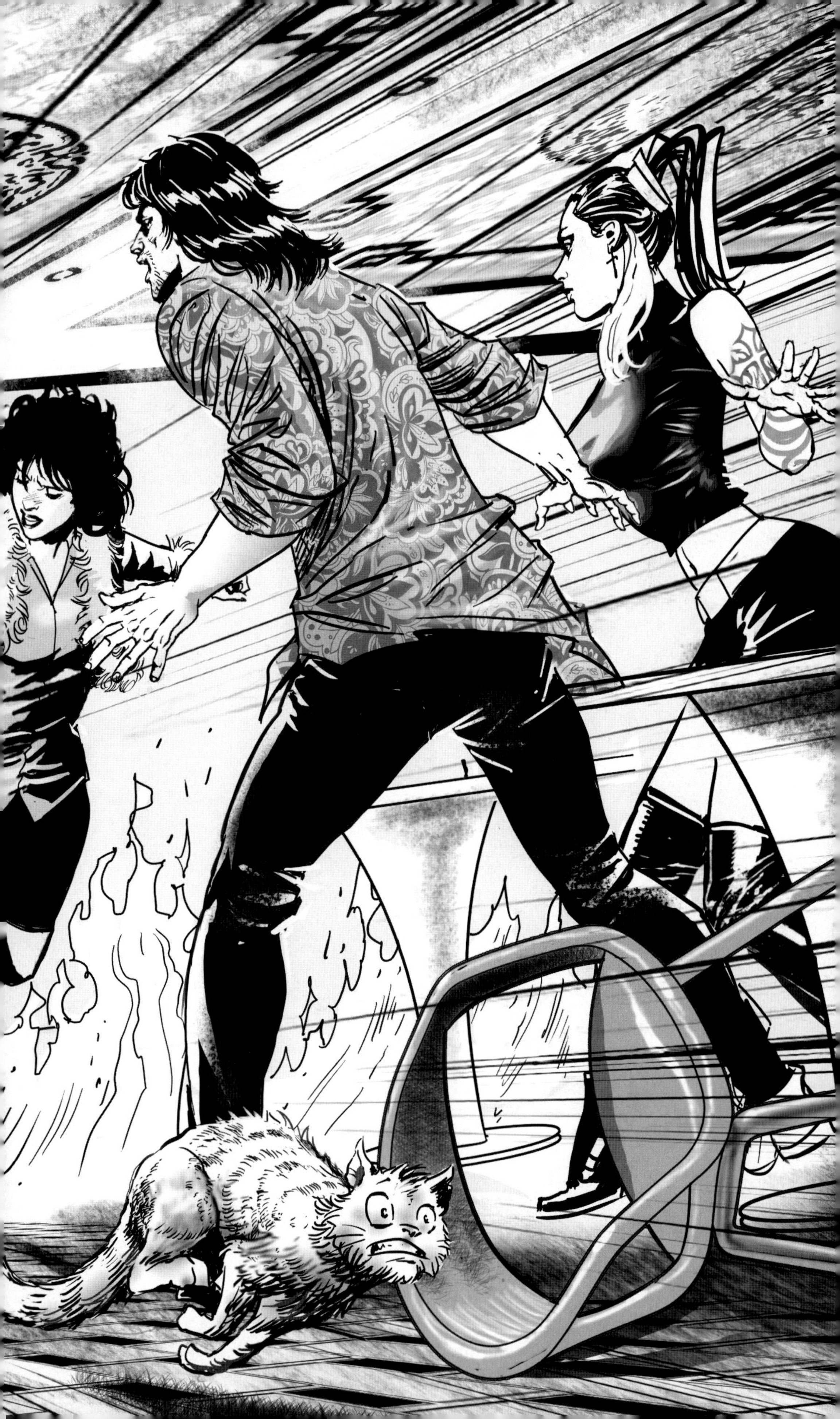

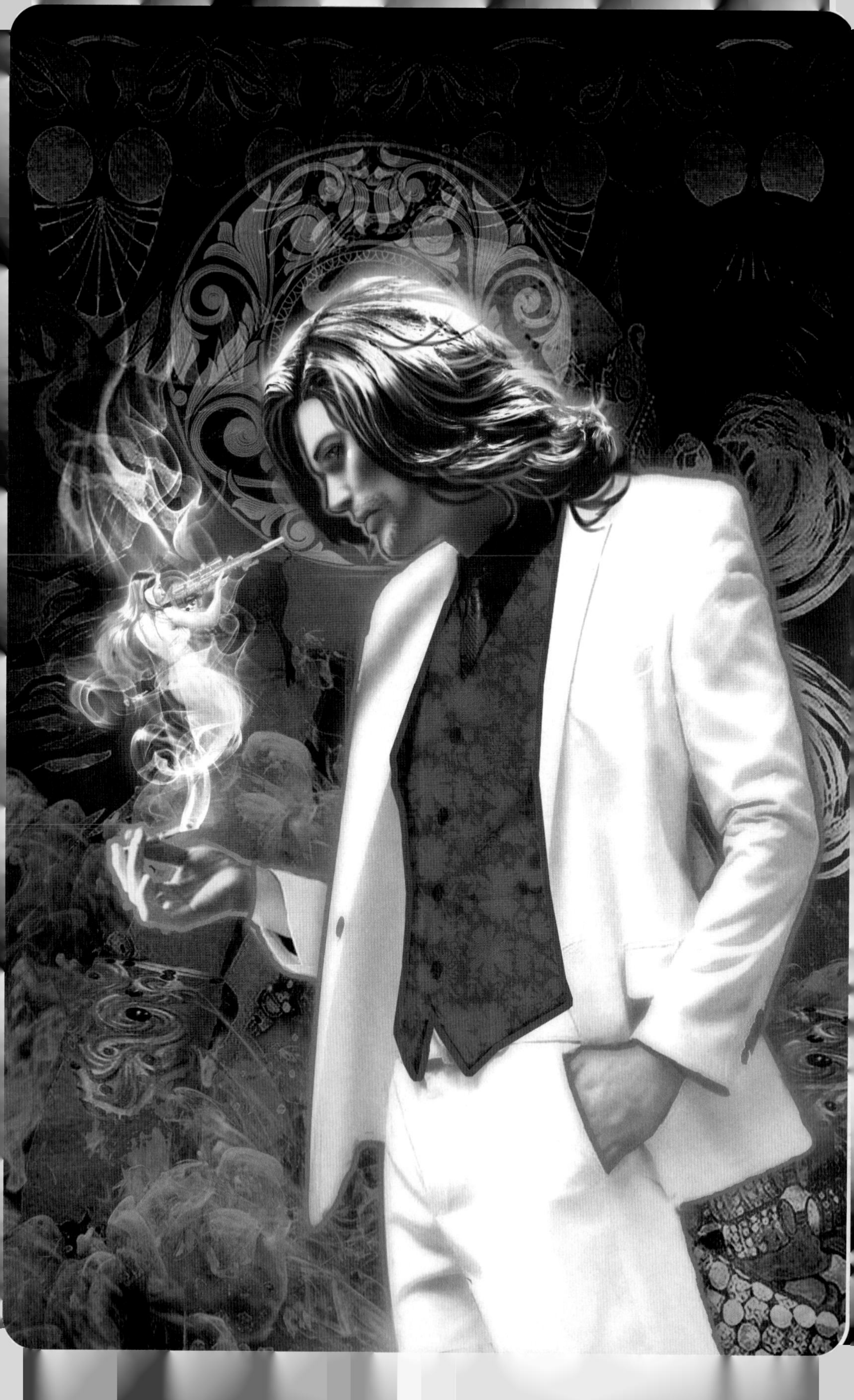

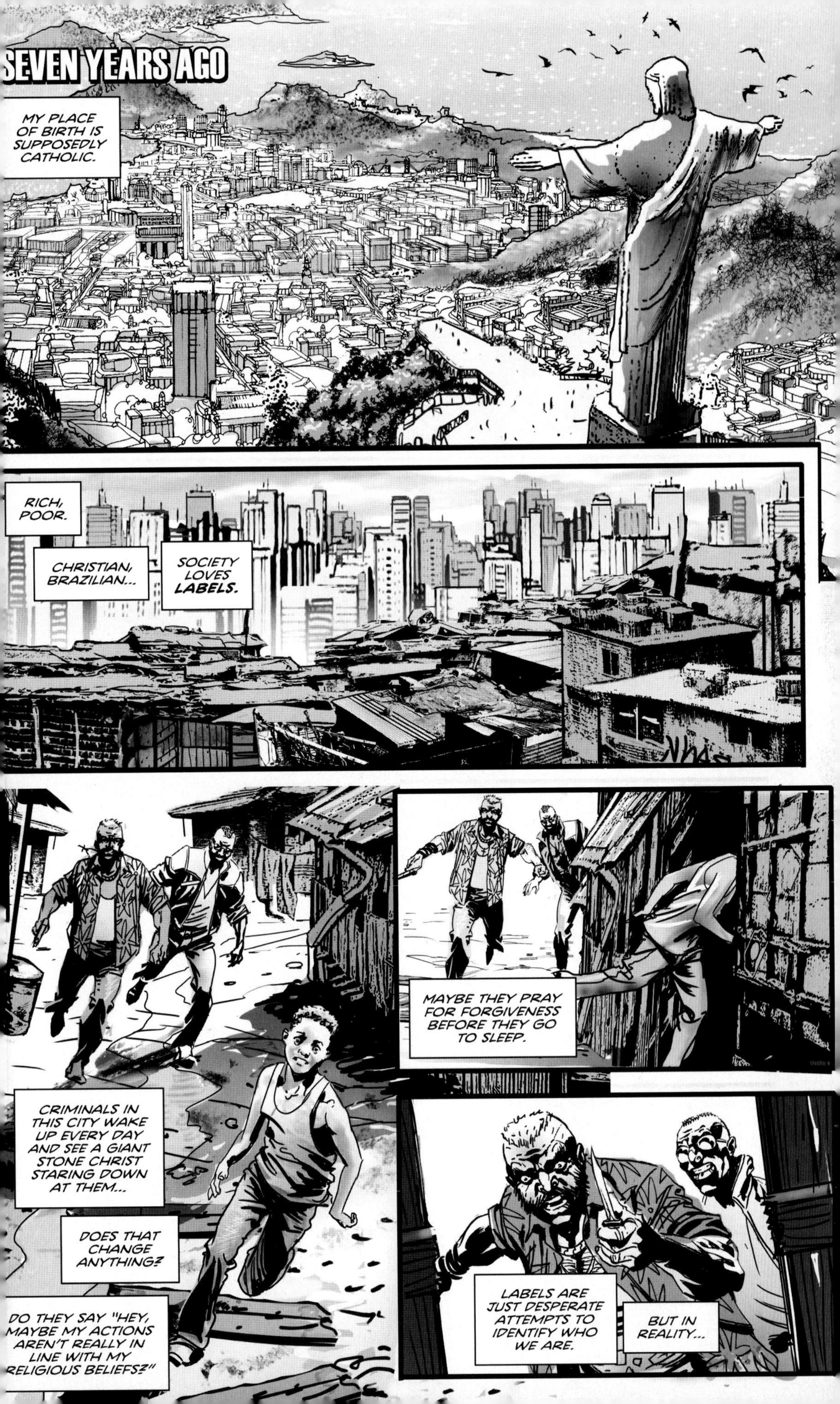
SEVEN YEARS AGO
MY PLACE OF BIRTH IS SUPPOSEDLY CATHOLIC.
RICH, POOR.
CHRISTIAN, BRAZILIAN...
SOCIETY LOVES LABELS.
CRIMINALS IN THIS CITY WAKE UP EVERY DAY AND SEE A GIANT STONE CHRIST STARING DOWN AT THEM...
DOES THAT CHANGE ANYTHING?
DO THEY SAY "HEY, MAYBE MY ACTIONS AREN'T REALLY IN LINE WITH MY RELIGIOUS BELIEFS?"
MAYBE THEY PRAY FOR FORGIVENESS BEFORE THEY GO TO SLEEP.
LABELS ARE JUST DESPERATE ATTEMPTS TO IDENTIFY WHO WE ARE.
BUT IN REALITY...

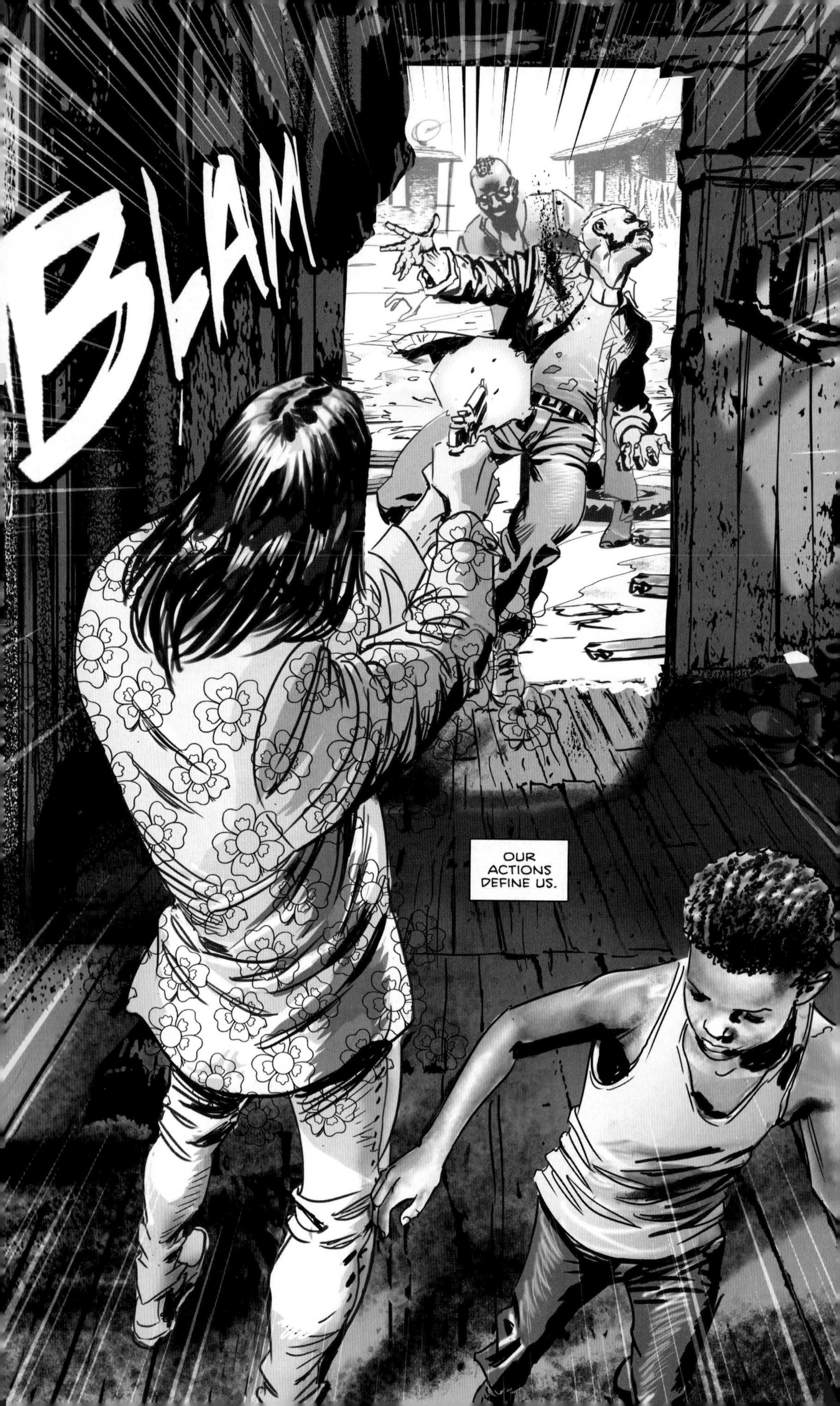
BLAM
OUR ACTIONS DEFINE US.

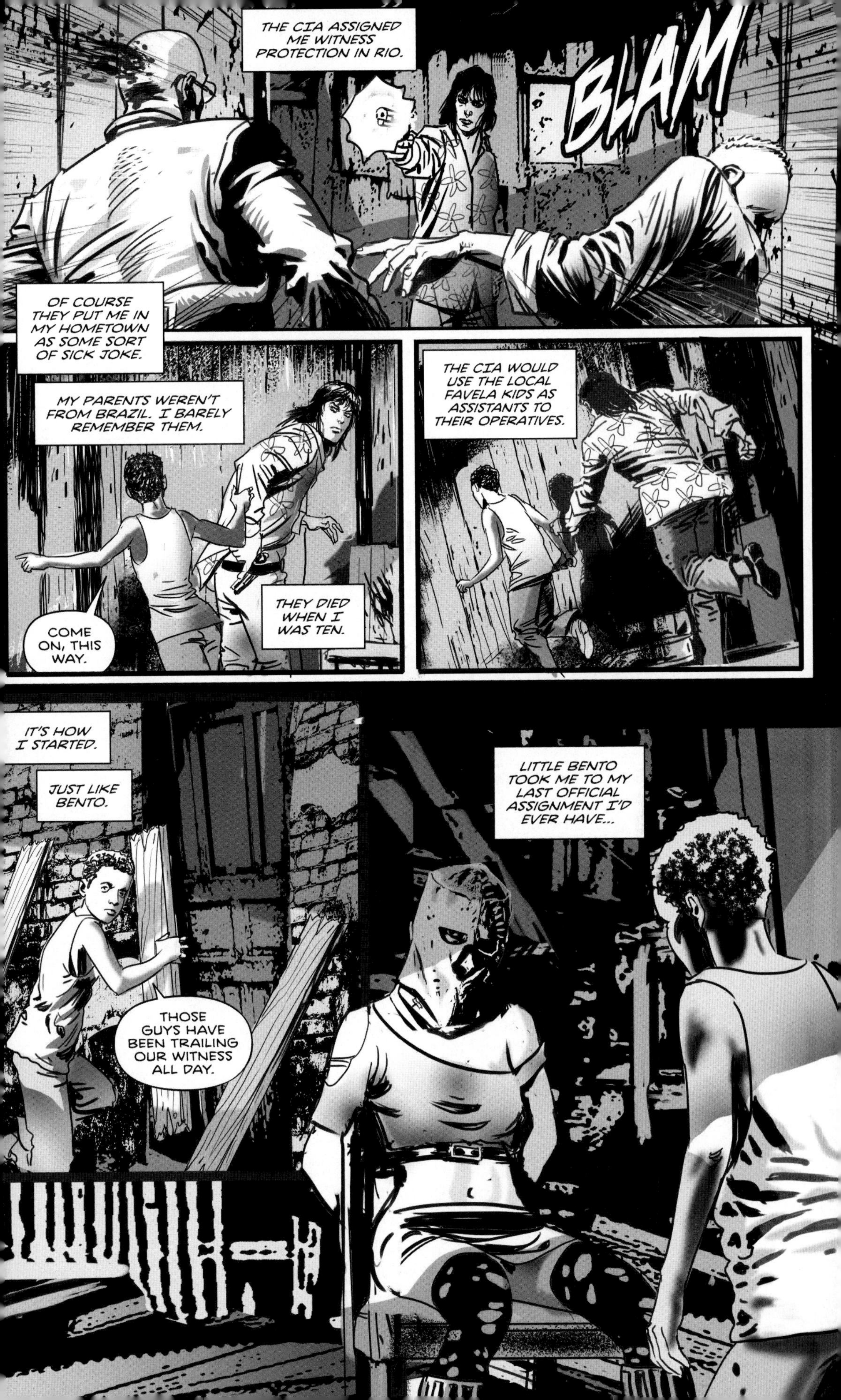

THE CIA ASSIGNED ME WITNESS PROTECTION IN RIO.
BLAM
OF COURSE THEY PUT ME IN MY HOMETOWN AS SOME SORT OF SICK JOKE.
MY PARENTS WEREN'T FROM BRAZIL. I BARELY REMEMBER THEM.
COME ON, THIS WAY.
THEY DIED WHEN I WAS TEN.
THE CIA WOULD USE THE LOCAL FAVELA KIDS AS ASSISTANTS TO THEIR OPERATIVES.
IT'S HOW I STARTED.
JUST LIKE BENTO.
THOSE GUYS HAVE BEEN TRAILING OUR WITNESS ALL DAY.
LITTLE BENTO TOOK ME TO MY LAST OFFICIAL ASSIGNMENT I'D EVER HAVE...

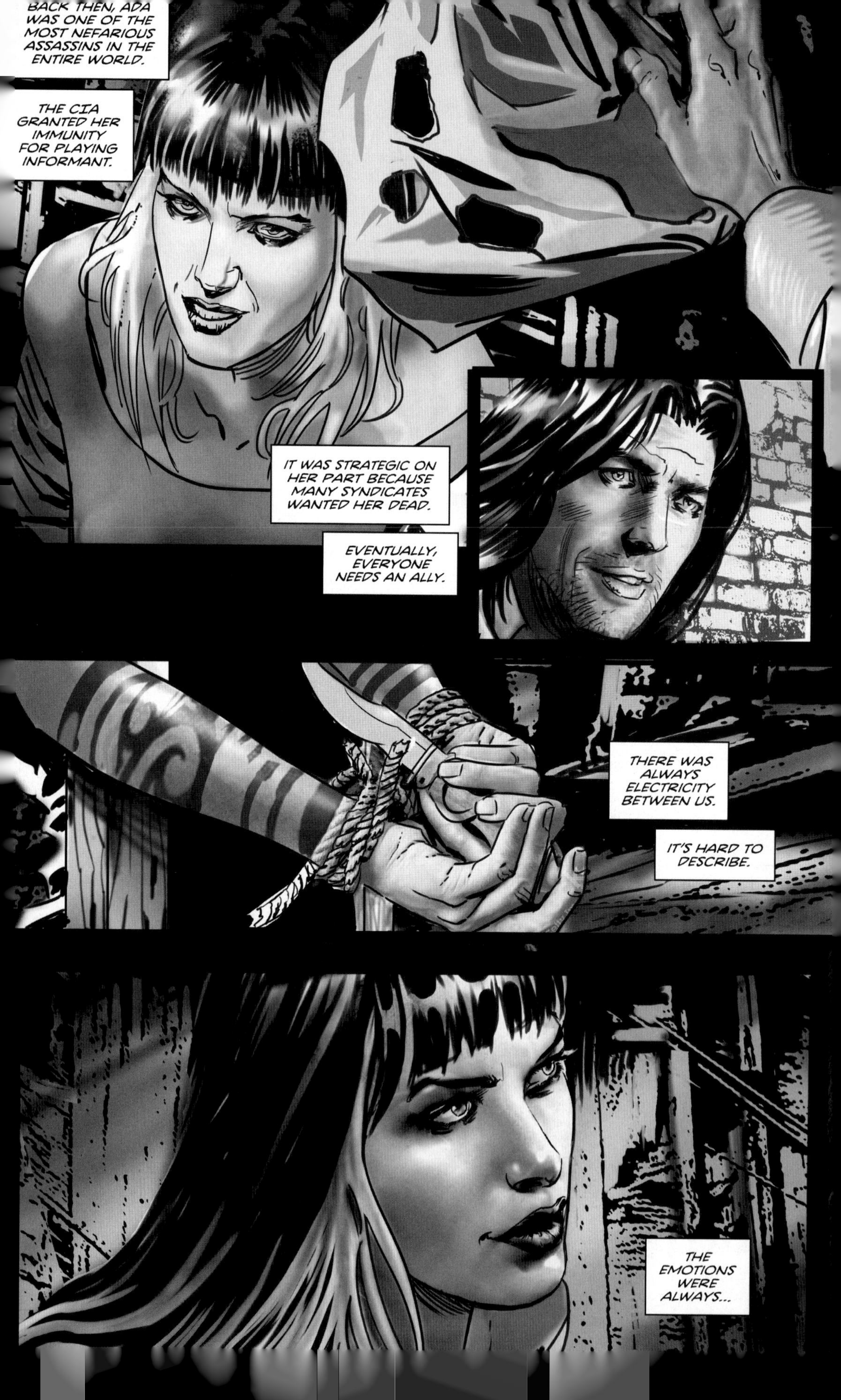
BACK THEN, ADA WAS ONE OF THE MOST NEFARIOUS ASSASSINS IN THE ENTIRE WORLD.
THE CIA GRANTED HER IMMUNITY FOR PLAYING INFORMANT.
IT WAS STRATEGIC ON HER PART BECAUSE MANY SYNDICATES WANTED HER DEAD.
EVENTUALLY, EVERYONE NEEDS AN ALLY.
THERE WAS ALWAYS ELECTRICITY BETWEEN US.
IT'S HARD TO DESCRIBE.
THE EMOTIONS WERE ALWAYS...

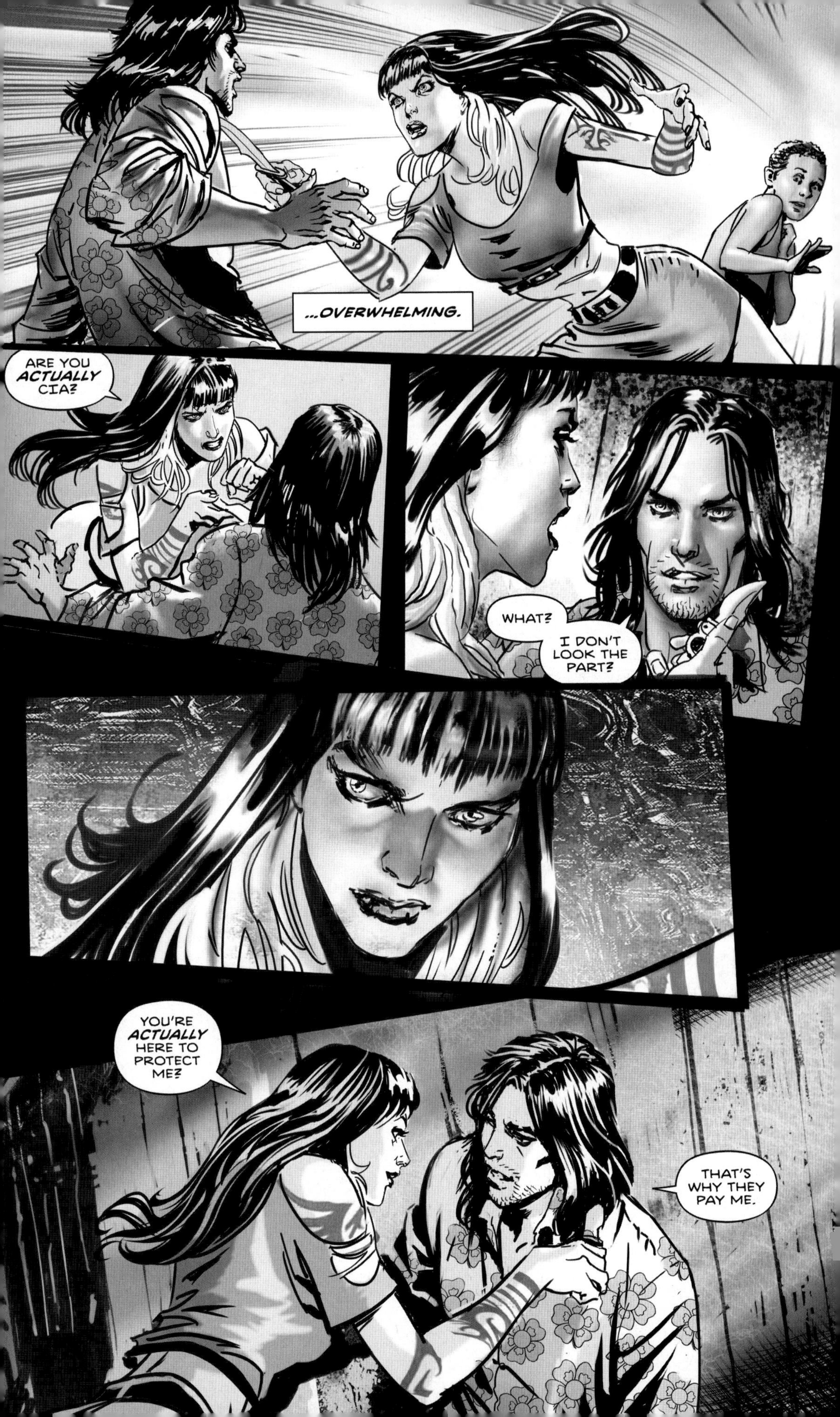
...OVERWHELMING.
ARE YOU ACTUALLY CIA?
WHAT?
I DON'T LOOK THE PART?
YOU'RE ACTUALLY HERE TO PROTECT ME?
THAT'S WHY THEY PAY ME.

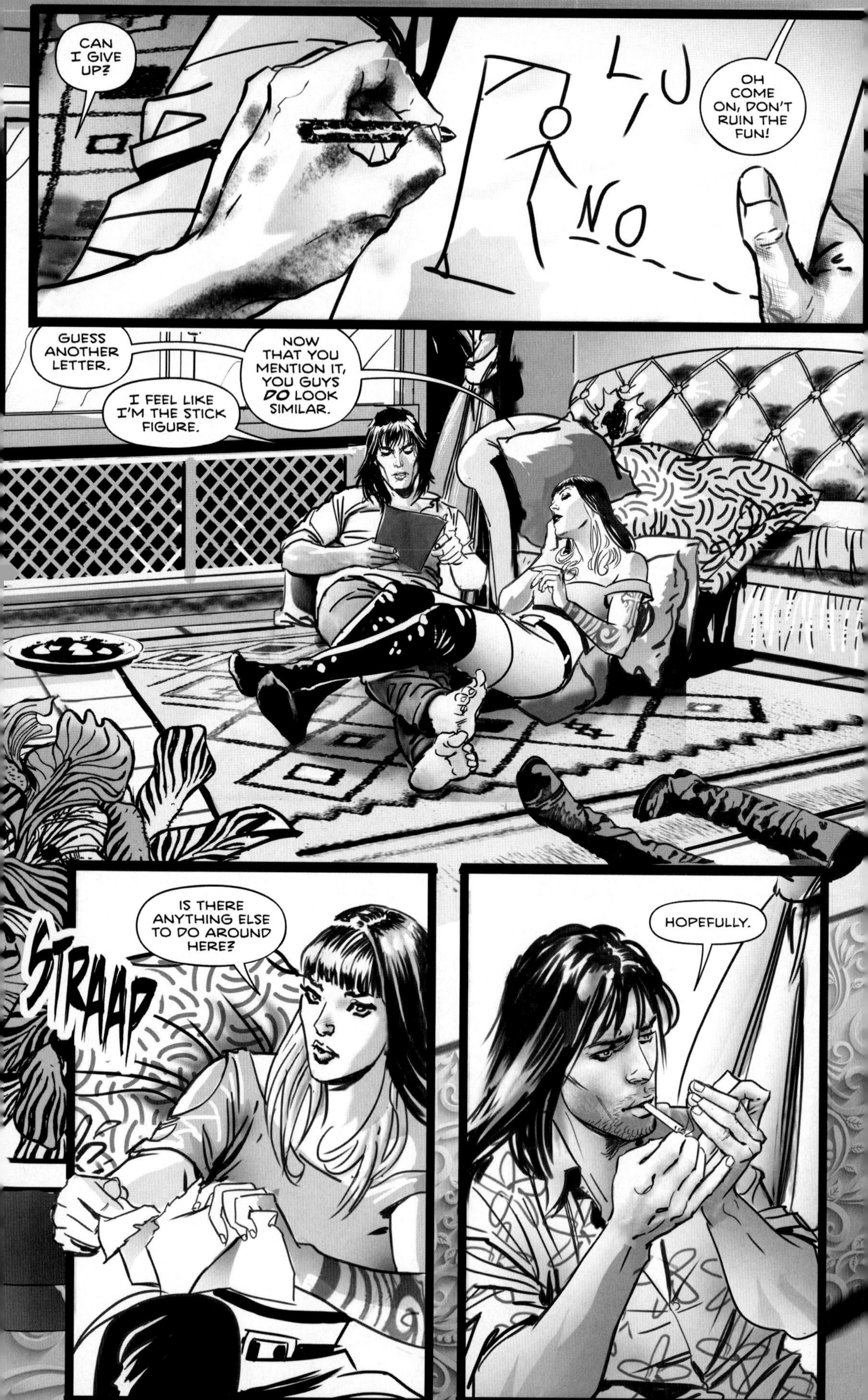
CAN I GIVE UP?
OH COME ON, DON'T RUIN THE FUN!
LU
NO
GUESS ANOTHER LETTER.
I FEEL LIKE I'M THE STICK FIGURE.
NOW THAT YOU MENTION IT, YOU GUYS DO LOOK SIMILAR.
STRAAP
IS THERE ANYTHING ELSE TO DO AROUND HERE?
HOPEFULLY.

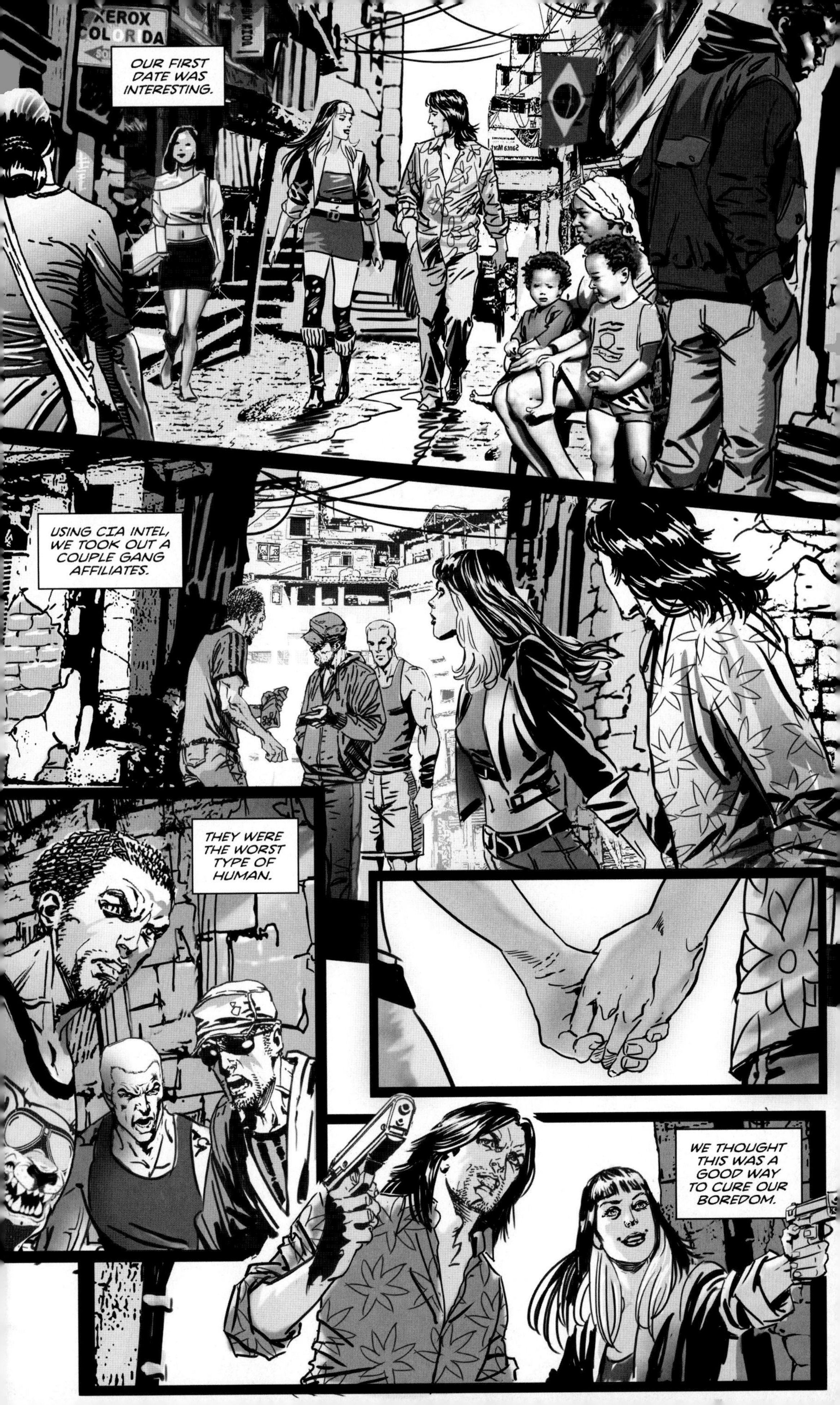
XEROX
COLORIDA
OUR FIRST DATE WAS INTERESTING.
USING CIA INTEL, WE TOOK OUT A COUPLE GANG AFFILIATES.
THEY WERE THE WORST TYPE OF HUMAN.
WE THOUGHT THIS WAS A GOOD WAY TO CURE OUR BOREDOM.

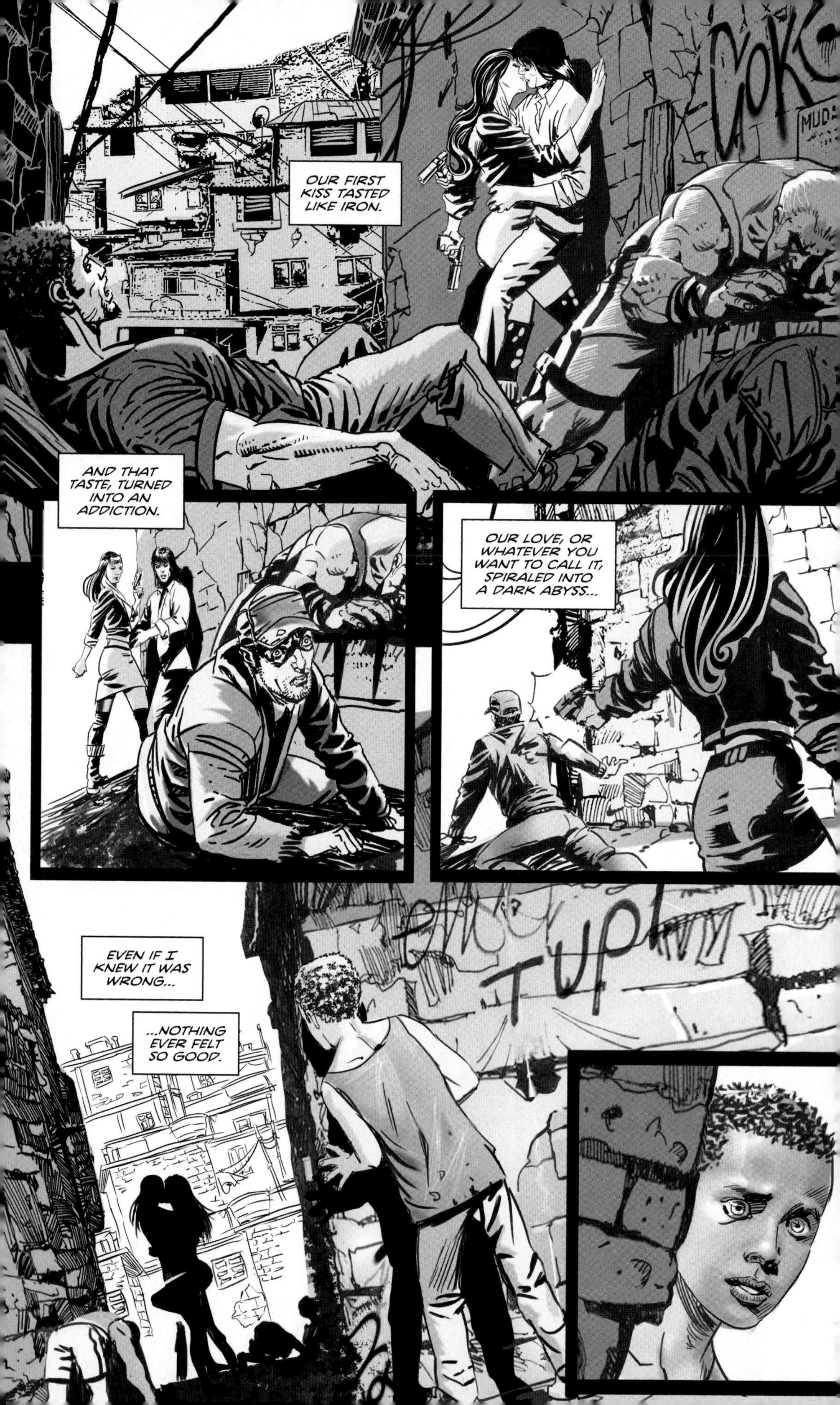
OUR FIRST KISS TASTED LIKE IRON.
COKO
MUD
AND THAT TASTE, TURNED INTO AN ADDICTION.
OUR LOVE, OR WHATEVER YOU WANT TO CALL IT, SPIRALED INTO A DARK ABYSS...
EVEN IF I KNEW IT WAS WRONG...
...NOTHING EVER FELT SO GOOD.
TUP

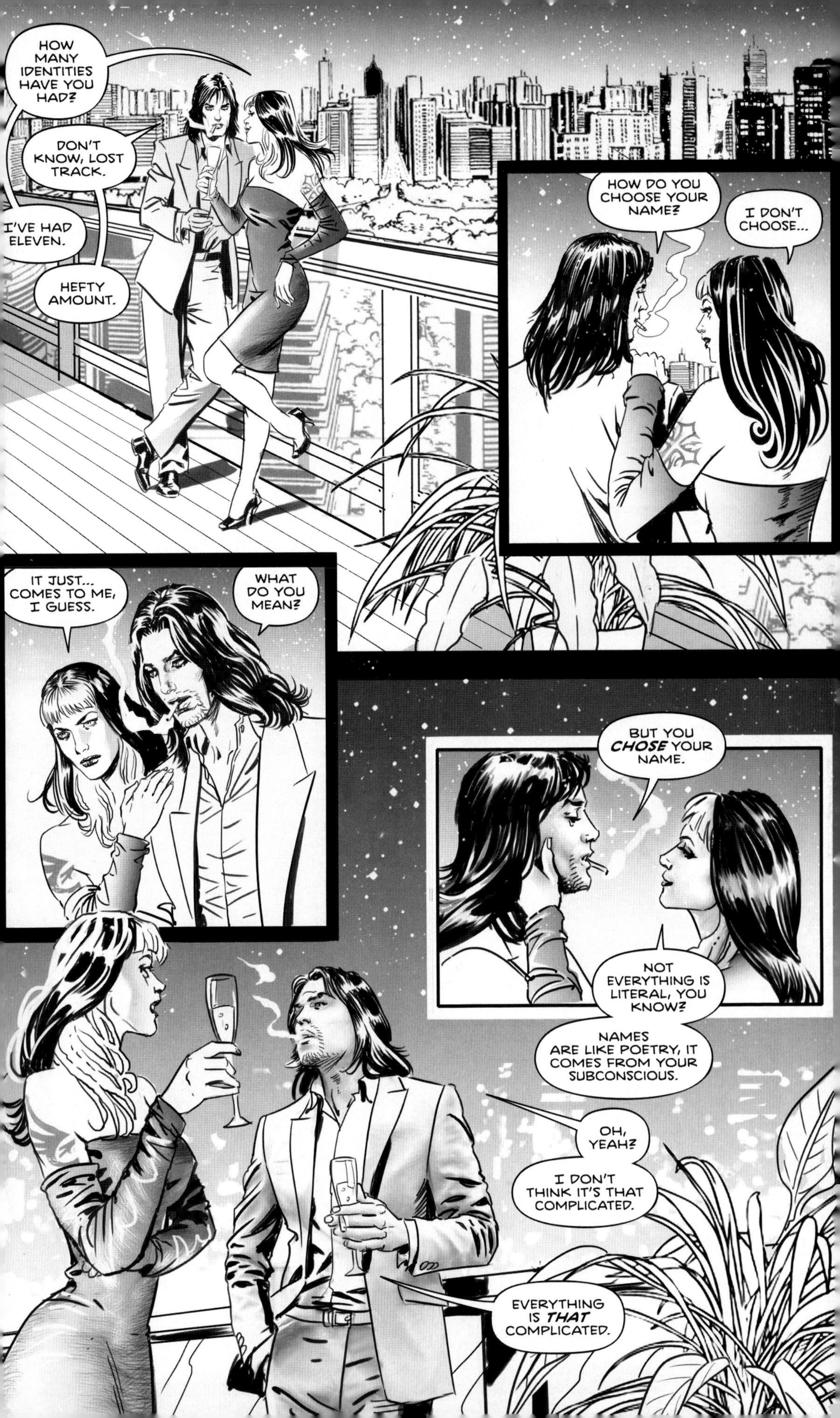
HOW MANY IDENTITIES HAVE YOU HAD?
DON'T KNOW, LOST TRACK.
I'VE HAD ELEVEN.
HEFTY AMOUNT.
HOW DO YOU CHOOSE YOUR NAME?
I DON'T CHOOSE...
IT JUST... COMES TO ME, I GUESS.
WHAT DO YOU MEAN?
BUT YOU CHOSE YOUR NAME.
NOT EVERYTHING IS LITERAL, YOU KNOW?
NAMES ARE LIKE POETRY, IT COMES FROM YOUR SUBCONSCIOUS.
OH, YEAH?
I DON'T THINK IT'S THAT COMPLICATED.
EVERYTHING IS THAT COMPLICATED.

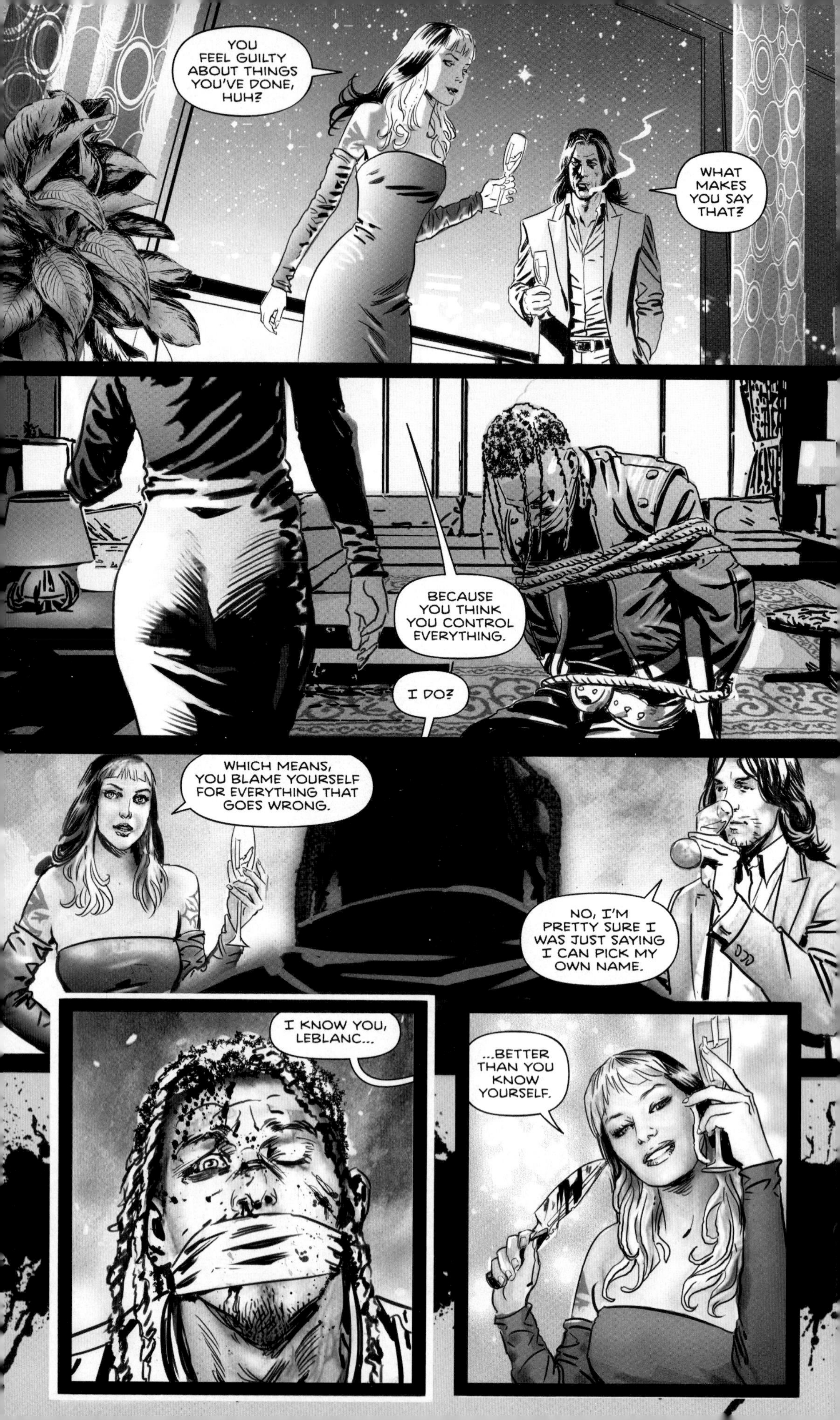
YOU FEEL GUILTY ABOUT THINGS YOU'VE DONE, HUH?
WHAT MAKES YOU SAY THAT?
BECAUSE YOU THINK YOU CONTROL EVERYTHING.
I DO?
WHICH MEANS, YOU BLAME YOURSELF FOR EVERYTHING THAT GOES WRONG.
NO, I'M PRETTY SURE I WAS JUST SAYING I CAN PICK MY OWN NAME.
I KNOW YOU, LEBLANC...
...BETTER THAN YOU KNOW YOURSELF.

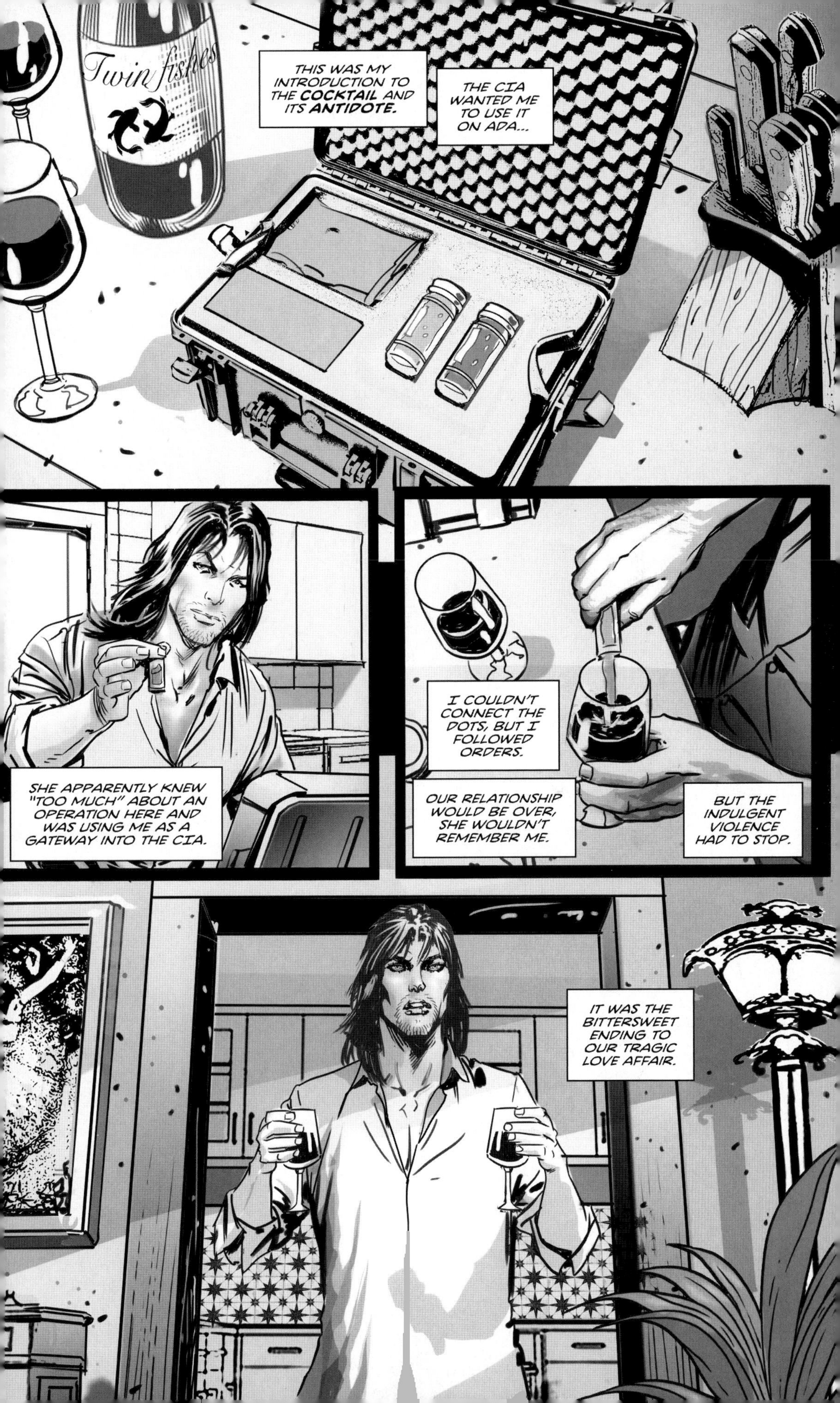
Twin fishes
THIS WAS MY INTRODUCTION TO THE **COCKTAIL** AND ITS **ANTIDOTE.**
THE CIA WANTED ME TO USE IT ON ADA...
SHE APPARENTLY KNEW "TOO MUCH" ABOUT AN OPERATION HERE AND WAS USING ME AS A GATEWAY INTO THE CIA.
I COULDN'T CONNECT THE DOTS, BUT I FOLLOWED ORDERS.
OUR RELATIONSHIP WOULD BE OVER, SHE WOULDN'T REMEMBER ME.
BUT THE INDULGENT VIOLENCE HAD TO STOP.
IT WAS THE BITTERSWEET ENDING TO OUR TRAGIC LOVE AFFAIR.

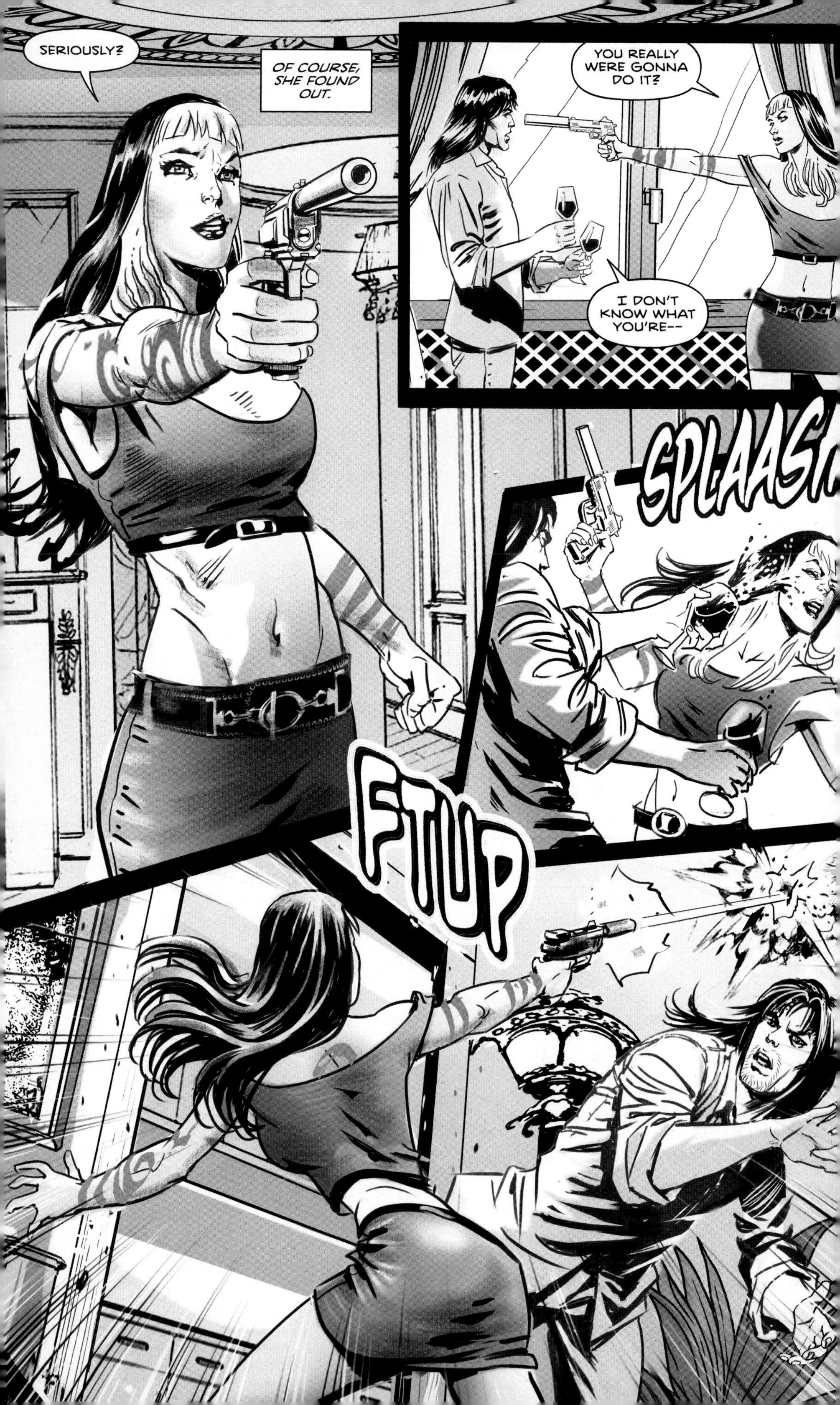
SERIOUSLY?
OF COURSE, SHE FOUND OUT.
YOU REALLY WERE GONNA DO IT?
I DON'T KNOW WHAT YOU'RE--
SPLAASH
FTUP

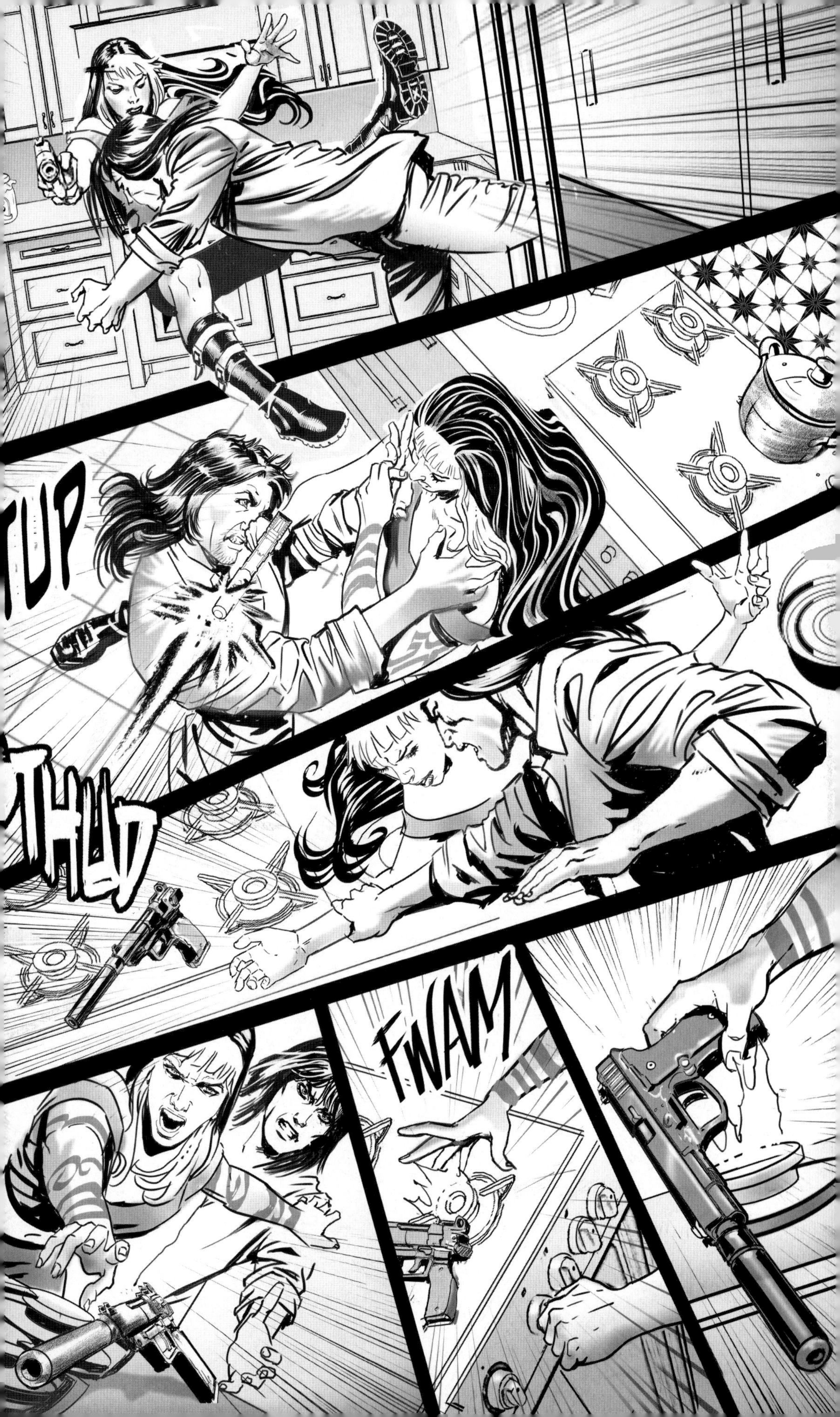
TUP
THUD
FWAM

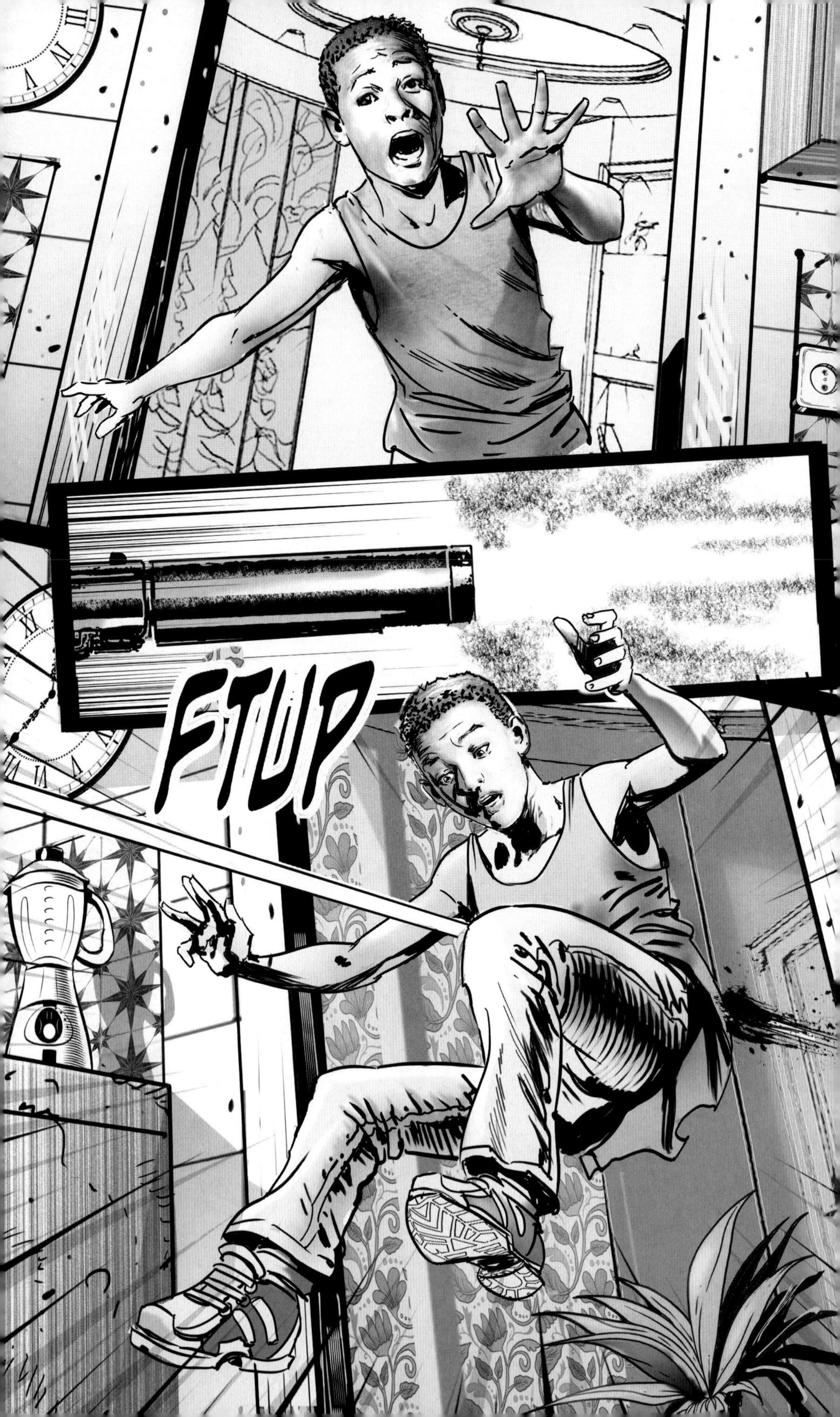
FTUP

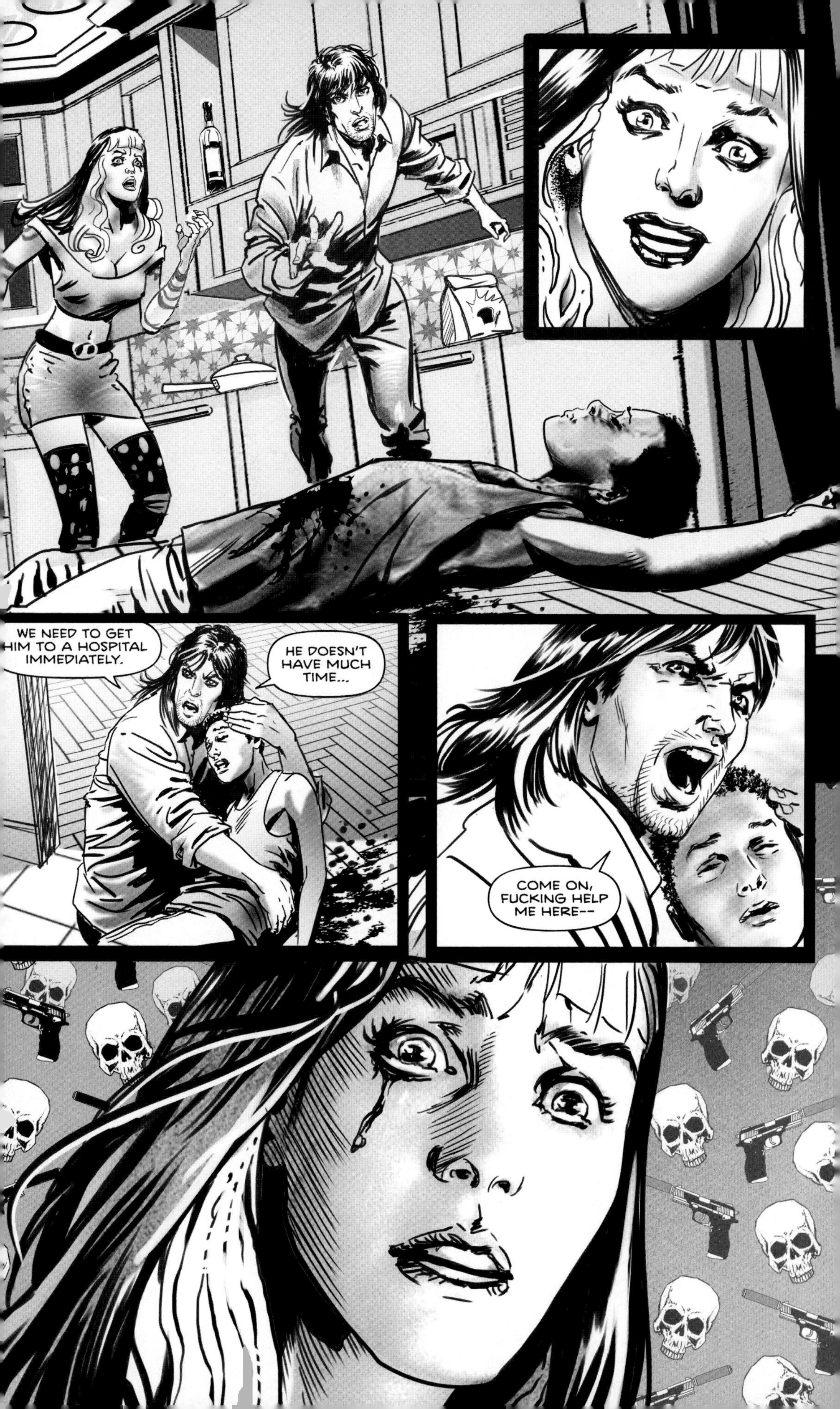
WE NEED TO GET HIM TO A HOSPITAL IMMEDIATELY.
HE DOESN'T HAVE MUCH TIME...
COME ON, FUCKING HELP ME HERE--

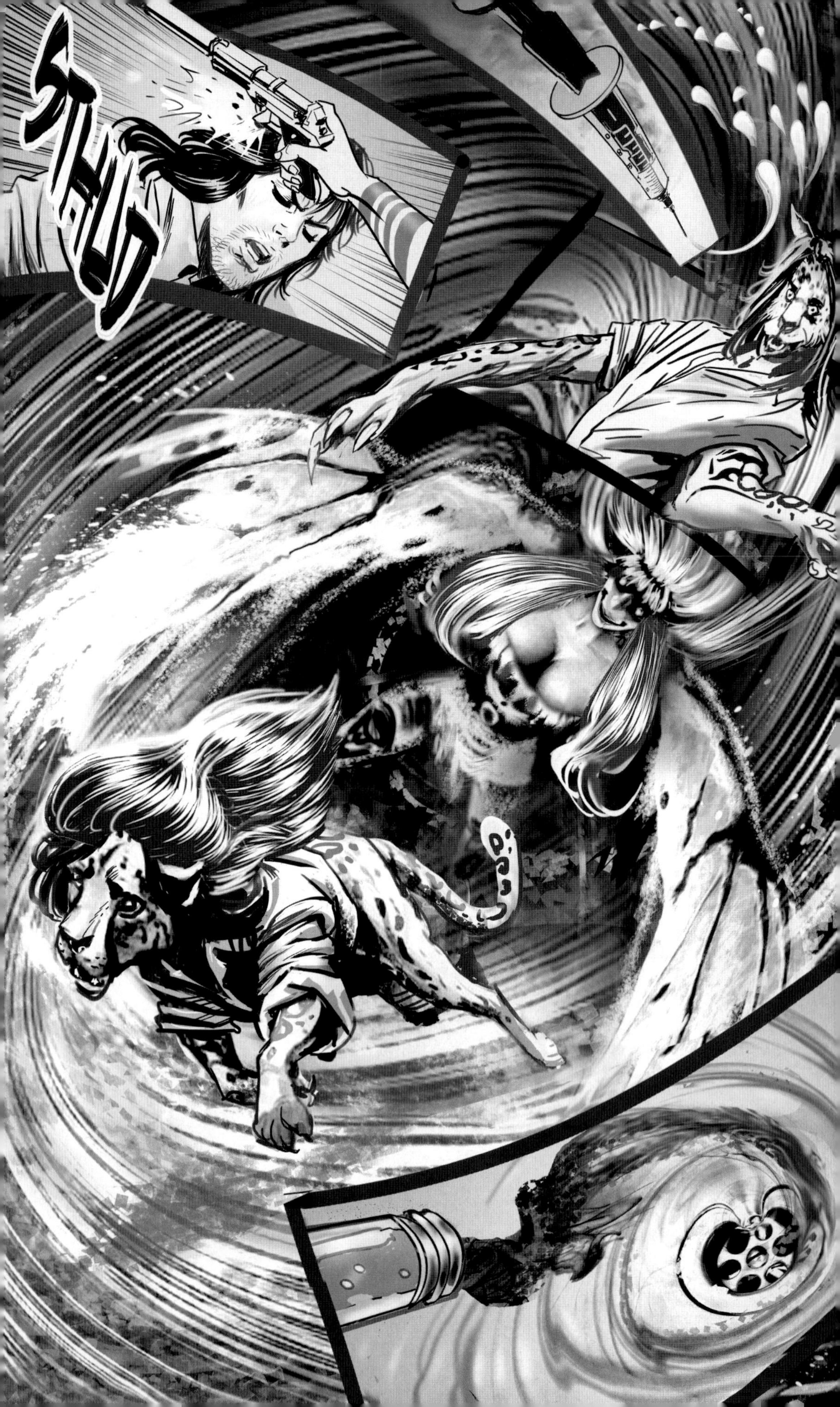
STHUD

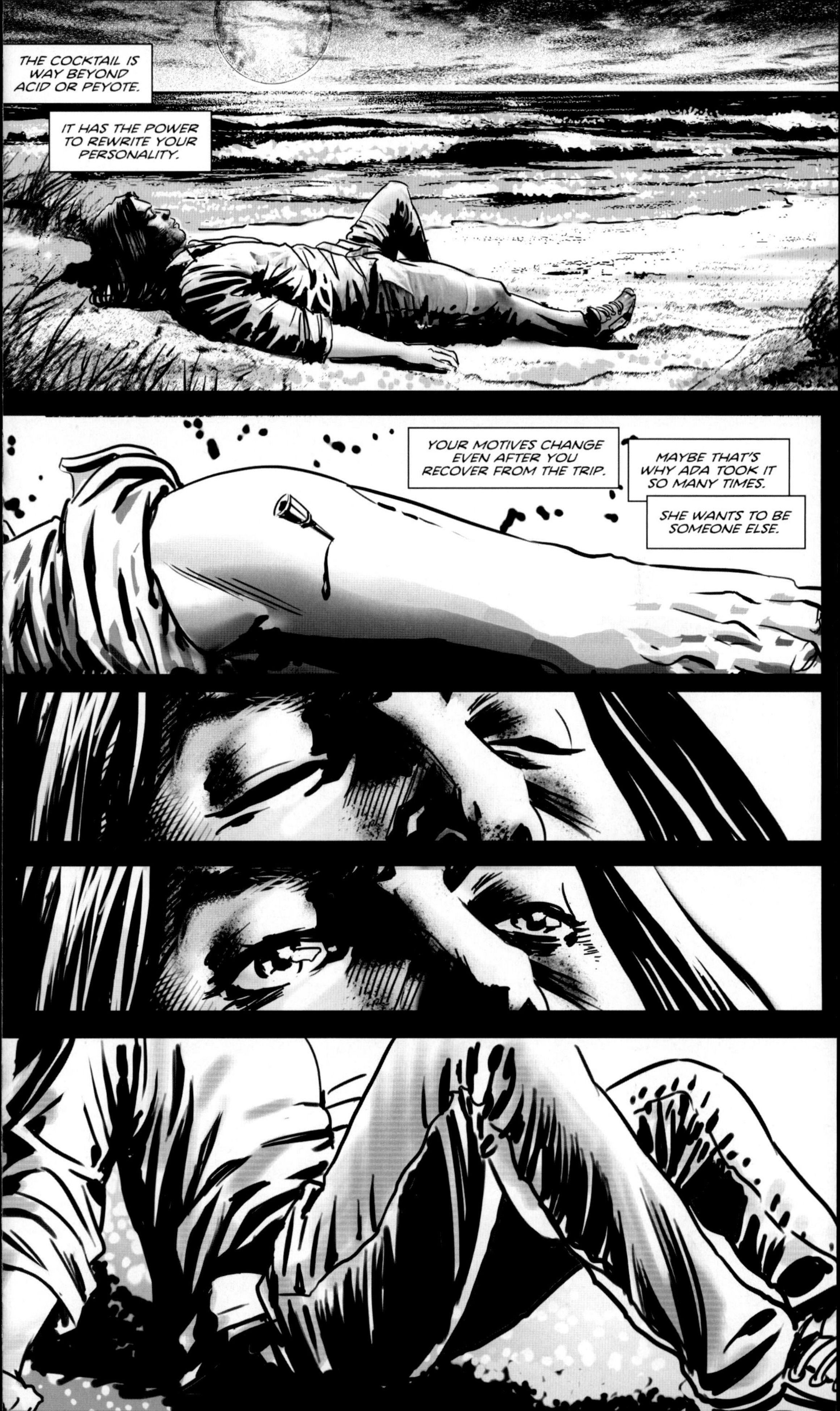
THE COCKTAIL IS WAY BEYOND ACID OR PEYOTE.
IT HAS THE POWER TO REWRITE YOUR PERSONALITY.
YOUR MOTIVES CHANGE EVEN AFTER YOU RECOVER FROM THE TRIP.
MAYBE THAT'S WHY ADA TOOK IT SO MANY TIMES.
SHE WANTS TO BE SOMEONE ELSE.

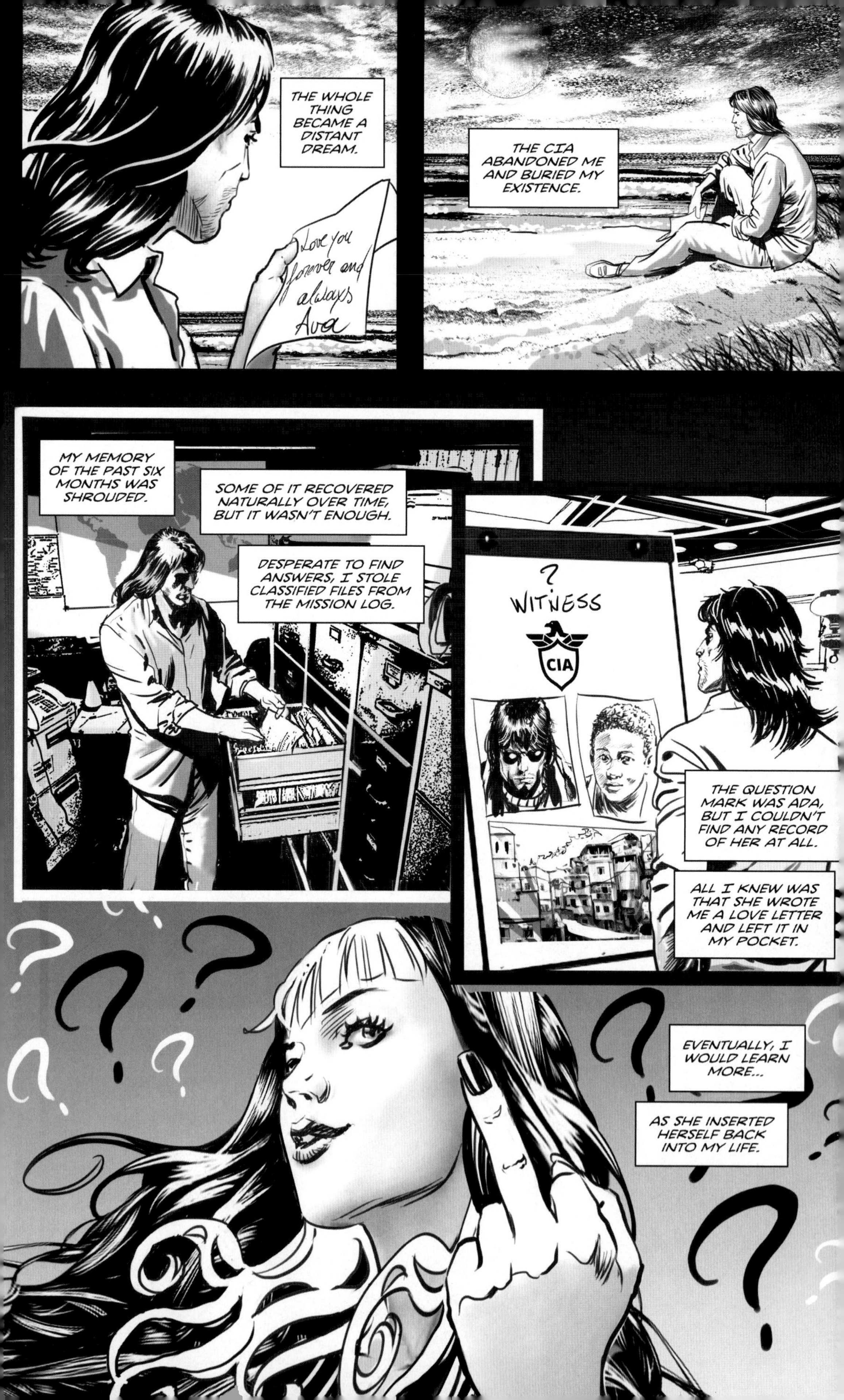
THE WHOLE THING BECAME A DISTANT DREAM.
Love you forever and always Ava
THE CIA ABANDONED ME AND BURIED MY EXISTENCE.
MY MEMORY OF THE PAST SIX MONTHS WAS SHROUDED.
SOME OF IT RECOVERED NATURALLY OVER TIME, BUT IT WASN'T ENOUGH.
DESPERATE TO FIND ANSWERS, I STOLE CLASSIFIED FILES FROM THE MISSION LOG.
?
WITNESS
CIA
THE QUESTION MARK WAS ADA, BUT I COULDN'T FIND ANY RECORD OF HER AT ALL.
ALL I KNEW WAS THAT SHE WROTE ME A LOVE LETTER AND LEFT IT IN MY POCKET.
EVENTUALLY, I WOULD LEARN MORE...
AS SHE INSERTED HERSELF BACK INTO MY LIFE.

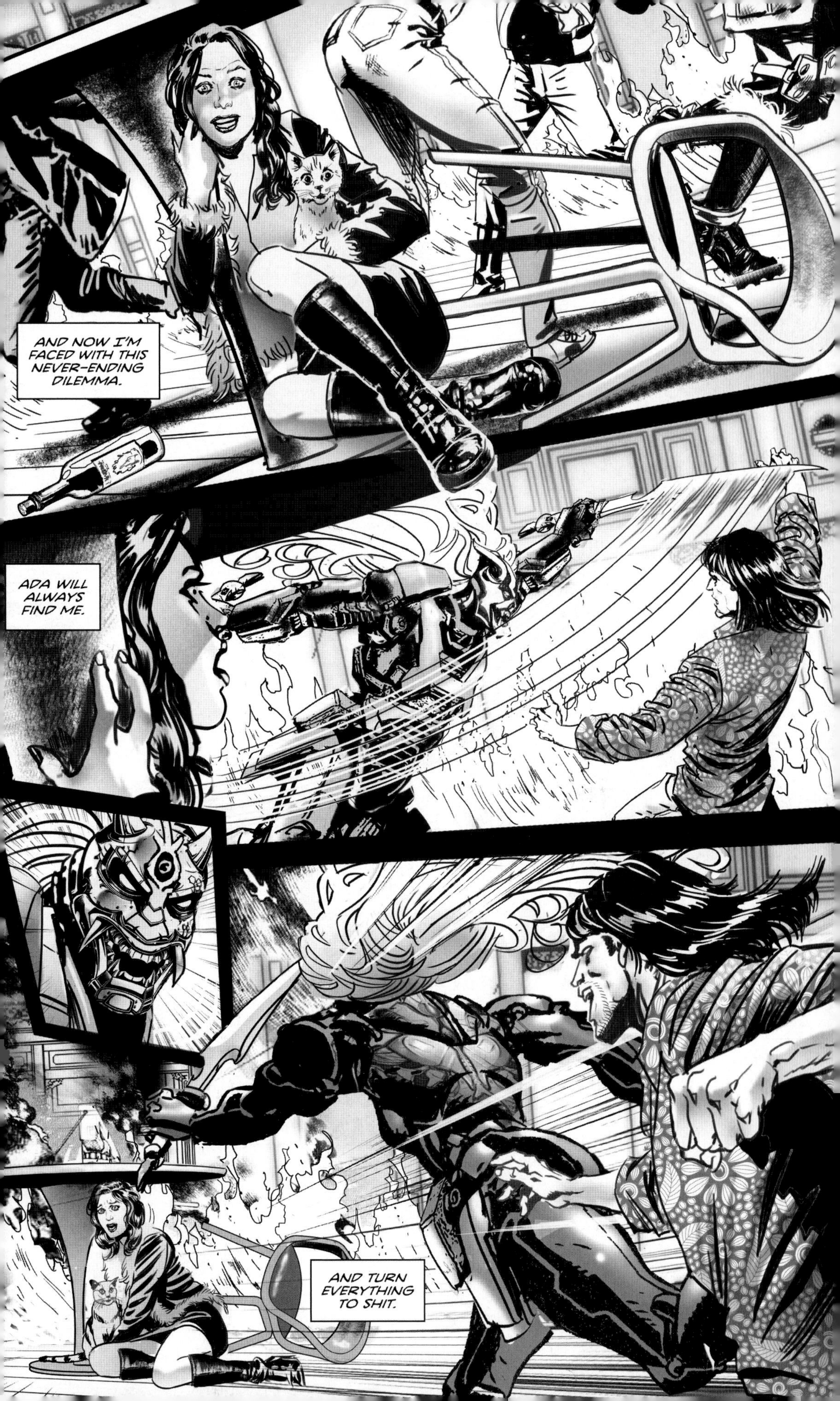
AND NOW I'M FACED WITH THIS NEVER-ENDING DILEMMA.
ADA WILL ALWAYS FIND ME.
AND TURN EVERYTHING TO SHIT.

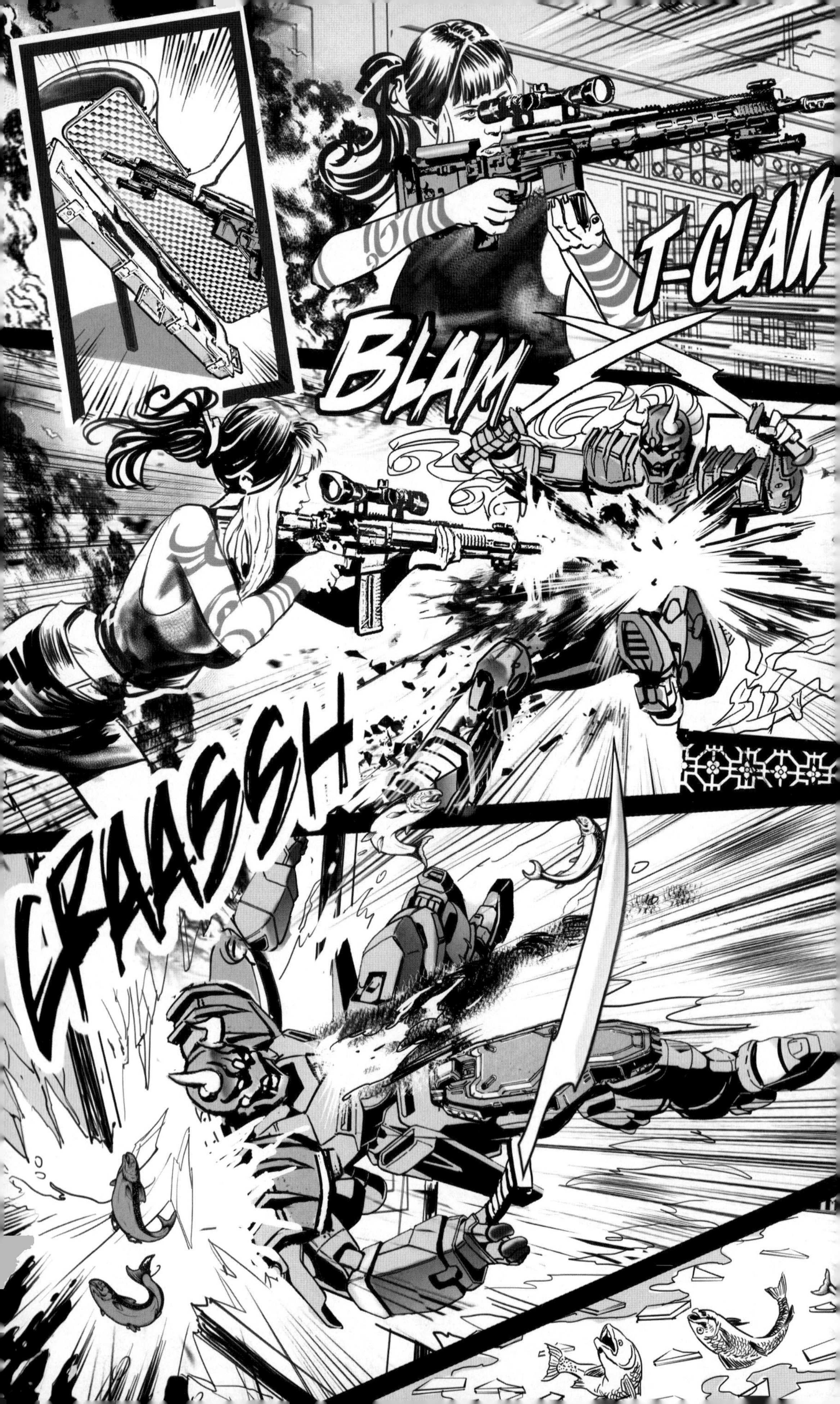
T-CLAK
BLAM
CRAASSH

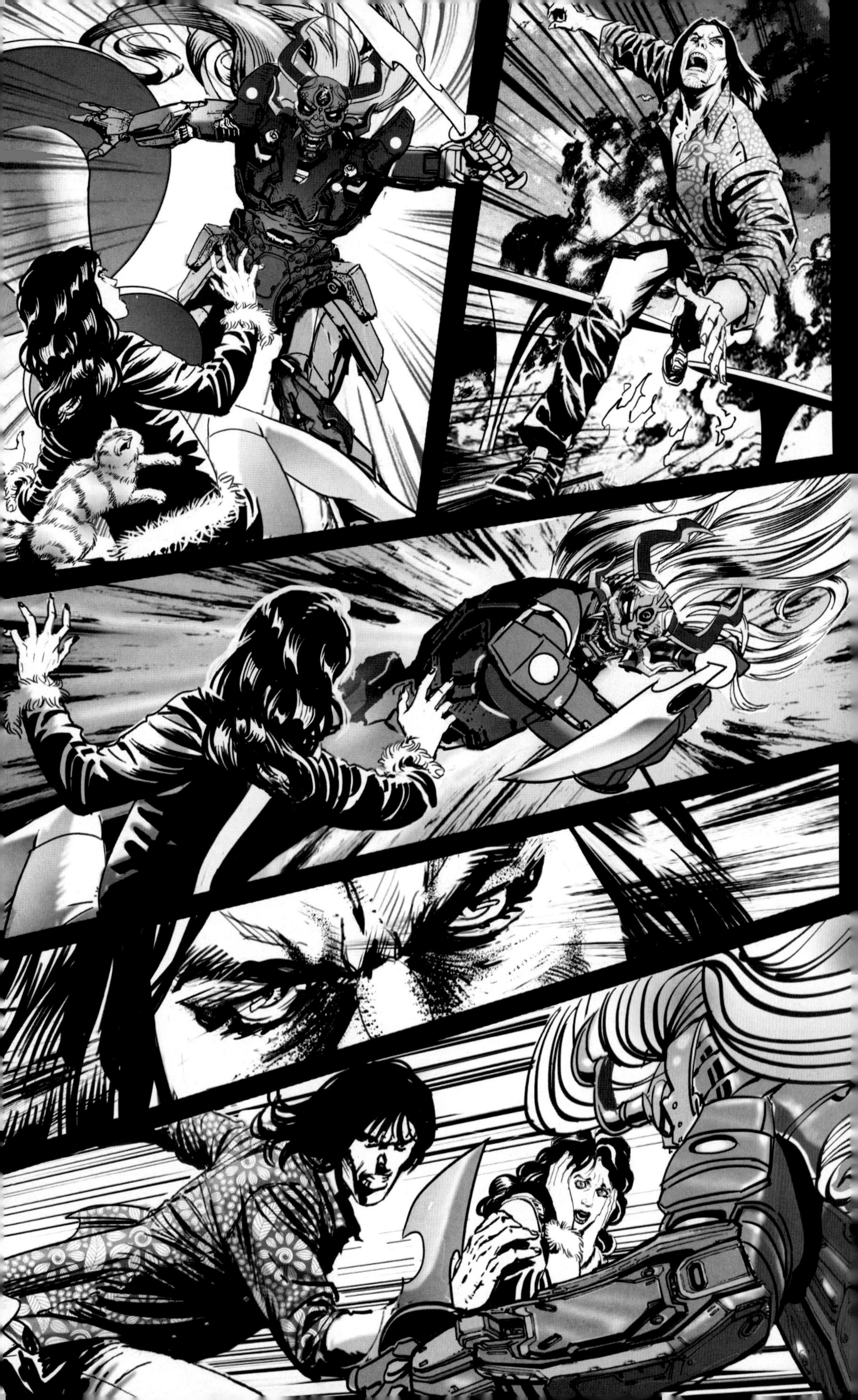

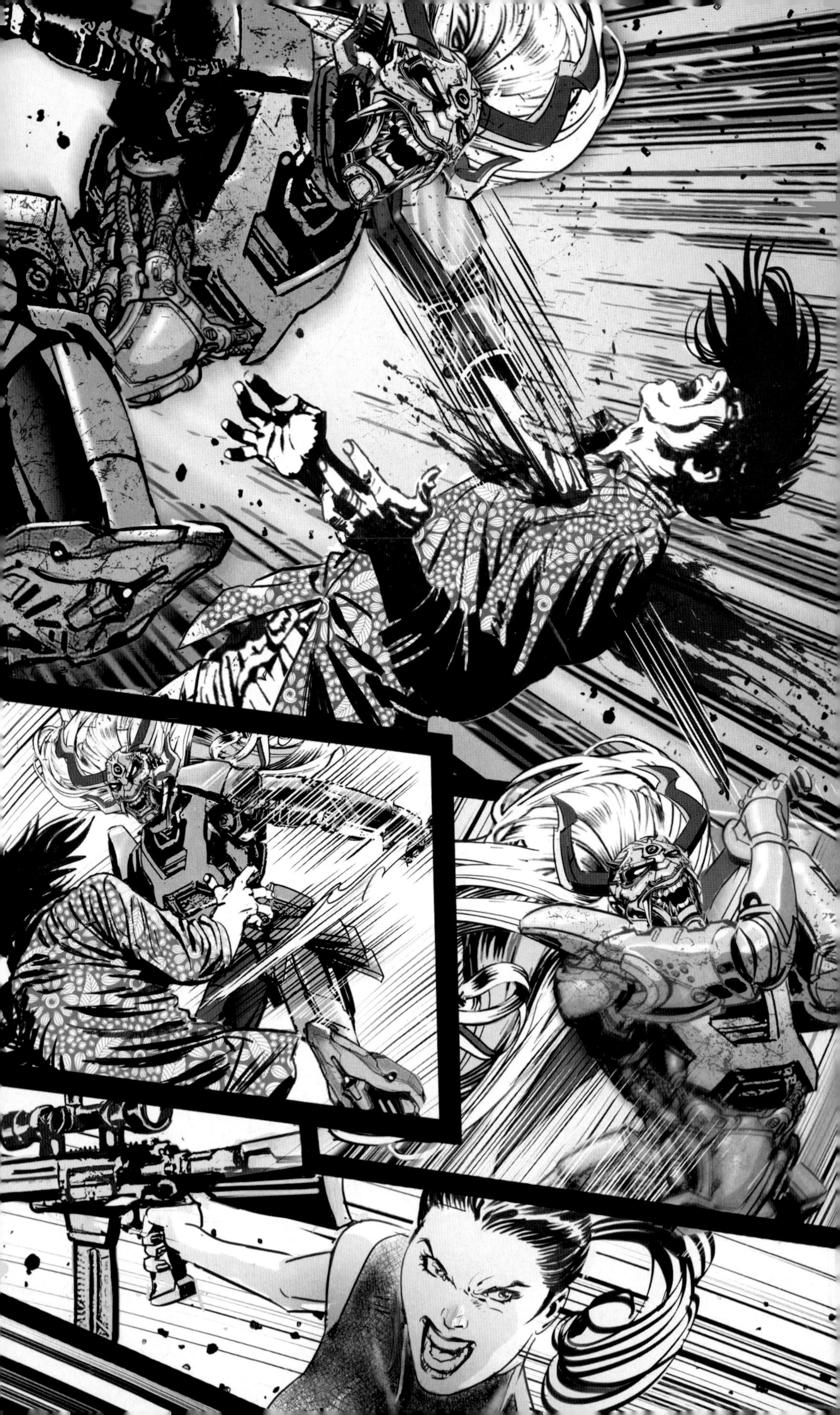

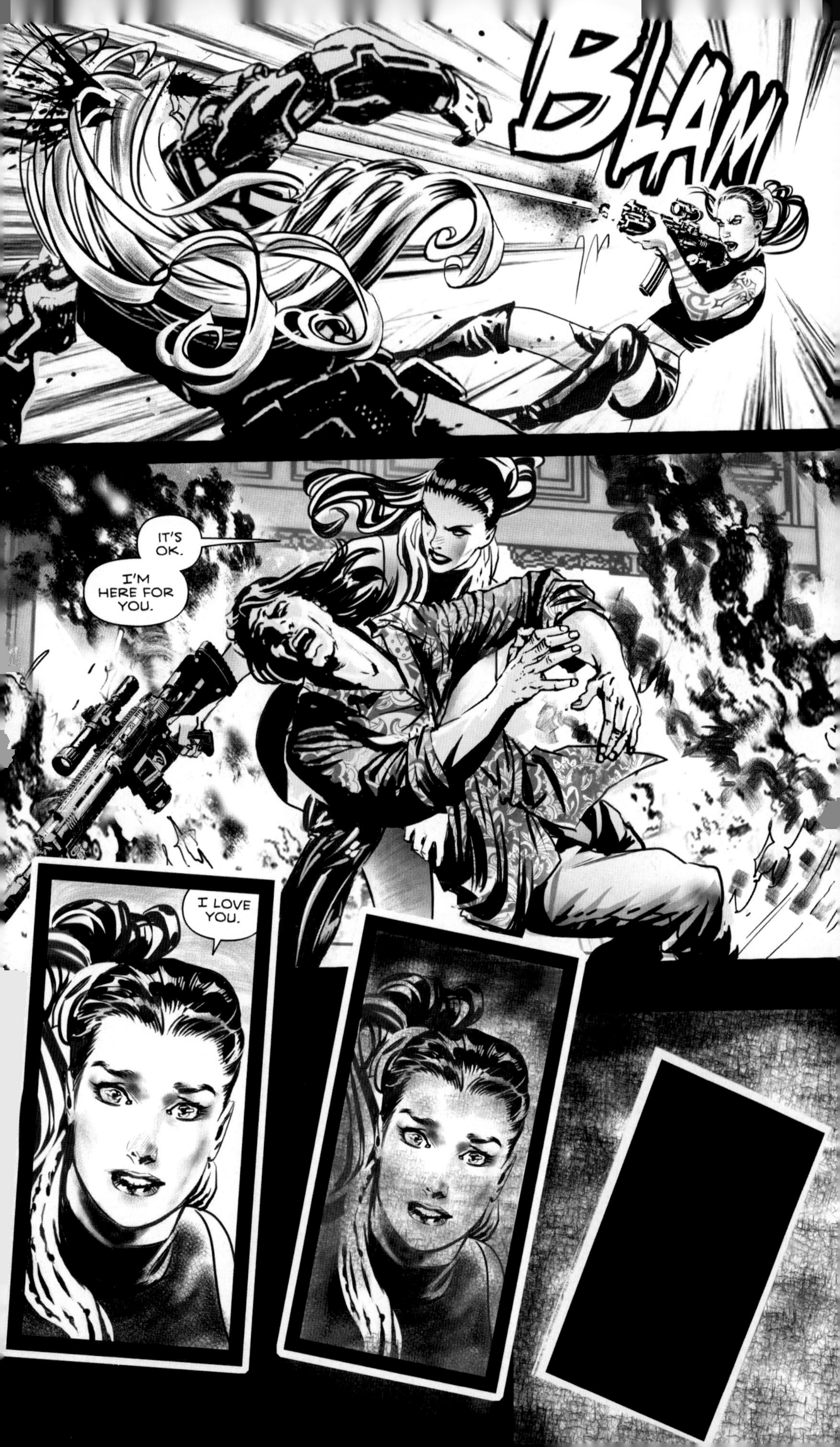
BLAM
IT'S OK.
I'M HERE FOR YOU.
I LOVE YOU.

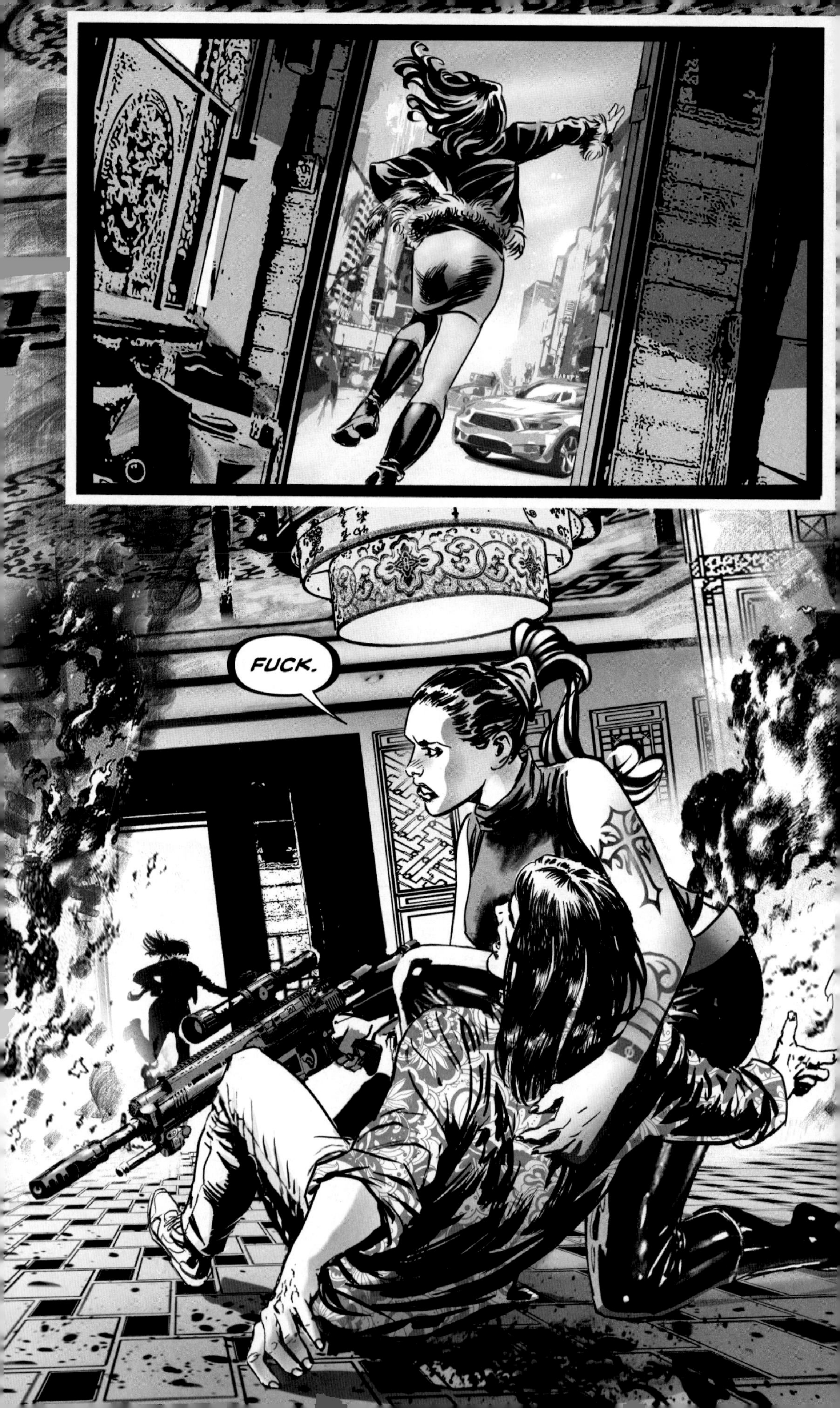
FUCK.

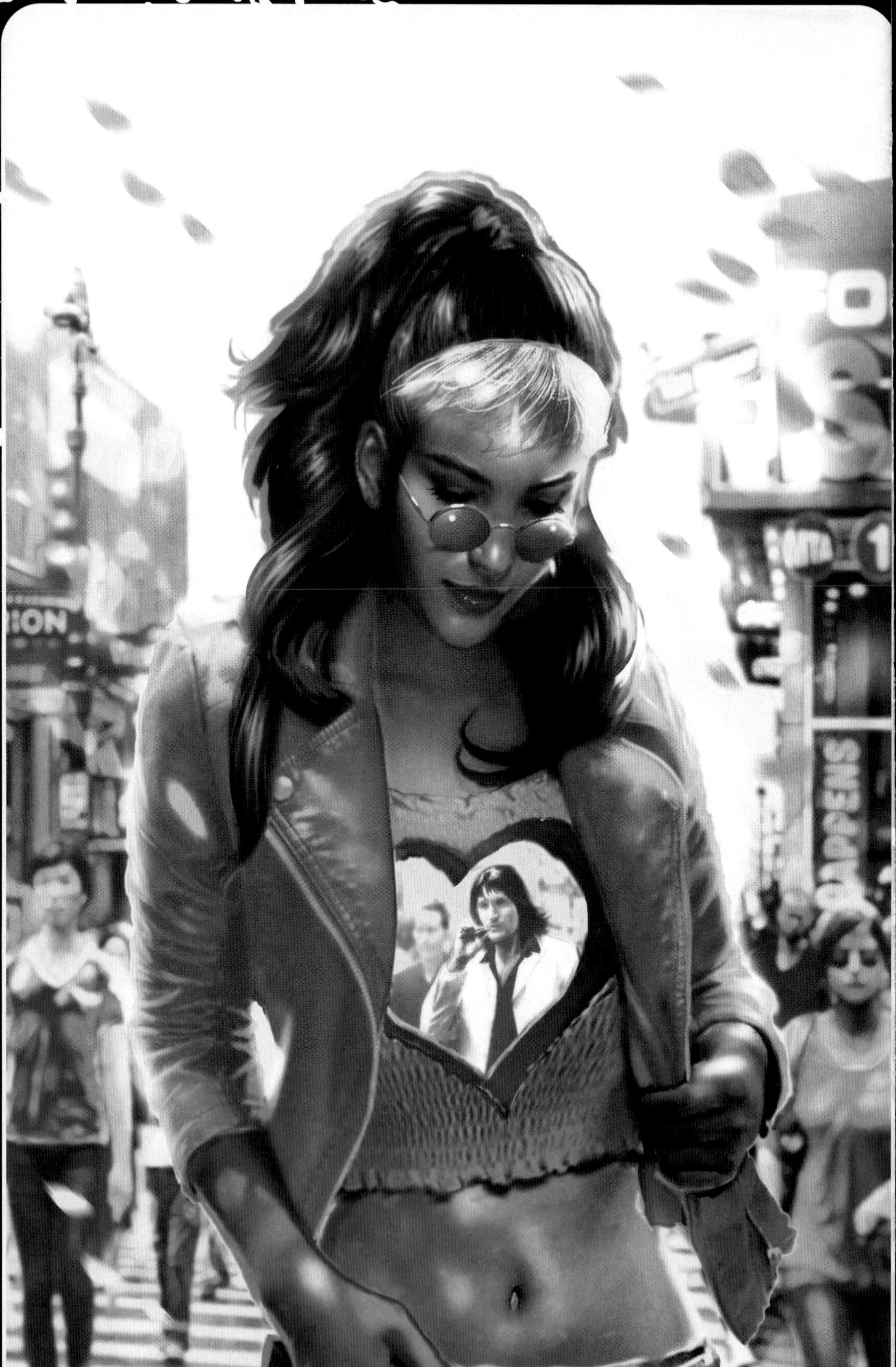

CHAPTER FOUR

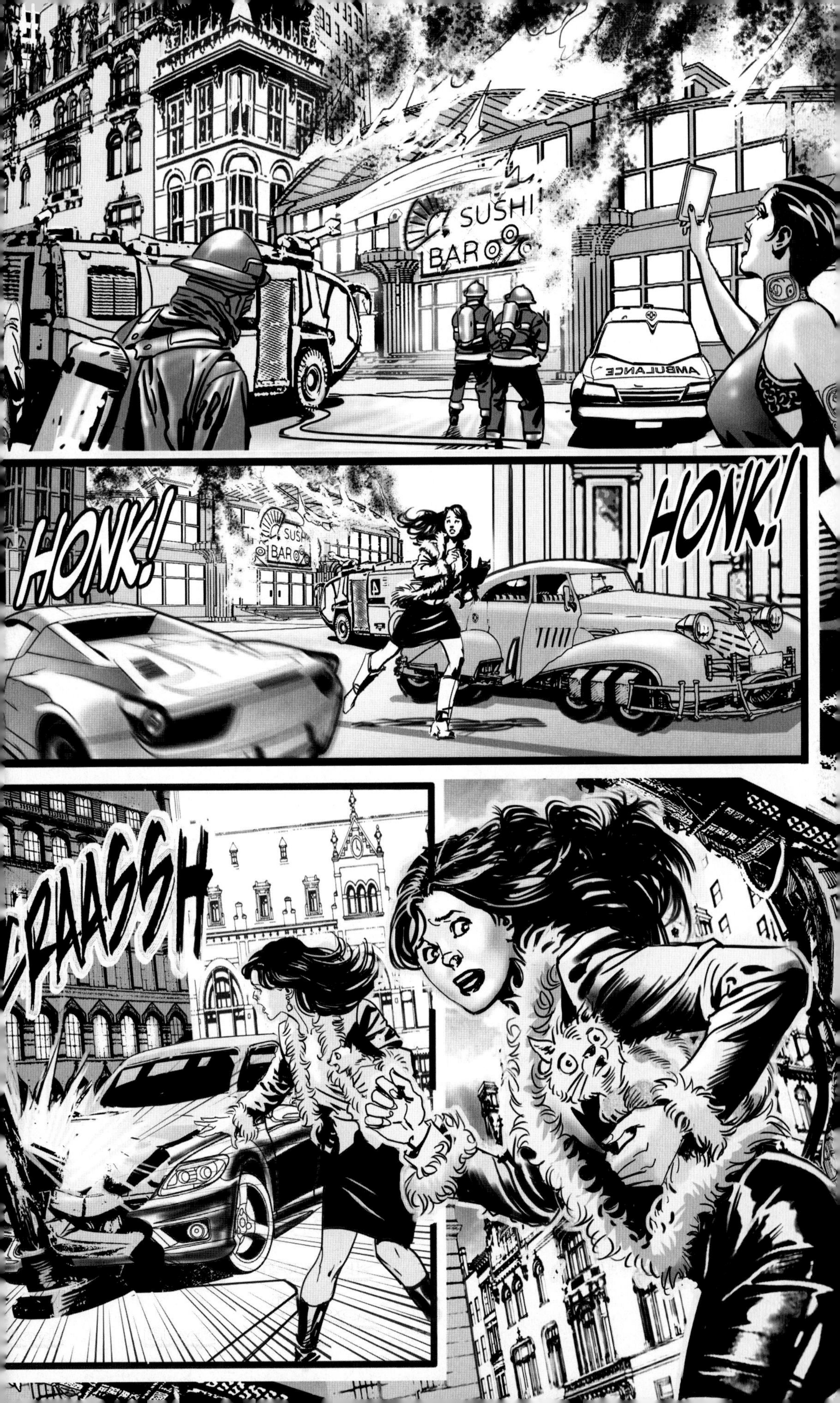
SUSHI
BAR
AMBULANCE
SUSHI
BAR
HONK!
HONK!
CRAASSH

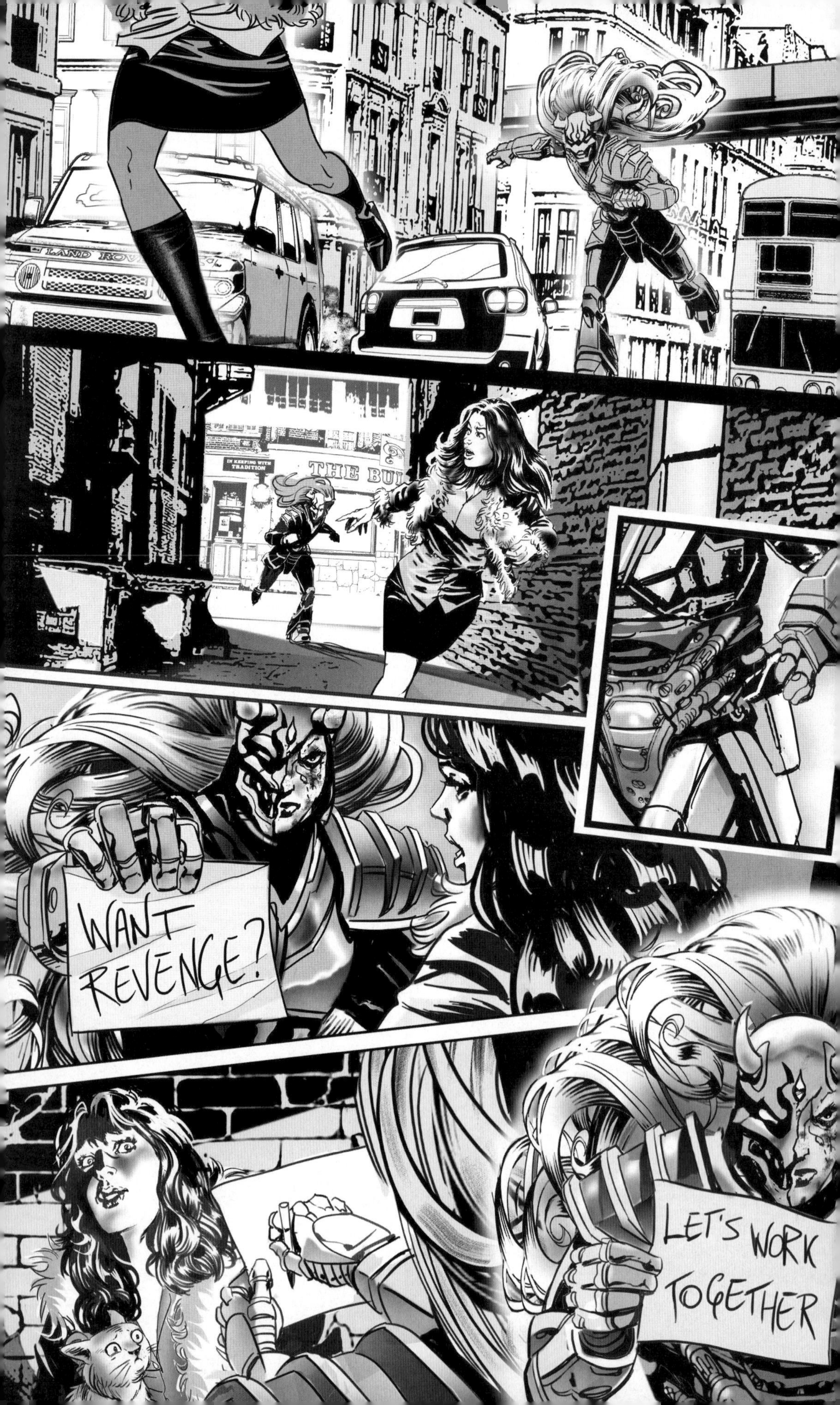

LAND ROVER
IN KEEPING WITH TRADITION
THE BU
WANT REVENGE?
LET'S WORK TOGETHER

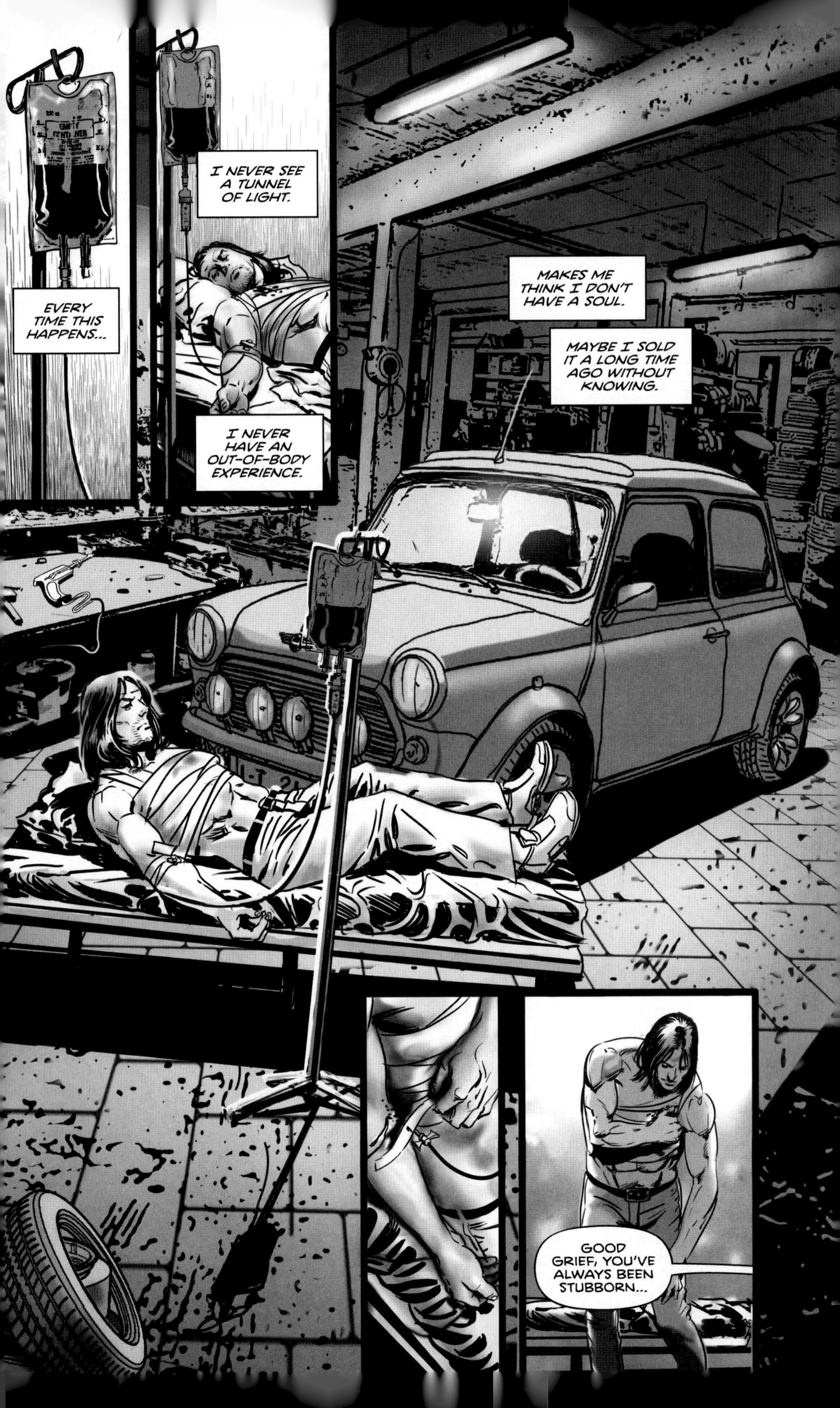

EVERY TIME THIS HAPPENS...
I NEVER SEE A TUNNEL OF LIGHT.
I NEVER HAVE AN OUT-OF-BODY EXPERIENCE.
MAKES ME THINK I DON'T HAVE A SOUL.
MAYBE I SOLD IT A LONG TIME AGO WITHOUT KNOWING.
GOOD GRIEF, YOU'VE ALWAYS BEEN STUBBORN...

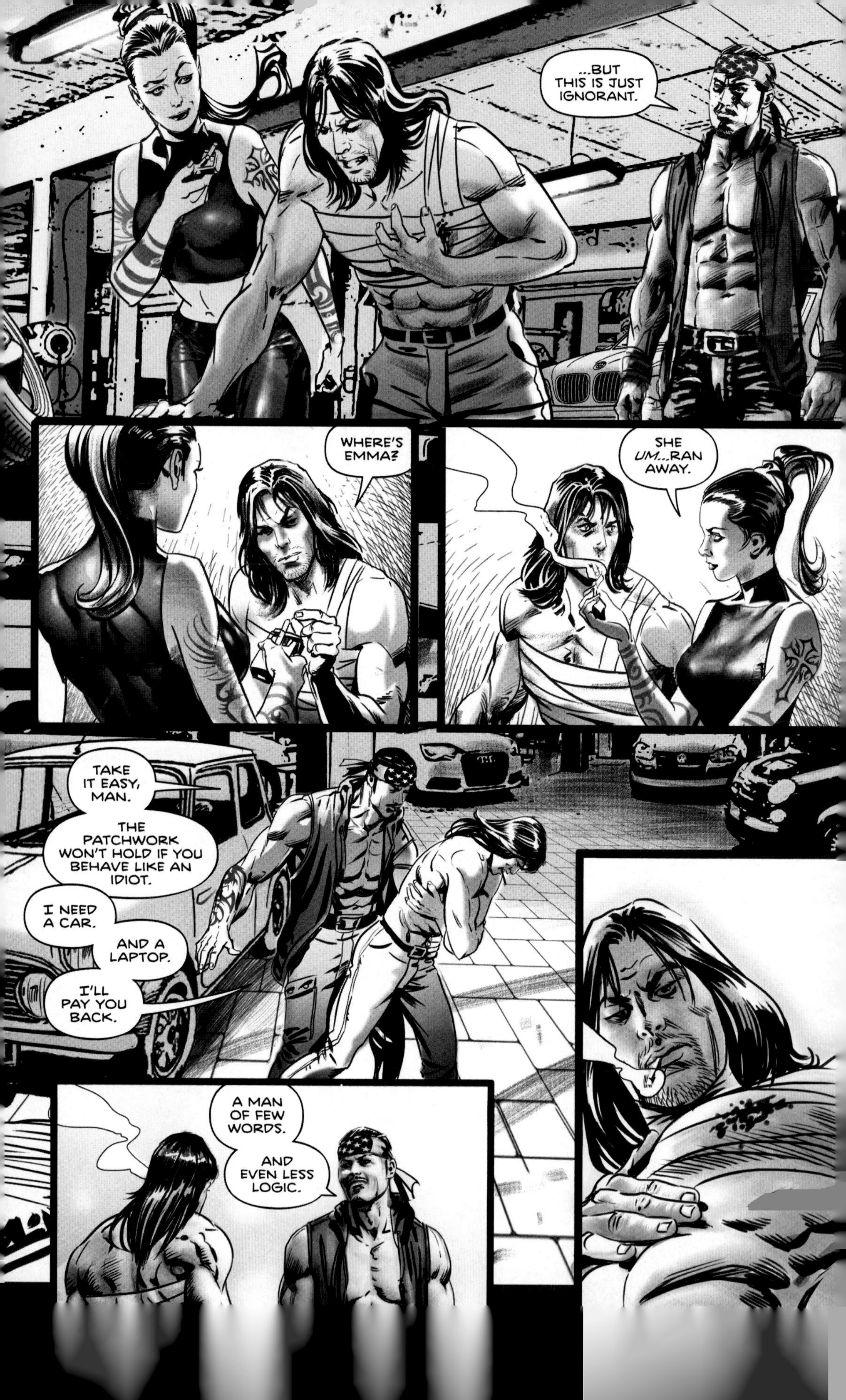
...BUT THIS IS JUST IGNORANT.
WHERE'S EMMA?
SHE *UM*...RAN AWAY.
TAKE IT EASY, MAN.
THE PATCHWORK WON'T HOLD IF YOU BEHAVE LIKE AN IDIOT.
I NEED A CAR.
AND A LAPTOP.
I'LL PAY YOU BACK.
A MAN OF FEW WORDS.
AND EVEN LESS LOGIC.

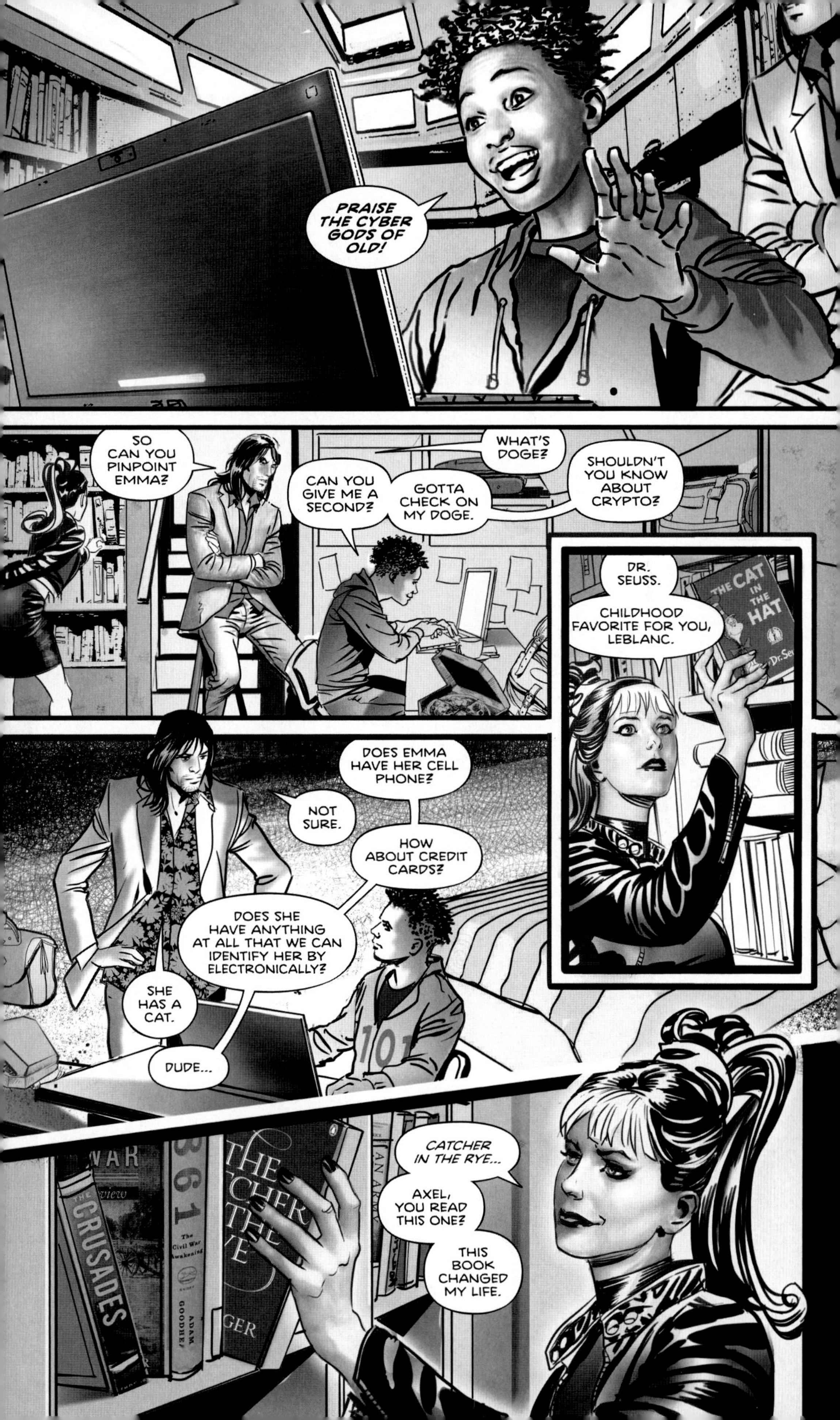
PRAISE THE CYBER GODS OF OLD!
SO CAN YOU PINPOINT EMMA?
CAN YOU GIVE ME A SECOND?
GOTTA CHECK ON MY DOGE.
WHAT'S DOGE?
SHOULDN'T YOU KNOW ABOUT CRYPTO?
DR. SEUSS.
CHILDHOOD FAVORITE FOR YOU, LEBLANC.
THE CAT IN THE HAT
DOES EMMA HAVE HER CELL PHONE?
NOT SURE.
HOW ABOUT CREDIT CARDS?
DOES SHE HAVE ANYTHING AT ALL THAT WE CAN IDENTIFY HER BY ELECTRONICALLY?
SHE HAS A CAT.
DUDE...
CATCHER IN THE RYE...
AXEL, YOU READ THIS ONE?
THIS BOOK CHANGED MY LIFE.
THE CRUSADES
ADAM GOODHEART

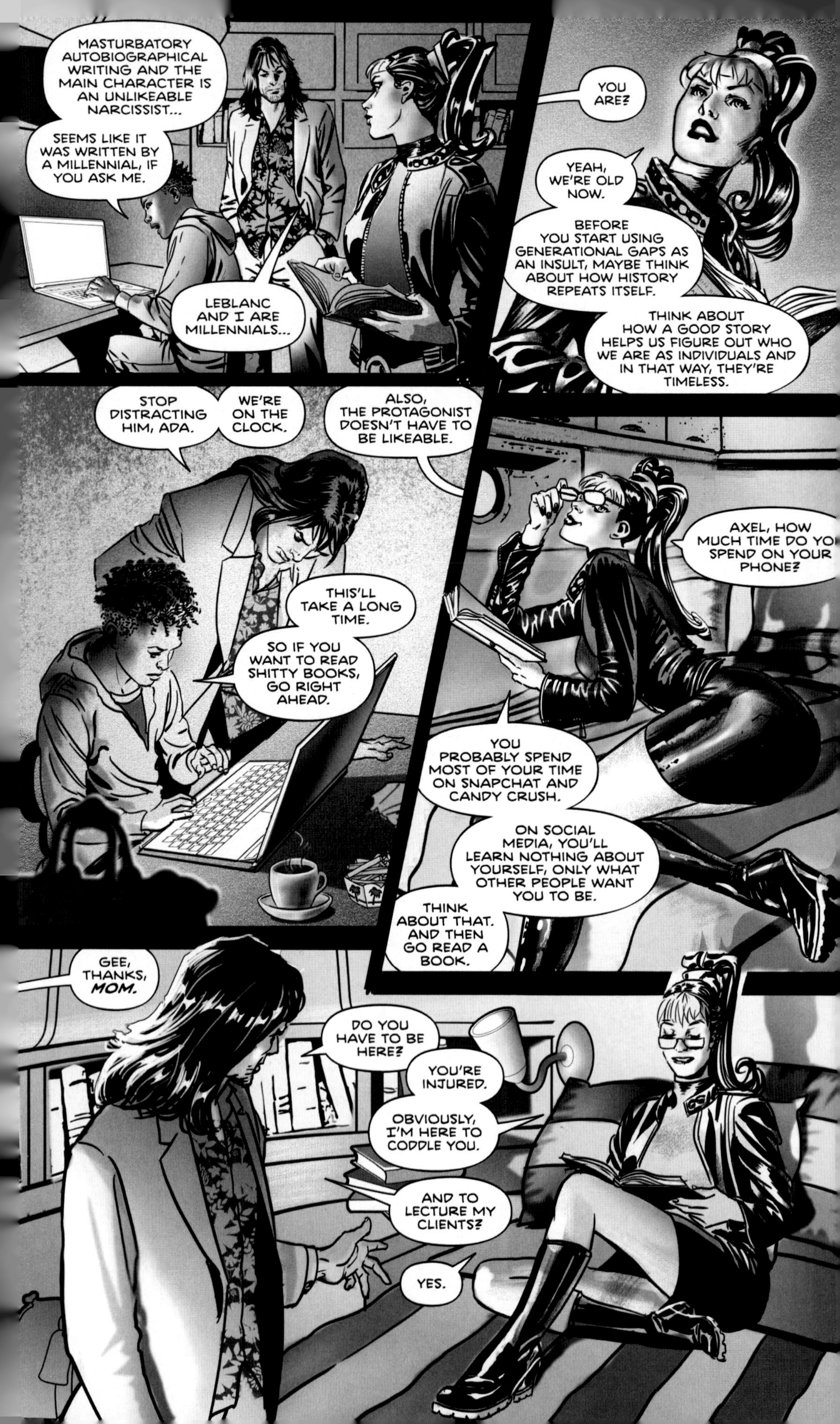
MASTURBATORY AUTOBIOGRAPHICAL WRITING AND THE MAIN CHARACTER IS AN UNLIKEABLE NARCISSIST...
SEEMS LIKE IT WAS WRITTEN BY A MILLENNIAL, IF YOU ASK ME.
LEBLANC AND I ARE MILLENNIALS...
YOU ARE?
YEAH, WE'RE OLD NOW.
BEFORE YOU START USING GENERATIONAL GAPS AS AN INSULT, MAYBE THINK ABOUT HOW HISTORY REPEATS ITSELF.
THINK ABOUT HOW A GOOD STORY HELPS US FIGURE OUT WHO WE ARE AS INDIVIDUALS AND IN THAT WAY, THEY'RE TIMELESS.
STOP DISTRACTING HIM, ADA.
WE'RE ON THE CLOCK.
ALSO, THE PROTAGONIST DOESN'T HAVE TO BE LIKEABLE.
THIS'LL TAKE A LONG TIME.
SO IF YOU WANT TO READ SHITTY BOOKS, GO RIGHT AHEAD.
AXEL, HOW MUCH TIME DO YO SPEND ON YOUR PHONE?
YOU PROBABLY SPEND MOST OF YOUR TIME ON SNAPCHAT AND CANDY CRUSH.
ON SOCIAL MEDIA, YOU'LL LEARN NOTHING ABOUT YOURSELF, ONLY WHAT OTHER PEOPLE WANT YOU TO BE.
THINK ABOUT THAT. AND THEN GO READ A BOOK.
GEE, THANKS, *MOM.*
DO YOU HAVE TO BE HERE?
YOU'RE INJURED.
OBVIOUSLY, I'M HERE TO CODDLE YOU.
AND TO LECTURE MY CLIENTS?
YES.

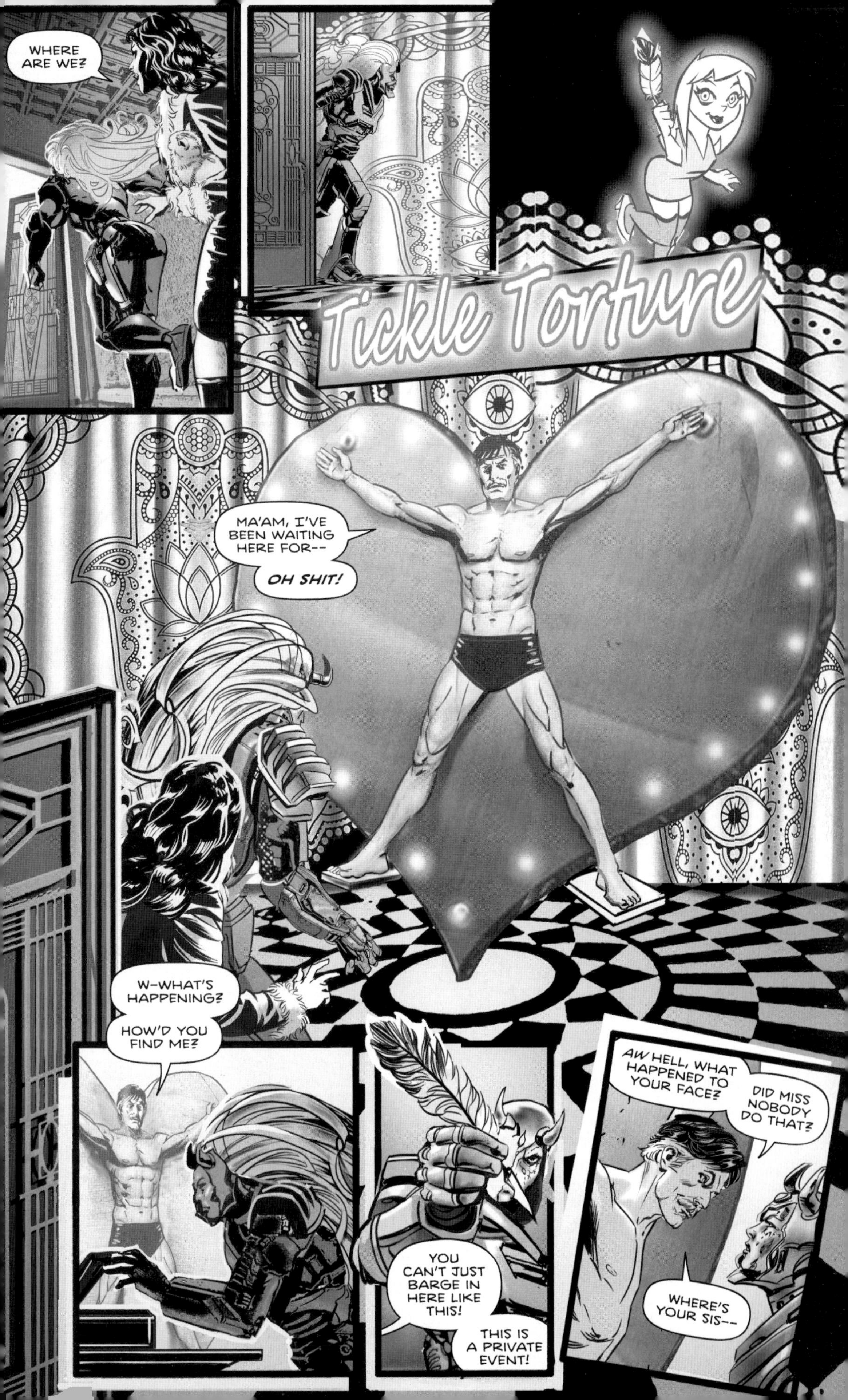
WHERE ARE WE?
Tickle Torture
MA'AM, I'VE BEEN WAITING HERE FOR--
OH SHIT!
W-WHAT'S HAPPENING?
HOW'D YOU FIND ME?
YOU CAN'T JUST BARGE IN HERE LIKE THIS!
THIS IS A PRIVATE EVENT!
AW HELL, WHAT HAPPENED TO YOUR FACE?
DID MISS NOBODY DO THAT?
WHERE'S YOUR SIS--

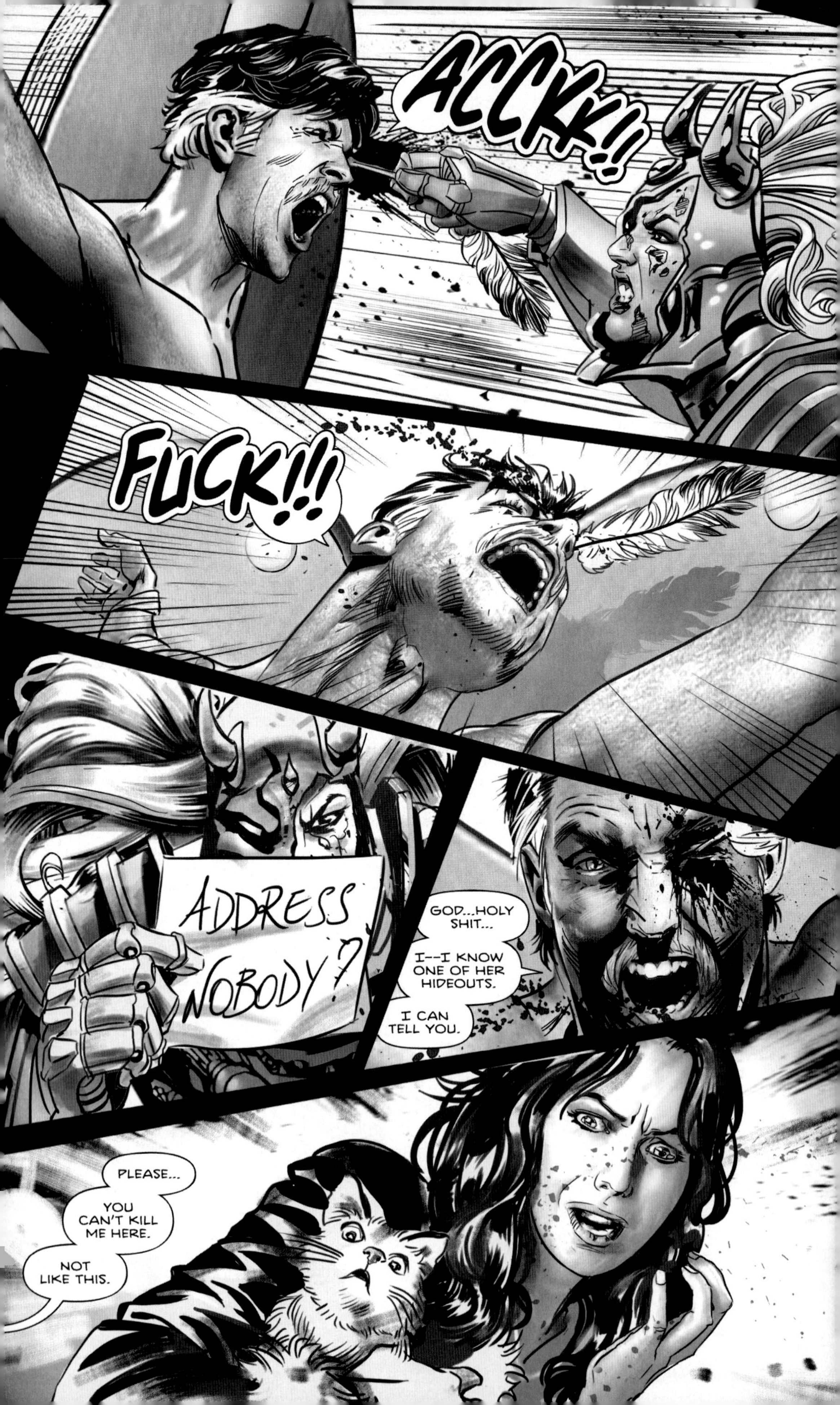

ACCKK!!
FUCK!!!
ADDRESS NOBODY?
GOD...HOLY SHIT...
I--I KNOW ONE OF HER HIDEOUTS.
I CAN TELL YOU.
PLEASE...
YOU CAN'T KILL ME HERE.
NOT LIKE THIS.

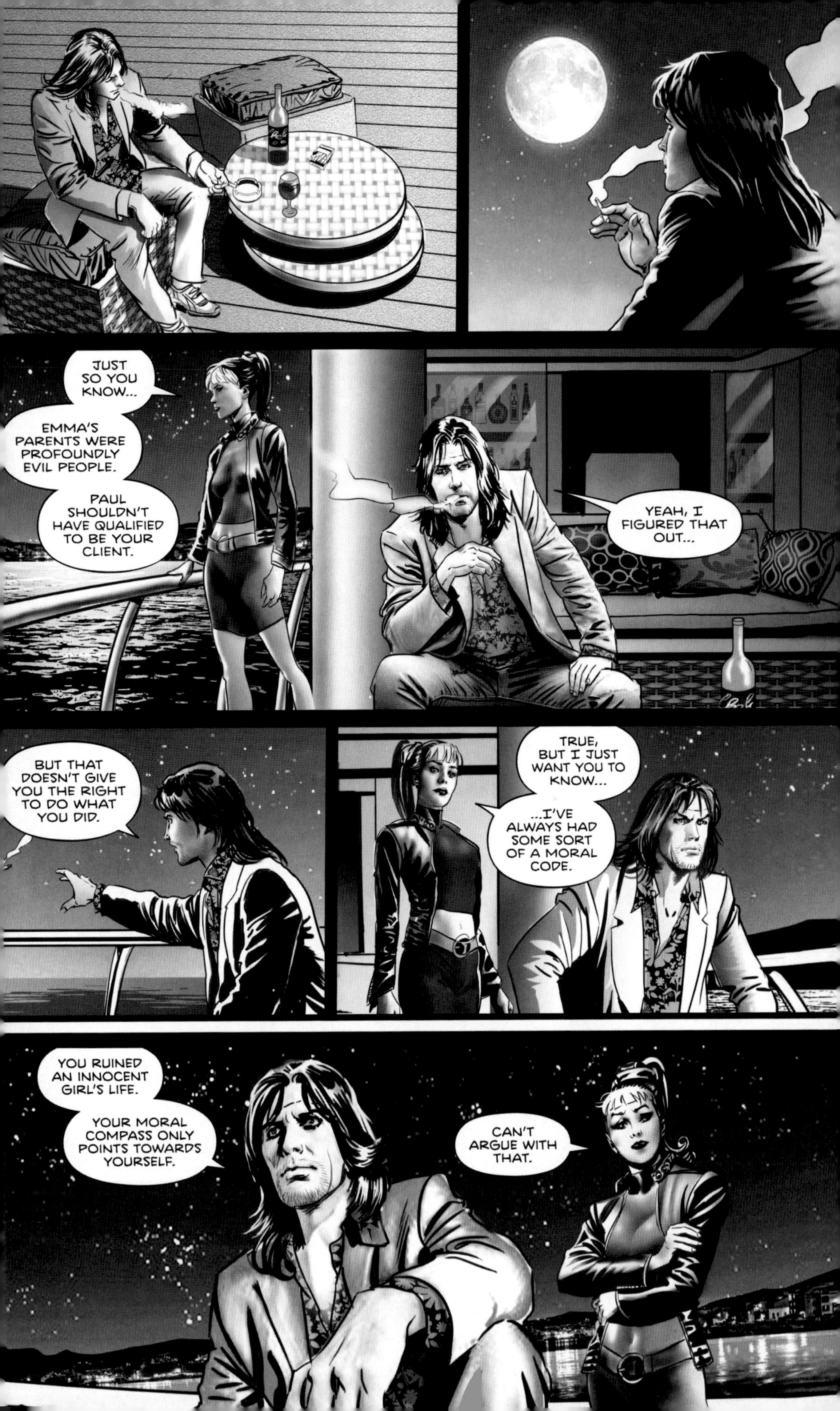

JUST SO YOU KNOW...
EMMA'S PARENTS WERE PROFOUNDLY EVIL PEOPLE.
PAUL SHOULDN'T HAVE QUALIFIED TO BE YOUR CLIENT.
YEAH, I FIGURED THAT OUT...
BUT THAT DOESN'T GIVE YOU THE RIGHT TO DO WHAT YOU DID.
TRUE, BUT I JUST WANT YOU TO KNOW...
...I'VE ALWAYS HAD SOME SORT OF A MORAL CODE.
YOU RUINED AN INNOCENT GIRL'S LIFE.
YOUR MORAL COMPASS ONLY POINTS TOWARDS YOURSELF.
CAN'T ARGUE WITH THAT.

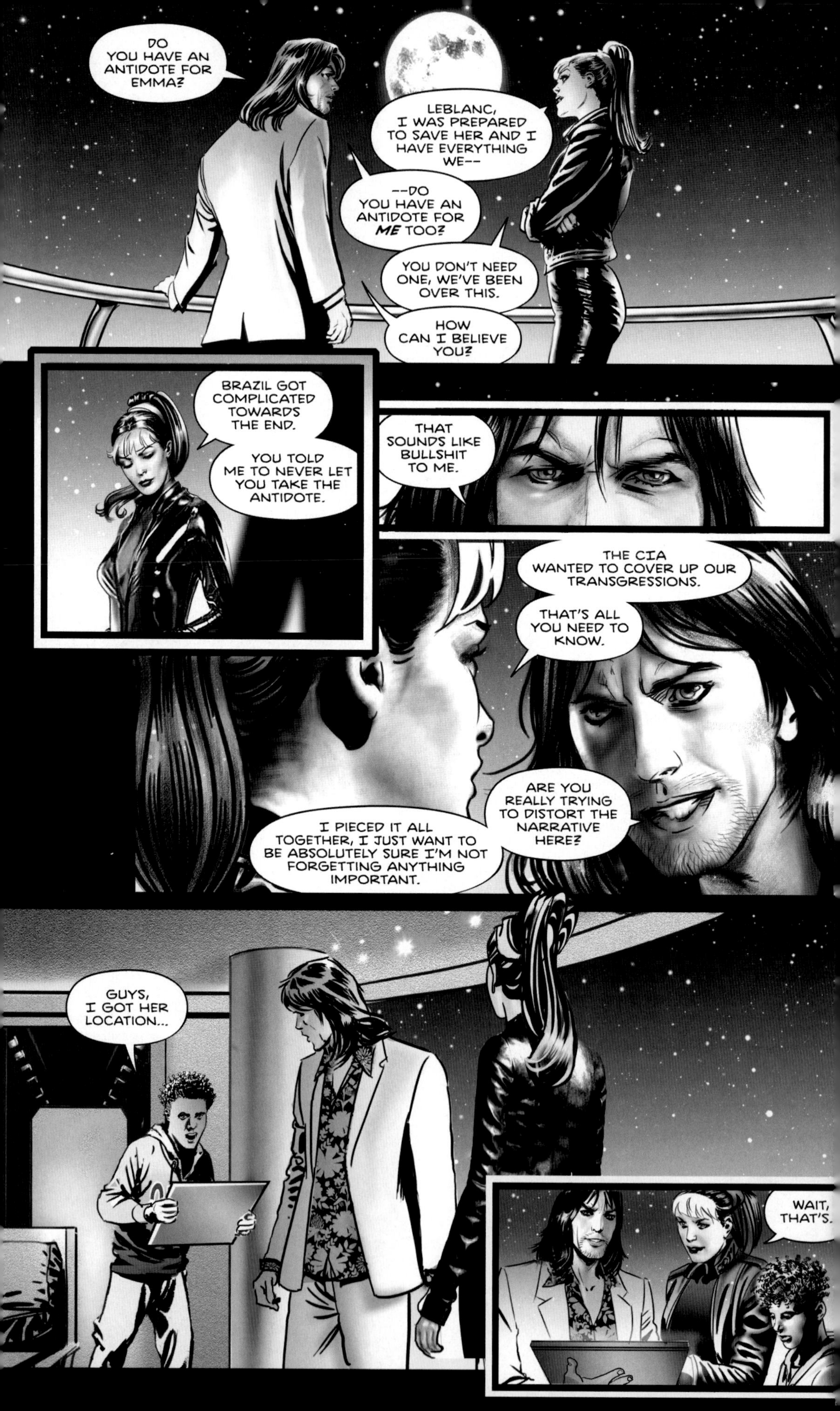
DO YOU HAVE AN ANTIDOTE FOR EMMA?
LEBLANC, I WAS PREPARED TO SAVE HER AND I HAVE EVERYTHING WE--
--DO YOU HAVE AN ANTIDOTE FOR *ME* TOO?
YOU DON'T NEED ONE, WE'VE BEEN OVER THIS.
HOW CAN I BELIEVE YOU?
BRAZIL GOT COMPLICATED TOWARDS THE END.
YOU TOLD ME TO NEVER LET YOU TAKE THE ANTIDOTE.
THAT SOUNDS LIKE BULLSHIT TO ME.
THE CIA WANTED TO COVER UP OUR TRANSGRESSIONS.
THAT'S ALL YOU NEED TO KNOW.
I PIECED IT ALL TOGETHER, I JUST WANT TO BE ABSOLUTELY SURE I'M NOT FORGETTING ANYTHING IMPORTANT.
ARE YOU REALLY TRYING TO DISTORT THE NARRATIVE HERE?
GUYS, I GOT HER LOCATION...
WAIT, THAT'S.

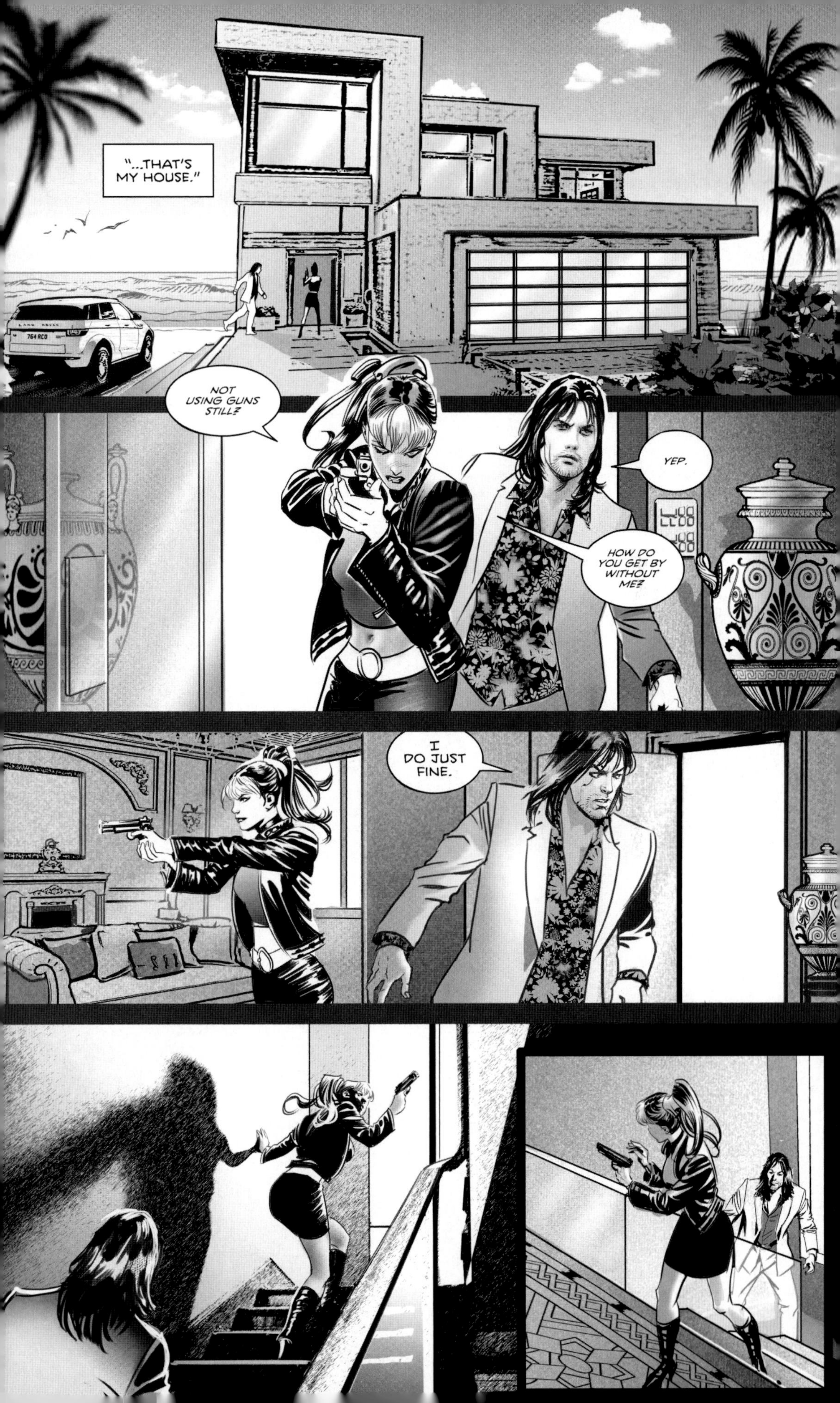
"...THAT'S MY HOUSE."
NOT USING GUNS STILL?
YEP.
HOW DO YOU GET BY WITHOUT ME?
I DO JUST FINE.

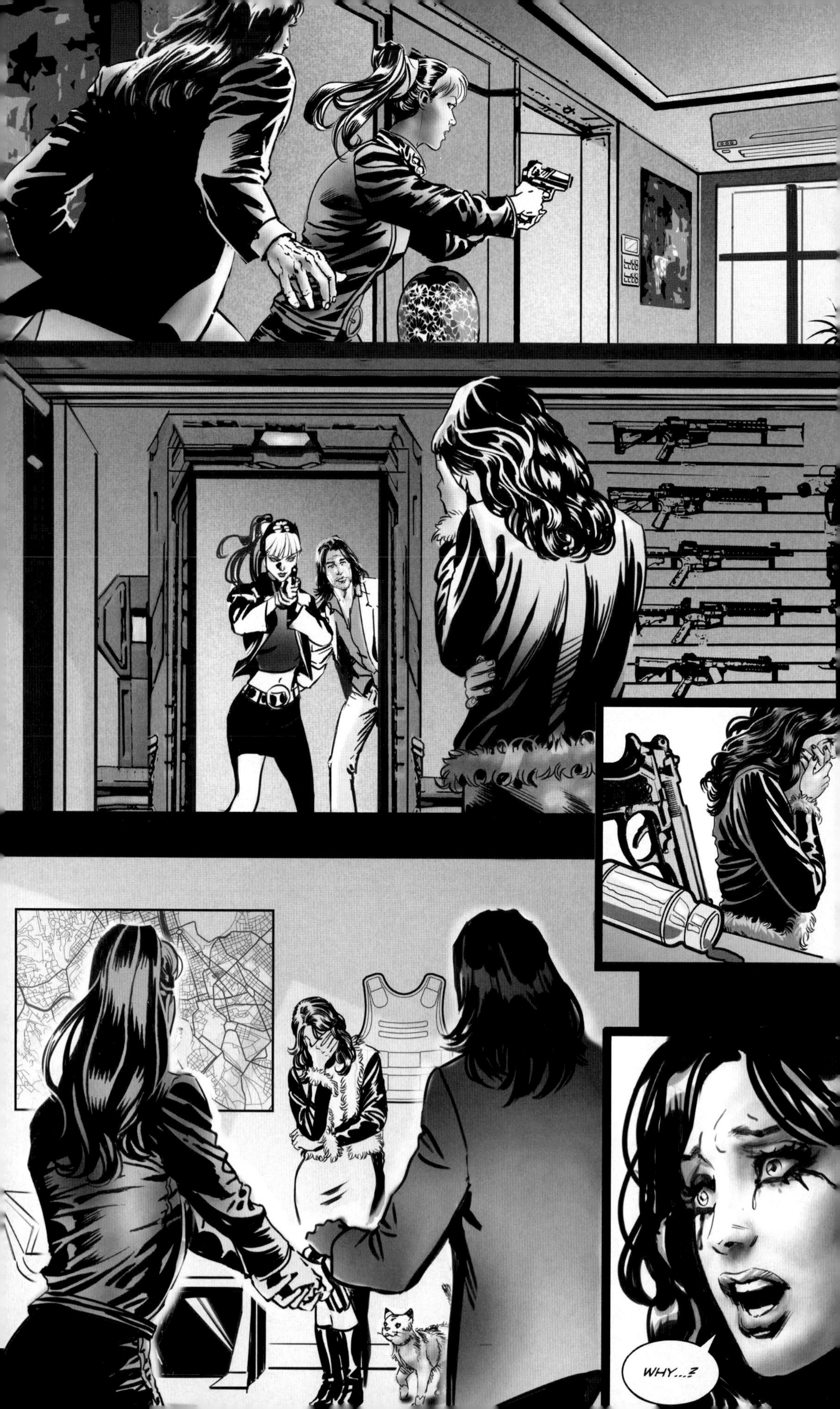
WHY...?

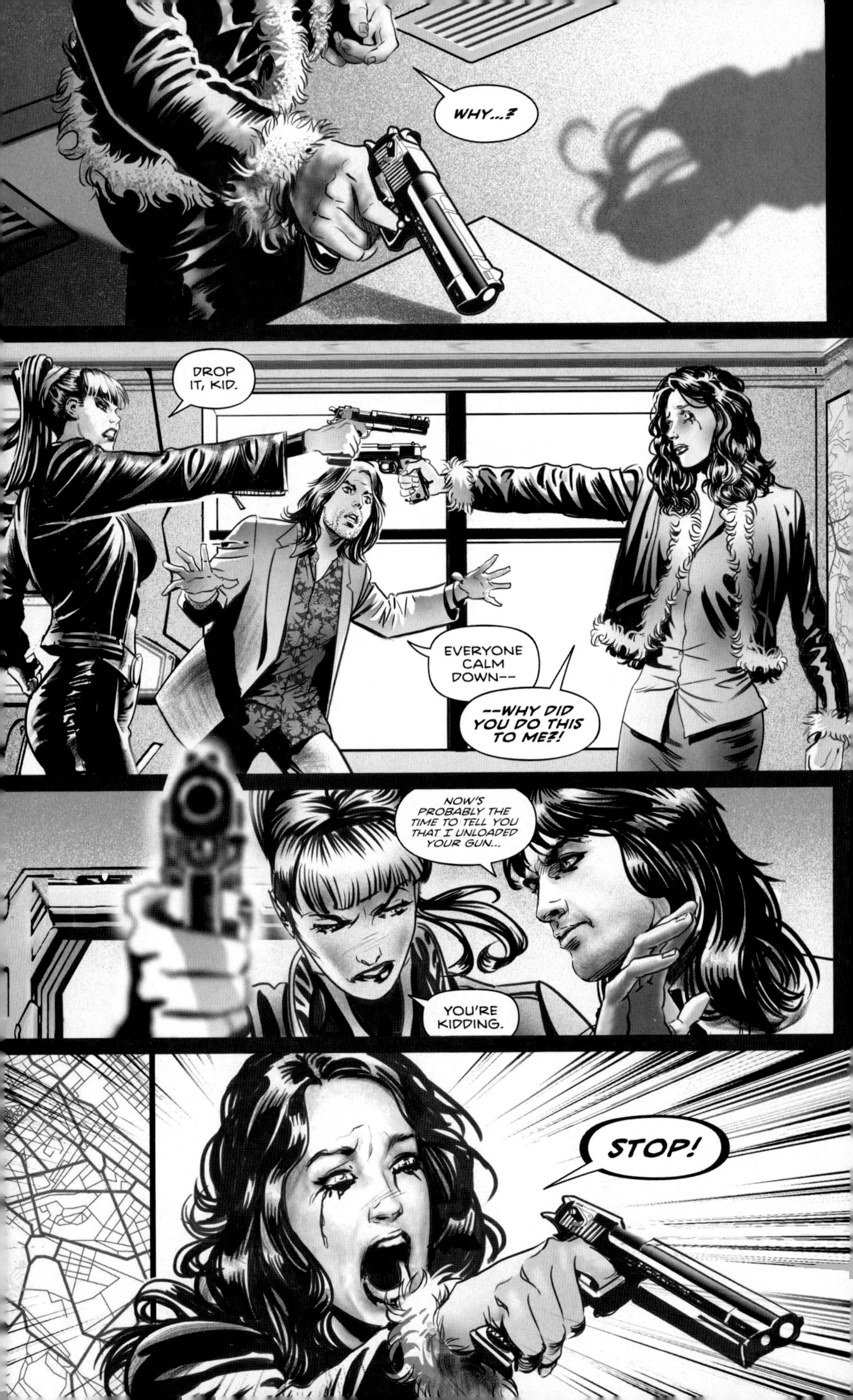
WHY...?
DROP IT, KID.
EVERYONE CALM DOWN--
--WHY DID YOU DO THIS TO ME?!
NOW'S PROBABLY THE TIME TO TELL YOU THAT I UNLOADED YOUR GUN...
YOU'RE KIDDING.
STOP!

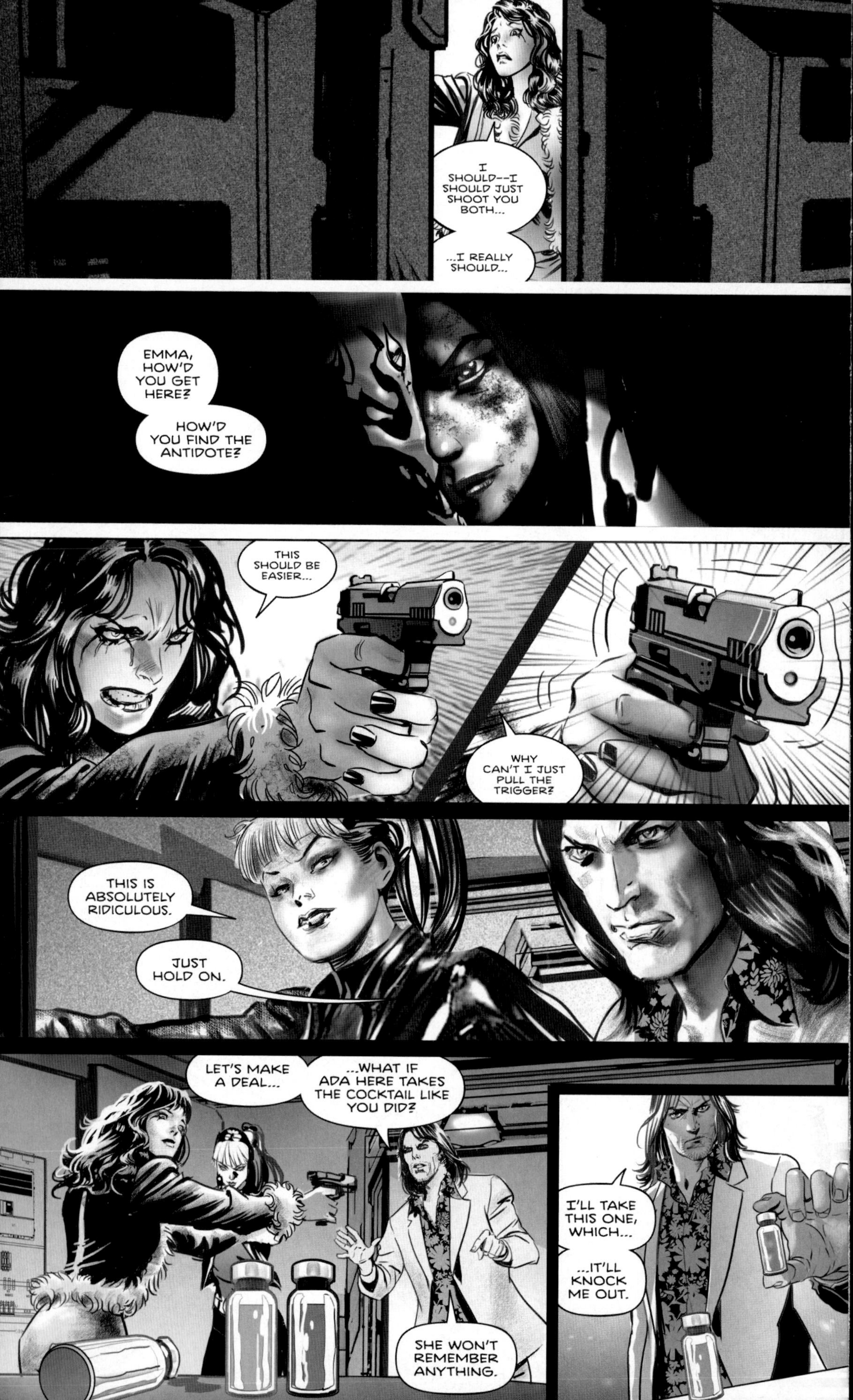

I SHOULD--I SHOULD JUST SHOOT YOU BOTH...
...I REALLY SHOULD...
EMMA, HOW'D YOU GET HERE?
HOW'D YOU FIND THE ANTIDOTE?
THIS SHOULD BE EASIER...
WHY CAN'T I JUST PULL THE TRIGGER?
THIS IS ABSOLUTELY RIDICULOUS.
JUST HOLD ON.
LET'S MAKE A DEAL...
...WHAT IF ADA HERE TAKES THE COCKTAIL LIKE YOU DID?
SHE WON'T REMEMBER ANYTHING.
I'LL TAKE THIS ONE, WHICH...
...IT'LL KNOCK ME OUT.

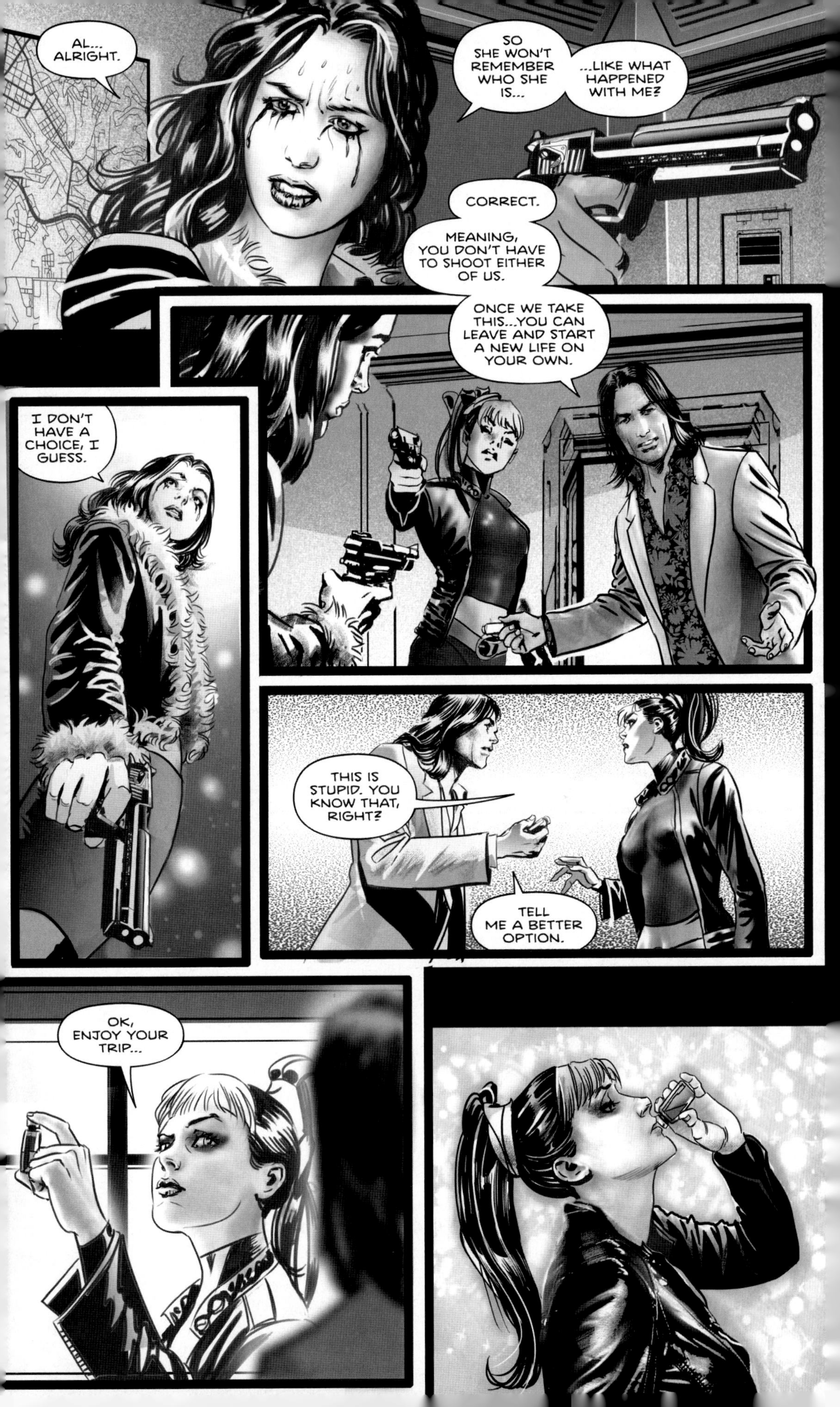
AL... ALRIGHT.
SO SHE WON'T REMEMBER WHO SHE IS...
...LIKE WHAT HAPPENED WITH ME?
CORRECT.
MEANING, YOU DON'T HAVE TO SHOOT EITHER OF US.
ONCE WE TAKE THIS...YOU CAN LEAVE AND START A NEW LIFE ON YOUR OWN.
I DON'T HAVE A CHOICE, I GUESS.
THIS IS STUPID. YOU KNOW THAT, RIGHT?
TELL ME A BETTER OPTION.
OK, ENJOY YOUR TRIP...

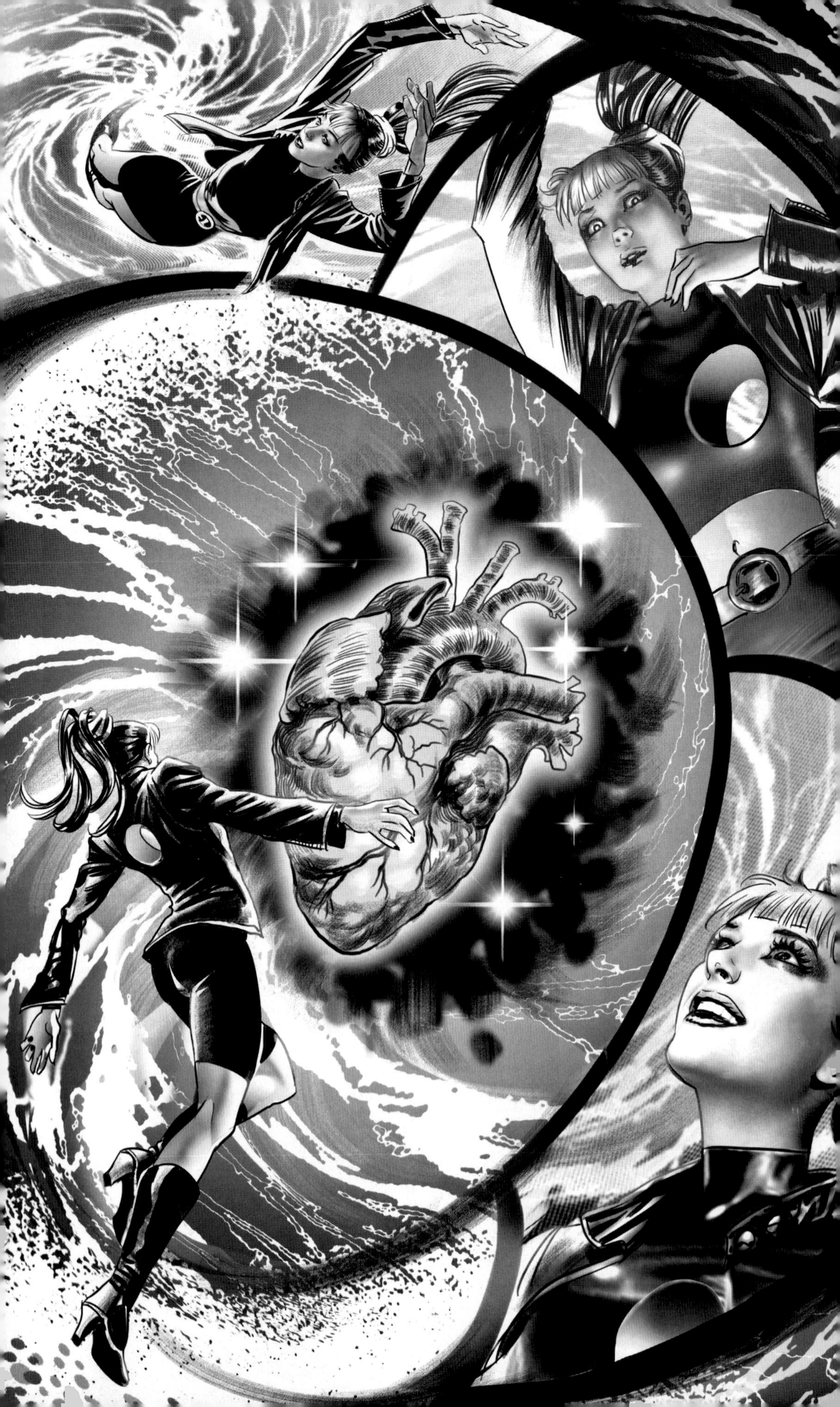

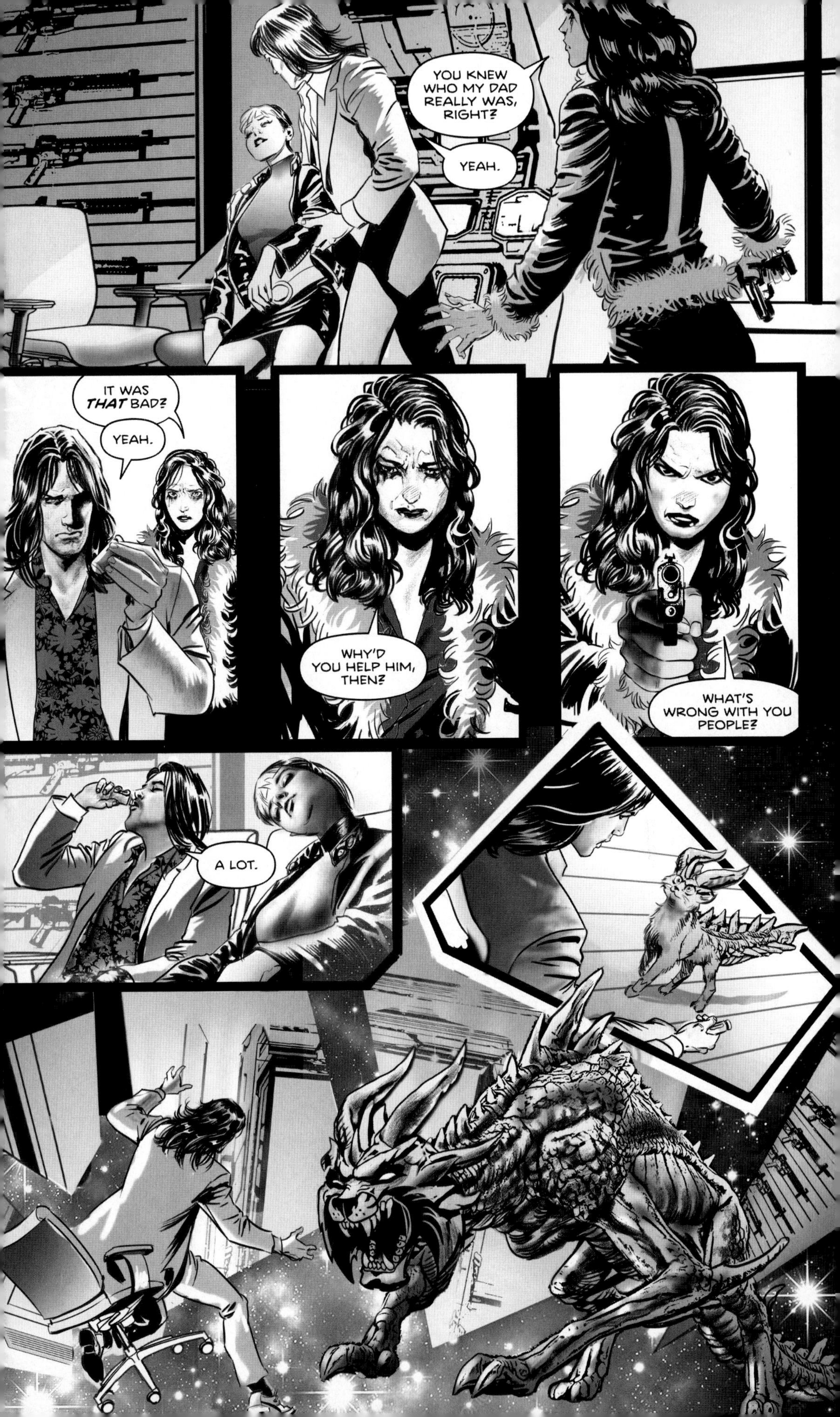
YOU KNEW WHO MY DAD REALLY WAS, RIGHT?
YEAH.
IT WAS *THAT* BAD?
YEAH.
WHY'D YOU HELP HIM, THEN?
WHAT'S WRONG WITH YOU PEOPLE?
A LOT.

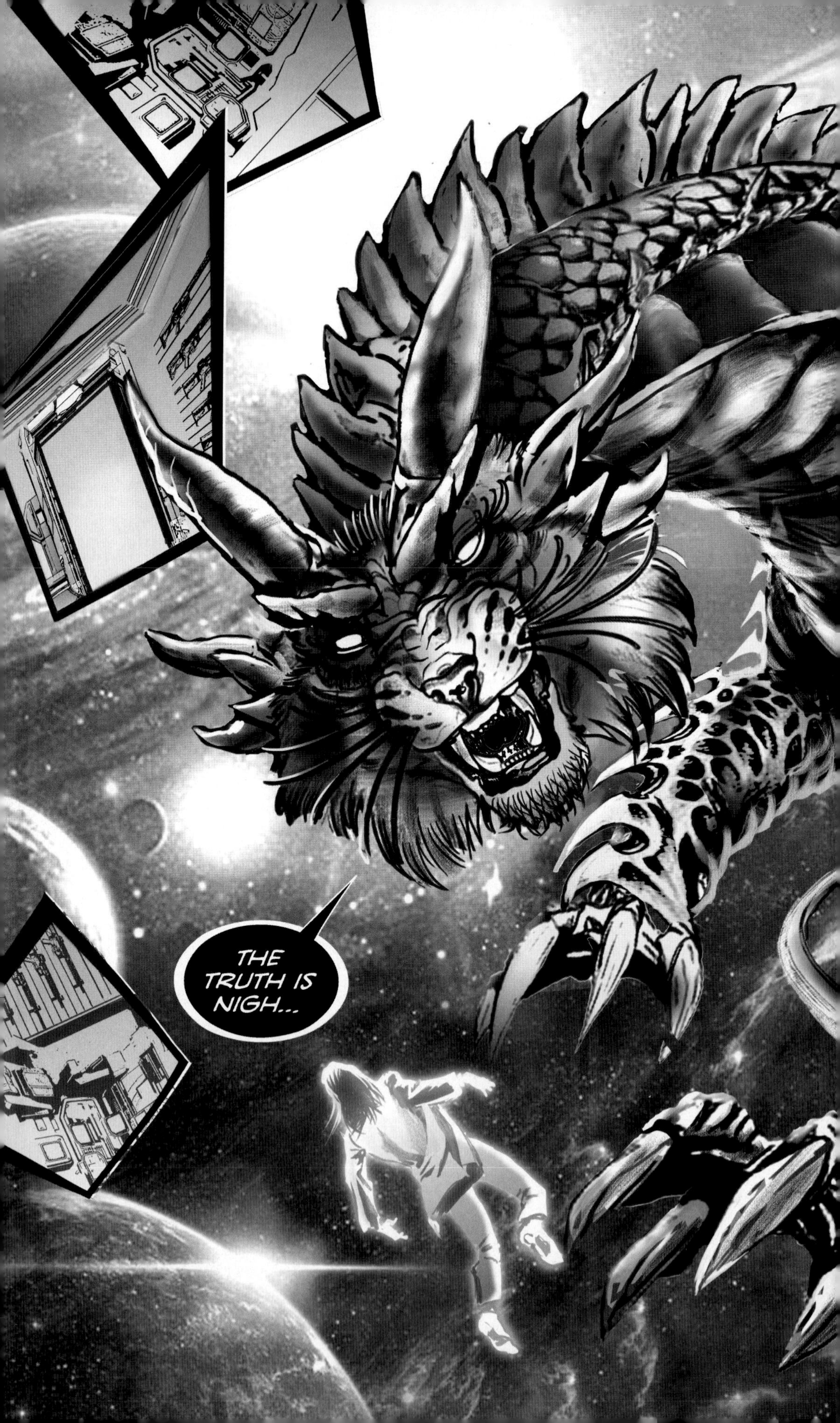
THE TRUTH IS NIGH...

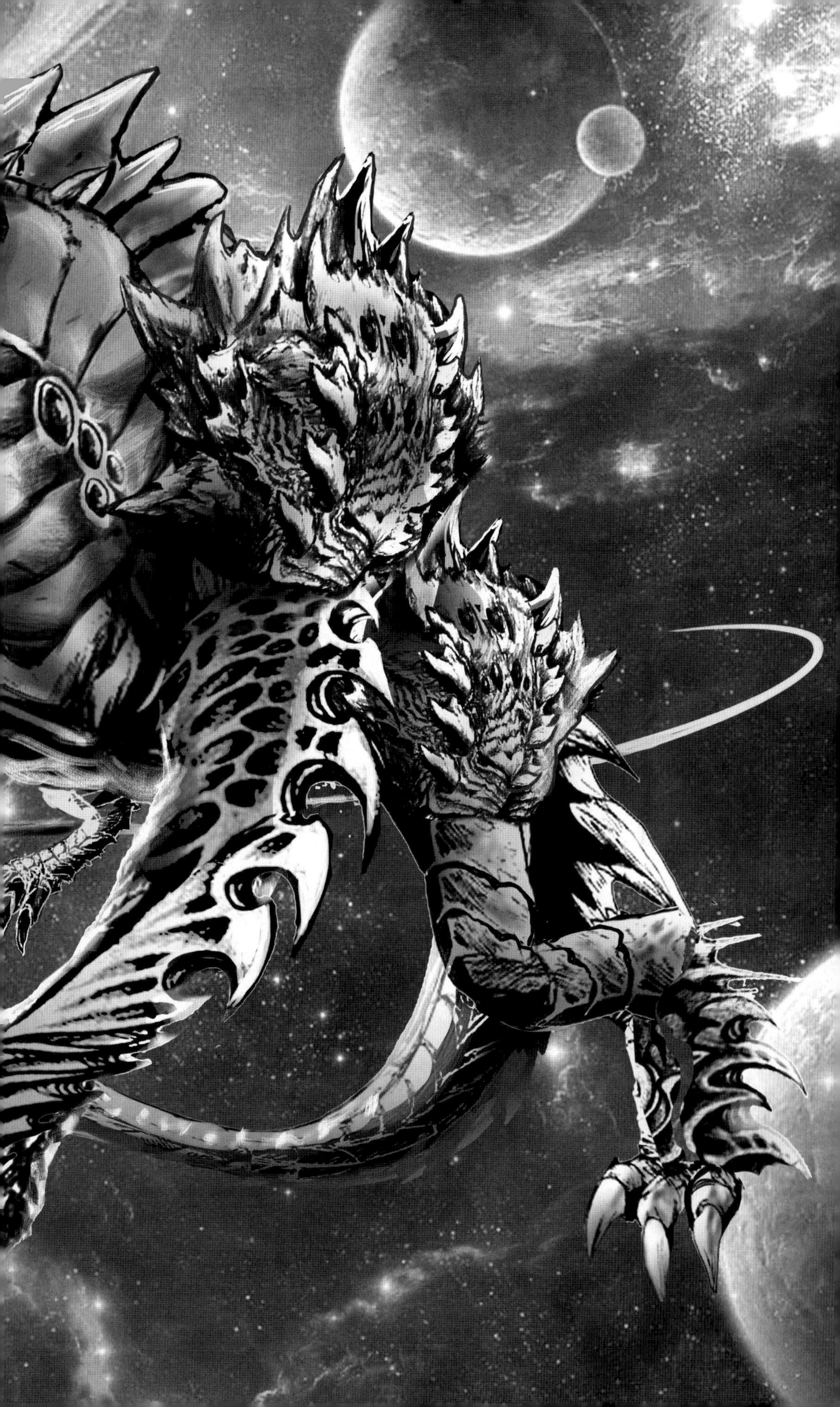

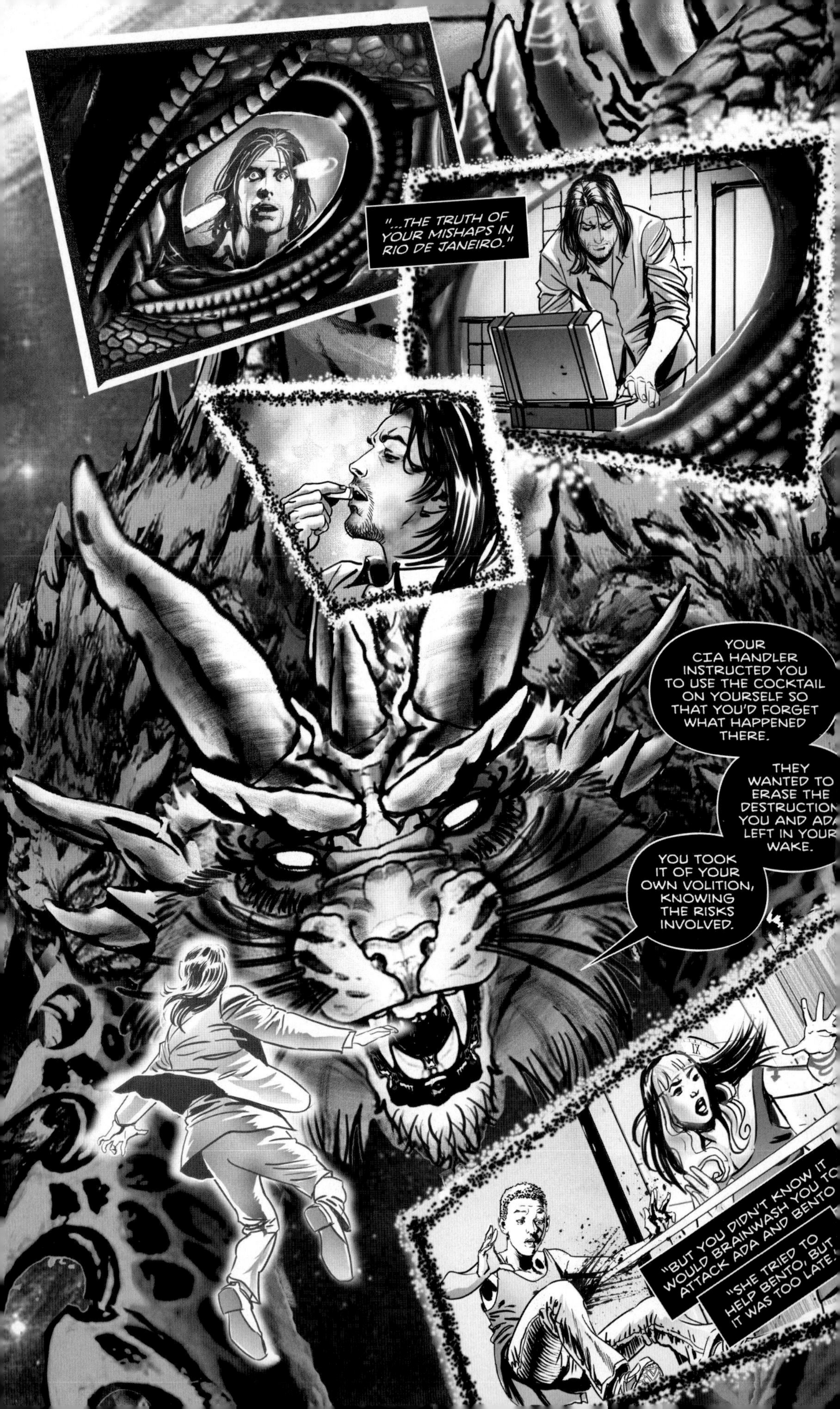
"...THE TRUTH OF YOUR MISHAPS IN RIO DE JANEIRO."
YOUR CIA HANDLER INSTRUCTED YOU TO USE THE COCKTAIL ON YOURSELF SO THAT YOU'D FORGET WHAT HAPPENED THERE.
THEY WANTED TO ERASE THE DESTRUCTION YOU AND ADA LEFT IN YOUR WAKE.
YOU TOOK IT OF YOUR OWN VOLITION, KNOWING THE RISKS INVOLVED.
"BUT YOU DIDN'T KNOW IT WOULD BRAINWASH YOU TO ATTACK ADA AND BENTO.
"SHE TRIED TO HELP BENTO, BUT IT WAS TOO LATE.

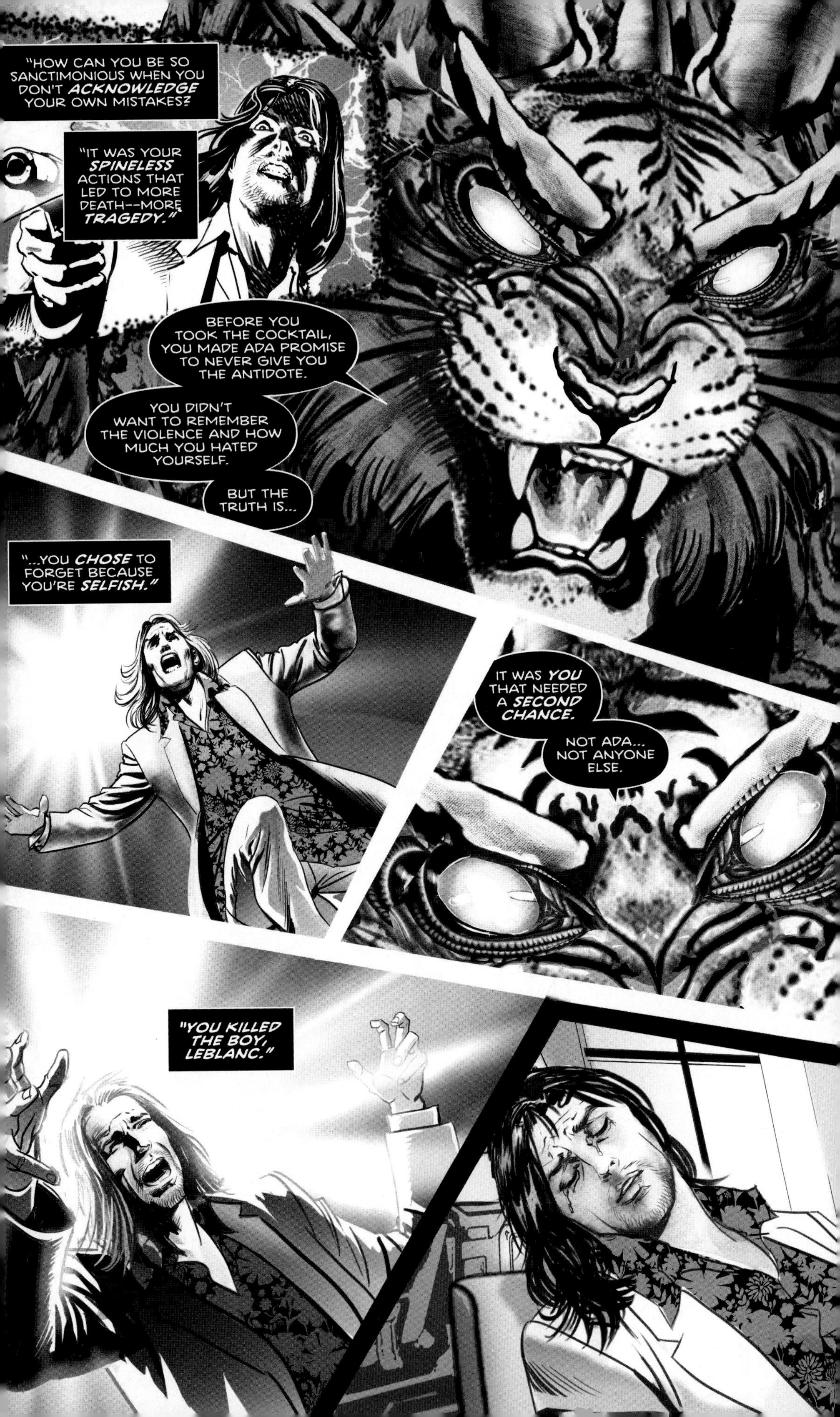
"HOW CAN YOU BE SO SANCTIMONIOUS WHEN YOU DON'T ACKNOWLEDGE YOUR OWN MISTAKES?
"IT WAS YOUR SPINELESS ACTIONS THAT LED TO MORE DEATH--MORE TRAGEDY."
BEFORE YOU TOOK THE COCKTAIL, YOU MADE ADA PROMISE TO NEVER GIVE YOU THE ANTIDOTE.
YOU DIDN'T WANT TO REMEMBER THE VIOLENCE AND HOW MUCH YOU HATED YOURSELF.
BUT THE TRUTH IS...
"...YOU CHOSE TO FORGET BECAUSE YOU'RE SELFISH."
IT WAS YOU THAT NEEDED A SECOND CHANCE.
NOT ADA... NOT ANYONE ELSE.
"YOU KILLED THE BOY, LEBLANC."

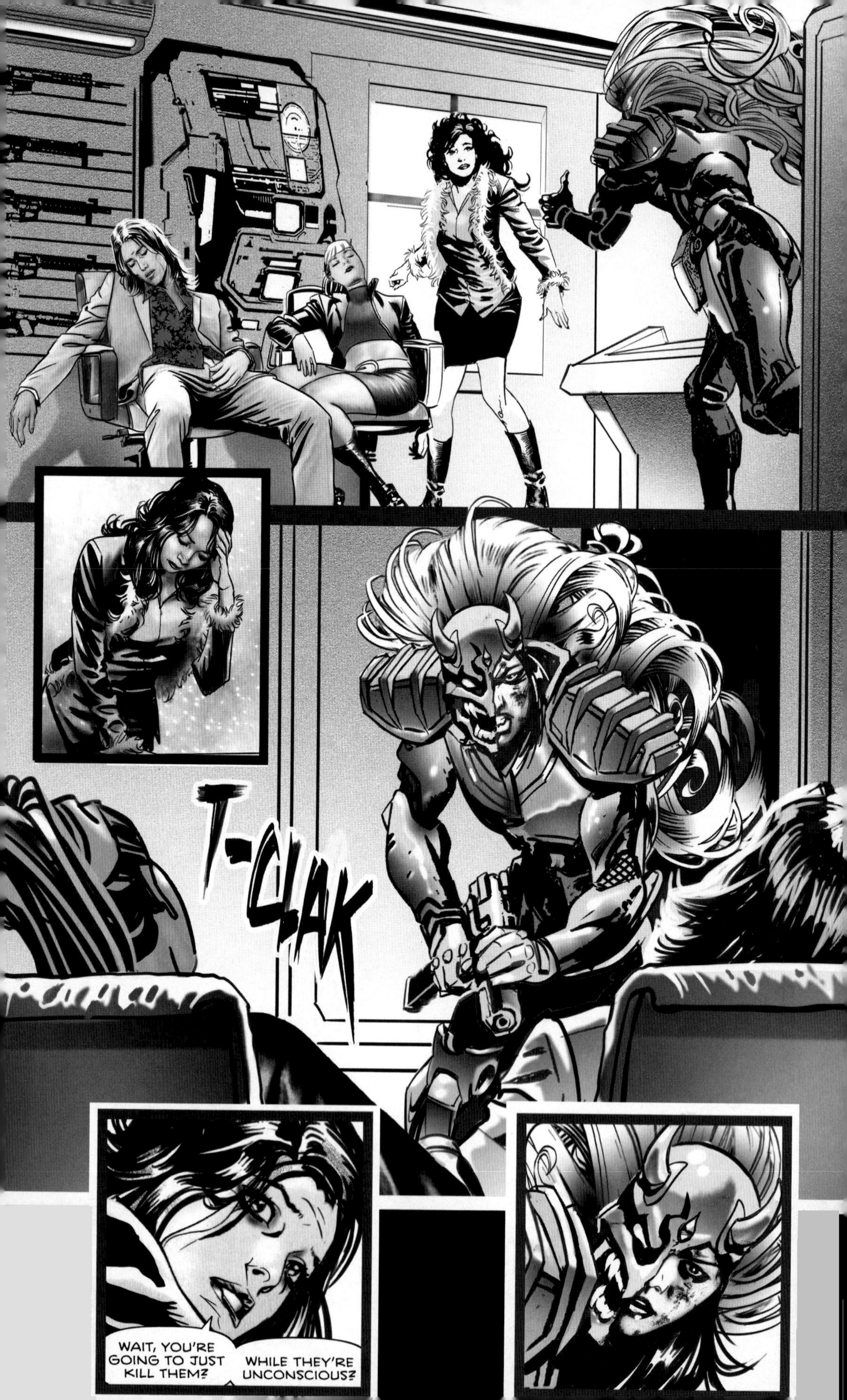
T-CLAK
WAIT, YOU'RE GOING TO JUST KILL THEM?
WHILE THEY'RE UNCONSCIOUS?

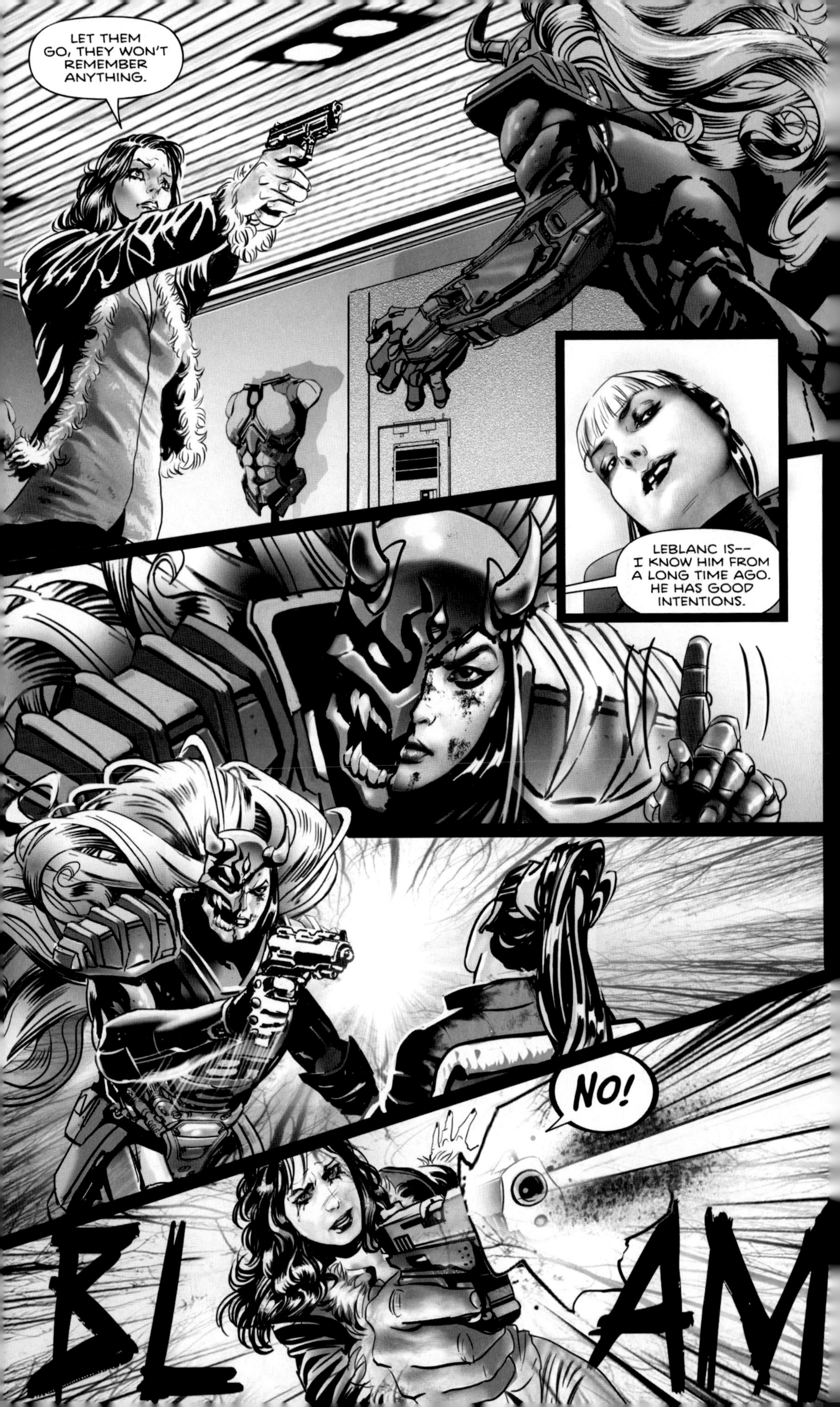
LET THEM GO, THEY WON'T REMEMBER ANYTHING.
LEBLANC IS-- I KNOW HIM FROM A LONG TIME AGO. HE HAS GOOD INTENTIONS.
NO!
BLAM

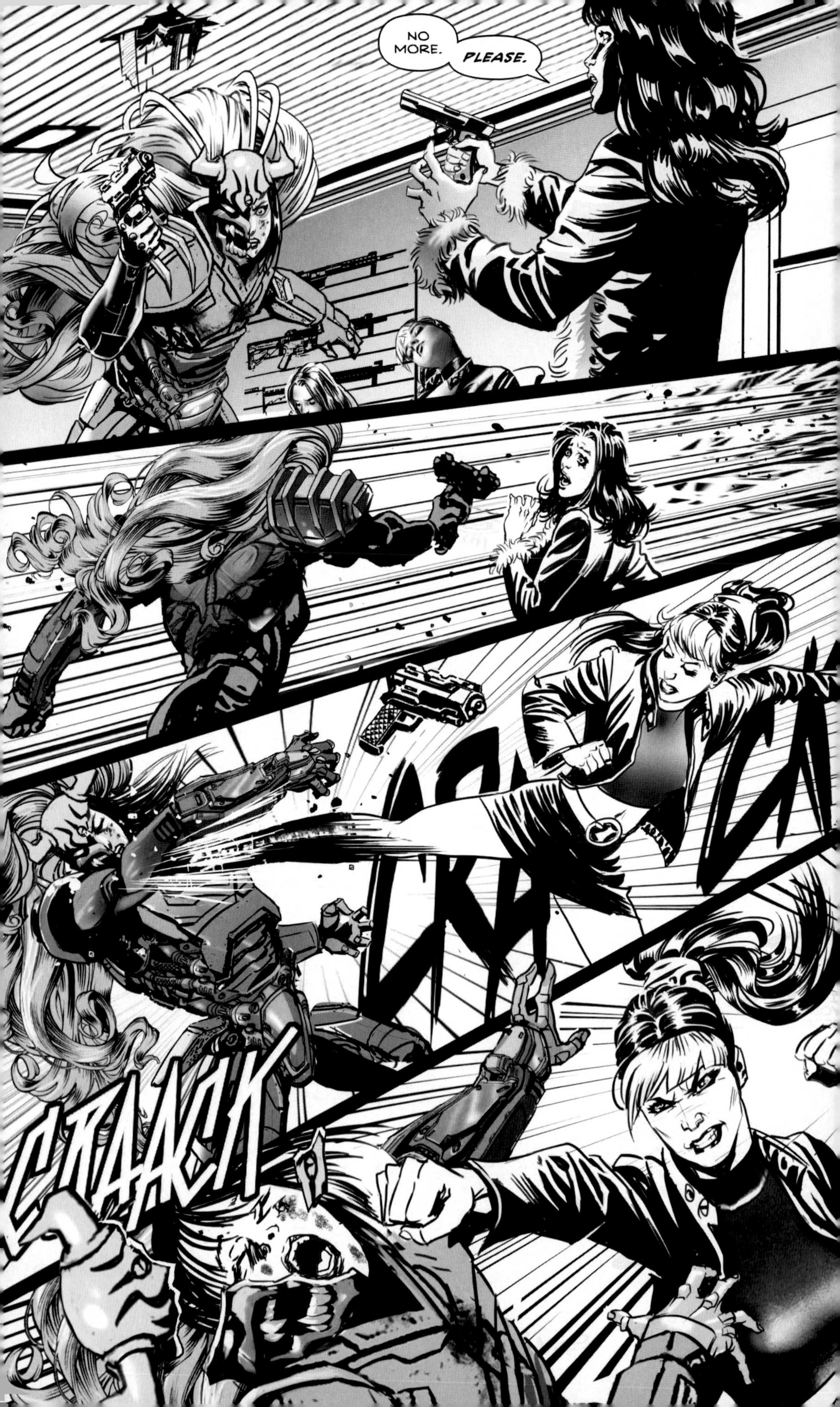
NO MORE.
PLEASE.
CRAACK

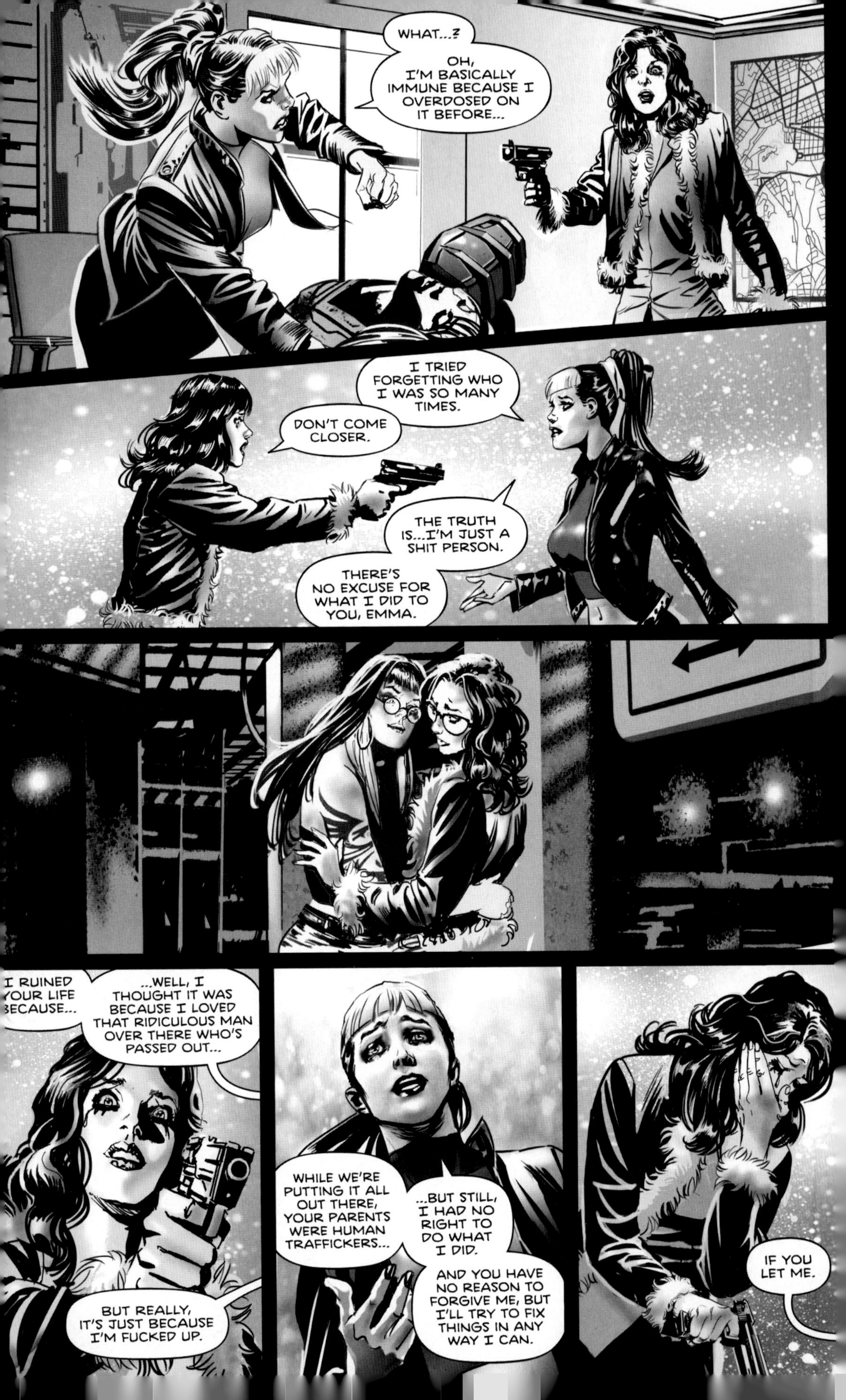
WHAT...?
OH, I'M BASICALLY IMMUNE BECAUSE I OVERDOSED ON IT BEFORE...
I TRIED FORGETTING WHO I WAS SO MANY TIMES.
DON'T COME CLOSER.
THE TRUTH IS...I'M JUST A SHIT PERSON.
THERE'S NO EXCUSE FOR WHAT I DID TO YOU, EMMA.
I RUINED YOUR LIFE BECAUSE...
...WELL, I THOUGHT IT WAS BECAUSE I LOVED THAT RIDICULOUS MAN OVER THERE WHO'S PASSED OUT...
BUT REALLY, IT'S JUST BECAUSE I'M FUCKED UP.
WHILE WE'RE PUTTING IT ALL OUT THERE, YOUR PARENTS WERE HUMAN TRAFFICKERS...
...BUT STILL, I HAD NO RIGHT TO DO WHAT I DID.
AND YOU HAVE NO REASON TO FORGIVE ME, BUT I'LL TRY TO FIX THINGS IN ANY WAY I CAN.
IF YOU LET ME.

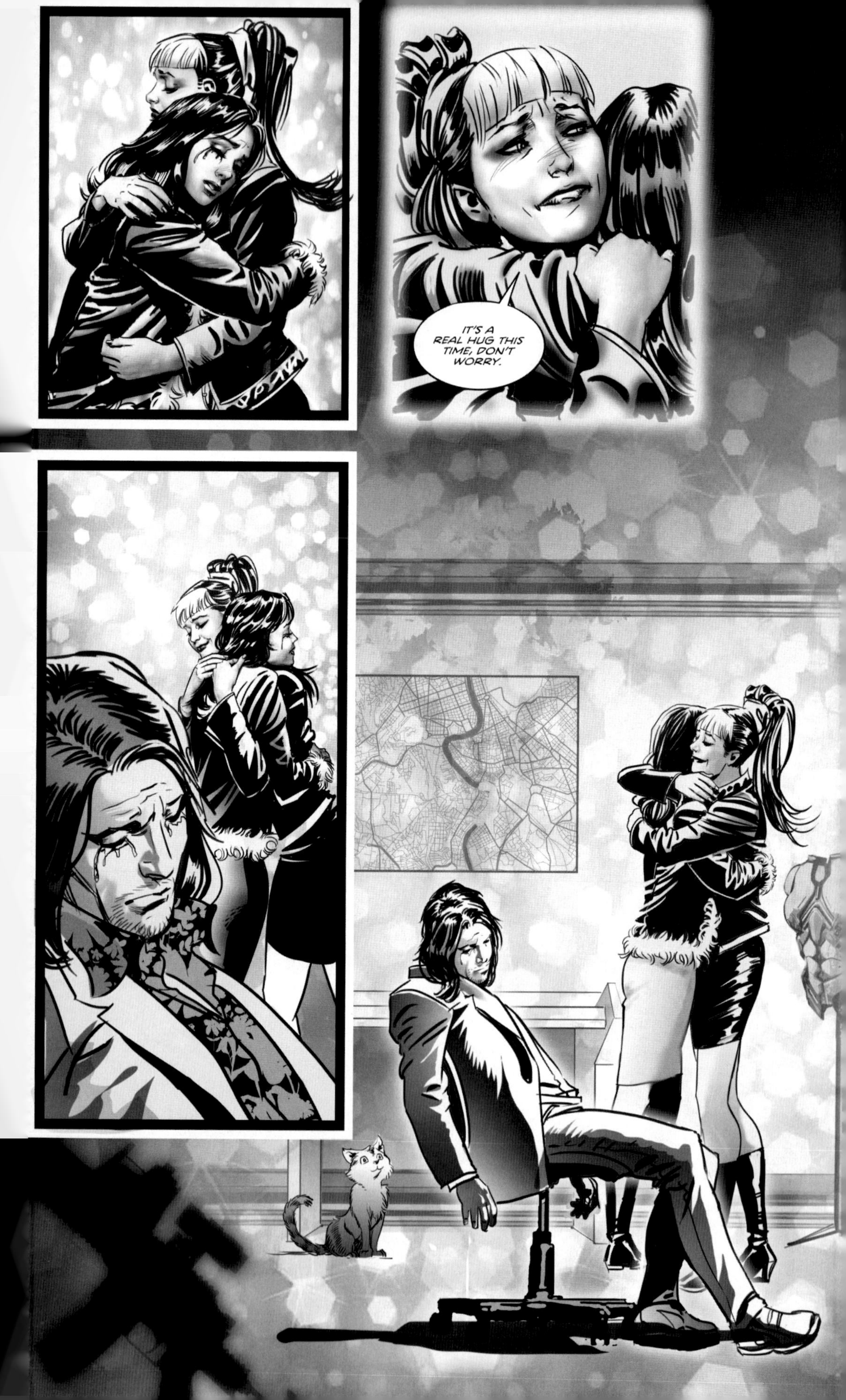
IT'S A REAL HUG THIS TIME, DON'T WORRY.

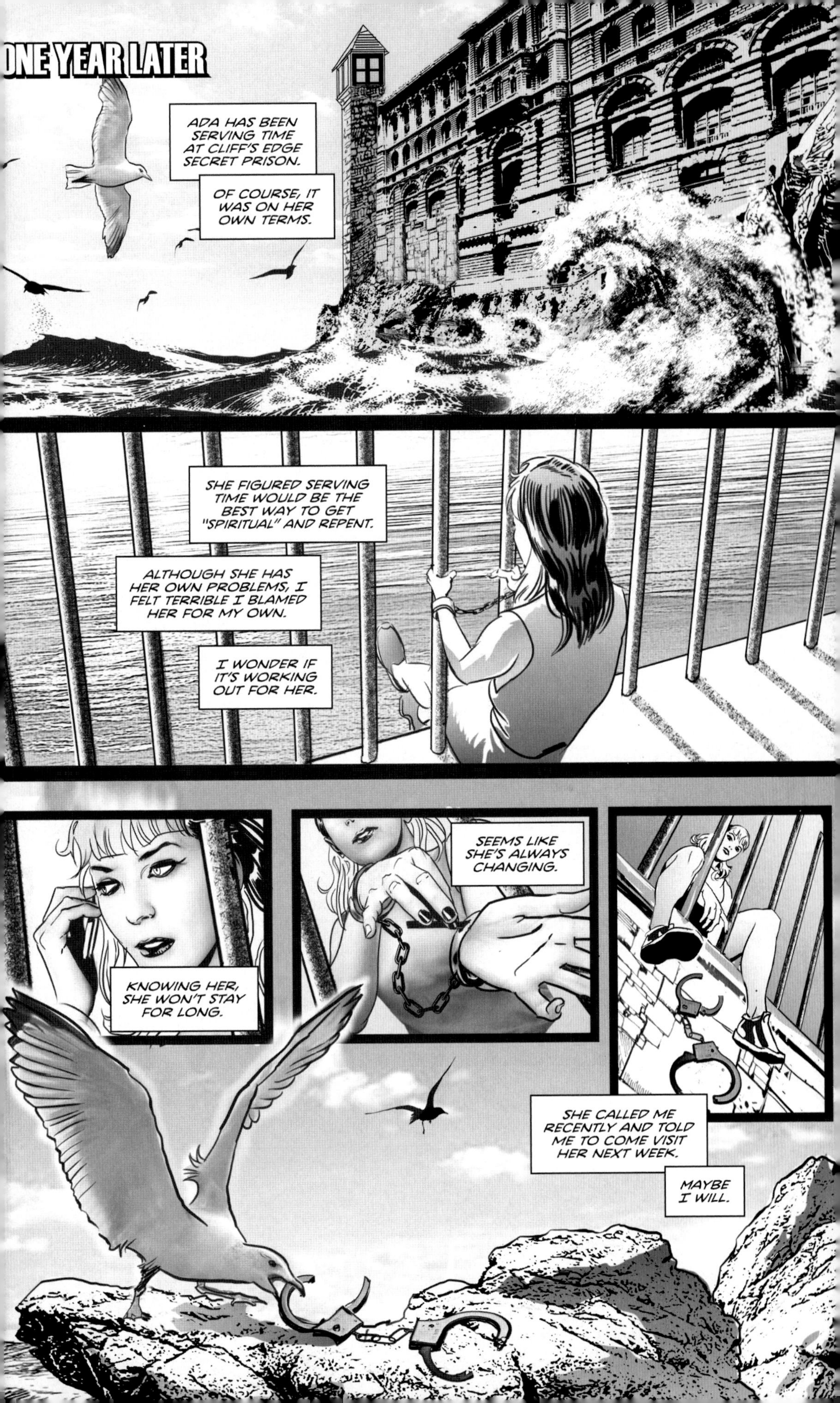

ONE YEAR LATER
ADA HAS BEEN SERVING TIME AT CLIFF'S EDGE SECRET PRISON.
OF COURSE, IT WAS ON HER OWN TERMS.
SHE FIGURED SERVING TIME WOULD BE THE BEST WAY TO GET "SPIRITUAL" AND REPENT.
ALTHOUGH SHE HAS HER OWN PROBLEMS, I FELT TERRIBLE I BLAMED HER FOR MY OWN.
I WONDER IF IT'S WORKING OUT FOR HER.
KNOWING HER, SHE WON'T STAY FOR LONG.
SEEMS LIKE SHE'S ALWAYS CHANGING.
SHE CALLED ME RECENTLY AND TOLD ME TO COME VISIT HER NEXT WEEK.
MAYBE I WILL.

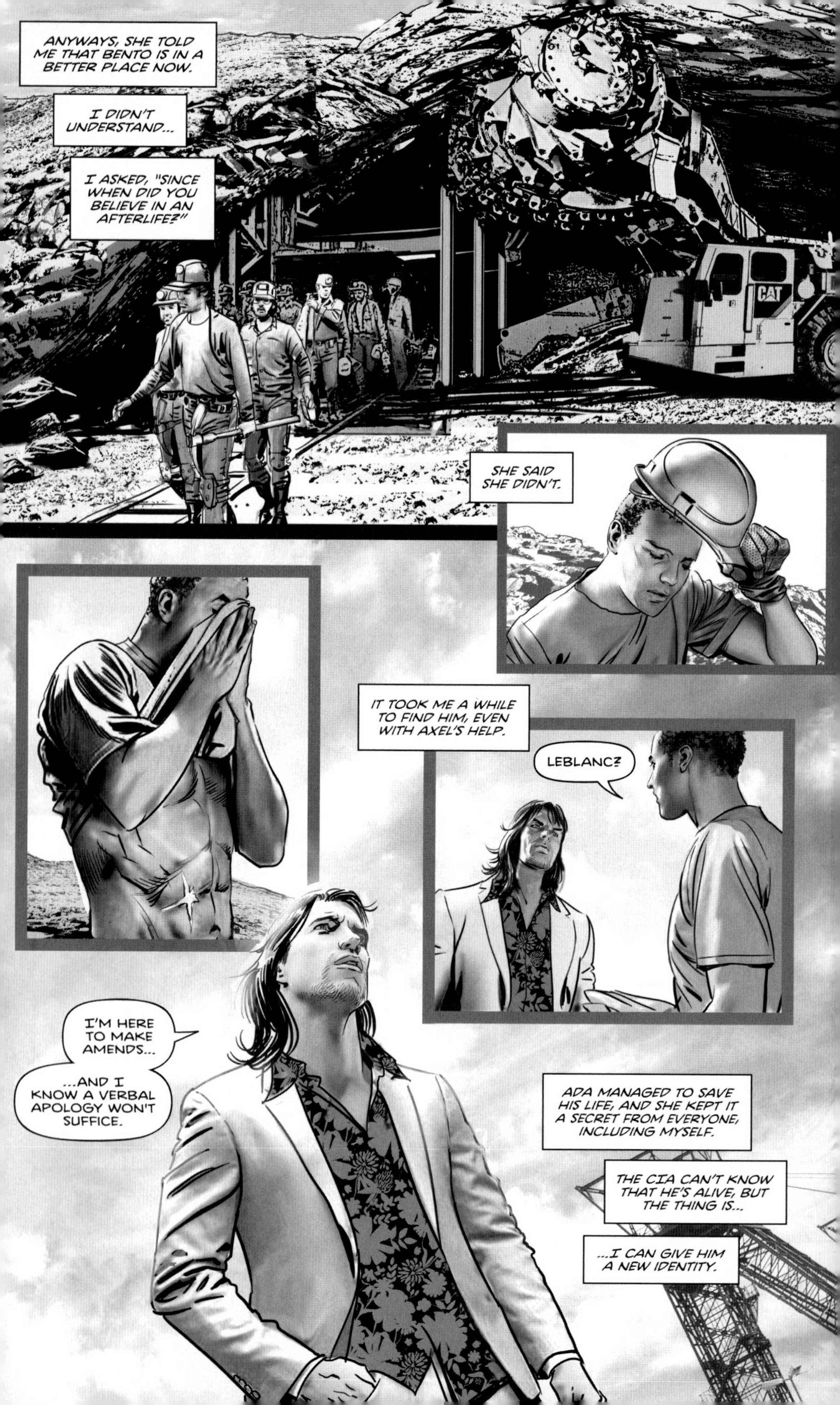
ANYWAYS, SHE TOLD ME THAT BENTO IS IN A BETTER PLACE NOW.
I DIDN'T UNDERSTAND...
I ASKED, "SINCE WHEN DID YOU BELIEVE IN AN AFTERLIFE?"
CAT
SHE SAID SHE DIDN'T.
IT TOOK ME A WHILE TO FIND HIM, EVEN WITH AXEL'S HELP.
LEBLANC?
I'M HERE TO MAKE AMENDS...
...AND I KNOW A VERBAL APOLOGY WON'T SUFFICE.
ADA MANAGED TO SAVE HIS LIFE, AND SHE KEPT IT A SECRET FROM EVERYONE, INCLUDING MYSELF.
THE CIA CAN'T KNOW THAT HE'S ALIVE, BUT THE THING IS...
...I CAN GIVE HIM A NEW IDENTITY.

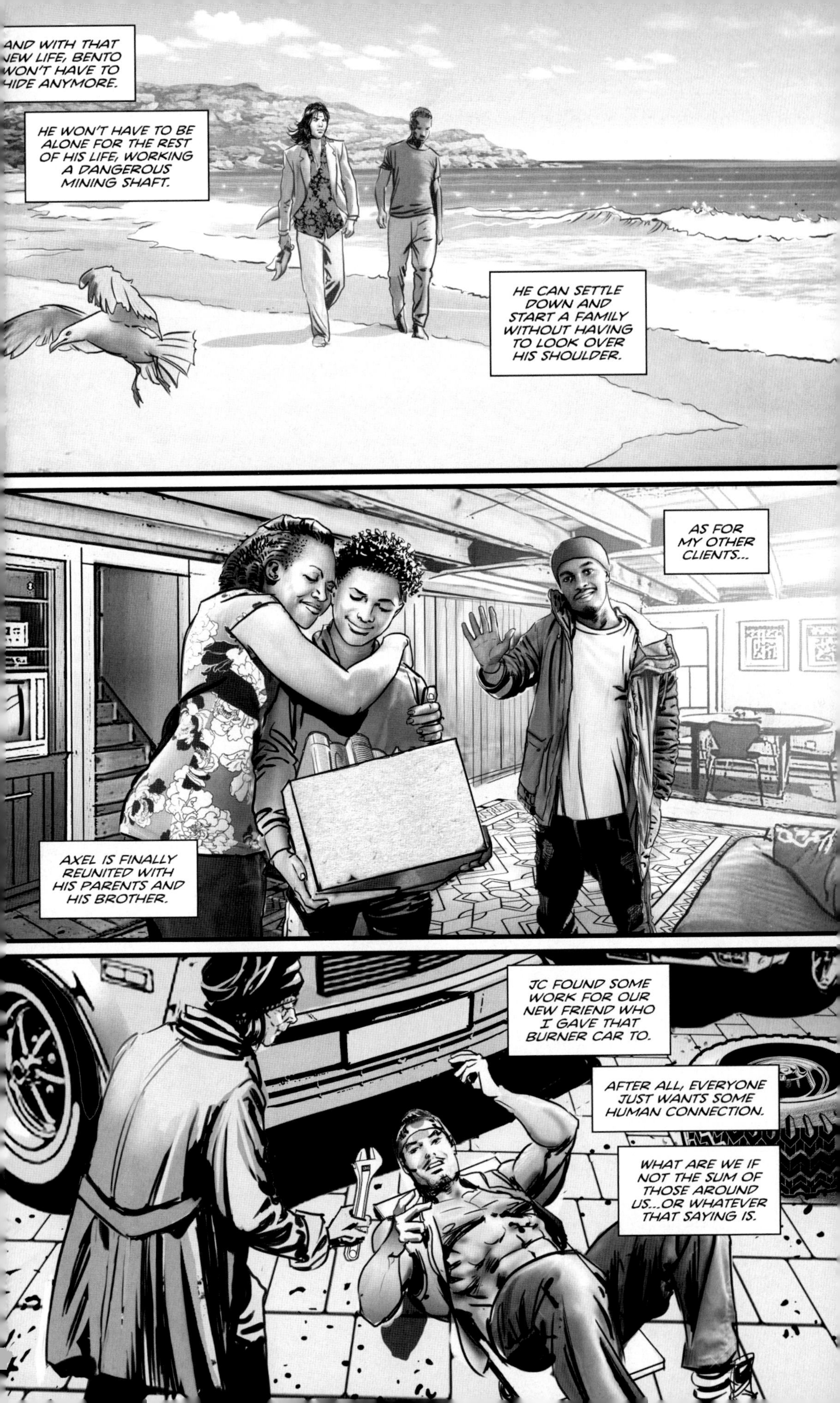
AND WITH THAT NEW LIFE, BENTO WON'T HAVE TO HIDE ANYMORE.
HE WON'T HAVE TO BE ALONE FOR THE REST OF HIS LIFE, WORKING A DANGEROUS MINING SHAFT.
HE CAN SETTLE DOWN AND START A FAMILY WITHOUT HAVING TO LOOK OVER HIS SHOULDER.
AS FOR MY OTHER CLIENTS...
AXEL IS FINALLY REUNITED WITH HIS PARENTS AND HIS BROTHER.
JC FOUND SOME WORK FOR OUR NEW FRIEND WHO I GAVE THAT BURNER CAR TO.
AFTER ALL, EVERYONE JUST WANTS SOME HUMAN CONNECTION.
WHAT ARE WE IF NOT THE SUM OF THOSE AROUND US...OR WHATEVER THAT SAYING IS.

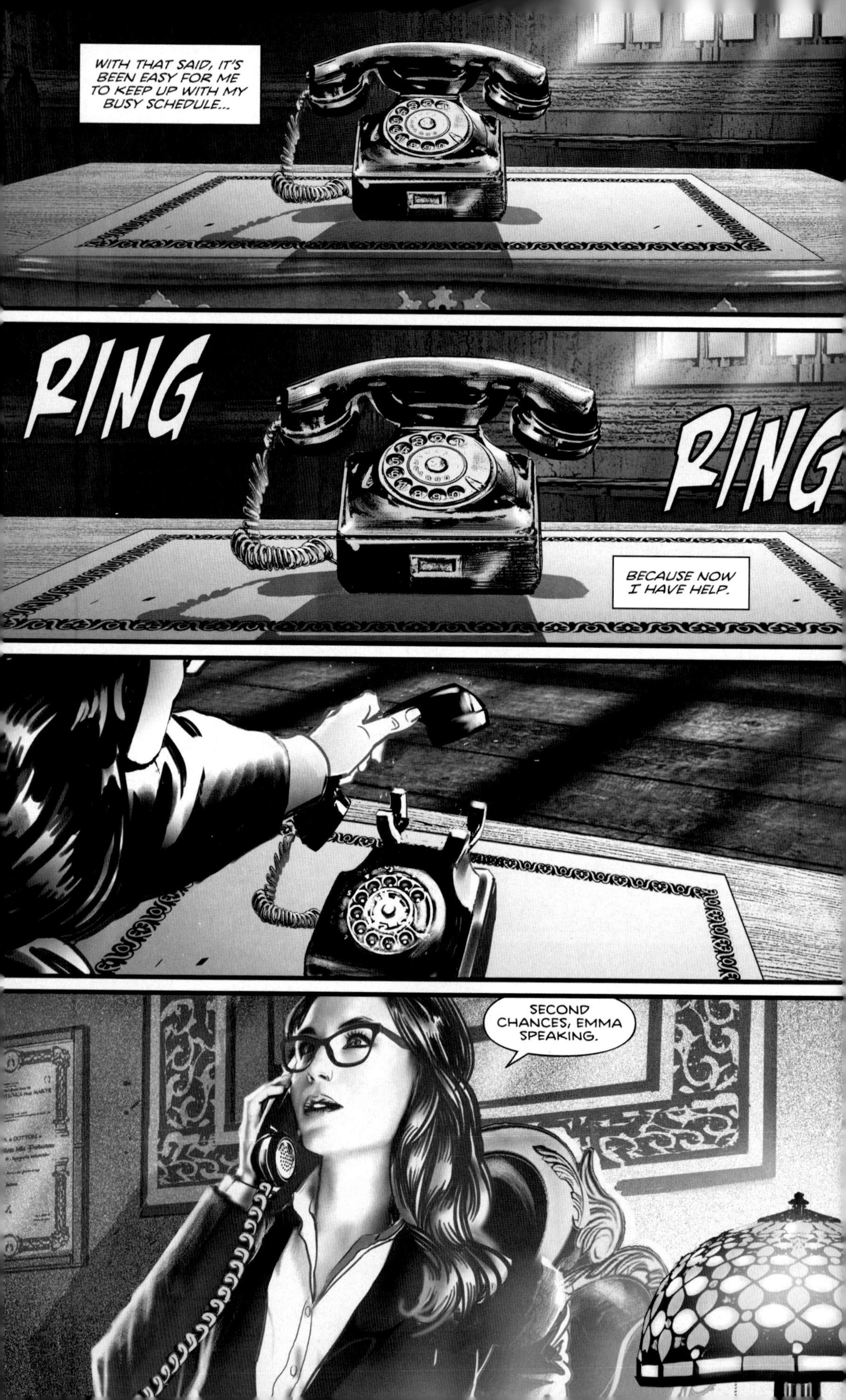
WITH THAT SAID, IT'S BEEN EASY FOR ME TO KEEP UP WITH MY BUSY SCHEDULE...
RING
RING
BECAUSE NOW I HAVE HELP.
SECOND CHANCES, EMMA SPEAKING.

EXTRAS

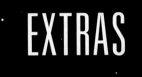

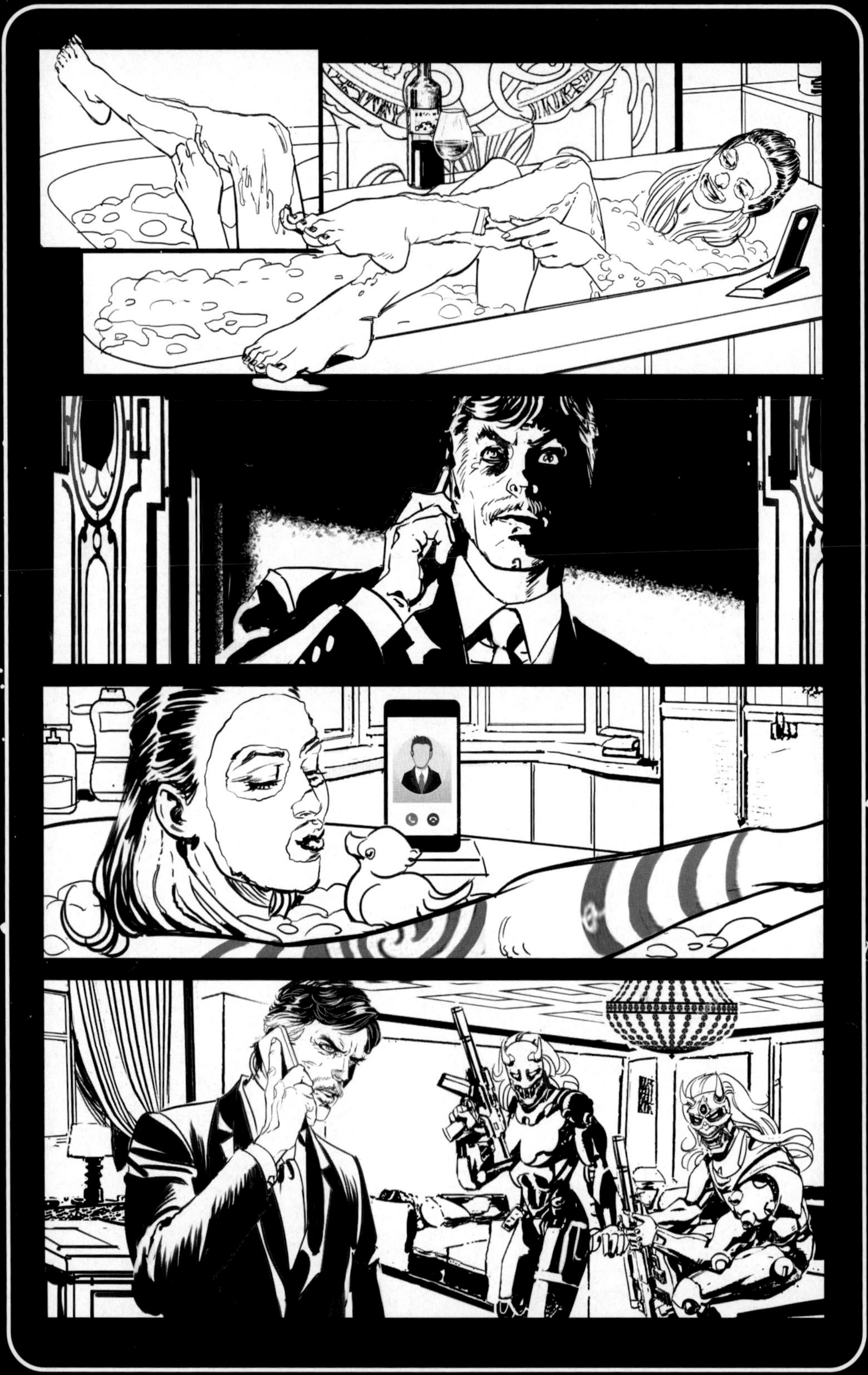

ISSUE 2, PAGE 9 INKS

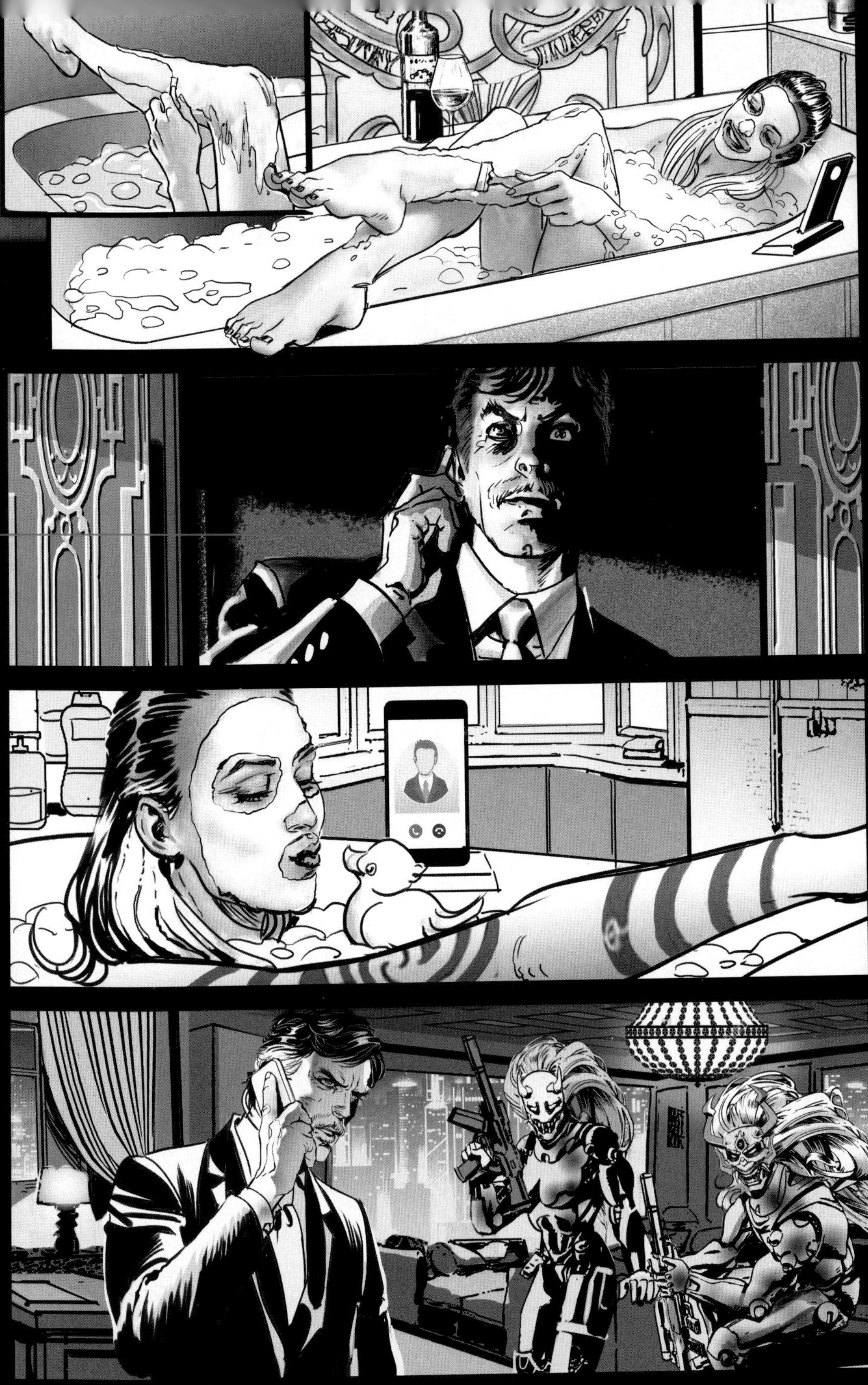

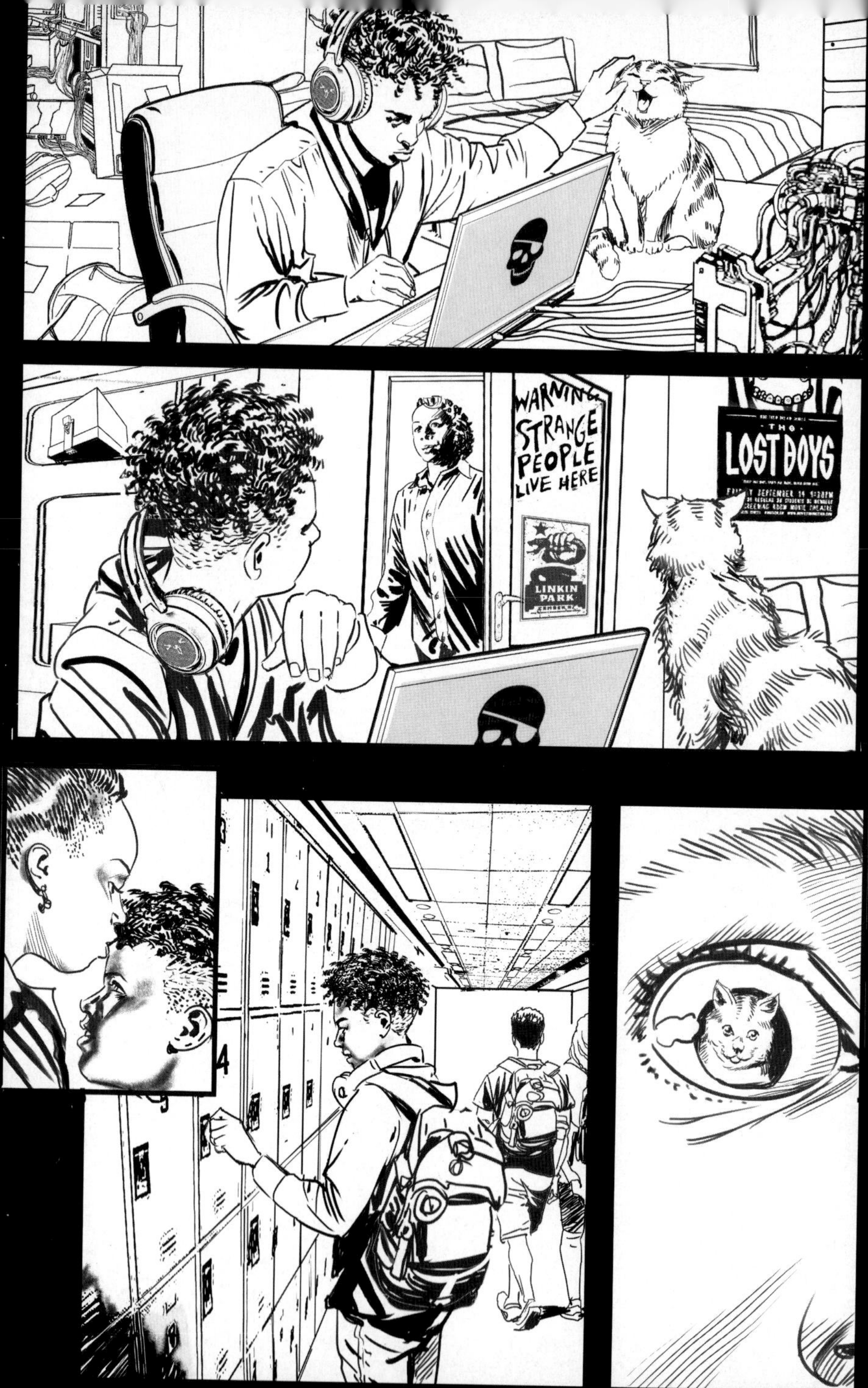
WARNING
STRANGE PEOPLE LIVE HERE
LINKIN PARK
LOST BOYS

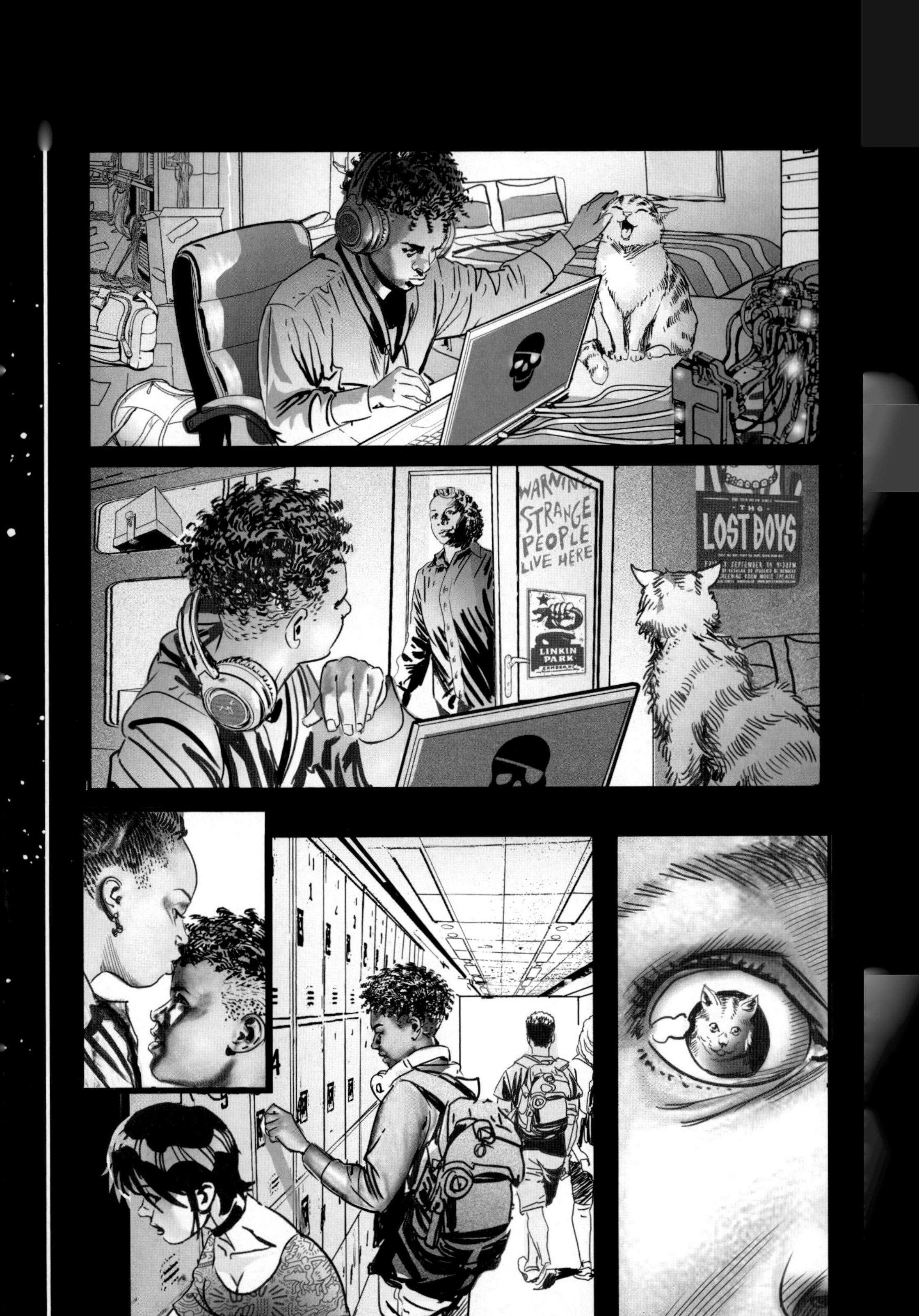
WARNING
STRANGE PEOPLE LIVE HERE
LINKIN PARK
THE LOST BOYS

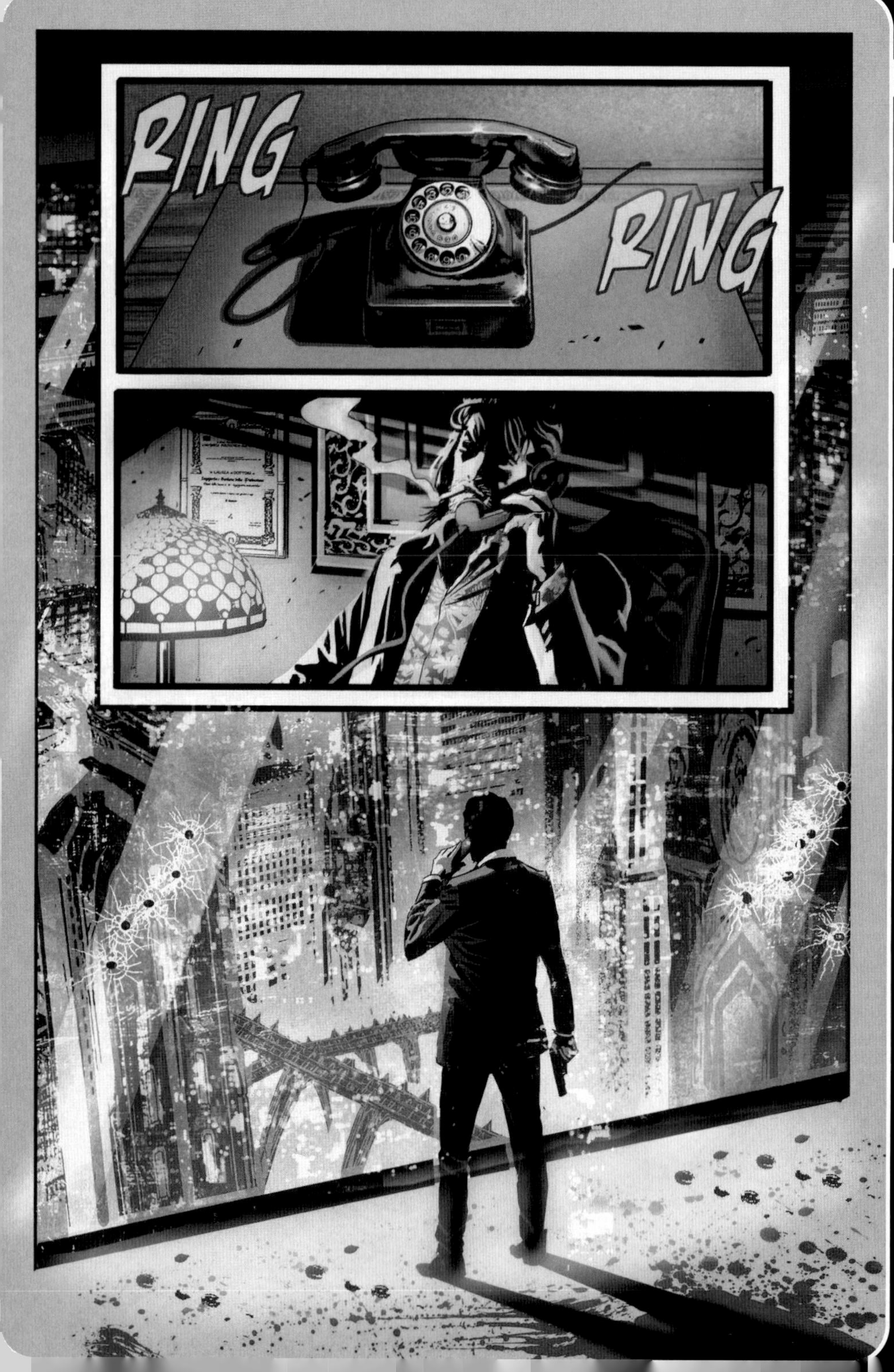
RING
RING

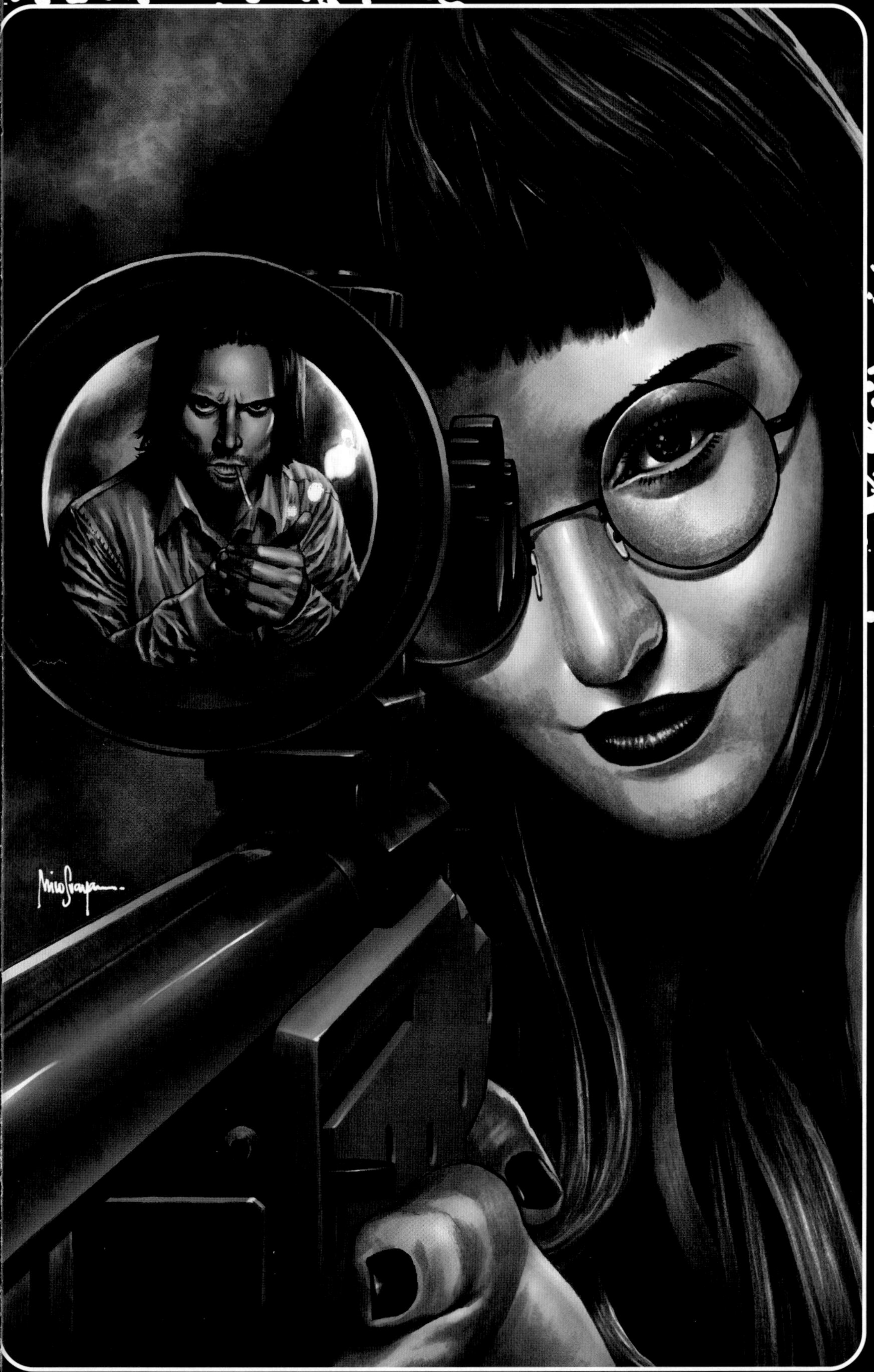

ISSUE ONE RETAILER EXCLUSIVE BY MICO SUAYAN

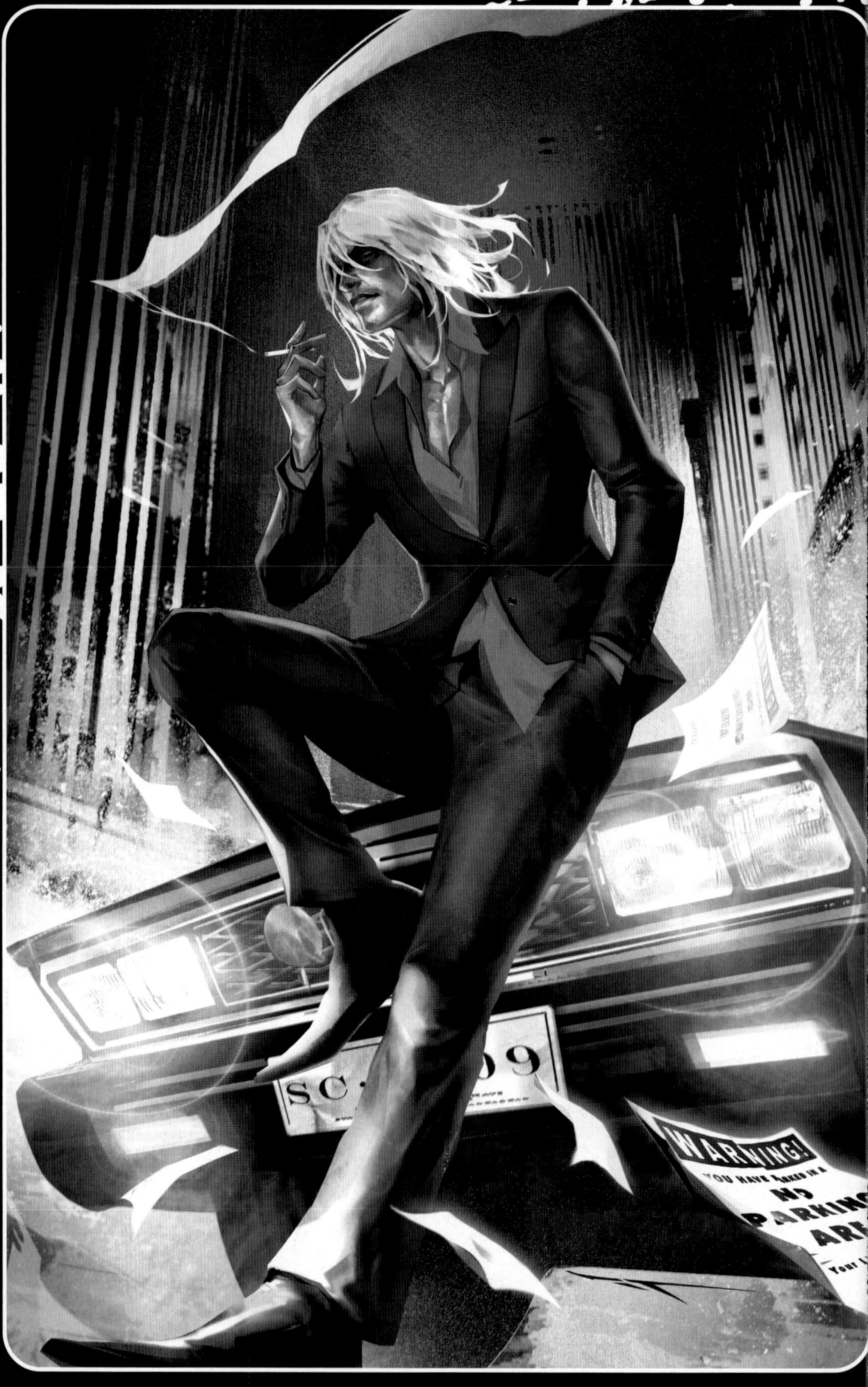
WARNING!

ISSUE ONE RETAILER EXCLUSIVE BY IVAN TAO

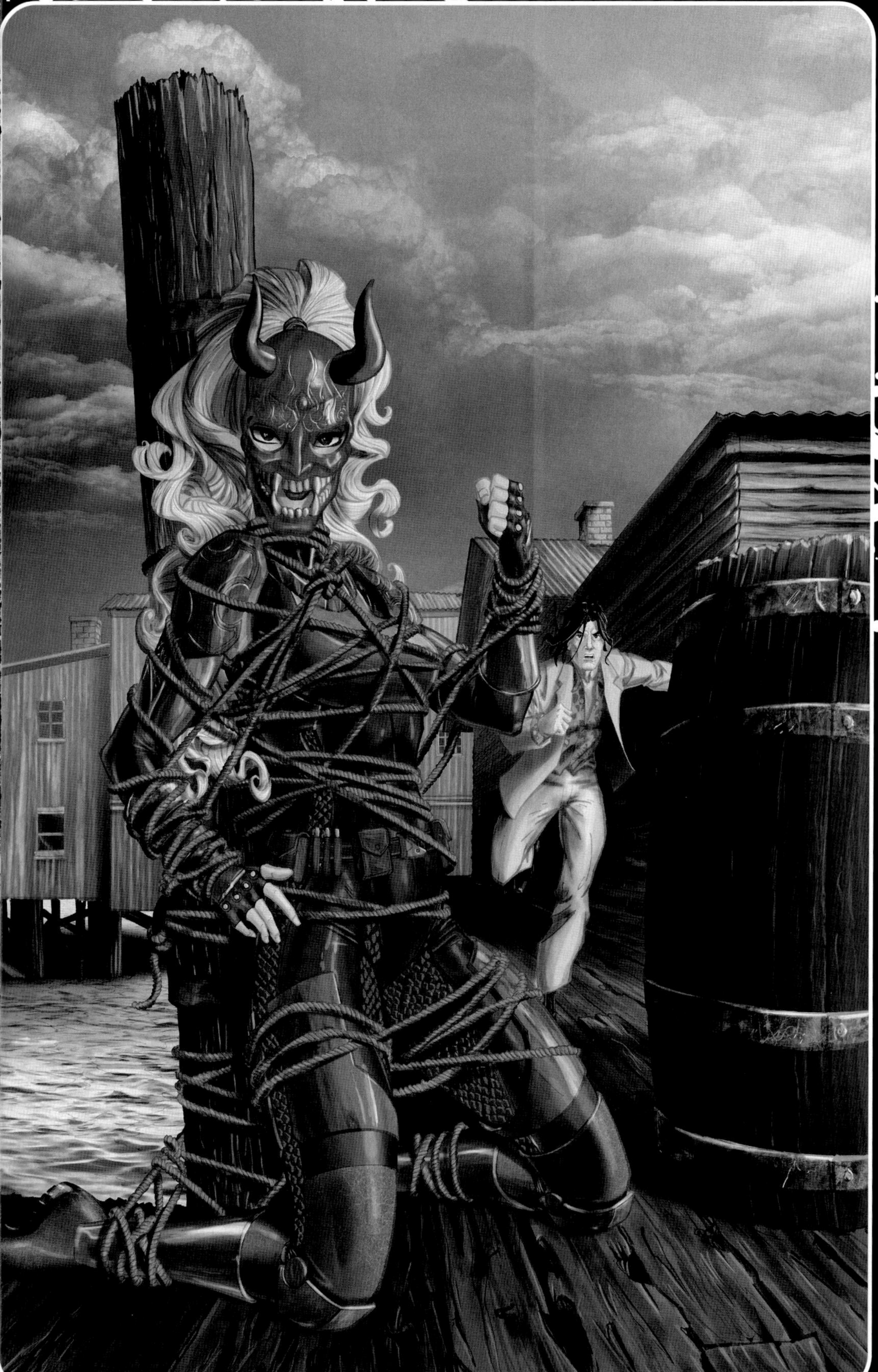

ISSUE ONE RETAILER EXCLUSIVE BY CHRIS EHNOT

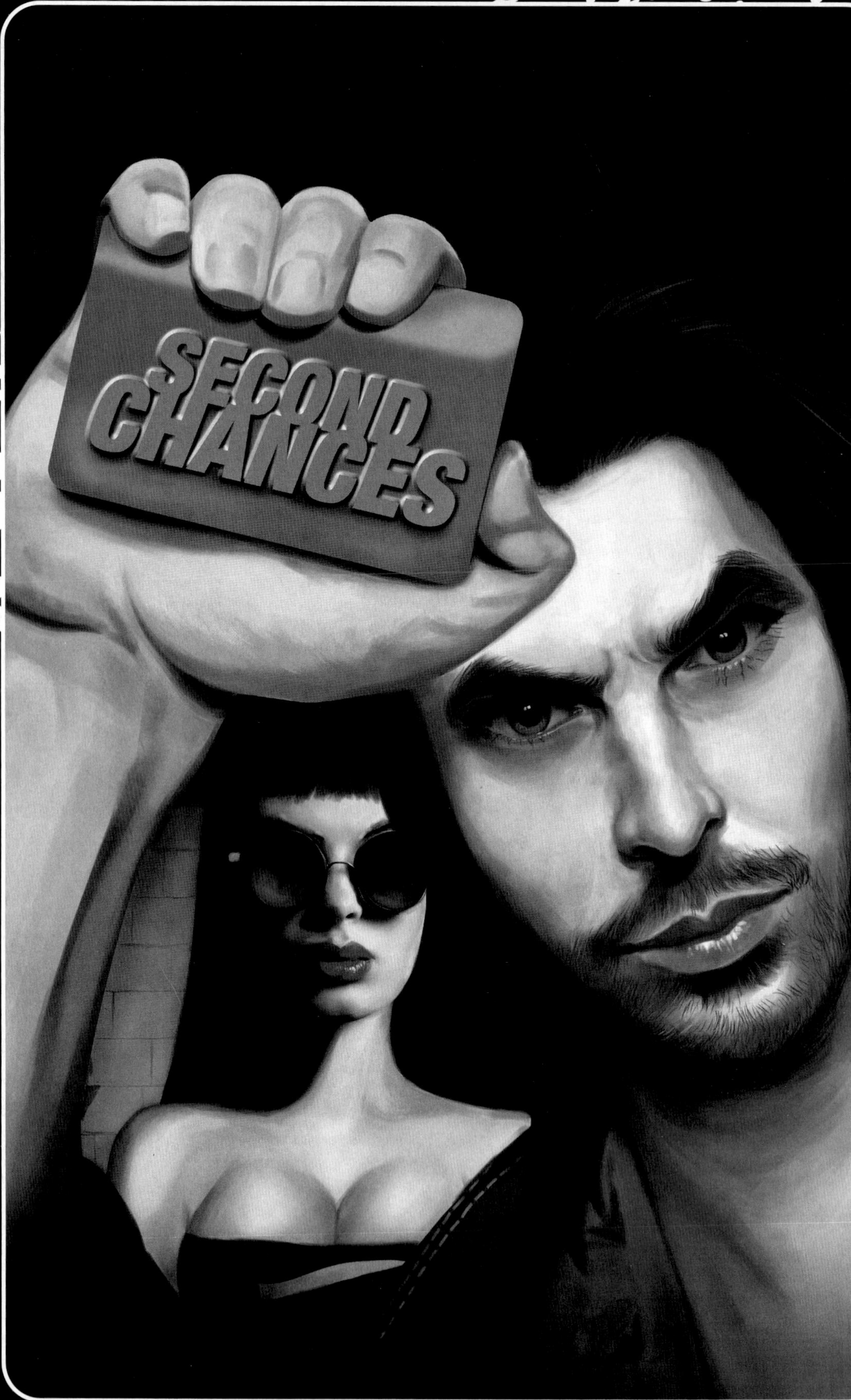
SECOND CHANCES

ISSUE ONE RETAILER EXCLUSIVE BY MARK HAMMERMEISTER